Naomi &
Adrian!

Stay strong!

Keep the
Faith.

Ron S. Chea
2019

ALFRED

AND THE QUEST KNIGHTS

VOLUME THREE

BY RON SMORYNSKI

Table of Contents
Book One

The Quest of Sir Murith

Chapter Twelve

Book Two

Book One

Chapter One

The Choices We Make

The mountainous region was snowcapped with evergreen trees filling the carved out valleys. The clopping of cast iron horseshoed hooves upon stone and gravel broke the quaintness of chirping birds. The great horses, heaving hot breath in the crisp mountain air, breached the rocky crest.

Noble men in shining armour on mighty horses with grand tunics and banners frenetically charged forth. They were not deterred by their gasping horses, faltering poles, tilted helms, or sagging bodies.

The armoured men pushed forth along the craggy rocks and narrow paths, up and down the rocky road.

One knight, wearing blackened armour that was richly ornate with leaves and vines of wrought silver, sat erect on his mount. Determined, he pushed the others on.

A screech was heard overhead. Horses neighed in panic and knights searched the bright blue sky. It was a loud booming cry that rocketed across the expanse. Only the Black Knight was unaffected. Several horses reared and their riders awoke from their exhaustion to try to control their mounts. There was some disarray amongst the heavy cavalry.

The Black Knight turned and raised his sword. Even the horses were calmed by his great pose. Knights reformed their line, passing him along the road as he looked back. Through his visor, his eyes narrowed.

Beyond the crest of the terrain, riding over distant ridges, goblins on large spiders charged forward. Up steep slopes, they came through the trees, some leaping from shadow to shadow, others large and heavy, crashing through. He waved his knights on and turned to take up the rear.

The road led to a monastery veiled amongst the monolithic rocks of the mountainside. Humble wood and stone buildings hugged the rocky spires. A green grove was its entrance. The sun's rays shown bright amidst the coldness of towering rocks and dark evergreens. It had a well-kept garden on a precarious platform of soil.

A woman stood there surrounded by many monks in modest attire. Several nuns were at her side. Their cloth did not fit with the rugged look of the austere monks. The embroidery and royal apparel revealed some sort of distinct nobility. They gently held the young lady. She waited with tearful fear. Again the screech boomed across the sky. Scratching horns echoed from the valley below like talons scraping rustic metal. Evil forces were converging.

The hooves of the horses tore the gardens and what little earth was upon the path. A young monk stepped forward, only to be held back by an elder. The garden plants were ruined as a score of knights reached the grove.

The Black Knight easily leapt off his horse and stomped forward with purpose. The young monk stared at him as the knight looked past him, to her.

"Take her! Save her and your child!" the elder monk said. The nuns cried, releasing her.

The Black Knight paused. His breathing paused. His eyes fixated. She ran to him. She was pregnant yet gripped his armour and him with ferocity. He lightly stepped back to meet her oncoming charge. He held her gently and seemed to weaken.

"MY LORD!?" the elder monk insisted.

The screeching of spiders and the flurry of shaken trees echoed from the vale. The Black Knight quickly leapt to his horse and lifted his love. Though with child, she was nimble and strong, holding his hardened steel body.

The knights quickly turned their horses around and formed up, pulling out their swords. It was a formidable group. All were ready to fight.

"No! No! You must go!" the elder monk said, stepping forward waving his staff. He hit the rear of the armoured horses to little avail. "The wizard awaits!"

The Black Knight galloped through his company and raised his arm. The others sheathed their swords and pushed their horses forward, leaving the grove and its grounds in ruin.

The monks and nuns stood in the grove for their last moments. The young monk stepped forward to help his tired master.

"You must leave as well. Quickly..."

"I'll stay."

"No, Brother Verboden, go... Survive! As Tirnalth ordered."

As the Black Knight and his men rode down the path, they could see the scattering horde of goblin riders and their vicious spider mounts dotting the valley below. The beasts converged upward through the forest vales toward their company. He turned to another path, a hidden one, and raced quickly away.

The path went around and behind the monastery. The goblin raiders converged on the secluded vale and up the road to the green grove. The monks and nuns held each other in silent prayer.

Those not outright killed by the cackling joy of goblin archers, were spun within morbid webs by leaping spiders.

The Black Knight pushed his mount on as never before. The others tried to maintain the same powerful treacherous gallop. They raced through a rocky narrow path, bursting through leaves and branches, up and down the rocky terrain.

A knight went down with his horse along the path, both crashing through the forest and upon sheer rocks. Another knight returned to his fallen comrade. The fallen knight pulled out his sword and quickly killed his maimed horse. He then motioned for the other to continue. He awaited his fate on the path – sword raised.

The Black Knight's horse frothed at the mouth as he pushed it up a steep rocky incline. They raced up a mountainside that was barren of greenery and filled with a forest of stones. In a massive rock peak was a cave opening where an old man, leaning against a staff, waited.

The horse faltered. The Black Knight climbed off, carrying the woman and setting her to his side. His mount tumbled to one side, choking on froth and spittle. He then knelt one last time with his horse as it frothed its last breath and shook to a frozen stillness. The Black Knight stood up as his men got off their exhausted horses.

The knights ascended the rocky terrain. They raised their swords and faced down the slope to the forest-veiled perimeter. They pointed and waved at each other, positioning themselves in squads amongst the rock spires.

The Black Knight unsheathed his sword and held her hand. He looked up through the rocky barren terrain to the cave opening and saw the old man, tired and bent. Even at such a great distance, their eyes met.

A screech permeated the air, and a vast shadow raced across the sky. Dark clouds began to spew as if formed by the explosive passing of a great beast. Goblins on spiders leapt and scurried from the shadows of the evergreens. Amongst the rocks, the knights stood their ground in their fighting groups. They were ready and able, slashing at spider limbs and webbings that spit forth. They attacked without fear and with cause.

The webbings hampered their fighting prowess, giving time for more goblins on spiders to leap forth. As knights aided each other in slashing the webs and scraping their sticky blades against stone, the spiders leapt in. The fighting was fierce and up close. Even as a knight would cut through one strand, another fluttered down from the sky to ensnare. A lone knight would be trapped and killed quickly. They hurried to each other's aid and grouped together, not to win this fight, but to give their leader time.

The Black Knight and his love scurried through the rock formations. He could see spiders leaping up to them from both sides, pushed by crazed goblins. A spider dropped in front of them and spewed forth webbings. The Black Knight leapt away as the woman was entrapped. He leapt from rock to rock and down upon the goblin rider. His blade quickly beheaded the rider and then twirled into the black arachnid beast.

Without stopping, he returned to the woman and sliced the webbing so she could pull herself out. She shook with a great fear. To be so entrapped by a horrific spider shocked her. Its body was as big as a fat pig, and with the spread of its limbs, even bigger. She swirled in his steel arms and couldn't help but see the nasty fangs and black orb eyes of the fallen spider. Was it dead or merely waiting to pounce? She almost fainted but awakened against his cold hard steel.

He lifted her up and hurried up the path. As great a knight as he was, she knew he could not retain such vigor carrying her.

"I can make it," she said too softly. "I can make it!"

He stopped to look at her through his black gilded helm. His breathing rose to a crescendo of choking exhaustion.

"Put me down!"

He complied. She landed on faltering knees but straightened and immediately traversed upwards. This gave him time to stand up and breathe in wanted air. He turned to assess the condition of his knights.

They continued the fight, bravely frustrating large groups of swirling arachnids and their riders. The knights used the tall rocks to avoid the webbings and slashed out as the spiders crept closer. Limbs were sliced, and goblins fell.

Larger spiders crashed through the smaller evergreens and lush summer bushes, methodically lumbering up the mountainside. Leaping from them were larger man beasts, troglodytes. With big jowls and tusks, some with horns, these beasts, part men and part warthogs, were much bigger than the goblins. They challenged the fatigued knights, who had already been dealing with the rush of spinning spiders and frantic goblins.

They pounded heavily with crude spiked clubs and heavy warhammers. The knights, on even ground and with energy, could easily defeat these brutish man beasts. But exhausted, surrounded, and stuck to webbings amongst rocky crags, the knights were failing. Yet they knew what they would be up against when they chose to go with the Black Knight many nights ago.

"Ethralia," the Black Knight whispered. Turning, he looked up to see her lifting her dirtied dress to get footing upon the sheer rocks. She was paces up, pushing upward to the old man at the cave.

The darkness of the clouds was shrouding the mountaintop as the Black Knight clomped upward.

A giant spider towered between him and her. Before the four troglodytes on it could leap off, he was slashing at the planted spider limbs. His blade cut though the chitinous armour, severing ligaments to crumble the great beast. As the behemoth tried to correct itself, his blade was up under its giant fangs and piercing out its spidery orbs. The troglodytes leapt or rolled off their dying mount and were met by the black death of armour and steel. They barely saw as they were rammed by a folded burst of limbs and put into their eternal ghastly sleep by the edge of his sword. Before the giant spider tottered amongst the rocks to its death, four trogs dropped or fell by his blade.

The Black Knight turned and hurried up, controlling his breathing.

At the ledge, the old man seemed unaffected by the screeching power from the sky or the onslaught of bestial attackers when Ethralia and the Black Knight finally reached him.

As they stood before him, breathing heavily, it seemed he waited there much too long. Ethralia and the Knight looked at each other, gasping, wondering.

The old man seemed to wake from a dream. "I am sorry. I am sorry for both of you. I am sorry we failed you."

The Black Knight rushed forward and grabbed the old man by the robe, yanking him back. "Finish it! Do it"

The old man grabbed the steel gauntlet of the Knight, trying to maintain his stance while stepping haphazardly back. The Knight held him up, even as he faltered.

The old man nodded repeatedly.

Ethralia hurried forward, shrinking as a horrific shriek blasted very close to them. Dark smoke exploded from above, cascading darkness around them. She grabbed at her heart and stomach in a wrenching pain from the fright.

"*She* is here," the old man said.

They rushed into the cave. The dark smoke seemed to cover the entrance, darkening the long stony corridor even more. The screech devolved into a deep rumbling roar that brought cracks to the stone and rained down dust and dirt from above.

The Knight pushed Ethralia violently toward the old man. She gasped at his ferocity, falling before the wizard. "Take her! Now!"

She reached up to him.

The Knight turned and faced several shadows of troglodytes lumbering through the dark clouds. Holding heavy spiked maces and stone axes, some wearing crude armour and others looking like bestial cave men, they charged forward like a stampede of bulls.

The wizard brought forth his staff and blasted light into their eyes. The Knight immediately dispensed with one as he raced against the stone wall, leaping past another. It grabbed its throat and dropped. Another swung ferociously, leaving itself open for the Knight's trained thrust. Even in such constraining armour, the Knight moved like a heavyset dancer and a violent wrestler.

One troglodyte managed to smash down on his armour, knocking him back. It made the fatal mistake of looking to the young lady bearing a child. The Knight leapt back up and charged into the troglodyte, piercing its torso and using the falling body as a shield against the others.

He tangled with them, moving about in unconventional ways that confused the simple beast men. He wasn't just a skilled knight with perfected swings. There was a brutality and haphazard fervor to his fighting that amplified the battle even beyond the beasts' comprehension. Six troglodytes lay dead as the Knight staggered to the old man.

"Tirnalth!"

The old man shook with fear, blinking through a sweaty, tearful visage.

"Open the doorway! Open the doorway!!"

The Black Knight pushed him back into the cave. Tirnalth grabbed him on his steel shoulders, standing strong and firm this one moment. The wizard's face came before the Black Knight's helm, as cut shapes of light. Quickly and amidst the swirl of a roar and crackling of stone, Tirnalth said, "Bedenwulf, your name will call me back."

A roar suddenly exploded around them. The wizard stumbled back, dropping his staff. Ethralia ran after them, tears streaming.

A black cloud of smoke burst into the cave right behind them as they retreated. The Knight held up his sword and swung at the darkness.

In the rear was an opening with torches lighting a room. Tirnalth hobbled to the center of it where there was a small altar. He looked up at a small symbol on the wall, a wooden circle upon a stick and spoke to it. "I'm sorry. I had to..."

He waved his arms.

Kurehnde, buht-thaguhm, muhrathum
Kurehnde, buht-thaguhm, muhrathum
Anrhi Mahn Neth Kuh Ruhm

A swirl formed, a vortex opened, and flashes of lightning exploded throughout the room. Ethralia stood at the entrance and quivered violently from the electrical summonings. She ran back out to the darkness of the tunnel, to the swirls of choking smoke.

She threw herself upon the Black Knight, holding him. "No, no, never! I can't!!!!"

She cried upon his steel as he faltered a moment, turning slowly to her. He held her even as the shadow of a dragon skulked ever closer. He looked at her through his helm visor. Their tearful eyes met, but they could not kiss with his helm on.

"I can't..."

"Run, my lady! To the gate! As Tirnalth said, trust him! Run, my lady! Now! Or all is lost!"

"I can't. I can't!"

The swirl of a dark drake reared, and the shadows seemed to darken even upon the armour of the Black Knight.

"Run, Ethralia! Run to the doorway! Now!"

He turned violently around, knocking her to the ground. He swung his sword at a giant dark limb. As it tried to grab him, he let the power of it force him against a wall. Then the Knight quickly leveled his sword. It cut deep into the giant claw. The powerful blade snapped, bursting white hot light. The claw, being pierced, retracted into the darkness. A roar bellowed with anguish. Then the beast began gathering air and force.

The Knight turned to her with shattered sword.

"I love you!" she cried.

The Knight paused, as if all the days to come were of gleaming sunrises. He yanked off his helm to reveal Bedenwulf, the handsome young man, and rushed to her, giving her one long violent kiss. He then released her. "Then go, my lady. I have lived a thousand lives in you, and I will always be with you! Now go!" He held his broken sword and pulled out a small blade.

Even with the billowing dark smoke, a glow of fire illuminated the caverns and shown on their sweaty tear-wrought faces. A guttural roar rose to its crescendo, denoting the imminent blast.

Bedenwulf put his helm back on and gently guided her back with his broken blade.

She nodded, sensing the growing power of evil. She hugged her child within her womb and in shock and fear, like a frightened girl, ran crazily to Tirnalth the Wizard.

He held out his arms for her, but she ran past him into the vortex. She ran as flames and fire engulfed the cave and as the screams of her love and Tirnalth, in horrific death, shattered her.

Chapter Two

Day In The Life

Women and children rushed past a police officer. He was a young black officer standing calmly and confused, peering a bit too long at each woman's frantic retreat past him. Finally, a mother came up to him and pointed back through the city park.

"There's a crazy man who has a boy!"

The policeman gulped and then shrugged, pushing his shoulders forward so his body would walk. His coat and uniform seemed a bit too large for his lanky body.

He walked along the asphalt path through well-groomed trees and bushes to the grassy knolls of the park. He saw what seemed to be a normal day of people leisurely sitting or walking about. Then he noticed a couple pointing and gasping at a commotion down the slope. He stepped forward purposely and saw a man swinging a stick at a boy. The boy rolled desperately away as the man advanced.

He realized the man was a homeless creep with a scarred face. The police officer quickly hurried over with his hand on his gun holster. He was new to the force and unsure of his footing on the morning grass or what exactly he would do in a public place with plenty of witnesses. He just knew he had to save the boy.

The man was armed with some sort of stick. But oddly, the boy had one too. It seemed the boy was fighting for his life.

"Hey, put the stick down!" the officer stuttered. He posed to a side, hiding that his hand was obviously on his gun.

Wooly looked up to see the officer and complied immediately. Alfred stood up and held his stick out like a sword.

"Sir... I mean son... get away from that man," the officer said. His eyes darted not just to Wooly but to all the eye witnesses gathering along the park's pathways.

Wooly raised up his hands in deference, as if it were routine. This comforted the officer somewhat, but he was still jittery, even when Alfred walked forward.

"Hi, officer." Alfred waved his sword.

The officer flinched as if the sword could fire lasers or something. "Hey son, where's your mom or dad?"

"My dad?"

"Yeah, I'll take care of this man, but where's your dad?"

"He is my dad!" Alfred pointed to Wooly with his wooden sword.

The officer looked at the creepy scarred visage of the homeless looking man. Wooly smiled politely. The officer's eyes were raised in fear.

"Are you sure he's your..." The officer then looked at Alfred, who was looking at his father. The officer's shoulders suddenly relaxed, and his smile could not be hidden by his stern look. He tightened his lips as best he could. He knew well, very well, that look. It was the shine of a boy.

The young officer stared for a bit too long. "Sorry about that," he said, smiling politely. Then he choked on something. He sniffed and shook himself. "Just being careful. Got reports of homeless folks bothering people at the park." He said this in a strange way, looking at Wooly's scarred face.

"We're training. Sword training!" Alfred danced about with his wooden sword. He actually did some well-timed moves.

The officer, knowing nothing of swordplay, was still impressed and gave a smug appreciative look. He noticed they had water bottles for two, snacks, and other typical dad-son stuff set to the side. "Okay, okay, you all have a nice day. Try not to, uh... get hurt."

As the officer walked away, Wooly picked up his sword. The officer inadvertently looked back with a jolt and stopped with his

11

sideways ready pose. Wooly froze, unsure. The officer shook it off, gave a bright white smile and continued walking.

Alfred charged at his father, and they tussled – it was a furious round of wood clacking wood. Joggers, walkers, and wanderers along the pathway gasped and pointed. The officer waved them all off, motioning them to move along. Some stayed to video the epic sword fight.

Deftly, without Wooly or Alfred knowing, the young officer swooped out his phone and took a video of the sword fight. He then went on his way, tapping furiously on his phone.

Alfred rushed into the apartment where his mom was busy sewing. It appeared that her work space was getting more and more crowded with odd jobs. Elegant dresses were hooked onto a pole across the fridge and a dresser. Stacks of classic curtains and embroidered clothes lay with orders paper-clipped to them. It appeared many were hearing about her unique antique-like sewing skills, which had not been done for many years, possibly ages.

Wooly followed in from behind, carrying a backpack and the wooden swords. Alfred plopped down in front of his mom and saw her eyes looking over at Wooly as he unpacked the belongings. Alfred didn't mind.

She blinked and shivered a bit and then looked at her son. "How was your day?"

"Awesome, mom! Wooly knows so much about fighting and swordsmanship! I am learning and learning!"

She smiled calmly, continuing with an intricate weave on a cloth that looked odd and ancient. Wooly remained in the kitchen, slowly unpacking the leftover snacks.

Alfred looked quickly from his mother to Wooly. His mind was racing, "Mom?"

She looked up slowly.

He bent in closer. "Do I call him dad?"

She looked at Wooly, who couldn't stop looking at her. She nodded slowly.

Alfred gulped. He turned to look at him. Alfred got up and went over. "This goes in the fridge. Mom wraps it in foil. This can just go in the cabinet. The dirty dishes can go next to the sink."

Wooly nodded, letting Alfred take charge of each item.

"Wooly?" Alfred finally stopped.

Wooly looked from Ethralia to him.

"Are you the Black Knight?"

Wooly looked back at Ethralia. Both of their eyes watered. She returned to her work, speeding up the motions of her delicate fingers betwixt needles and thread.

Wooly looked back at Alfred. "I am. I was."

"Awesome!!!" Alfred did a double fist pump in the kitchen, growling a cool hiss. Wooly looked at him oddly. It was difficult to tell with the scars what his emotions were.

"The Black Knight is my dad!" Alfred growled.

"Alfred!" his mother exhorted.

"It's true!" Alfred waved his hands in the air – like he just don't care.

"Is he going to move in?" Alfred stopped to ask.

Ethralia's eyes exploded into the brightest white glare. Wooly coughed.

"I should go. I have a lot of work to do." Wooly choked on some phlegm or perhaps scar tissue.

Alfred danced about the living room. There was something too giddy and joyous happening within him to contain.

Ethralia quickly stood up. Her work dropped to the floor. She hurried over as Wooly side-stepped to the door. Wooly opened the door and flinched as he realized Ethralia was standing very close. He almost calmed to share a look, but Alfred hopped up from behind and waved at him.

"Alfred?"

"Yes?"

"Say goodbye to your father."

"Bye... dad!"

Wooly nodded.

Ethralia spoke to Alfred while staring at Wooly, "Are you going to show me your new game?"

"Oh yeah, let me get it started!" Alfred said and hurried to his room.

Wooly stared after Alfred, but his gaze slowly and carefully returned to Ethralia, who stood below him, very close. He could have used the door as a shield, if he wanted to.

She looked up at him. He trembled. She grabbed the back of his neck and pulled him closer. She was going to kiss him but felt the scars on her delicate hand. Her fingers began to rub it too quickly and nervously. Her focus shifted from him, the man, to his scars. He pulled back in shame.

"No, no... " she cooed, tears flowing. "I love you. I love you. I love you."

He tried to cover his face and pull away from her hand touching him. He tried to use the door as a shield to separate them. But she wouldn't allow it.

"Mom, it's ready!" Alfred stepped out and gulped.

"Go to your room and close the door!"

Alfred stepped back into his room deftly and shut the door.

"Bedenwulf," she said softly. He stopped, looking sideways at her. "Bedenwulf..." As she said it, she saw his face, his true face, his young face. The face she loved so long ago.

"He is dead," Wooly said and walked away.

She stood there silent as he left.

Chapter Three

Ethralia

She ran to him in the dingy corridor of the apartment complex. She ran to him and grabbed his arm. He turned to her and pulled her to him, as a brave knight would catch a princess. She kissed him furiously along his scarred face and held him with a death grip. He stood stunned and in heaven.

Their lips met, his scarred and broken lips, her full luscious lips. Their tears melted together as they kissed furiously in that hallway.

Alfred leered from the doorway, dry heaving. But he couldn't help but smile. Then quickly turned away. His whole body shivered as he hop-skipped to his room.

Wooly faltered a bit as she kept giving him the death grip. He leaned against the wall. She couldn't help but giggle. He opened his love infused eyes. He was nearly on the floor as Ethralia stood over him, giggling and covering her mouth with her delicate sewing hands. He straightened up, standing tall again.

She stood under him and bit her lip, then pranced back to her door. He stood there, gazing after her.

She winked as she shut the door on him.

He turned with a light step and saw an old lady staring at him from another apartment. He walked past her, nodding.

15

The old lady touched her own face. "I got some cream for that."
He smiled, sort of, and went on his way.

Ethralia leaned against the door waiting for the heat to
dissipate. She wiped her face and fanned herself. She then saw Alfred
staring at her from his bedroom.

"We've been hanging out all these days, and I was wondering
when that would happen!"

"You mind your own business!" She pointed at him like a
funny witch.

"I am!"

She waved him off.

"Want to see my new game?" He rolled his eyes.

"Of course, Alfred, of course!"

She stood behind him. Her eyes glazed as the lights flashed
across his small monitor and the craziest of crashes, booms, screams,
and heavy footsteps crackled from the tiny speakers.

"Oh yeah! Whoop! Reload!"

"What is that? It doesn't look medieval?"

"You mean fantasy?"

"Yes... that, fantis-see? What is fantis-see again?"

"You know, the Westfold, the Northern Kingdom! Goblins and
castles and magic and ogres! That's all fantasy... to us here on Earth."
As Alfred spoke, he was furiously clicking his mouse and tapping his
keyboard. The sounds on the computer were definitely not fantasy.
They were gunfire and explosions. "They call all that fantasy here cuz
it's not real to them."

"Not real?" his mom asked, flinching with each explosive
sound and flash of light.

"Yeah mom, people here don't see goblins or monsters! No
powerful witch! It's all fantasy to us here. It isn't real. Magic isn't real
here. It's just for games and movies and stuff."

"Well, that is a relief! Then what is this you are playing? It
looks violent?"

"It's modern mom! Modern!"

"Those are guns? Like today? Like policemen?"

"Nah, like special forces, military!"

As they spoke, Ethralia flinched with each rumble of gunfire, or
a pull of a pin and toss of a grenade that exploded. Alfred was even

16

more active in his chair, swiveling from side to side and quickly tapping keyboard and mouse.

"I thought you only liked medieval fantis-see."

"Well... everyone needs a break!" Alfred shrugged, then jerked as he ducked, moving the onscreen point-of-view down an alleyway. "At least we don't have to deal with this in the Westfold! Imagine that mom, guns and stuff!? Special forces!! Phew! No way!"

"It looks so real Alfred, as if you are there."

The screen showed the point of view of the player, of Alfred, as his black-gloved hands lifted up his automatic rifle and dropped the spent magazine for a new one. The character then began firing bursts into enemy soldiers rushing to and fro in the distance. Alfred gritted his teeth.

"Why do you play all these games that kill? Why must it always be violent?"

"Mom? Seriously. It's just a game. I just need a break from it all. Sometimes medieval fantasy uhh... reality can get to be too much! Besides, I live in both worlds! Good to know this stuff too. Well, just for fun! Not like we will ever have to experience this!"

Ethralia stared for a while as Alfred's computer character rushed along, a special forces soldier, in and out of war torn scenery, rubble, and debris.

"Mom?"

"Yes?"

"Is Wooly... is dad going to move in?" Alfred talked with concern even as he typed furiously and slapped his mouse back and forth. There was furious gunfire on the screen.

"Oh, uh, I don't know Alfred."

"Just seems like, you know, now that you two know, well that we know, he's alive. You two aren't, you know... getting back together? I mean this is the first time he even came in!"

Ethralia's shoulders slumped. She looked at Alfred and rubbed his back. "Do you want him to?"

"I dunno." Alfred's character hid behind rubble and the screen switched to the zoom of a rifle scope. In quick succession, he shot enemy after enemy. The units dropped dead with one shot in each head.

"Why does it look different?" his mom asked, peering closer.

"I'm zoomed in, with my sniper scope. Uh, you know... I am looking through – like a spyglass. It's on top of my gun."

Ethralia flinched again as explosions rang out and the screen turned into violent chaos.

"Oh, I got blasted!" Alfred slapped his mouse down. The screen showed him on the ground sideways as enemy boots stomped by.

"It looks so much more real than the others, Alfred. Are you sure this isn't giving you nightmares?"

"Mom? Nightmares? After what I've been through?"

His mom shrugged, unsure of whether to giggle or cry. She held his shoulders and lowered her head close to kiss his hair.

"You two should get married."

Ethralia lifted her head, eyes wide.

"Wait, are you married? Aren't you? Did you two get together and have me and weren't married?"

Ethralia stared off as Alfred looked up at her.

"Mom? Marriage?"

"Oh. We were married."

"Were?" Alfred thought a moment. "Are????"

Ethralia's eyes darted back and forth. Her brows furrowed. "It was not allowed. We were married in secret, by a young cleric. We tricked him and had him recite the vows to us. He thought it was to practice... We betrayed a most sacred ceremony."

"A young cleric? Oh boy. Seriously!? Oh no.......... Verboden??"

"We were young – he was younger. We were friends." She clasped her hands to her face, covering her thoughts.

"But the King, your father, didn't give you permission, huh?"

"No."

Alfred couldn't help but smirk. "Well, you're still married."

"Not in this world."

Alfred scratched his chin. "Yeah, not in this world. Maybe we could have a small ceremony here? But first, you two need to go on a date. A real date!"

Ethralia looked up at Alfred, a slight glow in her demeanor. Her eyes darted to and fro.

"You have never gone out or been on a date! And now you can. Course, he's got a scary-scarry face, so it should probably be somewhere dark and not eating. Definitely not a restaurant thing! With his scary teeth lips! Oh no... Oh! ...Go to the movies!"

"Movies? Where they play the big TV?" Ethralia danced to Alfred's bed and plopped upon a luxuriously modern cheap mattress with clean sheets and not one, but two blankets.

"Yeah, yeah, it's dark and everyone is staring up at a screen. It will be perfect, you know, for his face!"

Ethralia blinked, sitting up. "Why do people do that?"

"Cuz that's what people do here! It's just like theatre!"

"But it's a TV?" she pointed to his small used antennae TV.

"It's a big TV! Just... trust me, you'll like it. You sit next to each other and watch something cool on a big TV! Everybody does it. Well not us, but everybody in this world does it."

She shrugged.

"And wear something... not so medieval," said Alfred.

"Like my work clothes?"

"Nooooo.... like jeans and a nice shirt or something."

"Jeans? Those are … yech."

"Mom... seriously, you're in this world. You should at least try to... you know... be part of it."

"I could probably get some from work. There are a lot of discarded clothes. I'll look through them."

"No!!! Buy something nice. Shop for one nice modern thing... one nice outfit!"

She stood and thought about it. She had a bit of a prance in her step as she left his room. Alfred followed her out to the living room.

"Oh, by the way, is dinner ready?"

Ethralia smiled at him and then noticed the dim flashing of red lights through their windows.

Alfred rushed over and looked down. "Oooh, was there an accident on the street?"

Ethralia was not bothered and went to the small kitchen.

Alfred peered for a while as Ethralia pulled out a pot of stew to heat.

"Mom? I think they are at Wooly's place."

Ethralia suddenly dropped the pot and rushed to the window. A swelling of fear rose so quickly, it was as if fate were never letting her go.

She grabbed the window sill so hard, her face was pale, and she saw them.

Police had Wooly handcuffed and were placing him in their car.

"Noooooo..." she gasped. "Not again." She became instantly frail and quivered, faltering among her seamstress projects.

"Mom, it's okay. Let's go down there. It ain't like they're evil Dark Lord servants."

"Don't say that! Don't ever say that!" Ethralia stood, her pale skin sweating, her tear-ridden eyes reddening.

Alfred stepped back, looking at her sudden change of disposition.

She swooned slightly and grabbed Alfred for support. He held her. She nodded, "Yes, yes, you are right."

"It's gotta be a mistake. They only arrest bad guys. Well, Wooly looks like a bad guy, but he's not! Okay, he's not a bad guy. They'll let him go once they realize it. Okay mom, it's gonna be okay."

"Yes, okay, let's go."

Chapter Four

Trouble in Paradise

They came out of the building and saw Wooly sitting in the back of a police car, behind a greasy dark window. He looked up at them but showed no emotion.

"Excuse me, officer. Why is he being arrested?" Alfred asked nervously.

"Step back, son. This is police business," a large officer with a clipboard said. There were two police cars and another official looking car. Several people with gloves on were inside the workshop looking around.

"He's my dad," Alfred said. The officer stopped and looked at Alfred, then at the lady behind him.

"You the mother?" he asked dryly.

"Yes, I am Alfred's mother."

"That your boyfriend?" the officer asked. A woman in a suit came up.

"Boyfriend?" Ethralia quivered.

"They're married! He's my dad. She's my mom."

"Then you must know what he's doing here? With no license, no rental fee, no identification? In a closed lot? He can't even prove his citizenship," the official looking woman said.

Alfred and Ethralia stared wide eyed.

"We're going to need to take you two as well, since you're related."

Several police officers walked towards them.

"Your husband is non-compliant."

Ethralia rushed from them to the police car window. She stared close at Wooly and began crying. She smacked her hand upon the window and pressed hard as if she were trying to push through. Officers rushed to her and held her back.

"Mom!?"

The woman came up to Alfred. "Son, do you have any documents of identification for you, for your parents?"

"Any whah?"

The woman leaned in closer, talking softly to Alfred, "What's your name?"

"I'm Alfred."

"That's a rare name these days."

Alfred shrugged, tears falling down his cheeks. To be king of a realm, savior of a land, and then to be here, surrounded by police officers and defenseless, stunned him.

"Alfred, where do you live?"

Alfred pointed up to an apartment window.

Policemen were handcuffing his mom and taking her to the second police car.

"Is that necessary?" the woman said, looking at the policemen and Ethralia handcuffed and sobbing.

"She's emotional," a cop shrugged.

The woman rolled her eyes.

"What are you going to do with my mom and dad?"

"We just need to know who they are. Once we know where they came from, what nation they are citizens of, we can figure this all out. Can you answer that for me?"

Alfred stared wide-eyed at her as tears continued to stream down his face. The police pushed his mother to their car. She suddenly seemed like any ragged crazed woman. People gathered along the streets to stare at the obvious criminals.

"Can you take me to your apartment and show me any paperwork, any identification?"

"I don't know."

"Wait, please wait, *he is a citizenship!* He is it!" his mother finally screamed as they were pushing her into the car.

The woman turned and waved them to bring her back.

The police rolled their eyes and lifted her back up.

"He was born here. I gave birth to him here. I have his birth certificate!"

"Oh, an anchor baby? How fortunate. Well, that's a start."

At the station Alfred and his mother sat in a stark white room with a mirror.

"Mom, these are those interrogation rooms like on TV."

His mom sat silent. Before them were two cups, one of water and the other of coffee. A half-eaten package of crackers sat before Alfred. Beside that there was a small worn manila folder with papers inside.

The woman on the street entered with a cup of coffee and some folders. She sat opposite them and placed another folder down.

"Well, you two, or three, are a big mystery."

"What have you done with my husband?"

The woman was calm as she stared at Alfred's mom. Ethralia looked worn out and tired.

"Obviously, you are illegal aliens. And guess what? We have a new sheriff in town. Have you been paying attention to the elections? Did you vote? Probably in this district, right? We are not going to allow illegal aliens to run around starting unlicensed businesses in condemned lots. Even white folks, okay? We're not racist like the news keeps reporting. We're equal opportunity! So until you, and your husband, tell us the truth, with who you are and where your citizenship actually is, well, there's going to be some difficulties ahead for you."

"We don't have citizenship here!" Alfred burst out.

"Son, you have citizenship because many politicians seem to want to flood this nation with as many foreigners as they can. And they'll use unborn children to do it. They pick and choose which laws they want to enforce. That's tyranny, by the way. But no more. We are enforcing our citizenship laws now. These years of your mother and father living under the radar are not going to fly anymore."

Alfred gulped and looked at his mother. She leaned forward and waved her hands. What was she doing? Alfred gasped. His mother stopped and looked at him. He nodded no at her.

"What are you doing?" the woman asked, flicking her hands about, imitating Ethralia's movements. "Is that some magical mind trick?"

Alfred nodded no again, desperately at his mother. She sunk in her chair, looking even creepier.

"We just need the truth, ma'am. Where did you come from?"

"From another world!" Ethralia said. Alfred glared at her. Her hair was ragged, and her eyes seemed sunken. He almost didn't recognize her. She seemed to fit in nicely with this room.

"Another world? That's not helpful."

"It's true!" Alfred said. "They're not from here!"

"Then where? What nation are they from? From England? Their English is quite good and very Shakespearean. Or Irish or perhaps some colonized African nation? And the apartheid movement had them forcibly removed? You know, if that's the case, we might be able to help you. Asylum is an option."

"Yes, asylum! I have heard of this. We want asylum!" Ethralia sat up, grabbing the edge of the table with her pale shaking hands.

"Well ma'am, that's fine, but you still have to tell us what nation you are seeking asylum from."

"What if it's too dangerous?" Alfred said.

The lady stopped and looked at them. Ethralia was breathing heavily, glaring up from a down-turned face. Alfred had a strange boyish smile and a furrowed brow.

"Okay, if you two are going to play with me, and the United States of America... then we can just put you in the..."

"We're not playing. Please!" Alfred changed his knowing expression to one of worry. "We don't know what to do."

The lady sat back. She rubbed her forehead. "I can't believe I'm wasting time on you two. Here's another question. If this 'Wooly' guy is your husband, why does he sleep in a condemned building?"

Alfred and Ethralia looked at each other.

"My mom didn't know he was her husband because of the scars."

The lady slowly blinked.

"She didn't know until a few weeks ago. He was hiding from her... from us... But he was protecting us."

"Protecting you? Now we're getting somewhere. From who?"

Alfred and Ethralia sat silent.

"How did he get those scars?"

"From those who want to destroy us," Ethralia said.

The woman looked at her. She sipped her coffee and formed a slight sneer. But then she saw Alfred's look. It was of fear, real fear. Ethralia looked like a crazed woman, ready to pounce. The woman casually took her hand down to unclasp her taser holster hidden under the table.

Alfred looked up and shuddered. He then reached out to his mom with an open hand. Ethralia flinched and seemed to melt into a mother. She took Alfred's hand and held it.

The woman casually brought her hand back up and tapped on the manila office folder, sipping more coffee.

"He'll have to live with you until we figure this out."

Alfred sat up with a stunned glee.

"You can't go anywhere. You must stay put till I figure out what to do with you. Understood?"

Alfred nodded vigorously. His mother closed her eyes as tears trailed down her face.

"I appreciate the fact that you have worked in one laundromat for over ten years and you," she nodded to Alfred, "go to school. So it seems you have made a decent life for yourself. But not all the 'i's are dotted, not all the 't's are crossed. I'm going to have to go to upper management on this one. You must stay put and stay together!"

"Oh heck yeah!" Alfred said, punching a fist into the air.

The woman couldn't help but sneak a smile. She hid it quickly with another sip of coffee.

"Alfred, could you wait outside while I talk to your mother for just a bit?"

"Outside, out there?"

"Yes, just out in the hall. There are benches there. It will only be a minute," she said softly, motioning for him to go.

Alfred nodded, moving slowly with each motion she made.

As the metal door closed, the lady turned to Ethralia. "Do you have any relatives, anywhere your son can stay?"

Ethralia slowly nodded no.

"Is it possible for you to find anyone?"

"We have no one."

"Is there anything you can tell me, anything at all, that your son doesn't need to know, but that can help this case? Is it drug related? Were you and your husband drug smugglers? Are you hiding from criminal organizations?"

"Drugs? No... not criminal..."

"Political?"

"No... yes... I think... is that of leaders?"

"So you are fleeing for political reasons. That's good, but you have to say from where. You have to give us more information."

"I can't."

"Then we can't help you."

Ethralia wiped tears and tried to think.

"We are cracking down on illegals. We can't have millions of foreigners swarming into our nation with no accountability. We need to know who you are and where you came from. It's that simple. And if we don't, if you don't tell us, well, I'm not sure what we'll do. If you don't prepare for the worst, for your son, he may end up in foster care. And moved around by social worker after social worker."

Ethralia nodded. Her face was red hot, swollen and moist.

"I'm sorry. You are a good mother, protecting your son."

Ethralia began to cry profusely.

Even the woman was touched. "I will do what I can for you. But please, figure out the truth, figure out your asylum case. Get a lawyer. And when you are ready, come back to me – while there is still time."

The woman put her contact card down on the table, took up her folders and coffee, and walked out.

Ethralia was busy sewing. Her delicate fingers worked robot-like and intricately on the embroidery of a dress. Alfred stood at the window looking down on the street below. He was eating a bowl of stew.

"Has he moved?" she asked, still focused on her work.

"Nope," Alfred said, taking in another spoonful of thick stew.

Down below, Wooly stood, with a few belongings in bags, staring at his taped off workshop. It had the yellow POLICE LINE - DO

NOT CROSS ribbon across the garage door and a lock bolted on the side door.

"He better not go in there," Alfred said, tearing fresh baked bread with his teeth.

"He'll come," she said.

Finally, Wooly turned toward their building and walked out of Alfred's view. "He's coming!" Alfred finished his food in a rush.

"Slow down, you'll choke on your dinner!"

Alfred plopped the bowl and bread down next to his mom. "Mom, where's he going to sleep?"

His mom slowly looked about the room as her fingers continued their needle work. There was a couch, a bit of floor space, lots of curtains, dresses, and classic wardrobe about. There was her pillow, sheets, and blanket she prepared each night for her bed. She shrugged and looked into Alfred's eyes.

Alfred returned the look with a gross sneer.

There was a soft knock. Alfred rolled his eyes and went to the door. She hid a smile.

"Dad!" Alfred said in a strange manner.

Wooly cringed as he stood still.

"Come in. Come in." Alfred waved.

Wooly leaned forward and walked in. He had a floppy duffel bag of stuff.

"They kept you awhile," Alfred said.

Wooly looked at his fingers.

"They fingerprinted you too?" Alfred asked.

Wooly nodded. "Why?"

Alfred looked at his. "Fingerprints are unique. We all have different fingerprints. And there's like a big database of them across America, even the world! Well, this world! Hah! Guess we're in the system now, though I doubt they'll ever trace you and mom's fingerprints from anywhere in this world!" Alfred spoke with aplomb. "You want some stew?"

Wooly nodded and set his stuff down. Alfred looked at his mom for assistance. She gave Alfred a look as she continued her sewing. Alfred shrugged and went to the kitchen. He had to remember where bowls and the spoons were. But he acted nonchalantly about it and finally got Wooly a piece of bread.

Wooly couldn't help but look at his wife most of the time. Alfred tried small talk, just about kitchen things, or mom things, or Alfred things.

"Ooh, wanna see my game?"

"Not now, Alfred," his mom said.

Alfred had a bowl of stew ready. He handed it to Wooly, who took it without even looking, and set it down on the counter. Alfred puckered his lips. He looked to and fro. Ethralia stared at Wooly, sewing mechanically. Wooly stared back, gripping the counter.

Alfred shivered and clapped his hands. "So... I'm the only citizen here! What we gonna do about it? Guys, we'll need an immigration lawyer?"

Silence.

He tapped his foot, realized he was tapping his foot, and then stopped. He gulped. He shuffled around Wooly and into the space between him and his mom. They did not seem to notice him.

He slowly walked to his bedroom door then turned to look at them, staring at each other so strangely. "Mom, I think I'll go to my kingdom, where I am, you know, a king. To the Westfold, to the Northern Kingdom, the one I saved from ogres and goblins and things. Saved the people. The farmers. Their families. Saved the gnomes from their Underworld prison. Yah know? Oh and Nubio and his kin, they were enslaved by the ogres. Big bad brutal ogres....??? Pretty scary stuff! Could have been killed many many times."

Nothing.

"Mom!?"

"Yes, Alfred?"

"I'm going... to the Westfold, to my kingdom," he said. He looked down at his hands as they were fading. "Yep, I'm going."

"Be careful, Alfred."

Alfred sneered as he was fading, but he did not fade fast enough.

Ethralia leapt to her husband.

Chapter Five

GROTHAM KEEP

Alfred stood in his cold damp room in Grotham Keep. It was still intact even though most of the castle was in ruins from the ogre bombardment. He stood wide eyed, gaping, then choking. He shivered, not from the cold but from seeing his mother be *sooo aggressive*. He did not expect that from his modest, humble, naturally beautiful mother, to see her leap at, well, his father!

He stuck his tongue out and wretched. He shook off the visual and the feeling. He looked about the room as he exhaled a cold mist. It was dark. Faint sunlight came from the window. He noticed there was dust and cobwebs. He looked about the room. His water basin was still there, but dry and crusty.

He became a little anxious. He opened the small wooden door to the corridor and spiral stairway. He quickly stepped out onto the upper walkway and looked out onto the Great Hall that was in ruins.

Except, it was not in ruins. Though the ogres had completely demolished it, it was now filled with canopies and tents and tables for work. It was riddled with a maze of scaffolding and tinkering gnomes. Candles and oil lamps dotted the space like Christmas time at a church. And the space was markedly larger! The Great Hall was going to be even greater!

He stood in awe at the prodigious affair. Everyone was quite busy. The sun was just coming up, and beautiful gold beams glowed in sparkling shafts of light through the structures. The rays spanned across work canopies and banners, fluttering light through laundry and fabrics.

Alfred rushed down the stairs to the main floor and ran out to see all the activity. He looked to and fro at the incredible array of men and gnomes hammering and tinkering away.

Several shadowy figures on the scaffolding were peering down at Alfred and then ducked away.

Lord Dunther the knight quickly walked past with scrolls of parchment, which Alfred recognized as designs for the Keep. He nodded, "Alfred."

Lord Gorham was just behind him, in casual attire, carrying several mugs of warm something. He nodded, "milord."

They passed. Sir Murith, the younger knight, suddenly appeared from between scaffolds and met Alfred's eyes. He paused a bit too long, seeming unsure of which way to turn, then bowed and retreated out of sight.

Abedeyan, the venerable castle steward, came out from under a tent. He stretched with his cane in hand, yawned and noticed Alfred. He bowed curtly. "King Alfred."

Alfred bowed back but then remembered not to bow and quickly stood. Abedeyan grimaced, then turned and went beyond his view.

Alfred furrowed his brows and rubbed his chin. He peered up and saw Captain Hedor's men working up on the wood scaffolds, hammering wood to extend the structure. The once scrappy bandits had now returned to their working ways. Beyond the tents and flowing canopies, he could see dozens and dozens of gnomes building new walls. It was a delight to see color and health return to these gnomes, after being isolated in their underworld caverns.

Before he had left, they were still in the planning stages of the ruined Keep. But now it was incredible to see the progress they had made, with several levels of solid silvery-gray stones perfectly placed. In no time the wall would be up, forty feet or more. And by the looks of the gnome's skillful stone cuts, they'd be precisely fitted pieces.

Alfred pondered everyone's behavior toward him, heading into the thick of it to see the work. He stood in what seemed the eye of the storm where everyone was quite busy and he, King of the Castle... was unattended. He straightened up and strutted, trying to use his kingship to get some attention. He then noticed Lady Nihan and her servants curtsying and hurrying up the stairs with brooms, a bowl of warm water, and folded wool blankets to his room.

Alfred crossed his arms and glared at them. Lady Nihan clasped her hands and obviously looked caught. She came back down to Alfred as her team hurried up to his bedroom.

"My lord, my King, so good to have you back! Forgive me your highness. We were not expecting you so soon."

"So soon? How long was I gone?"

"Weeks? A good month, perhaps?"

"That's it? Oh yeah, I wasn't really gone that long. My teleportation, just as it changes where I am, it can change time... based on how I focus... Seemed longer though, what with... well, never mind. Seems a lot has happened since I've only been gone a short while."

"Oh yes, my lord, the gnomes are a diligent folk. They love their work, their stone... and... OUR food."

"Oh?"

"As a matter of fact, you get cleaned up as we shall be breaking the fast shortly!"

"Ooh breaking our fast!?" Gib spat excitedly as he trudged by carrying an oversized stone. Gnomes could carry twice, no thrice, no *fier or funf* their weight in stone!

"Breaking?" Alfred shrugged and smiled, ready to say hi and get a hug.

"Milord," Gib nodded and continued on. Pep came up after him with an even larger stone. He appeared not to notice Alfred at all. After all, he was carrying a large stone!

Alfred blinked, arms splayed. He then looked at Lady Nihan who hid a smile and hurried away.

31

Alfred was dumbfounded. Hadn't anyone missed him?... Oh, wait a minute, he thought, he then skipped and sauntered over to Dunther and Gorham at a large table under a temporary wooden roofing. Several gnomes stood on stools and workbenches. It was obvious they were arguing or passionately discussing the design and workings of the new castle.

Nubio, the ex-slave Khanafian boy, suddenly rushed from somewhere and hugged Alfred from the side. He smiled with a big grin then looked closely at Alfred. "Ooops! I'm not supposed to..." He gritted his teeth, let go, and rushed away.

Alfred twirled about and then refocused his attention to the planning table. He walked up.

"The outer wall will be a third the height and on the slope," said Dunther. "We must also make sure the foundation is on stone or dig trenches and fill them with rubble to support it."

King Gup answered, "Our gnomes will not need to fill it with rubble sire! Solid stone, through and through!"

"If you can do that, we are much obliged! And the foundations of the outer walls?"

"Here and here, the rock is solid underneath," said King Gup. "On the north and west, we can dig from below and put in foundations. Plenty of good rock underneath."

Alfred stepped up closer to peer at the castle plans. His eyes widened like those of a boy at a medieval fair surrounded by knights and fantasy folk. Only, these were real ones.

Gorham casually handed him a warm broth. Alfred took it and sipped. Dunther glanced at Alfred drinking his broth and then glared at Gorham, who shrugged.

Suddenly, everyone laughed a huge guffaw as Alfred was in mid sip. He was slightly blurred by the steam and tried to look out at what was amiss. Dunther charged him and jostled him even as he held his mug of hot broth.

He bear hugged him. "Alfred!!! King! King! King! Alfred!! You're back!!! So soon??!!"

"I don't know. I guess, cough cough..." Alfred found a quick moment to set the mug down, splashing broth on the castle plans. No one noticed or cared. "I lost track of time!"

"Much sooner than we expected and plans are going well! The gnomes are a great, great hard working folk!"

King Gup, brother of Gib, bowed along with his engineers. Gib and Pep suddenly appeared, sans the burdensome stones.

Nubio rushed up. "Can we say hello now?!"

They all laughed again. "It was our plan, when you returned..."

"To ignore me or act like nothing new? I know, I know..." Alfred nodded.

"Oh well, not impressed I see!" Dunther yelled quite close. "Look here, Alfred, the gnomes are giving us the most solid wall known to man or foul beast! Solid stone all the way through!"

"Stone from the deep!" King Gup said. He was oddly dressed in simple wools, his gnome crown the only signifier of his title. "Our stone from down below is the strongest!"

"And they carve it to fit perfectly, making it stronger than anything man has ever made!" Dunther said.

"Hey ho! It's our king!" Captain Hedor dropped, literally, from above.

Hedor rushed up and hugged Alfred, who had already been hugged several times now. Ruig and the rest of the crew were there as well.

"BREAK'N THE FAST!!!!" suddenly rang out, along with the clanging of a crude iron bell.

The constant pinging and scraping of sculpted and placed castle stone suddenly stopped and was replaced by the excited chatter of scores upon scores of gnomes and working men. Lady Nihan directed cooks and servants as they came out of the half stone, half temporary wood hut kitchens. The ladies came in succession with tray after tray of biscuits and boiled eggs, honey and butter. Creams and milks were poured from vast jugs into tiny gnome cups.

Alfred was amazed at the setup. There was table after table with men and gnomes mixed. The benches were made to accommodate both. The gnomes placed smaller wooden boxes on the benches so they could sit up higher. All were anxious for the fare.

Nubio's people, the Khanifians, were there as well, mixed among the workers and servants, busy and happy as the rest, welcomed as family.

Dunther came up to Alfred and said, "We are a rich kingdom, Alfred. Very rich. The gnomes are a great ally. They work incredibly hard and long hours with little need for rest. And all they want in return is food, heaps of it.

Long have they lived in the Underworld, ailing generation after generation. And now, we are showing them a whole new world... or the world they should have known."

Alfred watched the gnomes' delight and enthrallment with each morsel of buttery steamy biscuit, the dollop of butter melting away or the oozing of honey. Each placement in their mouth of a cooked yolk or a drought of milk seemed like a drunken gulp of the finest wine. Not that Alfred knew what the finest wine even was!

King Gup sat amongst them, lowering his royal demeanor, his previous sheriff-like visage replaced by that of an excited child. Gib and Pep were in a flurry of not only tasting but gorging on the simple yet rich foods. They crossed each other's arms in trying to reach everything and put everything in their mouths!

The gnomes looked quite different from how they appeared when Alfred first saw them. Aside from their pasty white skin, they were now more visible all around. They had small bulbous bodies, thin in the joints yet with strong sinewy connections and round in the muscles, as if they were quite strong and virile. And most had the cutest of tight little bellies, extending outward in a perfectly round shape. They also seemed quite proud of their own, as toward the end of the meal they patted themselves on their stomachs.

They were wearing quaint woolen garb. They were quite simple and, well, ill fitted. Then Alfred realized why. During the meal Lady Nihan was not resting at all. She and the other seamstresses were measuring and fitting any gnome they could get their hands on. The gnomes ignored them as if it were routine. She and her lady seamstresses were trying to make them new clothes to wear, especially for the coming winter. Their outfits weren't the best, but better than the grimy dark leathery clothing they wore in the Underworld. Alfred saw gnome wives watching as they were learning to sew again. They were attentive to every remark Lady Nihan would make.

Up here was quite different from down there. The weather changed, and the gnomes were not used to the changes. As hardy as they were against stone and earth, the clinging cold mornings and burning afternoon sun were deleterious to them. Some had mitts, while others rubbed their cold fingers. Some had sweaters, while others still shivered in leathery mushroom skins. Lady Nihan and her servants were doing the best they could as quickly as they could, amidst the chaos of giggling, guffawing, chortling, and chewing gnomes. Alfred couldn't help but smile.

"Would you like to break your fast and eat, King Alfred?" Dunther asked.

"Breakfast?"

"Break your... *breakfast*? Hmph, that's much quicker," said Dunther, considering.

"Oh no, I just ate stew with my mother and..."

Dunther waited as Alfred seemed to peel off into thought. Gorham, Nubio, and Abedeyan stood nearby.

"...and... him... my... " Alfred seemed suddenly pale.

Dunther looked at him earnestly, unsure.

"...my father..." Alfred finally said.

Dunther's eyes widened. He looked at Gorham, whose jaw dropped.

Alfred faltered, lowering his head. Dunther went to a knee and scooted in closer, to peer at Alfred's downcast eyes. "Your father?"

Alfred nodded, trying to hide his face from everyone. Dunther was unconcerned.

"Your father – Bedenwulf?"

Alfred nodded. He brought one hand to his face, turning away, trying to hide his teary eyes with his trembling fingers.

The shanty-like temporary hall, filled with the incredible and cantankerous noise of eating gnomes suddenly quieted as all turned to peer at the King.

"Bedenwulf is alive?!"

Alfred nodded.

Dunther's eyes darted to and fro, trying to read every movement on Alfred's face. Gorham bent down to listen intently.

"He's scarred, his face," Alfred said, covering his. He cringed, muffling a cry.

Dunther gritted his teeth. "Burned by dragon fire?"

Alfred looked at Dunther and nodded.

"Your father, Alfred, you've been blessed," Dunther said, hugging Alfred, holding him dearly. "You've been given a great gift, to know your father."

Alfred tried a smile.

"How did he... how did you... when?" Dunther knew not what to ask or even if he should.

"He was there the whole time. Mom and I didn't know. He was protecting us. He was afraid they'd find us."

"He watched over you all these years, hidden by his scarred visage?"

Alfred nodded, then cried, and hugged Dunther tightly. Dunther teared as well, holding Alfred and softly rubbing his back. "He is a great knight."

"He's my dad," Alfred stood back, wiping what tears he could. "I have a dad."

"Alfred, could you do something for me?"

"Yeah, uh huh..."

"When you see him next, tell him I forgive him. I forgive him wholeheartedly. Tell him that, yes?" Dunther pleaded in joy. "That my jealousy of their love is cast out!"

"Yes, I can tell him."

"Alfred, your father was the greatest of us knights. The greatest!"

"Handy in a fight," added Gorham dryly.

Alfred finally got a smile out. He wiped his face quickly and sniffled to get a good breath and clear his emotions.

"After all these years, he's alive," said Gorham, nodding smugly. "Well that's adding a twist."

Dunther stood up and expanded his lungs. It was as if he had forgotten to breathe. He shared a look with Gorham but said nothing further.

Dunther looked at Alfred, who seemed dazed. Nubio came up to pat him on the back and share a bright smile.

Alfred noticed Nubio with a sword. "Hey, where'd you get that?"

"I'm a squire!"

"A squire?"

"To milord Dunther!"

Dunther nodded.

"It is not a slave! It is like a slave because I do so much for him! And he yells at me and makes me get everything for him!"

Dunther's brows raised. Gorham nodded agreement.

"But I get to choose!"

"Choose?"

"Yes... to be his slave... I mean squire!"

"And!?" Dunther waved a finger.

"And he trains me! To one day be a great knight!" Nubio then contorted his face to remember. "Oh... if the king allows it???"

"Well, duh, yep, heck-a-doodles yes!"

Nubio bounced with glee and clapped his hands.

Suddenly clopping was heard outside the makeshift hall. Beyond the slowly fluttering sheets, a beautiful grey horse could be seen. Its saddle and reins were of an elegant brown and green, finely sewn with embroidery of what appeared to be vines and leaves. Upon it sat Sir Murith in comfortable looking linens. And leaping from it was Loranna.

She rushed through the work area and up to Alfred. He opened his arms but was not quite ready for the charge. Loranna hugged him dearly and kissed his cheeks repeatedly. Alfred suddenly got visions of his mother and Wooly and gave a slight grimace. It was much to the pleasure of the men standing about. Nubio smiled a bit too enthusiastically as well.

Loranna, in archer gear, caught his look. "What was that? Not glad to see me then?"

"Oh no, no, no, not that! I am!" Alfred said, blushing.

"Not that? Not what?"

"Not... I dunno... I am glad to see you!"

"You've been gone thirty-four days and a morning!" she said.

"I was seeing my mom... and dad."

"Well, you don't have to be gone that... what? Your father?"

Alfred nodded again.

Dunther and Gorham nodded and waved as they went off to get back to work. Dunther had to pull Nubio out from the scene. "Yaahp!"

The gnomes and men began to depart the mess ridden tables to begin anew their work for the day.

"You must tell! Everything!!!" Loranna said, taking his hand. But she saw it in his face, that his revelation was a burden. So she hugged him gently. "I'm sorry, Alfred." She let go and stood back, looking down and away.

"Loranna?" he asked gently. "Can I come over for dinner tonight? And tomorrow, can you take me to all the farms, to see all the girls and boys!?"

Loranna looked up and hugged him again, whispering in his ear, "Tonight! Dinner!"

She ran off to Sir Murith and waved him to his horse. "Come, I have a dinner to make!"

Murith looked at Alfred and rolled his eyes. Back to his horse he went.

"My lady?" Murith bowed as Loranna giggled and was helped up to his great steed.

Dunther yelled from the worktable, "Alfred! Ready to be King again?"

Alfred nodded and hurried over.

Chapter Six

Castle Works

The dinner with Loranna, her sister Niranna, her brother Noren and her parents was wonderful. They had baked him a strange but tasty pastry dish they called a Westfoldham. It was salty pork and melted farmer's cheese wrapped in a light fluffy pastry. Alfred ate a bit too much.

Lord Dunther and Sir Murith were there as well. After all, a king always had to have his royal guards with him. And since they were there, they might as well eat too!

Nubio stood outside in the cold dark with the horses. He stared wide-eyed at the window. He licked his lips, pouted and sighed, for this was his lot in life. He peered out in the cold evening. There were many signs of activity at this farm. Fences and stockades were built. The barns were nearly complete with goats and sheep milling about. The Westfold farmers, rich with ogre treasure, were rebuilding their farmsteads.

Lord Dunther suddenly appeared. "How are the horses?"

"Oh, they are fine," Nubio said, standing straight.

Dunther peered at his noble steed, caressing its head. The horse knew its master and tilted its head to Dunther.

Nubio stood back and tried to appear servant like. Dunther eyed him.

"Nubio?"

"Yes milord?"

"You're terrible at the sword, you're not much of a rider, your arms are gangly, and you've just been freed from oppression. Why be a squire? I fret the day I offered it to you."

Nubio gulped. His eyes teared a bit.

"Answer me," Dunther asked softly, kindly.

"I have no home or place to go."

"You could help Verboden or attend to castle life. You are a good healer like your people, the Khanafians. You could train to be a healer? Or return to your home, your lands?"

"I was taken when I was very young. I do not know where it is or if any of my people are alive. I want to be with you, to learn to fight so my people will not be slaves."

"Everyone is a slave. To someone."

"But by choice. It is not a slave if you choose. I am not a slave. Anymore."

Dunther nodded, caressing his horse, taking in the cool night air. There was laughter from within. A warm light shown on Nubio's curious face.

"Have you ever had Westfoldham, Nubio?"

"What?"

"Go on! Try some! They are waiting for you."

"But who will watch the horses?"

"It is fine, Nubio. We are in safe lands..."

Nubio hurried in and upon opening the door, a loud chorus of "Nubio!" rang out. Everyone laughed as Nubio raced in. The door shut behind him.

Dunther remained outside. "In safe lands... for now..." He looked at his horse, staring deep into her eyes. They seemed to be quite close. He rested his head upon the horse's nape and looked up at the stars. He was looking... at her.

The next morning, Alfred and Loranna sat in the grove near her farm. At one end was a quiet brook. They sat on a rock under a tree.

The morning sun was well on its way to warming the rocks and trees around them. It was near the end of summer, at its hottest, and the air was full of buzzing, bumbling bees bobbing from flower to flower.

"You ever think about peace? What we will do in times of peace?" Loranna asked.

"Peace? Ah, I dunno. Build things? More farms for sure. Oh and we'll need watchtowers! A series of them to give warning or for weary travelers. Oh and better roads! I think the Romans were good at that. Probably have to study their work. Oooh... bridges! Definitely make bigger and grander bridges with lots of sculptures! There will be so much to build."

Loranna leaned back on the rock and stared up at the sparkling beams of sunlight coming through the full leaves of summer. "Build a family?"

"Oh yeah, that too," Alfred said, sputtering his lips.

"I like families," Loranna said softly.

"Me too."

"Mothers, fathers, sisters, brothers..." Loranna said, stretching out her arms in the warm summer morning.

"Yes. Fathers..."

Loranna looked at Alfred and saw he was now deep in thought. She brought him back. "And eating! I love eating!"

"Oh, I love eating!"

"Dinner time!" she chimed.

"That is an awesome time."

"I can't wait to call out 'dinner time'... and my children come running in. And my husband," Loranna said, turning just a bit toward Alfred.

He gulped.

Loranna sat up and stared at Alfred. He looked wide-eyed at her.

"Alfred. Do you love me?"

"Yes."

They smiled.

"Hey ho! We're ready to go!" yelled Cory from the other end of the grove. He had arrived with his spearboys. And coming down the slope were Setheyna and Niranna with the archergirls. Loranna got up.

"Wait, do you...?"

"Right, let's go!" Loranna hurried over.

Loranna flicked her string like a violin. It twanged a subtle sound, and the girls reacted instantly. Over their heads were ropes tied to a tree behind them with a gnome pulley system. She looked back and nodded. Noren and Cory, Alfred's right hand spearboy, quickly tugged at a release. A twirl of girls ran in and out as they fired arrow after arrow at their target. A giant hay stack strapped with metal pieces was hanging from the ropes. It swung wildly toward the girls.

The haystack swooped down like a lumbering armoured giant. The girls leapt out of the way, firing from all sides. Wilden, Nubio, and the boys threw large bundled hay balls at the girls, safely behind barricades on the sides of course. They yelled wildly as they threw them. The girls had to focus on firing and avoiding these giant balls of fiery grass... no wait... furious grass! A few arrows bounced off the steel plates, but most pierced the hay in quite violent ways. The haystack careened along the descending rope, finally bouncing and clambering to a stop at the other end.

It definitely looked like an armoured, albeit quite dead, haystack. Loranna, Setheyna, Niranna and the girls came up to examine their deadly result. They pulled the arrows out of the haystack. It seemed to grumble and gurgle in its death throes. Alfred shuddered as they yanked their arrows out and gave each other high fives.

Loranna turned to Alfred, staring deep into his wide boyish eyes. "Your turn."

Alfred gulped as he, Cory, Wilden, Nubio and the boys lined up with their spears. Loranna and the girls held the rope to the pulley system, giggling behind the boys. The giant haystack in armour stared at them, hanging precariously up the path. It looked ready to pillage and plunder.

"Ready, set, attack!" Loranna yelled as the girls yanked hard on the rope. The haystack bounded along the descending rope and right into the midst of the spearboy lines. It was immediately skewered by a dozen spears, and the bottom half of it fell off in a gory violent display of straw. The boys stared for a split second then all hollered in a near man-like glory – "Grrraaahhhh!!!!!"

Alfred hurried from farm to farm. He was enthralled by the incredible amount of work each farmer was accomplishing. They had bought sheep, goats, and chickens from farms further west, all made safe this last year by their victories against the Witch.

With the collapse of the goblin and ratkin raiders, farms and villages that spread westward had time to rebuild. Pigs and workhorses, oxen and cows, were also to be had. Large trains of distant folk came in, selling their livestock. It was a grand and wonderful sight to see.

Stockades, fencing, and barns were getting erected. The land was filled with the sounds of birds chirping, sheep baying, cows mooing, chickens clucking and hammers hammering.

Alfred noticed that the forests were being cleared of their trees. Lumber was as big a commodity as crops.

"Abedeyan," Alfred said commandingly, "we must hire a tree farmer! Someone who goes about planting and counting our trees, our forests. We can't be running out of them! We're going to need lots and lots of wood for many years to come."

Abedeyan dipped his quill into his small vial of ink. He said aloud, "To hire... Arborist!" and wrote it down on his parchment of to-dos.

Alfred continued training as a spearboy with Cory, Wilden, Nubio and the rest. The boys had grown in size and numbers. They were all growing, it seemed, quite fast. But that is how children are, especially those well fed with good food, cooked by their moms, and working hard with their dads and the animals, on their farms.

Dunther and Gorham watched from their castle construction as the boys maneuvered in the fields below them.

"They are going to be an elite core of lancers when they become men," Dunther said.

"Already are," Gorham proffered.

Dunther's eyebrow raised in agreement.

They then looked at Captain Hedor training his men and farmer volunteers. From a distance they could hear him yelling, "No, turn to your left! To YOUR left, this is my right arm. Look! It is pointing that way, to your left. Follow the arm that is pointing! The other arm!!!"

"It looks as if our soldiers may need some work," Gorham said.

Dunther's face twitched.

Loranna and her archer team were training younger, newer girls. A young Khanafian girl whose health returned also joined in. The incredible training camp they had in the groves down the slopes near her farm, the very same groves where she and her sister met elvish assassins and defeated them, was ever growing. Several areas were cleared out for more archery ranges and the indomitable giant haystack attacker!

Broggia and Boggin remained mostly underground. After all, their life was in the metal. And their forge and smelter were powered by molten lava at the underground Sanctuary. Gnomes were now their brethren. Many of the craftsman and master smiths made comfortable abodes under the blue mushrooms.

It wasn't a long trip to the surface, and they had plenty of regular visitors ever since the gnomes dug out a ramp way. It had a mine cart on rails as well as an adjacent walkway. The mine cart was fired by one of their infamous spring loaded contraptions. It shot the cart up the ramp way right to the level platform at the surface, and there it stopped.

At the surface, when loaded and ready, one merely pushed away at the stopper, and the cart flung down the ramp to the spring on the other end, ready to catch it. Many a child took the ride squealing and screaming. Farmers and their wives were the worst for wear, howling banshee screams of terror, holding on dearly to whatever supplies they were delivering or taking. The gnomes merely rolled their eyes at the prospect of their delivery system being "entertaining."

The farm tools were superbly made by the gnomes, and every farmer came with a bounty of baked and cooked goods. Not a single gnome could resist! Each one made the best axes, shovels, picks, rakes, plow blades... licking their lips for the trade.

Alfred came with the knights to see what new weapons and armour the father and son were crafting. And upon Dunther's insistence, Alfred and the spearboys were to be sized and fitted.

"Spearmen with thick frontal armour! Invincible!" Broggia yelled.

"What if they get us in the back?" Cory yelled back.

Everyone had to yell. The sounds of hammering and tinkering were loud, and the bubbling burning lava added a level of ambient noise. But the most prominent sound was that of the great underground waterfall. It roared stupendously nearby. The rushing waters were used often by the smiths running molten steel back and forth with the hot-cold strengthening treatment.

"Then you ain't a good spearmen, now are you?" Broggia yelled back.

"Your armour is strong in front, against the toughest of attacks. Having light armour in the back, allows you to be more mobile. You must train to keep the enemy from penetrating your lines and to protect each other's backs," yelled Dunther. "Your rear armour can take a hit, but not much more. All the weight and strength of your armour is in your front piece. There is always a balance, a trade-off!"

Alfred, Cory and Wilden nodded. They knew they needed more training and things to think about.

"The best armour is for the king! That is our goal here!" Boggin yelled. His eyes lit with life.

Dunther looked about at the incredible setup, the working gnomes, the anvils and directed pools of lava. The bridges and walkways were fashioned to expand the work area – and all of this was taking place in a secret underground cavern! He looked at Boggin, busy with his father measuring and notating how things fit the boys, readjusting straps and pieces.

"How are you doing down here, Boggin?" Dunther yelled.

Boggin looked up with a shrug. "I could use a wife!"

They all looked at him.

Back at the castle, the construction was moving along at a rapid gnome pace. Though the men building the scaffolding and temporary wooden structures needed many breaks, the gnomes continued their focused stone work, yelling and bickering with each other as stone after stone rose on a daily basis. The gnomes had the best pulley systems, utilizing well-crafted steel wheels and their very own steel cables. Seeing steel cables, twined threads of metal, was a fascinating experience for the knights and Abedeyan.

Alfred was amazed at the endurance of gnomes. But Dunther seemed not as appreciative. He kept apace with orders and direction. He yelled and argued with the gnomes as much as they did with each other. Gnomes knew everything there was to know about stone and placing it, but they did not know a whole lot about castle design, defenses and especially gnome-to-man scale. Dunther was constantly bickering, not at how incredibly solid and sturdy the stones were, but on where they placed them and for what purpose.

Dunther would have to wave his arms about and yell out things like "How do you expect us to get in here without first placing stairs!? We're men, not gnomes! These corridors need to be at least this high! See here! We are not crawling on all fours! We'll also be wearing splendid armour! We are not squeezing through! This is where the tower starts! Remove these stones! It's right here on the markers! Look at my stride and step, man-size! We need this spaced out for men! Where's that stone going! Here... not there! We have to look down on the field! Open this up! A walkway built for men, three abreast! Not gnomes! The fighting will be on a level platform! We aren't crawling up a wall!"

Oddly, as much yelling and frothing Dunther and the gnomes threw at each other, when it came to meals, the gnomes were the happiest lot, and Dunther found comfort and rest in his tent.

"It's amazing!" Alfred said, looking at the plans as Dunther rubbed his temples. "Now the castle walls are higher, thicker, and more solid. And Gorham said they can take on cannon fire!?"

"Yes, quite a bit as well. That stone will only chip at worst. They won't have enough cannonballs to break it."

"And you are going to start on an outer wall as well?"

"Yes, at this pace we could start on it by next spring! Never has a castle been built this fast or this solid. Never." Dunther, excited at his own comments, sat up.

"When will the Keep and courtyard be done?"

"It will be last. We need to construct the walls quickly, to have defenses in place. Then we will build a grand hall for the king!"

"You think she will attack us? Soon?" Alfred asked, a little enthusiastically.

Dunther looked at Alfred with sullen eyes. "We've weakened her. A witch, such as her, will inevitably come. But anytime soon? No. She has to rebuild. Concoct her evil armies from beasts and foul things."

"Then, we'll have a great castle! And be ready!"

Dunther tried to focus on the plans but eventually looked to Alfred. "Ready? You are never ready for war, Alfred. You know that. Things can happen. Vigilance, Alfred! Your vigilance! Keep your mind on our defenses! We are counting on you, King Alfred."

Chapter Seven

Tirnalth's Departure

"I have to leave."

"Whaddyamean you have to leave!? You're always leaving!"

Tirnalth gave Alfred a gentle smile and put his hand on his shoulder. Alfred buried his face into his hands. He was eating soup in the kitchens as the ladies were busy making dinner for the gnomes and men. There were now plenty of tiny wife gnomes in the kitchen learning the cooking trade. They were quite adept at finding small stools, buckets, and clay pots to balance atop and peer over the cutting tables and cooking pans. Their eyes gazed in wonder to see salts and peppers and herbs being sprinkled and rubbed. It was a busy and wonderful time. But at this small table, as if in a little alcove all by himself, Alfred sat sullen. Tirnalth stood next to him.

Lady Nihan came by and plopped a small plate of bread in front of him. She did not see Tirnalth, as he was in his ghostly form. "You okay, my lord Alfred?"

"Oh yes, Lady Nihan, thank you. I was…" and he glanced up at Tirnalth… "just missing Tirnalth the Wizard."

"Oh, he'll be around soon enough. Wizards are always off wizarding!" She patted his head and went on her busy way.

Tirnalth sat next to Alfred on a real stool but remained ghostly.

"Why Tirnalth? Why can't you stay and watch what we are doing? It is amazing, all the gnomes and the castle!?"

"Of course it is, King Alfred. Of course it is!" Tirnalth gazed as Alfred grabbed the grainy loaf.

"The girls are so much better and stronger and faster at archery! They could take down giants, I bet!"

"Of course they can." Tirnalth watched the steam curl out as Alfred broke the bread.

"And the boys, they're like spear'd'corps! Or whatever that phrase is! Top of the line spearmen!"

"Of course they are." Tirnalth gaped as Alfred swathed large dollops of butter on, these instantly melting across the hot steamy bread.

Tirnalth became more 'solid' as it were and waved politely as Lady Nihan rushed by.

She gasped, "Wizard Tirnalth!? Where'd you come from?"

"Wizarding! I came from wizarding!"

She gulped, holding many plates and bowls in the most adroit manner, trying to get out as much food as possible.

Tirnalth gently took a bowl of soup from her precarious pile. "I think I'll have some soup."

She grimaced a bit but was joyful to see him. She rotated her dishes. "More bread here, take it."

Tirnalth looked and saw one of many plates of bread. He took a serving. It steamed as it was fresh from the oven. His eyes lit up and so did hers. She nodded and went on her busy way.

"And what if she returns?!" Alfred said, gritting his teeth and looking somewhat meanly at Tirnalth.

"I'll eat some more then! A wizard off wizarding doesn't get to eat real food! Nothing quite like this in all creation," Tirnalth said gleefully. Noticing Alfred's serious look, he set his bread down. "Oh, you mean HER."

Tirnalth sat back and peered at him. Alfred looked down. Tirnalth continued. "My memories are full. I remember everything once again. I remember your mother and your father quite well. I remember the Silver Crusades, King Athelrod, Lord Dunther when he was young, and your mother's sister, who is now named Gorbogal. And I remember all that has happened, the expectations, the failures, the betrayals, and the love."

"Then why must you leave?"

"Because I am becoming powerful," Tirnalth said, tending back to his scrumptious meal. He winked and smiled with bits of bread and butter on his wizardly beard.

Alfred looked at him with narrowed eyes.

"I am not yet powerful enough to defend or repel her powers. But I am becoming powerful enough for her to find me. These last steps, becoming my former self, I must remove myself from this realm. Do you understand?"

Alfred nodded, smiling as best he could. He slowly took another sip of soup. His spoon shook slightly.

Tirnalth winced. "Alfred, my dear boy, you have done so much for this kingdom. You have saved the people of the Westfold. You have saved the gnomes from their underground tomb. You've defeated ratkins, goblins, giant hormig ants, bugbears and ogres! You've even tamed the crazed steward of this castle!" Tirnalth noticed Abedeyan stealing some bread and Lady Nihan chastising him for it. She then forced him to sit properly at the end of a cutting table and receive a proper bowl of soup and bread. "And I believe you have so much more to do. I will be gone only a little while. And when I return..." Tirnalth lifted a magnificent finger. Alfred followed it. "When I return, a witch we will contend with!"

Alfred smiled grimly. "Then I will hold strong. I will hold this position, defend it well!"

"Yes, King Alfred, you will! I know you will. Even alone."

Each slurped at his soup.

Alfred was washing his hands in a warm bowl of water. He was wiping off all the smells of the hard, laborious day. He had a root of a plant that he scraped against a stone. It foamed just as soap does. He lathered that in his arm pits and rinsed it off. He splashed water all over the place. He felt so refreshed that it woke him up, even though he was getting ready for sleep. His room was mostly dark, lit by a small candle and an oil lamp. He quickly dried and tossed on a long wool garment.

"Okay, Lady Nihan!"

Suddenly, the door opened, and Lady Nihan and Nubio rushed in. They seemed to know exactly what to do: removing the wash basin and replacing it with an empty one, taking the damp clothes out, putting up his new set of clean and dry laundry, and putting a small pitcher of cool water next to his bed with a small wooden goblet.

Lady Nihan spoke as she worked. "That word, 'okay'... it means ready? I thought it meant yes."

"Hah, no, 'okay' means, well it means all those things. It means ready, yes, and sometimes… things are so, so… it has a lot of meanings. It came from a president I think, a king…" Alfred said, wondering himself.

"Oh, a royal word? You have some interesting words!" Lady Nihan said. She clapped her hands. "Okay!"

"Perfect!" Alfred smiled. "It means that too!"

Nubio held a wad of Alfred's dirty laundry and the wash basin of dirty water.

"Nubio, you don't have to do this many jobs! You're a squire, a spearboy, and a page!?" asked Alfred.

"I like doing it! Lord Dunther told me to try everything to see what I like doing most."

"But you should be a squire!" said Alfred, waving his arms and getting into bed.

"He IS, King Alfred," said Lady Nihan, busily fluffing his bed, "but Dunther doesn't like to be served day and night. He's become a humble good man, thanks to you."

Alfred gulped and smiled.

"One day I'll be a great knight!" Nubio said. "And protect the King!" He looked odd, with his big smile, dreaming of heroic things.

"Right, that's it, my lord." Lady Nihan bowed. She elbowed Nubio, who bowed next, albeit carefully with his load, and then he exited.

She nodded and then said, "Have a wonderful rest. Much to do on the morrow! Okay?"

"Okay!" Alfred gave her a thumbs up.

Lady Nihan rolled her eyes and promptly shut the door.

Alfred sat quietly. He looked out his thick glazed window at the stars. He saw the stars twinkling through the hazy glass. He got out of bed and went to the window. He lowered to his knees and put his hands together.

"Dear… Father of Light… I don't know… you… what to say. I am just a boy, who happens to be a king, but still, just a boy. I'm kind of scared. Well, I should be. Verboden says you created everything. And watch over the good. But there is so much evil. I, I, can you watch over me? Over my mom and Beden… Wooly… my father? Can you watch over this castle and kingdom and all the people? Amen, I think."

Alfred tried to make a cross sign on his chest. He moved his finger across like what he remembered seeing on a TV show. "Wait, that's not for..."

"That was a wonderful prayer, Alfred," Tirnalth said.

Alfred looked up and saw Tirnalth sitting in a chair near the door. Alfred turned and went to hug him.

"Oh, you hug me as if you haven't seen me since... dinner!"

"I'm hugging you because you are leaving, and I don't know when you'll be back."

Tirnalth looked closely into Alfred's eyes. They shared a glistening reflection from the starlit night. Alfred stood up, rubbing his sniffly nose. "My dear boy, you are indeed a wonderful human being."

"I try to be," Alfred shrugged, plopping on his bed.

"And that is all one can ask, now isn't it?" Tirnalth said, clearing his own throat.

"Tirnalth? Are you part of the Father of Light?"

"Yes."

"Is he real?"

Tirnalth tilted his head gently.

"I mean, is he aware, is he watching, is he helping?"

"Up until the twelfth year of your life, you had no father. Do you think *your* father did not love you all those years?"

Alfred smiled.

"The Father," Tirnalth said with a deeper tone, and continued softly, "...loves you... always."

"Okay."

"Okay?"

"Yeah, okay," Alfred giggled.

"All is well then," Tirnalth said, sighing. "I must go, Alfred."

"I know."

"I have something for you to keep." Tirnalth pulled a tome from his robe as he stood. He put it on the table. It wasn't large but it wasn't small either. It had on the cover in small letters 'Tirnalth'. It was bound in leather and looked old and worn, but still solid.

Alfred came to the small table and peered at it, opening it quickly. Its thick parchment pages were blank, seeming to be new and crisp. "It's empty?"

"Oh no, it is not."

"What is it – Tirnalth?"

"Exactly! It is me. It is my way back. I am removing all that is me from this world, this realm. I am doing some powerful magics that will make me, well, powerful! And ready. You must hold out, Alfred, until I am ready. It won't be as long as you think, but it will be some time. That book is my focus, my return. Keep it safe."

Alfred closed the book and held it to his chest. "I will."

"Books are important! They are the way we, who have minds, truly communicate to each other, over time, over the ages, to the generations to come. It is how we record time backwards and forwards. It is how we witness and proclaim. It is how a father would talk to his children's children's children! A book!"

"Yeah, I got it."

"Do you now?"

"Yes, Tirnalth, I got it," Alfred hugged the tome tighter.

And with that, Tirnalth was gone. And Alfred stood alone in the dark.

Chapter Eight

Of Arms and Armour

Alfred returned to the crowded confines of the smithing hall deep within the cavernous realm. They stood on the stone walkway built by Sanba and her husband Deago – and by the gnomes, of course. It was a wide walkway for passing to and fro around the treacherous terrain of the stalactites above and stalagmites below. The walkway and cleared terrain had become the great foundry of the Northern Kingdom of the Westfold. It was their secret alcove for making the best steel known to man.

Broggia, Boggin and the gnome smiths had to yell, for the waterfall was ever rushing behind them. They spoke as if every moment were a sudden life and death situation, though it was not.

Boggin fitted the straps of the armour tightly against Alfred's body to ensure it covered him snugly. Alfred, though strapped in, was oddly quite comfortable. He stared at his fingers encased in metal. "It's like I'm a robot."

"A what!!?"

"I'm a robot."

Boggin cupped his ear, waved to the roaring waterfall right behind them.

"I'm a ROBOT!!!!" Alfred flicked his fingers.

"Row boat!!??" Boggin looked down at the armour then at the water fall. "No rowing, not a boat! Sink!!!"

"Robot!!!! Nevermind!!!!" Alfred waved him off and moved about in the armour. He did an odd dance as Dunther, Murith, Gorham and the boys stared at him. Loranna giggled. She too was being fitted by the gnomes. Her armour was smaller, lighter, focused on frontal pieces that did not hinder her movement or shooting. She looked amazing, like a silver arrow!

"You look sleek!!!" Alfred said, stopping his odd dance in front of her.

Loranna looked down at her cool pieces. Her forearm pieces were the strongest, to deflect blades and melee attacks. Everything the smiths fit on her and the girls were light pieces so they could move the way they did in practice. The gnomes were very skillful and meticulous with their armour.

Alfred did a forward roll to test his armour's mobility. They were all upon the stony bridge above the water. Dunther and the knights cringed fearing he'd flop over the side. Alfred leapt up with vigor and pomp! He raised his arms in the air victorious, jogging about. He tried some odd kicking and striking moves. They all shook their heads.

"This is awesome! It feels great!"

"Armour does that to you!" Gorham yelled back.

"Careful my lord! It doesn't give you swimming abilities!" Dunther yelled.

"It's the best armour in the world!" Murith added.

"Yer darn right!!" a gnome smith said. The others chuckled with him, excited at their work.

Cory and Wilden began moving about, copying Alfred's martial arts antics. Nubio merely stood and stared at his. The girls all began to pose oddly, in groups, as if someone were drawing their poses quickly on parchment and a town crier were showing it to everyone via some social medieval thing.

The knights had to stand along the edges of the walkways and gently nudge the spearboys and archergirls to keep them from falling into the roaring waters.

"Alright! Everybody is fitted and done! Out! Out! Out! Let's go!" Dunther yelled, pushing them along.

The knights began pushing out the armoured children as if they were readying for a parade. The kids were all excited looking at each other's new outfits. They couldn't have imagined them being so amazing.

"Just remembering the care-taking and maintaining of such armour! Follow the instructions given! Upkeep of armour is of upmost importance!" Dunther yelled out to no one in particular.

They marched through the Sanctuary lit in luminous blue under the glowing giant mushrooms. Many gnomes and a few farm wives delivering food were there. They stood and watched, many clapping at the armoured spectacle. A mother came up to hug her son. He tried to wave her off. Her skills at kissing his cheek surpassed his spear skills of deflection.

Captain Hedor, Ruig and his men were finally getting fitted in their armour too.

Ruig looked down at his armour. It's simple, like a town guard or a soldier. "It's nice. Not as nice as theirs but it's nice."

Captain Hedor shrugged. "Guess they won't need us for the parade."

"Nah... not that important. We're just guarding and protecting them all – is all."

They shared a glum smile.

"Hey, that's a bit tight!" Hedor said.

"You've gotten fatter since we measured!" Boggin said.

"Well, there's a lot of work at the castle," Hedor answered. "And food. Ohhhh, the food."

"Yeah, slowly walking around and keeping guard while everyone is hammering away is hard work!" Ruig added, patting his own tightly armoured belly.

Chapter Nine

Ninja!

"Who are you!?"

"I've come for you."

Alfred tried to scream in the dark cold night, to call for guards. But he realized – they had none. Lady Nihan and her ladies were in the rooms nearby, and Tirnalth's room was below him, but the wizard was gone. His book lay on the small table, where the shadowy figure's feet were placed. Dunther was below in the dungeons. Verboden's room was on the other side of the chapel. Who was to help or come to his aid in this ruined castle? Who would come in time to save him from this dark shadow?

The shadow stayed at the window. Alfred did not know how it came in. The glass window was sealed all along the frame of wood and stone with masonry. In these dark times, they did not have open or sliding windows in this castle. To have glass instead of wooden shutters was a luxury. And as Alfred was the Boy King, he was given the one room with glass windows.

"You should have better protections, boy king," said the shadow. It waved its hand quickly.

Alfred yelled, but nothing came out. He had no voice and felt the room shrink as if he were in some sort of vortex. It was like a nightmare, a real nightmare. He was drowning in paralyzed silence.

The shadow then waved his hand again. "Shhh, do not be frightened." Then it removed its hood and revealed a young Asian looking man. "I have come to warn you."

Alfred's eyes widened, and he couldn't help himself... "Ninja!"

56

"What?"

"You're a ninja! An assassin!"

"I am not an assassin, though my path crosses many."

"You're a ninja!!"

"I do not know what that is. I have not heard that word."

"You're Japanese, secret, stealthy, they uhhh... you know, they are a secret assassin group who go about doing secret assassin stuff!"

"Those of the Secret Order of Assassins are whose path I cross many times."

"Are you Japanese?"

"I am Hiro... of the Mu-shin Dynasty. Fallen long ago."

"Mu-shin... dynasty? That sounds Chinese!"

"I do not know this Chinese... I am Mu-shin. I am of a kingdom long lost..."

"Lost? How?"

"Lost to the Dark One, enslaved are my people, in the Mountain and River Kingdom, far to the East."

"Why are you here... Hiro?"

"Tirnalth sent me."

"Tirnalth!?"

"As a messenger, to inform you. And to watch over you."

"How is he? What is he doing? When will he be back?"

"Silence or you will wake the whole castle."

Alfred cupped his mouth. He should still have been afraid but couldn't help himself. He was sitting up in his bed and ready to prance about in excitement. The ninja, or Hiro, while revealing his ally affiliation, was still a scary dark figure. He was wrapped in tight black clothing with many blades and pouches. He looked like a veritable deadly assassin.

"You're not an assassin?" Alfred whispered, scooting closer in his bed.

"No. I was trained as such, as a slave in my own land. There is a hidden priory in my kingdom, a small monastery. It's a secret order of the Brothers of Light. They seek to free us from the Dark One. They found me near death after I was betrayed. Even under the iron grip of the Dark One, there is much treachery among his lord servants. The monks took me to their hidden enclave, healed me, and showed me the ways of freedom and the Father of Light."

Ninja!

Hiro stepped down quietly and softly from the table, then lit a candle. He sat on the small chair next to Alfred. The light warmed him and showed a young yet sad face, having seen much hardship. Yet still, his face was touched with a glint of hope. "Tirnalth asked me to serve his needs in Telehistine."

"Telehistine? You're from there?"

Hiro nodded and covered his eyes with his hand. Alfred grimaced as he was not sure why Hiro was doing that.

Then the door burst open, and Verboden slammed against the stone entrance with his staff in one hand and his other hand splayed out. He began with a burst of light that blinded Alfred's wide-eyed gaze.

Alfred reeled back, cringing and gritting teeth. "Verboden! Ow!!! Flash-bang! Ow!"

Hiro merely lowered his hand and opened his eyes as the flash was gone. Verboden rushed into the tight quarters ready to strike.

"I can't see! Aaaaggghhhh!!!" Alfred fell off his bed. "OW!"

Hiro blinked. Gazing wide-eyed and pointing his staff at Hiro, Verboden side-stepped to Alfred. He glanced to and fro. Dunther rushed in with blade raised, dressed only in his linen underclothing. He pointed his blade at Hiro, who was sitting beside Alfred's small quaint table. Verboden and Dunther were in a sweat and panic.

Dunther glanced at Alfred, who was blinking and flailing blindly. "Did he blind him?!"

"No, I think that was me," Verboden said, lowering his staff.

Dunther, with blade still pointed, glanced at Alfred, Verboden, and the stranger. "Who are you?"

"He's Hiro, a friend of Tirnalth!" Alfred said, rubbing his eyes and seeking balance.

"Then why didn't he come through the front door, during the day?" Dunther asked.

"I have many times, easily. Too easily," said Hiro, standing before them. "Three are the number," Hiro showed three blades suddenly, causing Verboden and Dunther to raise their weapons again.

"Three are the number of assassins whose paths I have crossed in this Keep."

"Paths you crossed?" Verboden asked.

"Killed," Dunther said.

"Poison, blade, and mishap were their skills."

Dunther and Verboden blinked.

"Phew, I can see again, oh man." Alfred leapt back into bed. "Seriously? You stopped three assassins from killing me?"

"A woman died of sickness, a butcher stopped showing up for work, and a strange old man was crushed by a stone, an accident," Verboden said.

Hiro nodded.

"Perhaps you are the assassin, killing our folk," Dunther said.

"Your kindness to strangers, while good in the eyes of the Father, is also Gorbogal's ploy to kill the boy king. And you have no protection for him, even as assassins have slept on these very grounds. You let too many strangers in."

"I can sense evil intent," Verboden said. "I cast protections on him every night."

"They are not strong enough," Hiro said.

Verboden grimaced.

"Okay, okay, we get the point!" Alfred said. "Let's all just relax and sit and have a secret meeting." Alfred waved for them all to find a sitting place. "Shhhh... Let's not wake... anyone else."

"We've yelled loud enough for the others to come," Dunther huffed.

"They will not come. He cast a shell of silence around us," Verboden said, looking about.

"I must remain hidden, secret, to perform my task," Hiro said softly as he sat again.

Verboden sat on Alfred's small bed. Dunther stepped back and leaned against the wall.

"Want to sit, Dunther?" asked Alfred, scooting over.

"No, I'm fine." Dunther shrugged and held his sword a bit too casually.

"It is not safe for Alfred to be here, not while you have so many people coming and going and no system of protection."

"You are not taking him!" Dunther said, stepping forward too quickly.

Alfred eyed Dunther, who backed off.

"I cannot. I must leave soon," Hiro said. "That is why I had to reveal myself. I cannot protect you any longer."

"Why?" Alfred asked.

"My success here has become a focus. The Order will send many more. My brothers are still strong in Telehistine. There will be a war of the assassins, and I do not want it to be here."

"So you are an assassin!" Dunther said.

"I am a spectre," Hiro said, standing. "We have committed our allegiance to fight the Dark Lord and his assassins."

"A spectre!" Alfred said. "A ghost... a ninja! Oh yeah. My very own ninja!" Alfred did karate chops and-or a robotic disco dance while still in bed.

"I do not know what this is?" Hiro mumbled. "What are you doing?"

"Oh yeah, so cool! A freaking ninja! Pft! Pfoosh! Pffewwah!"

"Your king is strange."

"Agreed," Dunther replied.

"Then where do you propose he be taken? A farm on the outskirts of the kingdom?" Verboden asked.

Hiro nodded no. "Further. There is also much more danger to this than Alfred's assassination."

"Oh, well that's good," Alfred said.

"You have defeated Gorbogal's forces with astounding courage. I bow to your mastery of war." Hiro bowed suddenly and for a long time. Alfred, Verboden and Dunther were unsure of what to do. Alfred somewhat bowed while sitting in bed, then remembered not to. The others waited.

Hiro finally rose up. "She has been building a force much greater and more powerful. Perhaps this force is even greater than the forces she has sent against the provinces of Telehistine. Our spies have seen armoured troglodytes, war trolls and legions of black orcs."

Dunther couldn't help but grab his chin and rub it quite violently, pacing Alfred's small room.

"It will take her some time. But she works day and night on breeding this dark force. Meanwhile, she has sent agents to the borders of your kingdom, Agents of Scourge, to sow discord and dissolution. She seeks to destroy some regions and control others. You must send out your knights to counter these agents. You must anoint them Quest Knights."

"Quest Knights? Oh hoh hoh..." Alfred jostled in the bed. Verboden put a hand on him to try to calm him.

"We cannot leave this kingdom! It sounds like you want to weaken us!" Dunther said.

"You are already weak. Without alliances, border alliances, you will be attacked from all sides and with a far greater force. You must build up this Keep and its forces, while administering to border kingdoms and realms. Her force will lay siege to this unfinished citadel next summer."

"Next summer? That... is... so... soon. How can she build an army like that?" Dunther moaned.

"Her land of slavery and tyranny under the power of the Dark Lord is immense. You will run out of time very soon. Her siege army was built from long ago, to fight the forces of Telehistine, but now she directs them toward Alfred. You must complete these quests this winter." Hiro spoke with no expression.

Dunther and Verboden both sank in their thoughts.

"What are the Quests? What is going on?" Alfred asked.

Dunther waved away any answer Hiro might give. "This is ridiculous. We are needed here."

Hiro ignored Dunther and focused on Alfred. "To the north and west, there is dark sorcery cursing the lands. It will soon destroy the farmers who come here to provision your land with food. A beast that will never die is destroying them."

"A beast that will never die?" repeated Alfred with a gasp.

"To the east, in the mountain villages, there are troll hunters, stout dwarfmen and barbarians. They live near Gorbogal's Spire and have fought off her forces and never been defeated. Yet, no alliance from the west has aided them. Gorbogal is now using the tactic of payment and mercurial services to entice them. It appears to be working."

"They are hardened and powerful fighting men. However, they have been isolated all these years from us... if she were to procure their services..." Dunther huffed. "But we cannot do these quests! We are needed here! We should not spread out. We must remain to ensure the castle is well defended."

"To the south a sorcerer is conspiring with wood beasts for the attack. He is using the magic of the forest realm. Florina, Queen of the Faerie Realm, has returned and is fighting the sorcerer..."

"I'll go. I'll do it," Dunther said. "I'll be a Quest Knight. That Quest Knight. I'll go. I can do it."

Chapter Ten

The Quest Knights

"Sir Murith," said Verboden, "you and I shall go to the north, to see this beast that never dies. It has cursed the land these last two summers. I have spoken to families who fled and are here. The people that remain in those lands live in terror of this bestial blight."

All stood or sat crowded in Dunther's abode in the dungeon of the unfinished Keep. Sir Murith was once again plopped on Dunther's small bed. Lord Gorham stood next to Verboden. Dunther and Alfred stood opposite them, all peering down at the map of the lands. Hiro was there as well. Abedeyan and the gnomes, King Gup and Gib, found spaces between the larger men. They were all stuck together in the tight confines and peered as best they could at the map.

"What do you mean, a beast that never dies?" Sir Murith asked.

Verboden responded. "From what I gathered, a wolf beast. But one that never dies? I do not know what is meant by this. Each new moon, the beast attacks. One bite, and the curse is passed to another. Sadly, they've had to burn any of their own people that were infected. After many tragedies, the warriors rose up and hunted the beast. Moon after accursed moon, they'd find the wolf beast at great loss to their own. The people live in fear, many fleeing. The only way to kill and end the beast is with fire. They have to burn it to ash. They trap it with much difficulty and sadly always lose more of their best fighters. Then another full moon, and the beast that never dies terrorizes them again. And the nightmare task begins anew. Their people are being destroyed."

"Wait, why fire?" Alfred asked.

"Blades do not kill it. When wounded, it heals quickly."

"Why not silver?"

"Silver?" Verboden looked at the others to understand Alfred's question. They all shrugged.

"Yeah, we're talking about a werewolf, right?"

"A were-wolf?" Verboden repeated.

"Yeah, where I come from, we call them werewolves. You guys don't know about werewolves? Verboden, there was one in the forest when we first met! Don't you remember?"

"Yes, I remember. Well, he was..."

"Well, for us, or for where I come from, werewolves are men, ...or women... equal opportunity curse... heh heh..." Alfred looked up to see if anyone chuckled, but no one did. He cleared his throat. "Anyway, a werewolf is a cursed man, bitten by another werewolf. They change on a full moon to a wolf-like beast. Just like that one in the forest when we first met Verboden!"

Verboden winced when Alfred nodded to him. Alfred continued, "You have to kill it, or him. Fire works for sure, burning anything to ash, sure... but the best thing to kill them with is silver. A silver sword or something like that."

"At least with a silver sword, you could defend yourself!" Murith said, sitting up.

"Yes, the farmers said their greatest warriors tried killing it with blade and arrow, but the grievous wounds only made it more vicious, attacking them, cursing and killing many," Verboden said.

"Right, silver actually hurts them!" Alfred added.

"How do we know these werewolves from your world are the same as the cursed beasts in this world?" asked Verboden.

"Oh, this is getting tricky," Gib, the gnome, spoke up.

"Well, we'll have to test it, I guess," Alfred shrugged.

"We can make fine blades of silver," King Gup said.

"Best to make steel, coat with silver, stronger." Gib mumbled.

"Right, yes, I was going to say..." King Gup answered nonchalantly.

"What's this place like, where you're going?" Alfred asked, pointing at the map.

"The moors: a dreary, foggy cold region," responded Verboden. "Only the roughest of folk can live there. They say there's more moon there than sun. Most are sheep or goat herders. The terrain is difficult, soggy, crowded with hillock after hillock of bog growth."

"Do not attempt to climb them. You'll sink right in," Abedeyan added.

"I shall travel north with Sir Murith. It isn't far," said Verboden. "There may be many people who are in need of my blessings."

"And hope," Alfred added.

"Yes, hope," Verboden nodded.

"Perhaps King Alfred should go with you," Hiro said. "Given what you know of this ...werewolf."

"Ah, I wanted to go with Dunther to see the faeries," Alfred said.

"No, you should go with them," Dunther said suddenly. Everyone glanced at him. He shrugged.

"But the Queen of Faeries and faeries... they're like really beautiful, right? And a faerie forest? I totally want to see that. It must be so magical and amazing there. And to see a queen, a faerie queen, she must be like the most beautiful enchanted woman ever."

As Alfred spoke, everyone looked at Dunther and his dreamy eyes. He shook out of it and cleared his throat. "No, no, faeries are deceiving and quite dangerous! They, uh... hate little boys. They sacrifice them, to their wood gods... idols. Very nasty folk, these faeries. So... you go with Murith and deal with the werewolf beast – that never dies. Plus, you have Verboden the Cleric. Best you go with them. I will deal with this woman... I mean Queen... faerie... folk."

Alfred sighed, "I thought I was the king..."

"I suppose I must go eastward then," said Gorham.

"Of course, Gorham," Dunther interjected. "Your lineage awaits!"

Everyone looked at Gorham. He spoke with an annoyance. "Yes, my father's brother is one of the troll hunters. They are a barbaric lot. My lineage rules as a clan near a well-known and roughshod tavern in the Crag Mountains where the hunters congregate."

"Could you persuade them to join us to fight the Witch?" asked Dunther.

"They've repelled her since her attacks upon the West began," said Gorham with a sigh. "There is no limit to their boasting of this. They live in a very difficult mountainous region, full of sharp rocks and deep crags. They hunt trolls and other beasts with some skill and much more ferocity. If they joined us, they'd be a match for any of her foul minions. But they are known to love secluded lands."

"The last I heard was that the Witch hired a small band of them with coin. They helped quell a rebellion of good people," said Hiro.

"The troll hunters hate the Witch and have successfully fought her off from their mountainous crags," Gorham spoke with contempt at Hiro's remark. "They are a powerful force and could easily defeat her armies. How do you come by such an accusation?"

"It was my priory of monks, a hidden monastery in the mountains of the East, which they destroyed," he said with sadness. "The monks fought well. But against the ferocity of the troll hunters, they could not prevail. The hunters have resistance to brothers' magic, somehow... I fled. It was the last time I ever saw the monks."

Gorham's face softened, with only a brow lifted.

"They have resistance to our powers of Light?" Verboden asked.

Hiro nodded. "Yes, if they attacked here, I doubt even the gnomes fortifications would hold."

"Oh now, that's for us to decide!" King Gup spoke up. "Our stone can withstand cave drakes, and they are stronger than any man or foul beast under the sun!"

"That's right! Our stone would repel any pounding or hammering, even cannon fire!" Gib chimed in to reinforce what Gup had said.

"Troll hunters do not pound or hammer. They climb their steep crags just as you gnomes do in the caves below. Their armour is thick troll hides, hardened, and able to absorb arrows and spears. Their strength and ferocity with bladed weapons, the sharpest and most piercing, is unprecedented."

"Sharp? Piercing? Oh..." King Gup sighed.

"He's got a point there, literally," Gib said, pouting his lips.

"So you believe they may be siding with Gorbogal, at least through coin, through greed..." asked Gorham with a weighted voice, bracing himself upon the table.

"Yes," Hiro answered.

"Well, there haven't been any treaties or alliances from our kingdom, from men of the West, to these remote places. Indeed, a quest to open up communication is probably all that is needed. After all, for years it seemed as if the West was lost. But it is not! When my distant cousins know of our victories, they will join us in this great fight against the Witch."

Gorham stood proud at the end of his speech, ready to take on this quest.

"Then we are all agreed. The Quest Knights must go out and unite these lands against the Witch and her conspiring," Dunther proclaimed.

Alfred saluted.

Chapter Eleven

Preparations

"Now, why is it that you all get to go gallivanting off while I must stay here?" asked Hedor.

"You are the captain, Captain Hedor!" Dunther said, looking over parchments of the castle's design. Gnomes came in and out with more scrolls, pointing and nodding with Dunther. There was still much planning to do on the construction and design of the Keep's new fortifications. Dunther was trying to do that and keep a sense of order before he left.

"Captain Hedor, the inner walls must be done after this winter, by spring, to give us enough security to protect the King and defend the land. There is no telling when Gorbogal may begin her siege," said Dunther.

Captain Hedor nodded with a grim look.

Alfred sauntered over to the large group of children training in the fields away from the chaotic castle construction. All the children were there, including Setheyna and Loranna's younger sister Niranna and brother Noren. Wilden was working with Nubio and some other boys on spear maneuvering.

Alfred went up to Cory and Loranna. "You two are coming with me!"

"What? Where?" Cory asked, twirling his spear around two boys trying to attack him.

"To the moors! A dark and dreary land full of cursed werewolves!" said Alfred excitedly.

Cory's eyes widened. "Werewolves? The moors? I've never been anywhere!" He dropped his spear's angle, forcing his two trainees to fall in front of him. "I can't go, King Alfred! There is much training to do and the harvest! My father will need me."

Alfred rubbed his chin.

"Take Nubio!" Cory suggested. They looked to see Nubio training. He was not faring well jousting against Wilden. "Well, he's good at mending and tending."

Alfred shrugged. "I suppose. This journey will probably go past harvest, and you and the other boys will need to be here for that. I'll take him."

Loranna hop-skipped to them, away from the other girls who were maneuvering and shooting arrows. "Ooh, I've never been anywhere outside the Westfold! Oh, and the Underworld, of course. Would have been nice to see the faeries though. But I guess a dark and dreary land full of tombs and crypts will do."

"Tombs and crypts?" exclaimed Alfred.

"Yes, many kings far and wide used the cursed land as their resting place. Grave robbers and tomb raiders would not go there. The land is difficult to traverse and full of foul cursed things. Sounds exciting!" said Loranna.

Cory rolled his eyes along with his spear as several boys tried desperately to get past his defensive moves.

"Hmm..." Alfred thought. "Best I talk to Verboden then. We must be well prepared. Oh, and I'll talk to Broggia, Boggin and the gnome smiths. We must make sure to get silver spears, blades, and arrows!"

"Silver?" asked Cory.

"Yes, silver!" yelled Alfred as he rushed off.

"I'm not much into praying, cleric," grumbled Dunther, kneeling in the chapel, fidgeting as Verboden prayed next to him.

"Where you are going, to confront her, the most beautiful Queen of the Faeries... you'll need plenty of prayer," said Verboden.

"What's the use, when we all know... the Father of Light has abandoned us!?"

Verboden opened his eyes and looked calmly at Dunther, who looked obviously uncomfortable. "I still have my blessings and my incantations. He gives us fortitude and miracles yet."

"But they have all the power, the Dark One and his servants. They rule with the dark magics, the conjurers and necromancers, and enslave or destroy everyone before them!" said Dunther, wringing his once praying hands. "Where is the Father in this!?"

"He is in us," said Verboden softly.

"Don't tell me you haven't lost the faith, Verboden. I came across you many years ago when I was a knight without a king, in our suffering, and you were not a man of faith then!" Dunther wagged a finger at Verboden.

Verboden closed his eyes, bowed his head and spoke from there. "I did. I lost faith and went on that perilous path of denial. But I couldn't... it was far worse. I hated myself and everyone. I became my own god and wanted to force others to my will. Wanton and selfish... nearly poisoned by the dark arts. I knew then... in all that vileness, drawing toward it... that there was truly an Evil force."

"Yes, so, how did that make you come to a faith in a feckless Father?" asked Dunther under his breath.

"If there is truly an Evil drawing us, then there is also Good... waiting for us."

Dunther rolled his eyes.

"You have lost faith in the Father? You do not believe he exists?"

"No, no, I believe..." sighed Dunther, trying to look forward at the empty looking symbol upon the altar. It was just a circle atop a small pole. "It seems so empty, though, unfinished. I'm an impatient knight! There is so much evil, so much power out there. I want peace. I want peace for the people!"

"Peace?" Verboden looked up. "We can have peace in slavery."

Dunther's head jerked around to look at Verboden.

Verboden continued. "Peace is easy. Just submit to the Evil and peace will come. Yes, even in slavery until one's death. Freedom is what Goodness always yearns for. Freedom to choose, to be, to live a life of good or bad. Freedom to make mistakes, to suffer and live in joy. To decide one's own loves and hatred, one's own toil and play. Freedom to worship the Father or not to worship anyone or anything. Evil will never allow that. It seeks only tyranny, slavery, submission... and the worship only of its dark magics and of death, yes, much death."

Dunther seemed to lose strength, kneeling there, sinking down into the small pew, the weight of Verboden's words upon him.

"There is Good, which is of the Father, the way of true peace and freedom. And then there is Evil, which can look beautiful, can look enchanting, can say soft lovely words, can entice you and be of the most magnificent wonders... but it will inevitably ask of you to fear the Light, to hate the Light, to choose sacrifice, death, killing, slavery, inevitably, always – inevitably."

Dunther looked up, seeing a vision of her, the Queen of Faeries as Verboden spoke. He saw her beauty, enchanting yet forbidding. His mouth gaped as his eyes blinked. He was madly, deeply in love, but with what? Good or evil?

"She, she, she... you healed her with your blessing. You said she was of the Light? You said that, Verboden, upon our encounter, with her... You said she is of the Light!?" Dunther mumbled.

"I pray she is. Yes, she was created by the Light, by the Father. But she has... not chosen him... and that can be the most dangerous of them all. For when they choose Evil, they may take others with them, willingly. The faerie realm is of the land and not the Father... They have hidden themselves from that struggle, worshiping the creatures and not the Creator... The darkness seeks her, to enslave her. The Light waits..."

"And if she chooses the Light?" Dunther asked.

"She may lose her authority over the faeries..."

Dunther gritted his teeth, unsure.

"Whoa, hoh! Dunther on his knees praying!?"

Lord Dunther and Verboden jerked their heads around to see Alfred rush in. He plopped himself next to Dunther, who was feeling quite uncomfortable on his knees for so long.

"Dear Father of Light!" Alfred began.

"Do not be mischievous, King Alfred, not in prayer!" warned Verboden.

"Right, sorry," Alfred nodded. He cleared his throat and began again, softer, in earnest. "Dear Father of Light, bless Lord Dunther, Sir Murith and Sir... Lord... Gorham on their quests. Please bless us and help us to do what is good, against the evil. Please be there and strengthen Verboden the Cleric, so he can strengthen and bless us. And keep us safe from all that want to harm us. And keep the castle safe as well. Amen."

"Amen," Dunther and Verboden repeated together.

"Well, I have much yet to do before I go questing!" Dunther slapped the pew he was leaning on and got up quickly. Verboden and Alfred flinched. "I shall see you on the morrow, quite early, when we go to the smiths for our silver swords! Till then!" He patted his king on the head and then left quickly.

Alfred blinked and looked across at Verboden, who sat back on the pew. "Loranna said there were tombs and kings there. Dead kings! Does that mean there will be scary ghosts and uh... undead!?"

"Undead? What is this?"

"Undead, you now, ghosts, zombies, scary things like that? They died but are now undead!"

"Hmm... tombs of kings? Ah yes, the crypts and mausoleums of ancient kings. Yes, quite a few of them were placed in the moors. Wraiths, revenants and ghouls... oh yes, some of that," Verboden said, shrugging.

"Bu, bu, but... isn't that a problem? A werewolf and now wraiths and ghouls?! Problem!!!" chimed Alfred.

"Yes, I suppose they could be a hindrance. I will do my best to keep them at bay. We will stay near the locals, who know their way around these tombs, to avoid them. The tombs have been there many ages. The herders have lived there alongside them. I do not see them as a threat."

"Okay, makes sense. But I think we should still have, you know, some sort of ghost repellent." Alfred held an imaginary can of spray and twiddled his finger. Verboden looked oddly at it.

Once again at the Sanctuary's smithing hall, Alfred and Dunther where there to pick up the silver swords. Alfred had brought along several spears and scores of arrows for Loranna's bow.

"I want these to be tipped with silver as well," Alfred said, handing the bundle to Boggin.

"Right away," Boggin said. The gnomes and Boggin immediately went to work heating more ingots of silver. They had hardened clay crucibles where they placed the silver ingots. Several furnaces were built next to the "Dragon's Maw," as everyone called it. It was the place where the molten lava bubbled, surrounded by an upper row of stalactite teeth and a bottom row of stalagmite teeth. It looked like a dragon all right, with its mouth open and the intense red glow of volcanic lava swirling about.

They placed the crucibles within the furnaces using long cast-iron tongs. The furnaces were merely stone housings that covered the lava as it heated the enclosure to a very, very hot temperature. The silver ingots did not take long to melt. The gnomes deftly pulled out the stone crucibles containing the liquid silver. They then used limestone rods to stir the silver and clear out any impurities. Boggin brought forth steel arrow tips and spear heads. Using tongs, he quickly dipped them into the silver. Once done, they moved to the roaring falls to cool the silver plated arrow tips and spear heads. Alfred got excited watching the process.

The final process was to grind and sharpen the heads. They went over to good ole Broggia, who was sitting at the grinding wheel. He examined each head and used a steel hand grinder first to break off any tiny lumps of silver. Then he'd take it to the grindstone to sharpen the silver to a deadly point. Alfred peered closely, wanting to see the process, when he suddenly sneezed. He realized the grinding spewed forth a lot of silver dust.

"Oh... wow, that's very irritating!" yelled Alfred amidst the roaring waterfall and bubbling lava.

Broggia nodded, waving Alfred to stand back. Dunther stood back as well, still examining his completed silver-plated swords.

Alfred rubbed his nose and watched as Broggia worked the silver heads. He watched as the silver dust sprayed out again. Alfred rubbed his itchy nose then snapped his fingers. "Dunther! I got it!"

Dunther looked at him and cupped his ear to hear better.

Alfred rushed to the grinding wheel and breathed in again, then sniffled and sneezed, reeling backwards. Broggia looked at him oddly. Dunther caught Alfred. "What are you doing? That dust is quite irritating?!"

"Yes it is!" Alfred nodded. "Silver dust! Werewolf!"

Dunther tilted his head, not sure what Alfred was saying.

Alfred pretended to grab the silver dust from the air, then with a fist, turned to Dunther and opened his fist, blowing the air into Dunther's face. Dunther was not amused.

"An air bomb! A... uh.. silver air bomb! We can use it to blow silver dust into the werewolf!" Alfred turned to Broggia. "Broggia, I need that silver dust! Or can you make more of it?"

Broggia looked up and then reached down under the grinding wheel and pulled out a dirty tray. "Help yourself!"

It was filled with silver dust and bits, collected from all their work testing out silver plating on the swords and now the arrow tips and spear heads.

The sun was just rising as a rooster crowed. Gnomes and castle workers were waking up, stretching their stiffened muscles. The castle construction was going along nicely. King Gup, Gib, and Pep saluted Lord Dunther as he passed all the plans along to them. Before Dunther even left, gnomes brought in a wide stone table and placed it under the wooden table. The gnomes lifted the wood table and carried it out under Lady Nihan's direction. "Yes, we'll take that! Place it in the kitchens. We can always use another table!"

Gib and Pep slapped the new and quite low stone table in joy as King Gup organized the parchments. Dunther shrugged and exited.

Alfred stepped in quickly. King Gup, Gib and Pep looked up as Alfred brought in rolled parchments. "I have some plans I want you to work on. Top secret! Only the most trusted gnomes may look at and work on this. Aaannnd... I want you to work on it, when the others are asleep, quietly, secretly, in some Underworld cavern..." Alfred rolled out his small parchments.

The gnomes' eyes widened as they rubbed their knobby little hands together. "Whoa!"

Lord Gorham and Sir Murith brushed and cared for their wonderful steeds, given to them by Florina the Queen of Faeries. Dunther came to his white steed, touching it with open palms, anxiously waiting for the moment to leave.

"Eager are we?" Gorham said, calmly brushing his black steed.

"I can see why she gave you a horse for freeing her. But, why us? And how did she even know two other knights remained in this realm?" Sir Murith asked, brushing his beautiful grey steed.

"She must have faerie spies in the trees around us!" Gorham posited with a jocular smile.

Dunther eyed the distant trees. They looked beautiful in the morning sun. He smiled softly.

Alfred came out from the kitchen with Loranna and Nubio. They were still munching on biscuits. The gnomes hammering and picking away at the castle works, all turned to see the luscious biscuits. "Wait your turn!" yelled Lady Nihan, shooing some gnomes away. "Plenty of those coming up for break'n the fast!"

"Oh, I love breakfast!" a gnome yelled, rushing off to work.

The gnomes hop-skipped along with large bundles of rubble and brick, busying themselves and anxious for meal time.

"Be our last warm meal for a while, I think!" Alfred said, crumbs on his chin and clothes.

Verboden came up with a small wagon with two large goats pulling it.

"What is that?" Nubio asked, examining the large black goats and the thickset wheels.

"It is our traveling wagon, given to us by a family who fled the moors. The goats have splayed hooves, and the wheels are wide, perfect for travel in the dire bog drenched land."

Alfred, Nubio and Loranna threw their few belongings on it. Silver spears, silver arrows, and pouches of silver powder were most definitely amongst their gear. Lady Nihan came up with a wrapped bundle.

"These are more biscuits, stinky cheese, dried ham and sausages, and dried fruits and nuts. There is plenty for you all for many days. But you'll have to find other foods as you go. Northern berries are acrid and will give you bit of a stomach ache, but are sustenance nonetheless! And the stinky on the cheese isn't bad. It means it's good! If it weren't stinky, then it's gone bad. But Dehrman's cheese is always stinky." She had difficulty finishing the last words, nearly sobbing.

"Do not worry, Lady Nihan," said Verboden. "I am well aware of living off the land in the northern moors. The wet cold lands provide more than one realizes. And these goats are both female. They will provide milk."

Lady Nihan noticed their milk sacks and smiled. "The family was most gracious."

"They pray our quest will be a success. Tragic is their tale," said Verboden. Lady Nihan nodded with difficulty, doing her best to not cry in front of the children.

Lord Dunther raised his arm. He was in his splendid armour and atop his white steed. Next to him was Lord Gorham, in his amazingly designed armour too. Sir Murith was behind them, alongside Verboden, Alfred, Loranna and Nubio in the wagon.

Captain Hedor and his men kept the path open, pushing people back. "Now, now, no crying. They'll be back! They're just on diplomatic missions, except for an undying wolf beast, crazed barbarians, and a seductress of the forest. But other than that..."

Dunther lowered his arm, and the small troupe began their three separate journeys.

Cory, Wilden and the spearboys saluted as Alfred and Nubio passed. They returned the salute.

The archergirls were next to them. Loranna's younger sister Niranna and Setheyna with her pronounced forehead scar waved goodbye. Loranna's parents were there, showing courage for their daughter but unable to stop the tears. Loranna waved back.

"I thought this was supposed to be a secret exit by you," Verboden whispered to Alfred sitting next to him... "to hide from would be assassins."

Alfred shrugged, waving, and seeing Hiro cloaked amidst the castle workers and farmers who were unaware of his presence. Hiro nodded, then turned and left the crowd, to where Alfred did not know. The wagon turned northward as Dunther headed south and Gorham east.

"We're off," Alfred sighed.

The Quest of Sir Murith

Chapter Twelve

JOURNEY TO THE MOORLAND

The path northward wound through the fields and pastures of the farms. As the day ended, they reached the outskirts of the Danken Fuhrs. There were still plenty of scary looking trees around their small campsite. Alfred, Loranna and Nubio were busy with the cooking and entertainment while Verboden kept watch over them. Sir Murith looked out at the darkness of the land toward the north.

Traveling northward the next day, they skirted the Dark Forest on the west by a field and a half. As the days progressed, the fields became grey and sallow. Yes, sallow, having sickly yellowish and brown colors. Mist began to rise from the myriad of puddles dotting the landscape. Eventually, there were foggy fields and foggy fallows. Yes, fallow, untouched fields, perhaps once farmed but now desolate. There were many stone walls, very low and in ruin, stretching along the narrow muddy paths, going up and down rolling hills.

"How come we see these small walls but no farms or people?" Alfred asked Verboden, as both sat rocking side to side on the lumbering wagon.

"These lands were once filled with great farms and much sunshine. But as the kings laid in their tombs and crypts, the land was filled with haunts and curses," said Verboden somberly.

Alfred shivered from the cold. Loranna and Nubio huddled in the back amidst the small sacks of food and blankets. Sir Murith rode ahead a short distance, ever looking about.

Alfred had never seen such a land. He thought the misty grey of Westfold was well... misty and grey, but this was really, really misty and grey. He looked to his right as they passed a large looming hill fading into fog. Just beyond that, there was another hill visible as a grey shape, and this was during the day. The patchy earth was becoming more and more alien to him, like some strange bumpy world full of spidery bushes and giant sized moss beds. All around them was a land of mud and puddles. There would be a shine to the drenched ground if enough light filtered through the fog. But for the most part, everything had an eerie grey glow, even the shadows.

The goats were impressive. Their wide hooves and dreary drudging kept the wagon going at an even slow pace along the old narrow road. Even in the squishiest of blackened goo, the goats and thick wagon wheels continued. Alfred, Loranna, and Nubio held their noses and waved the air, trying to clear the boggy smell away, to no avail, of course.

Sir Murith controlled his grey steed as best he could. "Whoa girl, these lands are not meant for you." He patted her as she pulled precariously, hoof after hoof, from the sinking sod. Verboden stopped the wagon and got out, stepping deep into the goo. He was less concerned about that than the predicament of Sir Murith's mount. He plodded over, calming the horse with open palms.

"Sir Murith, careful, a break here will surely spell doom for your horse," said Verboden. Sir Murith leapt off quickly, sinking deep in the mud. Both looked at each other and knew what must be done.

"She will return south. She knows the way," said Verboden softly

Sir Murith tensed his expression but seeing her stumble again in the sucking mud confirmed the only choice. He nodded.

"Such a beautiful mare. I thought for sure with her enchantments she could go anywhere. I was wrong." The horse neighed as Murith removed the man-made reins, leaving on the exquisite faerie crafted horse tack. The faerie bridle and saddle were so finely crafted that they seemed to be part of the enchanted horse. "To the Keep, my fair lady, to the Keep go yee. I shall return," said Sir Murith.

His horse seemed reluctant to leave as Murith and Verboden pushed her back to somewhat drier land.

"Beyond this, it is leagues of wetlands. No horse, enchanted or not, will fare well in the brackish moors," said Verboden.

Murith's mare looked at them one last time and then galloped away, fading into the mist.

Chapter Thirteen

The First Encounter

Along the path they sat huddled together next to a small fire. The faint orange light was surrounded by the dark grey of night. Though few stars could penetrate through the fog, the mist seemed to brighten the night from the diffused light of the campfire and light from the stars above.

"It is the last of our wood," Murith remarked, placing a small branch to feed the small flame.

"It seems bright tonight," Loranna said, tucking tighter and scooting closer to Alfred.

Alfred scooted away, you know, to make more room for Loranna, of course. He looked up and away, staring at the bright clouds. He noticed one area where it shone brightest. "Is that the moon behind the clouds?"

Verboden looked up.

"It's a big round light," said Nubio.

Just then, the mist seemed to open up for them. Peering from behind it was indeed the moon.

"A full moon!" Loranna said with joy, seeing the light brighten their night.

Alfred gulped, "A full moon?!"

And then there was a great yet distant howl. It was most definitely a full throttled wolf's howl.

The First Encounter

Murith stood up and quickly pulled out his sword. Verboden stood with his staff. The children leapt up and huddled behind Verboden. It was difficult to tell which side of Verboden was opposite the echoing howl.

They could hear the approach of clomping feet. The goats neighed and became rightly anxious. Verboden quickly uttered words and patted the goats, dulling their senses.

"A silver sword indeed," said Murith through gritted teeth. "It best work. Our fire is too small, and we have no kindle!"

The clomping got louder along with a salivating growl. It seemed to echo all around them, as if it were reflecting off the very mist.

"Where is it?" Nubio waved his spear around, hiding behind his small shield.

Loranna strung her bow quickly and strapped on her quiver.

"Are there more than one?" Alfred feared. He hurriedly untied a small pouch of the silver powder from his belt.

"No, it is just one," said Murith, glancing about with narrow eyes. "The burrows of the moor echo harsh noises."

The growl grew and the clomping of feet was close enough that the squishing of the moisture rang out. The mist of the night still hid whatever beast was out there and where it was exactly. Alfred tried to untie the pouch's leather string, but it was stuck. Shaking, he clenched his teeth into the string, yanking desperately. The growl crescendoed and turned to a bestial bark. Nubio stepped back and bumped Alfred, causing both to slip in the mud and fall.

Murith rolled through the mud and swung his sword. A hairy beast flew past and howled in anguish as it swung evil talons against Murith's exquisite armour. Its loud scrape against steel was to no avail as it disappeared into the folding mist.

Loranna aimed blindly as she fell over Alfred and Nubio. All three, stuck in the mud, pointed their weapons in the wrong directions. They quickly got up, slopping precariously.

Murith leapt up from his roll. He looked at his silver blade and saw black blood. It then turned red and steamed from the blade. He smiled and held his open hand toward Alfred and the rest. Knowing his signal, they froze and were silent, even in their fear and dismay. Nubio mistakenly held his breath. Alfred turned, knowing the instinct and silently motioned for Nubio to breathe through his nose – albeit silently. Nubio nodded, the strain lessening on his face.

The growl in the mist subsided to an angry whimper. The mist suddenly rolled to the side, and the silhouette of a werewolf was only paces away. Verboden aimed his staff but Murith waved him off. The knight trod through the mud with sword ready. The beast turned with a limp and howled with claws raised. Murith thrust forward with a knightly aim and quickly dispensed with the wolf beast as it fell before him.

"Ah hah! Stupid foul beast! A silver sword brings you to your end! The beast that never dies is dead!" Murith said, wiping the very blade on the hairy fallen creature.

They quickly advanced, all pointing their silver weapons at the fallen werewolf. Verboden knelt before it and whispered, "It isn't him."

"Who?" Alfred asked, less concerned with the answer than with the fallen beast before them.

"It's kind of small for a scary beast," said Loranna.

"Look, it's turning!" Nubio said.

They watched as the fur retracted, the snout shortened, the limbs softened from bestial to human, and the large hairy ears shrunk.

"What is it?" asked Nubio.

"Who..." said Verboden. He quickly took up the forepaw, whose black claws softened to that of a small hand. The wolf suddenly coughed up blood, and its eyes opened. They realized it was a boy. Loranna gasped. Verboden scooted even closer and spoke ancient words of peace and rest, grasping the quivering hand tighter and resting his other on the boy's head. He gave him peace as the boy went to eternal sleep.

"A boy?" Murith hissed, "I killed a boy?"

"No, Sir Murith, you ended his curse," said Verboden, turning back to the boy, comforting him. "Be at peace, child. Your heart is of the Light."

"It was... I mean... he... was infected. The scratch or bite can infect any of us, anyone. And if it does, we will turn into a werewolf," said Alfred sadly.

"And the only cure is death by this silver sword?" asked Murith, raising his sword with the blood of a boy on it.

The First Encounter

"I don't know. I think so," said Alfred, kneeling next to Verboden in the mud. "I remember an old movie, uh story, saying it was a curse that could only be cured by killing with silver."

"Should we bury him?" asked Loranna, trying to hold back her tears.

Verboden looked up and around the moors, still caressing the poor boy's hair. "No, not here. We shall wrap him, place him in the wagon, and when we find a hamlet, ask if they may know his family."

Chapter Fourteen

The People of the Downs

"Is that a ghost?" asked Nubio, peering into the mist. They all looked up to see a bright orange light dancing along.

They stood behind Verboden and Murith, a line ready to fight. Alfred and Nubio held silver spears on each side with raised bucklers. Loranna had her bow taut and ready. Verboden leveled his staff and spoke a blessing over them. Murith was ready with his sword.

Another orange light appeared along with the first. Both bobbed up and down as they got closer. Then more appeared, a half dozen, all in a row, bobbing.

"Well, it isn't a werewolf, a poor werewolf at least," said Loranna.

"Nor is it evil," Verboden said, lowering his staff. "I sense people, and those lights must be their torches." He stepped forward carefully through the muck. "People of the Downs! Farmers and fair folk!"

"Hooh, hey? Who comes to our barren lands?" one responded from the mist.

"It is I, Verboden the Cleric, from the Northern Kingdom and Grotham Keep."

"Aye, we know you well!" the voice called out. "And be cautious! A curse covers this land. We seek the beast now!" The men suddenly appeared in the midst. They were the People of the Downs, a ruddy lot of farmers and herders living in the moors of the Northern Moorland. Their attire was thicker than the Westfold farmers, and they had many belts and pouches. They wore peculiar wide leather boots with what appeared to be down-turned flaps. As they stepped along the mud, the flaps splayed outward and kept them from sinking in. As they stepped up, the flaps folded back in, sloughing off the mud. Their gait was wider, tending to shift from side to side. It was obviously due to their living on such a wet soggy land.

All were armoured with thick leather-hide breastplates and greaves. Verboden could see in their eyes, the fear and near panic. But the leader, he could tell, carried the burden of their courage. He was a large stout man with a torch in one hand and a handaxe in the other. He could see the tears of the man, the reddened sad face. "Is this the boy you seek?" Verboden asked, stepping aside so they could see the fallen boy.

The man looked at the boy on the ground. He stepped closer, lowering his torch. "We seek a wolfkin. This boy is not known to us," he said with a hoarse tired voice.

Verboden glanced at Murith and the others and then stepped closer. "This boy is not your kin?"

"No, was he the curse then?" asked the man. "The wolfkin who attacked our hamlet, struck a curse on my brother and his daughter."

"Your brother and daughter, bitten? You killed them?" Alfred asked with a gasp.

"No, not yet. We'll pray until the night of the next full moon. They await their fate in the cage," said the man, peering close at the fallen boy. "Who is he?"

"He was a werewolf," said Alfred.

The scruffy man leered at Alfred, then at Verboden and Sir Murith. "Who is this boy that speaks to me?"

"He is King Alfred, boy king, defeater of ratkins, goblins and ogre enslavers of the Orient. And he has come here with silver swords to save you!" Sir Murith spat harshly, raising his shiny silver sword.

The man cowered, looking fearfully at Sir Murith and his sword. Then seeing Alfred, he realized, "The boy king and an archer girl who knights bowed to?" They each nodded from his affirmation. "I'm sorry! We all know about and heard of the great victories of our sunlit brethren to the south. Forgive me. I am under much angst with this curse."

Alfred shrugged with a smile, looking at his muddy self. "Well, I don't look much like a king..."

"What is your name, man of the downs?" Verboden asked gently.

"I am Chief Runnik. These are my sons. We hunt the wolf beast, knowing each full moon, our demise is ever nearer." He stood, with a glint of hope in his bloated tragic face. "And now the boy king comes."

"We've come to help you," said Alfred.

"To save us," Chief Runnik implored, dropping to one knee in the mud. His sons dropped as well. "Please, save us." He sobbed, hiding his emotionally wrought face in his muddy elbows, while still holding his axe and torch.

"We've come with silver blades. They stopped this werewolf," said Alfred, gesturing to the boy.

"Silver?" Chief Runnik replied with a breath of hope.

"Yes, in my world, ...well, where I come from, it is silver that is their weakness. Do you have silver? To make weapons?" asked Alfred.

"Yes, yes, some," answered the Chief, shuttering from this positive revelation.

"Can we take this boy back to your home to give him a peaceful burial?" asked Verboden.

The Chief looked up with anger in his reddened eyes.

Verboden spoke peacefully, "The boy has carried the same curse you now deal with. We must set his soul free."

The Chief nodded reluctantly.

Sir Murith gently wrapped the boy in a blanket and set him on the wagon. Nubio helped and noticed the boy's wrists. He began to tear and cried softly, "Look, Alfred!"

Alfred and the others came to see what Nubio was crying about.

"His wrists, they have the scars of slavery," sobbed Nubio, showing the same scars on his wrists.

"Shackles," Verboden touched the boy's wrists gently. "He was enslaved, imprisoned... and now having this curse?"

"We enslave no man, no boy, no girl in these lands. Never!" said the Chief with conviction.

"Take us to your hamlet. I wish to see your family that is cursed," said Verboden, covering the boy's hands.

"Can you save them, cleric?" asked Chief Runnik.

"I do not know. This curse is ancient and powerful. It may be beyond me. But the silver sword gives us a hope against this curse that I have not known for ages." He looked at Alfred and nodded.

Chapter Fifteen

The Hamlet

As they traveled along the muddy roads of the moors, Chief Runnik and his people slopped along quite well in their mud flap boots. They stepped high and wide, going through mud and sod at an even pace. The goats fared even better, pulling the wagon along. Sir Murith had the most difficulty in his regular leather boots covered with well fitted steel sabatons.

Chief Runnik and everyone else noticed Murith yanking and pulling his legs from the mire. The armoured knight finally became so stuck in the muck that he had to unbuckle a sabaton, pull his leg out, then bend down and dig it out. The Chief came back to Murith. He motioned for his sons to help. They pulled out leather pieces and leather straps and tied mudflap platforms under his boots. Though awkward, with these Murith could finally plod along.

Verboden and Loranna watched amused as Murith walked with a wide gait. Murith waved off the wagon-riding hooligans. Alfred did not notice Murith's pitfalls or the strange land as he was busy tugging at the string on his pouch of silver powder to open it. Nubio noticed. "What is that? A magic dust?"

"No, no, it's silver powder. I meant to pull it out and throw it at the werewolf, but I tied the leather too tight, and I think the wetness has made it stick," said Alfred through gritting, pulling teeth.

"Remember, when we fought the giant ants, we put the hot lava into clay pots?" Nubio said. "We threw them and they burst upon the vicious biters!"

Alfred nodded, remembering.

"I can make you small pots from the clay?" Nubio offered.

"Great idea. Then we can throw them much easier!" said Alfred, putting the pouch away.

"Will it kill the wolf beast then?" asked Nubio.

"Well, the sword definitely worked. So this will burn them for sure! Probably slow them down or keep them from jumping right at us!" Alfred said with an almost malicious grin. Nubio was impressed.

They stopped before two very large mounds in the mist. They seemed to have stone ruins atop them, which could just be seen in the early morning light. The Men of the Downs were used to the travel and the late hours, but Verboden and the children were practically asleep on the wagon. Murith trudged along by pure willpower, for his shoulders and head had drooped hours before.

"Our hamlet lies beyond these tombs. We usually take a long route, but with you Verboden, the renowned Cleric, to protect us, may we go through?" Chief Runnik inquired with a smile, bowing.

Verboden raised his head sullenly. "Go around."

Chief Runnik's smile waned as he looked at Murith, who looked quite exhausted, trudging through the soppy terrain. Sir Murith shrugged, breathing heavily. "Take the long way."

"As you wish," the Chief responded. They turned away from the mounds and headed the long way.

Hours later, passing through the moorlands, they came to where many goats and sheep of that particular wide-hooved and muddy fur type roamed. It was a land of gritty tufts and foggy fields. Several of the herders came up to the Chief, inquiring of the cursed wolfkin. They were surprised and most curious to see Verboden, Murith and the boy king.

They followed along, and more gathered as the Chief led the wagon into a rustic fortified hamlet. The walls of the hamlet were made of earthy bricks, sod-stacked, criss-crossed and up twice the height of man. However, it seemed any kind of creature with ferocity could easily traverse its roughhewn surface and overcome the walls. The gate wasn't much to speak of either. It seemed more like a giant wicker basket than a sturdy wooden door. It was woven together with thick branches, layer upon layer. It was obvious to Alfred that this hamlet and land were most definitely in shortage of lumber and trees. They made do with the sod, branch-ridden thickets, and lots of goat skin.

The Downs people, in all their thick furs and hides, quite dirty in their life of mud, surrounded the wagon and reached in to touch Alfred and Loranna. They thanked them for their glorious victories against the goblins. They were also quite curious about Nubio and his dark skin. Some showed fear, but the Chief waved them off.

"No, he is not a demon!" the Chief had to finally yell amongst the whispers and mutterings.

Nubio turned to look at their wide open eyes, seeing their apprehension in who or what he was. Loranna put her hand on his shoulder, patting him.

"His skin is just, he is," the Chief tried to explain and then turned to King Alfred. "What is he?"

"He is Khanafian, from a land far to the south," said Alfred. He stood up quite proudly atop the wagon. "He is a boy, just like me. His skin is darker, but he fought alongside me against ogres and scary giant bugs! He is my protector!"

The people clapped politely.

"Our apologies, we have never seen a Khanafian before, King Alfred and..." Chief Runnik proffered.

"Nubio, my name is Nubio, a Khanafian. And I am Royal Squire to Lord Dunther, Royal Baron Knight of King Athelrod!"

"Well, that is a name! And Lord Dunther, we are well familiar with, though he was once a bane to our people, a curse years ago. In these times under your kingship, Alfred, he has made his amends and traded fairly with us!" Chief Runnik said. "And now you come to save us! To fight the curse for us! I am so very grateful, as are our people!"

Chief Runnik bowed again, as did all the people surrounding the wagon. Alfred realized looking about that there were so few, indeed. He noticed over their bowed heads, a cage housing simple furniture and a stone oven. It was covered with a thatched roof. It contained two people, a father and daughter, who gripped the bars and looked on with the most desolate of expressions.

The hamlet was made mostly of sod, of clay bricks with a few bits of lumber and larger branches for frames. Everywhere and everything was either muddy or of mud. Nubio noticed many clay pots and cups and inquired of their potter. Another thing they seemed to use quite a bit of was rope and thatch. There were many rope things crafted, mats of rope, many articles of clothing and doors of rope and the clay bricks and sod were netted or matted together with rope. They used the widely available tufts of moorland grasses to make them.

Chief Runnik mumbled orders to some elders who took the fallen boy. "We will give him a fire funeral. We must make sure his curse is completely gone."

"Yes, I will pray over him," Verboden nodded reluctantly.

"When you are ready..." the Chief answered.

"May we see your brother and his daughter?" Verboden stepped down from the wagon.

"Yes, yes, of course," Chief Runnik answered with hope. He hurried along to lead them to the cage. "When one of our folk is cursed, for many have been these many moons, we place them in here and pray daily hoping the curse will not come. But on the eve of the full moon, the curse begins."

Verboden stopped. "Then what?"

The Chief stopped and looked at Verboden with dead eyes. "Then we immolate them."

Verboden noticed the cage the father and daughter were in. It had blackened bars, a grass tuft roof covering, and many dried peat moss bricks as furniture. Verboden looked about and saw that they used the dried peat moss bricks like wood for fire. It was in their stoves, their kilns and atop small torches to light the hamlet even during the foggy day. "All of that burns?"

"Yes. It is the only way," said the Chief. "Well, until now, with you here to save my brother and my niece, I pray."

The father and daughter held each other as they looked on with some courage. The father had a bandaged arm, and the daughter had one on her leg. Verboden came closer and then felt a dizziness. He wavered and stood back as Murith and Alfred passed him, then looked back at him.

"I sense their curse. It is powerful. Woefully," said Verboden, trying to breathe calmly.

The father heard and cried, holding his daughter.

"They have wounds now, but once they heal, the curse will take hold. They will heal like the wolfkin and will become very strong. We have all accepted our fate if wounded and reside in the cage. And when they fully turn, at the next phase of the moon, we end their suffering," said the Chief, keeping a safe distance from the cage and from his own brother. The brother nodded with tears, whispering comforting words to his daughter.

"She's so young. We have to save them, Alfred," said Loranna as she stepped up next to him.

"I don't know how," Alfred said. "In my world, the legend says there is no cure." A dreariness came over them both. They had been traveling in the cold damp moorlands for many days and were in need of a comforting rest.

"Chief Runnik, do you have a place we can rest?" asked Verboden. "Perhaps with rest, my sojourners can think anew of how to defeat and end this curse."

"Yes, yes, of course," Chief Runnik replied. He led them away from the cage. "You know this hamlet is not our home. Before the curse began, seasons ago, all of our families lived on farms and herded our sheep. This hamlet is what is left of our clan. We built it hastily. We will make our last stand here. There are abodes for rest just over here." The Chief hurried ahead of them.

Verboden spoke softly to Murith, "Agents of Scourge indeed. She seeks to destroy these regions..."

Chief Runnik opened the wicker door to a small hovel. It was a small brick shelter not much longer or wider than a man lying down. On two corners, it had beds with layers of woven tuft grass and rope. The layers built up to floors and dry beds which Alfred and Loranna immediately claimed. Both were snoring before Verboden or Murith could enter and decide their own resting situation. They smiled, looking at the young yet great warriors sonorously asleep.

"With great rest, I'm sure Alfred will think of something. He always does," said Murith, yanking off their muddy boots and placing them in a hanging basket outside the doorway.

Verboden nodded with a peaceful look. He found enough room at the end of one of the beds to sit. It was adjacent to the stone stove in the opposite corner. The weight of the cursed land and wolfkin seemed to float away as he pulled off his boots and handed them gratefully to Murith.

Chief Runnik brought in two clay mugs with grass tuff tea and handed them to Verboden. Murith, wiping his boots off and hanging them in the basket outside, spotted Nubio, as awake as ever, at the potter's kiln. He was working with the potter on something. Murith turned back into the hovel to speak with the Chief and Verboden, as they sat next to the stone stove. He took a clay mug from Verboden.

"This is my brother's humble hovel," the Chief said. "I hope your presence will bless it and him. He is my last brother, the last of my family. The curse of the wolfkin is destroying these lands. Many farms have been destroyed. Whole families killed or cursed. Many have fled south to your kingdom. We fated few are trying to hold on, to stay here, in our land, as dreary and moribund as it is."

"This boy that fell from the curse, you do not know him at all? He is not one of your people?" asked Verboden.

The Chief shrugged. "No, he is not. He is the first of the cursed wolfkin that we have ever seen. The others, at much cost of our own lives, we burned in their wolf form. We never knew of this silver. I will have our blacksmith coat our weapons immediately. We have time. This moon's three nights has ended, and the beast that will never die will not return till the next full moon."

"We can't wait till the next moon!" Alfred said, sitting up. The men jolted, surprised he was awake. "We must find where this boy came from!"

"Came from? He's not one of us. He is a foreigner," the Chief answered.

"Did he escape as a werewolf from another land?"

"Where?" the Chief replied. "This land is filled with leagues of moors and bogs. There are no other people but our own, the People of the Downs. And that is the way we like it. It is a remote harsh land where we thought no one would bother us, not even a horrible curse. We are simple sheepherders, believing the Father would give us this refuge, even in all its foul fields. But it appears the Father of Light cannot give us peace, not for my brother, not for his daughter, and not for any of our families." The Chief's face swelled with a red anger as he stared into the small stove. It slowly burned a peat moss brick.

Alfred got up from the bed, jostling Loranna who was still in a deep sleep. He stepped through the men crowded about on the weed woven mats. "The beast that never dies? You have fought and killed this werewolf every full moon?"

"Yes, for several seasons now. Each time, we thought we ended it. When we discovered the bite was infectious, we tried to save those who were bitten. But they turned... and many healers were lost. It was... a nightmare, knowing you had to kill your own, to eradicate this curse. But the beast has returned each full moon. We had to fight, burn, and sacrifice even our own, thinking we had cleansed the land each time." The Chief looked up, breathing in air to cool his reddened face.

"So the beast returns each moon, even if you kill it?" asked Alfred.

The Chief nodded. "We kill it and any who were bitten. But even after that, the beast never really dies!"

Verboden looked sunken. "The curse, it is powerful. I sense it in your brethren. It is beyond my powers, even of blessings... even... of prayer."

The men sat silent, sunken, but not Alfred. He stood in the small area, jittery, going back and forth. He bent down and lifted his mouse playing hand, then the fingers of his left hand flicked, as on a keyboard. He was in a trance. Chief Runnik, still in his reddened facial frustration, looked confused by what Alfred was doing. He then looked at Verboden and Murith, who seemed to look at Alfred with some strange kind of hope.

"Agents of Scourge..." Alfred sneered. "Then, there is a source. A werewolf that is infecting..." Alfred kept his odd stance, looking at something the others could not see. They leaned in to see what he was looking at but could not see anything. "A high level boss lord!" Alfred suddenly blurted out.

"A high level boss lord?" Murith squinted his eyes trying to understand.

"Yeah, in my games at home, there's always some boss who is the main goal in a level, a high level NPC. You have to get through all of his minions to defeat him!" Alfred said.

"Ennnpayseh??" Verboden repeated.

"N-P-C! Non player character!" Alfred yelled back, much to their surprise. "That's it! There's a werewolf lord out there in the moors, infecting... he's got slaves! Oh wow... oh no! This is terrible! He's got this boy and others as slaves. And each full moon, he bites one to send it out to curse the land!"

Verboden stood, gritting his teeth. Then feeling the burden of such a terrible evil, he leaned on his staff.

Murith stood as well, pulling out his silver sword deftly in the tight confines. "We must find this evil Nnn-pay-Ceh boss and kill it!!!"

"And save the children!" exclaimed Loranna, who suddenly sat up.

"Sacrificing children... a boy... girls? Enslaved?" Verboden's face became ashen white. He wavered. Alfred caught him, and both sat on the bed.

"Verboden, we need you. Be strong. Please!" said Alfred earnestly, holding him.

Murith spoke softly, staring at his reflection in his sword, "There is no limit to evil. None."

The cleric nodded and took a deep breath. "I'm okay. I must seek strength in prayer. I must. I shall attend to the boy's funeral." He stood again, stronger, and stepped carefully through the crowded hovel to the door. Murith put his sword away and tried to offer help, but Verboden gently pushed his arms aside. "I just need to pray."

Verboden stepped outside onto the squishy mud with his bare feet. He felt it between his toes. It actually seemed to calm him.

Alfred, the Chief, and Murith watched silently as Verboden walked out into the cold of the hamlet and to where the boy was laid for cremation.

"What do you need from us? How can we help, King Alfred," asked Chief Runnik, putting another peat moss brick into the stove.

"I'll need a map of all the crypts and tombs of the moorland!" said Alfred.

"Oh, we have very good maps to help our shepherds avoid them."

"We're not avoiding them. We're going to them," said Alfred.

The Chief looked at Murith with his mouth agape. Murith, brows fluttering, nodded grimly.

Chapter Sixteen

The Tombs and Crypts

"Did we have to reach our first kingly tomb in the dead of night?" Loranna asked, getting off the wagon.

The mound was like a small perfect grassy hill. It had a perimeter of low crumbling stone walls and spear-point cast-iron fencing.

Alfred stared at the map with a candle. Nubio was juggling little clay balls filled with silver powder -- juggling them carefully, that is. He was feeling their weight in his hands, ready to throw at the sign of any howls of a wolfkin.

Alfred noticed. "It won't be a full moon for weeks. Put those away – carefully."

Nubio nodded and wrapped them in a clothe with a few others and carefully placed them inside a clay jar.

Verboden took care of the goats, unfastening them and tying them to a thicket of bramble nearby. The rustic goats began chewing on the greyish leaves.

"It is an odd land. It is very dark at night with the stars and moon veiled by mist. Yet the light seems trapped down here, making day and night seem washed together," Murith noted, laying out wicker mats provided as bedding by the People of the Downs.

"Washed together like dirty water," quipped Loranna. "Dirty, dark grey water." She shivered and set her bow and quiver next to her bedding.

Verboden brought bramble and pulled out a peat moss brick from the wagon to make a fire. Nubio helped him, and a fire was flickering soon enough. They sat about it, sipping a warm soup from small clay bowls.

"We shall investigate the nearby tombs in the morning. Everyone get some sleep," said Verboden.

"What if ghosts come out tonight?" asked Loranna.

"I do not sense any. No malice, no unrest, it seems quite... quiet..." Verboden said, peering into the dark mist.

"Clerics have a way with such things," said Murith.

"We shall see in the morning what is amiss in these cursed lands, in these tombs. Now rest," said Verboden.

The gate grated loudly as Murith used a strong iron crowbar, a tool given by Chief Runnik, to open it. Murith poked in a torch and waved it about. He stepped into a dark clammy dungeon corridor. It was filled with hanging roots and dripping ooze. He passed the crowbar back and pulled out his sword. "The gate opened too easily."

"Something has been here before?" asked Verboden from behind.

"Most assuredly," Murith said, carefully stepping in and peering down the squat, narrow corridor. He used his torch and sword to move the dense, dripping roots. He stepped carefully around the puddles and on the stone walkway. "There's another gate at the end. I see it. It is open."

"Careful, Sir Murith!" Alfred shouted too loudly.

Murith rolled his eyes. "Yes, my King." Stooped over, he hurried to the second gate and stood tall within a crypt.

Verboden and Alfred came up behind him. "I sense nothing," said Verboden.

Murith waved his torch about. "This is not the work of grave robbers or tomb raiders." The room was filled with chests of treasure, furniture, and weapons. A sarcophagus sat at the other end.

They walked carefully through the crowded tomb. Alfred glanced to and fro at all the ancient ornate trappings. He was intrigued at how all these things were hand-made, as opposed to the mass production of things back home in his world. When he'd see a chest or piece of furniture with a lock on the lid or handle, it was perfectly made by machines in his world. But here, each lock, each hinge or handle was handmade and had all the distinct and personal touches created by human hands with human tools.

"It is a king, but not a rich king. He is very old as well," said Verboden, looking carefully about. He went to the sarcophagus and noticed it was slightly open.

Verboden motioned for the torch. Murith found an ancient kingly candle. "Well, he won't be needing this." He lit it and handed it to Verboden. The cleric peered closer at the slight opening, trying to shed some light within. He had to get closer to look into the dark slit. The lid was of stone and would require leverage on both sides to open. He got just a bit closer to the opening, bringing the candle as close as possible.

"Ow!" he yelled, and retracted. He handed the candle to Murith, whose heart skipped a beat. Murith held it with trembling hands in his gauntlets.

"Hot wax! Hot wax!" yelled Verboden. His hand was caked in candle wax. He quickly wiped and scraped it along the sarcophagus – rather rudely!

Murith was shaking a bit, holding the stupid candle he immediately set down on a nice table. He stared at Verboden, who was peeling off the wax. Verboden noticed Alfred and Murith's disheveled impatience.

"It's empty," said Verboden, nodding to the sarcophagus.

"And?" Murith wanted a bit more info.

"I don't know. It's empty, ahhh..." Verboden peeled off a large chunk of wax and waved his poor red hand about.

Murith gave his sword to Alfred, who knew how to handle it. Quickly and with surprising strength, Murith pushed the lid off the sarcophagus and over to the other side. It dropped with a loud rocking clamor as dust and webbing exploded into the air.

There was nothing within but dust and some torn and aged pieces of cloth and leather.

"Gone," said Murith under his breath.

"Ah hah!" yelled Nubio from the entrance, pointing his spear. Loranna aimed her arrow from behind.

Murith, Alfred with a knight's sword, and Verboden, blowing gently on his red hand, turned to stare back at them.

"Oh, thought you were crushed or killed in some cruel way," noted Loranna, lowering her bow.

"Was there a stone trap you avoided?" asked Nubio, lowering his spear.

"You're supposed to be guarding the entrance!" said Murith, taking his sword from Alfred and sheathing it.

"Oh well, we... wanted to rescue you," Loranna said.

Murith flicked them both away with his gauntleted hands.

Reluctantly, they went back out.

Verboden looked in the sarcophagus. He peered at and then touched the dust. He closed his eyes as he slowly moved his hands about. Alfred carefully took up the thick, squat candle, pouring the excess hot wax to one side.

Murith, miffed, found a candle holder, grabbed the candle and stuck it in, handing the whole thing back to Alfred.

"I sense... evil, old, ancient... but gone... long gone," Verboden said softly. "I can't tell what. I am not a diviner."

"Well then," Alfred pulled out the old parchment map. "We've got lots more to search!"

Chapter Seventeen

Ghostly

The tombs and crypts they searched seemed to have similar tells to tale, silent and foreboding. Each sarcophagus, mausoleum, tomb, and crypt, while generally intact, contained empty coffins. The kings of old were missing.

"I don't get it," Loranna said, sloshing atop the puddles and muck with her moorland boots. "All these weeks and no wraiths, no ghosts or banshees. Only cluttered tombs with great treasures, but no corpses! No decaying rotting skeletal kings! What I'd give to hear a banshee wail and shiver me to my very bones and make us all quiver in utter fright!"

"Not even a single NPC! A wolf lord! A mini-boss!" said Alfred, booting alongside her. Both were traveling along a field of sod just to stay active as Verboden kept with the wagon on the narrow cemetery-like road. Nubio slept soundly in the wagon, his head bobbing along with each snort.

As they sloshed further, kicking mud at each other with pounding steps and giggling, they came up to Sir Murith standing in the midst. He pointed to a small mound silhouetted in the fog.

"Is that another tomb?" Murith asked nonchalantly.

Alfred stopped and unfurled his parchment. "Ahhh... yeah, but it's a small one. Has a marking here that it was actually robbed years ago."

"Must have been a lowly baron or duke then, no nasty traps or ancient locks like the kingly ones," said Murith shrugging.

"You mean like all the ones that were already set off or bypassed by someone else," Alfred said. "Who, Sir Murith?"

"Well, I thought that was why we've been out here these many days, to find out, and find your wolf lord enpaycee," Murith answered.

"N-P-C... non-player character. The N stands for... nevermind," Alfred said, rolling up his parchment. "Just pass this one. Let's go to the bigger, kingly tombs."

"Whoooohhooo comes hereerreereeree???!" a haunting voice rang out.

Murith pulled out his sword deftly and swirled in the muck. Alfred and Loranna dropped all pretension of boredom and stepped even closer to Murith, pulling out their weapons.

"Whhhoooohhh disturbs me??!" the voice boomed louder with a gargling vileness.

"Will silver work on ghosts?" Murith whispered to Alfred.

"I dunno? Why you asking me?" replied Alfred.

"It was your idea," hissed Murith, pointing his sword from one side to the other.

"My idea is to fight werewolves! And it worked. Hullo!?" Alfred responded, haughtily.

"You know, it was your idea to come to the tombs," added Loranna.

"Oh yeah..."

"Howwwwwhhh darRRRrreee youuuu disturbbb meeee!"

Verboden jumped off the wagon and sloshed through the field from the pathway. "Is it a ghost! A wraith!?" he asked rather too excitedly.

"Yes, yes, cleric! You can finally use your priestly powers!" Murith said, waving his sword about.

"Ooh! I want to see what 'turning the undead' looks like," said Alfred under his breath.

Verboden oddly plopped in front of them with his own mud flap boots and waved his arms about. They all stood listening, but the voice did not wail out again. They waited longer, peering into the cold mist to see if they could see anything.

"It's cold. Is that the ghost?" Alfred whispered.

"No, that's winter coming upon us," Verboden said, glancing to and fro.

"There!" Murith pointed with his sword.

A grey ghostly figure was sloshing along the mud. It was a distance away, somewhat hidden by the mist. It began to advance toward them, howling like a ghost and not like a werewolf. Okay, so it was moaning.

Murith and Verboden stood in front, ready to defend Alfred and Loranna. Suddenly, Nubio crashed into them from behind. They all tottered a bit and gave out gasps as they managed to keep from falling into the sod.

"Hold the line!" Murith yelled, pushing them back up and gritting his teeth in all seriousness.

Nubio shook in fear. "I'm sorry! I heard Verboden get up, then the ghost moans and came running!"

They looked out and saw the ghost. It trudged along rather haphazardly. Then it suddenly fell in the sod and with much ado, got back up.

"Is that a ghost?" Loranna asked.

Murith lowered his sword a bit.

Verboden tapped Murith's sword to raise it up again. "It is a ghost. I sense it strongly."

"Clumsy ghost?" Alfred wondered aloud as they waited impatiently for the ghost to approach and begin its cursing or wailing.

"Howwww... darrree... yeee... OOOF!" the ghost got stuck in the mud again and tottered.

"Do you need help?!" Alfred blurted out. Everyone else, not amused, stared at Alfred angrily. Murith feigned an elbow strike to Alfred to get him to shut up.

"I'm alllll righhhh!" the ghost yelled out. He stood up once again, then carefully with high lifted knees came towards them.

The group straightened up and leaned on each other, waiting. Posing in fighter-ready positions can get tiring, after all. Verboden checked his fingernails, picking out some of the delicate sod.

Finally, the ghost was within paces, and the group decided to return to their fighter-ready-ish poses – not completely ready to fight but at least a modicum toward that disposition.

"Welllll thhhhheeennn... eck, akk... pffffeww... cough cough!" the ghost suddenly bent down as if choking on something.

Murith advanced to help him in some way.

The ghost waved Murith off as he cleared his ghostly throat. A mud toad suddenly spurt out from his throat. "Ahhh... there you are my warty friend. Off you go, back into the warmth of the mud!"

The toad seemed to smile as it shimmied into the puddles of mud and sank within the moorland sod.

Loranna gagged.

The ghost stood up. "Well well well... what do we have here? Visitors?!"

Verboden, Murith and the children stood with mouths agape and eyes wide open, gazing. This ghost was certainly ghastly looking and much more solid than expected. He was in pompous garish garb with many flares as it were. But of course he had that dead dreary laid-in-a-coffin-for-ages look.

"What? Haven't seen a scary ghost before! Ehy?" the ghost suddenly twirled his fingers at them, pretending to advance to scare them. He then realized he was stuck in the mud and tottered once again.

"Who are you?" Verboden asked stunned.

"And why do you get stuck in the mud?" asked Alfred.

"Why are you so strange?" Murith muttered.

"Not very scary for a ghost," Loranna confided.

"I like him," said Nubio.

The ghost suddenly smiled and pointed at Nubio. "Now that's a nice chap, that Khanafian!"

"You know my people?" asked Nubio excited, stepping forth.

"Of course, of course, I am a worldly man!" the ghost bowed, then stood up, and remembered. "Oh yes, allow me to introduce myself. Been awhile since I chatted... I am Baron Oswahl von Schnikerstahn! Lord of Manorial Klepturstah..goh.. vol... something or other... heh heh... been awhile. Been a long while. I'd get my papers from my burial cloister." The baron turned to look at his dismal little burial mound. "But, I've been robbed!" He turned back to them, trying to make the best of it with a smile.

"Why do you get stuck in the mud? I thought ghosts floated?" Alfred asked, coming forward.

"Oh, me? Stuck? Oh well... I'm just trying to fit in, you know. I could float, I suppose..." the Baron thought for a moment, then recalled. "Ah yes... is this it?" The Baron rose a bit, and his muddy feet faded. He then floated about slowly and waved his arms around in a scary ghostly floating way. "Ooooo... Ooooohhh!"

"Yes, that's it, much scarier!" Alfred nodded.

"Alright, what's the meaning of this?! Who are you and why are you here?" said Murith impatiently, stepping between Alfred and the ghost with his sword pointed.

The ghost floated back. "I told you, I am Baron Oswahl, and that is my tomb! If anyone should be asking anything, it should be me, upon thee!"

Verboden stepped forward and spoke, "We are searching these very tombs for wraiths, ghosts and banshees, and you are the first we have come across. We were expecting, well, much more maligned specters than yourself."

"I was maligned... very, once... long ago... But I realized my fate... It was... deserved." He floated back down, his feet solidifying into the mud. "You see, in life, I was an incredibly rich baron, full of pomp and flare. I lived in the pageantry of life, full of splendor and grandeur! But it was all for naught, it seems. Even in my death, my wife, my ex-wives, my children, my illegitimate children... all fought over my wealth, and I was left with but a small decrepit mausoleum." He pointed to his small humble mound. "Forgotten. Easily robbed. What few possessions in there were taken, and my bones... scattered. Scattered across the moorlands! I am forever doomed to the bogs and brambles of this cursed dreary land. Deservedly so... I suppose..."

They stared at him, wide eyed and in wonderment. Not even Verboden had seen such a resigned ghost as him.

"Are you at peace then?" asked Verboden.

"At peace?" the ghost with a faint smile found that amusing. "I suppose that could be a word... resigned, fated, accepting, deserved, at peace, yes... I suppose I am. Bored..." He turned to look gently at the living. "But enough about me! What brings you all to these remote, barren, cursed moorlands?"

"The tombs of the kings, they are gone," said Verboden. "Their souls, their bones, none are present. Their sarcophagi have been opened. Their bones and bodies removed."

"Oh yes, yes... a wretched horrible *necromancer* took them after the moor folk left this region. A wolfkin or two has scattered the people," the Baron said calmly, flicking his fingers as if it were no big deal.

"What? A necromancer?" Alfred slapped his forehead.

"Yes, a powerful one. He came with a cadre of nasty revenants of one kind or another and cursed tomb raider villains. He was a very powerful necromancer, easily entering each tomb and removing all my friends. They were not very good friends, as all were quite snobby and greedy in their rich pompous crypts. But, hah hah, they were no match for the necromancer! He showed them! Took their bones as well!"

"Why their bones?" asked Alfred.

"The bones are their... anchor, their connection to this world," Verboden said.

"More like their chain and shackle! Their bones are their most precious... But yes... cleric... you know... the necromancer now owns them. They are servant to him!" the ghost said, chuckling. "Stupid kings, buried in extravagant crypts, only to become slaves in their death."

"Where is this necromancer?" asked Verboden.

"Oh, he is long gone! He took all the kings' and lords' corpses and bones and went to the Far East, probably where the Dark Lord himself resides. He has an army of the undead under his power, to be used at a later date methinks. An army of wraiths, powerful wraiths... quite formidable..." the ghost figured.

Verboden tottered in the sod.

"And he didn't enslave you?" asked Alfred.

"Couldn't find my bones! Hah! So, it actually looks like this cheap burial mound saved my soul. Well, as saved as it deserves to be. My bones are scattered here in the moorland. They weren't worth finding, anyway. I was just a pompous, self-loathing, arrogant fool in life, and now a fated meandering, lonely soul in the hereafter."

"We should leave this ghost and continue our quest," said Murith, sheathing his sword and turning away.

"No wait!" said Alfred. "You mentioned wolfkins? Do you know where they came from? Who... who started them or created them?"

"Mmm... can't say that I do... I know these lands quite a bit... take long arduous ghostly walks amongst them... regularly... can't say that I've come across... how did you ask it... started them? Created them?" The ghost folded his arms thinking... thoughtfully.

Ghostly

Alfred stepped forward. "We are looking for a wolf lord, one who must have captured slaves and keeps them in one of these tombs. Then each full moon, he infects one..."

"...and sends them to terrorize and annihilate the People of the Downs?" the Baron interrupted.

"Yes," Alfred said sadly.

"How quite wicked and evil!" the Baron said.

Chapter Eighteen

LORANNA'S CLAIM

"I've seen these children, sad, lonely, these many moons. Once in a great while, would I come across one. I cowered from them. I didn't want to scare them. But how could I help them? I am just a cursed prisoner of the ethereal world."

The Baron brought them to a crossroad, a dark and sickly intersection that went in all four directions. Verboden rode the wagon while the children walked alongside the Baron ghost. Murith followed behind, eyeing the ghost.

Bramble and thickets covered the hilly paths, and the road was littered with puddles and patches of black goo. A steamy peat moss mist rose from the ground, warming the land even as the fog of winter rolled across the sky.

"They came from the north, walking alone upon this path, southward, toward the moorland folk. Take this road south and in a few days you reach the farmsteads of the People of the Downs. The children looked like they were fleeing... or escaping, but with much fear and despair. I could not add to their calamity by revealing myself to them, by trying to help them. I'm sorry." With this the Baron began to fade away.

"Don't go!" said Alfred.

The Baron suddenly returned to solid form. "Oh, yes?"

"Come with us? You can help us?" Alfred offered.

106

"Not a good idea," mumbled Murith.

"He's probably right," the Baron nodded, scowling at Murith.

"No, I want you to come with us!" said Alfred, pushing. "You know this land, the tombs we seek. Please, come with us! You can help us and the children – now."

"He may not be able to come," replied Verboden, sitting on the wagon. "Ghosts tend to be limited to their burial site or haunting."

"I am limited by my precious materials, my bones..." said the Baron, fading, then solidifying once again. "However... it appears a fragment of my bones may be that way!" He pointed northward with a gleeful smile and motioned for them to follow. "Come then, I shall be your tour guide on this most precarious adventure to find a powerful wolf lord... mini-boss... ennpaycee!"

"N-P-C!" Alfred said, sloshing along. "...Nevermind..."

He offered his arm, "Milady?"

Loranna suddenly smiled and reached out to hold it but realized it was ghostly, ghastly and somewhat dead looking. She backed off with a polite wave.

"Oh, sorry," the Baron noticed and shrugged. "I'm a ghastly ghouly ghost!"

He hop-skipped along the road as Alfred, Loranna and Nubio hastily slopped along in their mud boots to keep up.

The wagon was parked outside an elaborate mausoleum with a gothic gate and many ancient stone sculptures of knights and priests. The children sat around a small flickering peat moss fire warming up goat's milk. Verboden watched over them as Murith stood waiting and peering into the gate of the mausoleum.

"Well, he makes for a fine scout, searching out the crypts for us," Murith said.

"Yes, these ones in the north are much more sophisticated and elaborate than those near the hamlet," replied Verboden.

A loud KLANG CRUNCH was suddenly heard echoing from the tomb.

"Another trap!" Murith hissed.

"I'm alllrigh.... I'm allrigh..." the ghost yelled from the dark entrance. "Just a large stone with spears in it! Reconstituting my corporeal form now. No worries. No need to come rescue me or keep me company in this dire situation. No need!"

Murith and Verboden stood at the gate, waiting for the Baron. The children were sipping and enjoying their nourishing milk. They had milk mustaches and were giggling.

The Baron came out with huge holes in his torso that were slowly reforming. "Aside from untriggered traps, there was no kingly corpse."

"Another empty tomb in the north, this necromancer was quite thorough," said Murith.

"And no wolf lord hidden within," answered Verboden.

"Nope, nothing but gaudy rich treasures. I'd suggest you all take that and finance your own powerful army of mercenaries or start a kingdom or two, far away from this dreary moribund place," the Baron said.

"We are running out of time, Verboden," muttered Murith.

Verboden nodded. "The next full moon is almost upon us."

"And Chief Runnik's brother and daughter are nearly at their end," Murith reminded.

Alfred stood up with his milk mustache. "When's the next full moon?"

They all looked up into the dark fog and could not tell. Verboden then calmly whispered to himself, closing his eyes and tilting his head. He leaned against his staff and quietly waited.

He opened his eyes. "Two days."

"Whoa!" Alfred gasped. "We will never save Chief Runnik's brother."

"And daughter," sighed Loranna.

"They will burn them alive," said Nubio, lowering his head.

"And we will have a werewolf on us soon, here or at the hamlet," Murith added.

"I sense a child," the Baron said softly.

They all sat silent in their own ways: Alfred, Nubio, and Loranna at the small fire; Verboden leaning against his staff; Murith shouldered against a sculpture of a knight; and the Baron staring off into the dark grey fog.

Verboden looked up. "What do you mean, you sense a child?"

The Baron pointed into the dark mist.

They stood. Verboden quickly walked up to the ghost to peer into the dark fog. They heard the faint sobbing of a child.

"Careful, Verboden. It's a werewolf," said Murith, quietly unsheathing his sword.

Loranna quickly walked up. "It's just a child, Verboden. Don't kill it!"

"Don't worry, the child will not turn yet. The moon is not full yet," said Verboden.

As he said that, they looked up to see the fog clear for a moment, and there, shining down was not a full moon, but almost. It gave Verboden pause.

Alfred and Nubio rushed up holding small clay pots with the silver powder in them.

Verboden noticed. "I think those will be unnecessary. Let me seek this child alone."

"Not a good idea," Murith said.

"Quiet," said Verboden quickly. Their rustling subsided as they stood still and the moaning of the moors gave way to the soft sobbing of a child. It then began squishing steps in mud that faded farther away.

"It's leaving! Southward," the Baron noted.

Verboden waved everyone to stay as he rushed out into the mist. Murith hesitated and looked at Alfred, who finally motioned for him to go.

As Murith rushed forth, he looked about in the mist and could not see anything. Apprehension rose in him as he retreated back to Alfred. "I can't see a thing and cannot leave you, my king!"

Alfred nodded. Fear rose in him as the mist, in its blinding obscurity, was isolating and demoralizing.

They waited and heard the sobbings rise again and the sloshing of mud. Then they saw the large shadowy shape of Verboden come forward. He was carrying a ragged girl with blazing red hair.

They all gasped at the gaunt, gangly figure in Verboden's arms. She was dirty and weak, in rags, and had a grievous wound on her forearm that looked diseased. It was a festering bite.

She may have been the age and height of Loranna, but due to her diminished state, she looked half the size. Verboden set her down upon the wicker bedding next to the small flickering fire. She had a gaunt face and pale eyes.

Murith was not thrilled. "She's infected. We must end her curse now. We have no choice."

The girl shuddered at Murith's claim.

"Stop it! Just stop it and have mercy!" exclaimed Loranna. She took her own clay cup and ladled a small bit of warm goat's milk from a clay bowl and held it out, ready to serve.

Alfred stood back and stared, aghast at her gaunt form. Nubio had seen it all before and helped Verboden with her comfort. He also waved at Loranna. "Only little sips. Do not let her take too much or it could hurt her."

Loranna stared wide eyed at Nubio, realizing he knew and had seen this form of enslavement many times. She carefully put the small clay cup to the girl's lips.

The girl suddenly became ravenous for the milk and squealed and grunted as she tried to gulp the small portion. Nubio knew well how to grab the starving child's hands and use a knee gently upon arm to keep her from reaching up and gulping the milk too quickly. Verboden held the other side as Loranna wept, seeing the suffering before her.

"We can't risk this," said Murith, standing above them with his hand on his sword.

"Ask her where she came from! We must know! We are so close," said Alfred, a bit too excitedly and not compassionately. Loranna looked up at him with angry tearful eyes. Alfred gulped and stood back.

"Her wound is of a werewolf bite most assuredly. She has the curse," said Verboden. "And she was heading along the road south, straight to the People of the Downs."

"Ask her where she came from," Alfred pushed.

Verboden looked down at her and spoke a blessing.

Strength upon us
Light upon us
O domme rai
Vee bede mohn

She seemed to breathe in air and fill her lungs, focusing her eyes upon him.

"What is your name?" asked Verboden.

"The others call me Red," she whispered.

"Red? Others?" Verboden muttered, then cleared his throat. "Where are the others?"

She nodded no, fearful.

"Tell her we've come to rescue her," said Alfred behind Verboden.

The girl was able to focus her eyes now. She looked at Alfred, then the others. "Run... run away."

Alfred stepped in. "Red? Look, we have a knight with a silver sword. He can defeat any scary wolf lord."

Murith raised his sword to show her.

She shivered. "Not strong enough."

Verboden looked back at Murith and Alfred, then back at her. "Not strong enough for what?"

"Them," she said, shivering and cowering, trying to cover her eyes with her wounded arm and weak hands.

"We're so close, Red. We can stop them. We have a powerful cleric, a powerful knight, and well, me and my archer and bodyguard," Alfred said, sort of unsure if they really were powerful enough against *them*.

She glanced frantically, lying there in her weak form, fearful of their intent. "Please... run... please... me... run away."

"We can't let her go," said Murith sharply.

Red began to cry. Loranna stood up with tears in her eyes and faced Murith angrily. He turned away and looked out into the dark mist.

Loranna looked down at Red and sat next to her on the wicker bedding. "Sister, this is my bow. Its arrows are silver. They kill wolf beasts outright. I have killed many goblins and ogres and assassin elves. I aim to go and kill as many of *them* as have hurt you and your brothers and sisters. I will do so even unto my own death. Show me the way."

Red looked up at Loranna's glorious elven bow and her elven cloak. They were oddly clean in this mud filled land. They seemed to glow. Loranna looked oddly at them too.

"Courage," Verboden said. "I sense it in your bow, Loranna. You have awoken it."

Loranna looked at her bow and felt her hand tighten around it ... or the bow tightened around her hand. Red stared in awe at the glistening bow as she sat up and then pointed northward.

111

Chapter Nineteen

The Black Tower

"There are no tombs in the Black Rocks," said the Baron, hovering before them, staring past the moors to a vast mountainous wall of black rocks. "She's taken us another day to the northern borders of the moors. There are no kingly crypts beyond the moorlands and especially in those dire rocks."

Red sat in the wagon, sipping a bowl of goat's milk, but also hugging the festering wound that was bothering her.

Verboden and Murith shared a glance. Verboden spoke softly to him. "We must hurry. But be ready." Murith grimaced.

Red pointed. "The tower."

"What tower?" asked the ghost, his ghostly image wavering.

Then the black fog seemed to roll aside, and there before them, nestled in the cliffs of the Black Rocks, up a rocky winding path, was a menacing thick squat black tower. Several small windows were lit with flames, and goblins could be seen squabbling amidst rocky encampments surrounding the base.

"Oh, that tower," the ghost said, turning back to them, with a glum, nervous look.

Once Red saw it, she began to wail. Nubio, sitting in the wagon with her, tended to her fragile disposition. He carefully tried to shush her. Verboden immediately turned the wagon behind some bramble to hide it and petted the goats to keep them still.

Murith went to the wagon and put on his great knightly helm and unsheathed his sword, "We've got some goblins to kill." He then looked about. "Where's the King and Loranna?"

Verboden perked up and looked about, then made a rare snarl and peered up the path to the tower.

Several goblins meandering about, chewing on bones, suddenly dropped. A blurry shadow seemed to quickly advance behind the rocks and animal hide tents. More goblins dropped with arrows in them.

"Blast her! She won't leave any for me!" grumbled Murith. He hurried up the path.

Verboden shrugged. "What a terrible plan!"

Goblins began to react to their fallen brethren by panicking and scowling. They hurried back to the gated entrance of the tower.

Alfred suddenly appeared from behind a rock. He was limping and trying to get away. Murith noticed and hurried to help.

The goblins saw him and gathered together with their crude blades, spears, and measly bows. They hollered in excitement then chased after him.

Alfred held up his shield as a few arrows fell around him. He was frantically hobbling away. Murith yelled and rushed forward but was too far away to help in time.

As the goblin group neared Alfred, many fell from arrows in their backs. Then Alfred turned and quickly dispensed with goblin after goblin after goblin. He was not wounded in any way when Murith finally reached him slashing at the remaining single fleeing goblin.

"I thought you were wounded!" Murith said, breathing heavily.

Alfred shrugged a smile.

"And your moves, Dunther never taught us that. Where'd you learn such skill?"

"My father," said Alfred. He turned and hurried to the entrance.

Murith stood stunned, then hurried after him.

All the goblins lay strewn dead across the dirty, grimy goblin encampment. Passing quickly, Sir Murith figured over a score lay fallen. He never knew of any knights who could dispense with twenty or more goblins so quickly. He said under his breath, "And she collected her arrows as well!" He rolled his eyes and shook his head, but hurried on as a dutiful knight.

Loranna was barely visible in her elven cloak. The gate was still open but was covered by a small portcullis with many sharp spears pointing downward. A lone goblin made it in and was waiting for them to enter so he could drop the spears upon them. He had an evil malicious smile and cooed a giggle at Loranna as she stood beyond the gate. Though her cloak could hide her in forest and green terrain, up close and upon carved stone, it was not as effective.

The goblin had his hand on the lever and waved a finger at her, daring her to come in.

Alfred and Murith rushed up, stopping just before the dreadful trap.

Loranna moved in such a way that not even Alfred and Murith anticipated it. The goblin's arm was suddenly pinned to the wooden frame with an arrow and unable to pull the lever. He was stunned to see his arm stuck and Loranna slowly walking under the sharp spears of the portcullis.

The goblin quickly turned to use his opposite arm, only to see it get pinned as well. As he realized his immovable predicament, Alfred finished him off, and they were in the tower.

"Go Verboden and Nubio! I'll stay back here with Red," the ghostly Baron said with a ghostly smile. "I can go no further beyond the moorland anyway. This is the edge of my haunting realm." Verboden and Nubio quickly got off the wagon and rushed off. Red cowered in the wagon, and the Baron tried to comfort her with a tuh-tuh wave of his ghostly hands. He looked to see they were far off. "Well, just you and me. Red?"

Red rolled her eyes back in pain, turning to lie in the wagon. She then grasped her arm as the pain had become much greater.

The ghost looked up to see the full moon rising... "Oh my..."

They carefully ascended a narrow stairway as Verboden and Nubio finally caught up. They were breathing heavily but still ready.

"I sense great evil above us. It has awoken and knows our approach," warned Verboden. Loranna, Alfred, Nubio and Murith were ready. "Wait... I sense something else... below us, in the dungeons..."

"Shall we split up?" Murith asked.

"No way!" said Alfred. "We are not in some stupid scary horror movie!"

"What's a stupid scary horror moovy?" asked Loranna.

"Well, I saw it explained on a TV show, actually... the kids were talking about..."

"What?" Murith wondered. They looked at him.

"Let's just get going! Together!" Alfred finally yelped. "Up, let's go up first!" Alfred pointed his silver spear up the stairs. "Knight, you lead."

Murith shrugged, "Of course!"

Murith ascended the stairs to the next level. There was an open trapdoor of sorts. His helm rose above the wooden flooring and quickly ducked as goblin arrows flew at him.

An axe fell down upon his helm and glanced off. He growled a fierce roar and charged up swinging skillfully at the goblin guards. Loranna stepped up the stairs quickly, angling her bow, firing several shots during the cloistered fighting. Alfred charged in ready to fight.

"Whoa, great job my royal guards," Alfred smiled, seeing the half dozen dead goblins.

Loranna and Sir Murith shrugged, ready for more.

The next level, above the goblin guards, was not occupied. But it had many scary items: torture devices, wracks of pain, chains and shackles.

"A sorcerer resides above us," said Verboden grimly.

"Oh, he is so dead," said Loranna angrily, seeing the contraptions.

"We must interrogate him," said Verboden.

"Interrogate his soul," replied Loranna, twanging her bow string unconsciously.

"He could know how to cure the werewolf curse, and there's a full moon tonight!" Alfred said. "Don't kill him."

"Not yet," Loranna said, standing back as Verboden, Murith and Alfred advanced.

115

Nubio stood amidst the torture devices, tears streaming. He looked at Loranna. "They are small, for smaller... children."

"Oh... he's dead, DEAD!" said Loranna firmly, tears streaming down her angry face.

Verboden stepped up the narrow stone stairs to a door. It was at the top of the tower. There was little room on the wooden platform for him to lean against the door and try to push it open. Murith stood below him on the stairs, ready to leap up. Alfred was behind them.

Verboden then paused and felt the door, then realized something. He calmly turned the latch, and it opened. He walked in to the candlelit abode to see a room full of rich furniture and red drapes.

A lone man in velvet and black robes stood with his back to Verboden. He was mixing a concoction at an alchemist table, quite casually.

Soft music playing from a flute seemed to weep throughout the room. Verboden then noticed a small boy, frightened, in clean garb sitting and playing a flute. Verboden blinked.

The sorcerer turned with a misty vial in his hand. He was hairless, gaunt, pasty white, and his skin wrought with black spider web tattoos, though most were covered by his adornments. He smiled at Verboden.

"Kill him!" Murith said, charging up and into the room. Verboden stood there. And so did Murith when the sorcerer splayed his fingers outward. Murith shook in his incredible plate mail and raised sword, stuck amidst ornate furniture. He strained furiously for one step. The sorcerer stood firm, though his spell hand quivered a bit. He looked down to balance his misty vial, then looked up, impressed at the knight's resistance.

Alfred entered between them and pointed his spear at the sorcerer. "Let them go!"

Loranna came up, ready to fire, but saw Verboden's sad look and she stood back, in the shadow of the stairwell.

The sorcerer smiled. "I am only holding your brutish knight. Your cleric is quite taken by me and my sanctuary." The sorcerer lowered his hand, and Murith stepped forward, crashing through chairs and tables, raising his sword to strike.

The sorcerer was saddened by the wanton destruction of his beautiful furnishings.

"Stop, Murith!" Alfred ordered. Murith stood very close to the sorcerer with his sword ready to strike. He looked like a giant robot towering over a small sickly man.

"Silver?" the sorcerer noticed the sword. "Impressive."

Alfred looked at Verboden, who stood back in some strange derangement. Alfred noticed the boy playing the flute, quivering. "Stop playing that!"

The boy lowered the flute and stared, frightful.

"Oh, he is a fabulous player. So soothing, a natural," the sorcerer cooed.

Alfred looked at the sorcerer and the misty vial he was holding. "Put that down!"

"This?" the sorcerer raised the vial. "Oh, it is not an enchanted elixir, a powerfully cursed tonic, or a potion for summoning a greater *daemonic* force..."

Murith was ready to strike, quivering in anger. "Just say the word, King Alfred!"

"King Alfred?!" the sorcerer repeated. "Oh my... oh my... you are the great King Alfred! I am honored. Defeater of the armies of my queen, impressive indeed. It is an honor to encounter you on this great struggle of the Great Lord of this Land versus the incognito Father of Light." The sorcerer raised an eyebrow as he slowly twirled the wide brimmed vial to stir the red clear liquid. "Oh, and this tonic, it is my favorite, and no spiritual dweomers or spells here. Just a fancy drink, for fancy times." The sorcerer raised his hand in peace as he slowly took the tonic and drank it.

Alfred was ready to order a strike but merely watched as the sorcerer imbibed the drink fully.

"Ahh... my favorite concoction," the sorcerer said. "Light, fruity, with a reminiscence of decay."

"It is demonic!" Murith warned from his steel armour.

The sorcerer looked up at the great knight and winked.

Murith hissed and could not control his desire to strike. But it was for naught, for the sorcerer began to swoon and totter. He found the nearest ornate chair and sat down. He dropped his delicate vial, and it shattered on the floor.

"My powers are of deceit and conjurings. I have no power to stop or destroy you," he said with a smile as he closed his eyes and dropped his head. He then began to steam, and his skin darkened.

Before long, he was but a burned corpse steaming in his ornate robes and bedizened chair.

Alfred blinked then waved away the smelly smoke.

"So ends the evil sorcerer and his vile sufferings," said Verboden.

Murith turned and pointed his sword at Verboden. "Why didn't you stop him? Why didn't you use your powers, cleric?!"

Alfred and Verboden shrank at Murith's temper. Alfred looked up at Verboden, who seemed quite weakened.

"I don't know. I felt an end to him - so powerful and so... cowardly," said Verboden.

Alfred looked at the boy, quivering and tearing. Alfred reached out with his hand and motioned for him. "Come, show us the way to the others."

The boy took his hand, and they exited down the stairs.

Chapter Twenty

Dungeon of Despair

At the entrance to the dungeon the boy was too scared to go any further. Nubio noticed the shackle scars on his wrists. Nubio showed him his own. The boy realized that Nubio was like him, so he took Nubio's hand. He looked quite odd in his ornate child's suit while the place was made of crude stones, shackles and chains. He pointed down the corridor. It descended a stone incline to a large dungeon area, a carved out space much larger than the tower rooms above.

"We must hurry for the full moon is almost upon us," Verboden said sadly.

"There is no hope, since the sorcerer is dead, for a cure," Alfred sighed. "And Chief Runnik will kill his own brother and his daughter soon."

"Then we must end it!" said Murith, stomping forward.

They followed behind the knight except for Nubio. The boy tugged at him and was on the verge of a panic. Nubio tried to pull away, spear and shield ready, but could not. Alfred looked back and nodded for Nubio to stay with the frightened boy.

Murith descended the stone way as goblins suddenly appeared, charging at him. He raged in anger as he swung viciously and deftly. Goblins dropped to each side as Loranna's arrows flew and Alfred's spear jabbed. Verboden walked amongst them as he sensed a dread far greater up ahead. As he peered beyond the fray of fighting, down beyond the landing, against the wall of the lower dungeon, he could just see a small erect cage.

Murith finished the barking squealing goblins and reached Verboden. "Another sorcerer!"

119

"No, nohh...." Verboden wailed, leaning on his staff. "Brother?!..."

A gaunt, gruesome, mangy man was shackled inside a fitted cage, ragged and forever erect. His neck was manacled to the very top of the cage with his head out in the open. The cage covered him from the neck down.

Murith lifted his visor to see better. "What devilry is this? Upon this suffering man?"

"Brother Harkonen?!" Verboden wailed again, tottering to one side as Murith caught him.

Alfred rushed up, gasping, "The wolf lord!?"

"Verboden???" the man moaned. "My brother... Verboden?" He began to whimper, tussling weakly within his confined shackles.

Loranna, having retrieved her arrows, finally came and stood beside them. "Did he curse the children?" She then saw on her left and right, beyond the rows of shackles and manacles, cages against the walls. And within them, blighted and scourged children. "No, no, this is too much!"

Alfred stepped to Verboden, who gathered his strength.

Lord of light, give us strength
courage and might.
Lord of light, cast hope
into the pain that rises
the suffering within our sight!

Verboden straightened himself up as Murith stepped to one side.

"He is the Wolf Lord, isn't he?" Alfred asked, coming to Verboden's side and giving him courage, focus. Verboden put his hand on Alfred's shoulder, to hold himself up.

"Yes, I was guarding him in the forest those seasons ago when we first met," Verboden said, looking at his fallen brother with gentle eyes. "We sought a cure for this curse. Praying, praying, desperately and losing faith... Brother Harkonen dispensed with a wolfkin or werewolf as you say, but was wounded. We sought a cure, a salvation together, away from all contact of man in that cabin in the Dark Forest. When he turned on his first moon, I guarded him, from others, from the flesh of man."

Brother Harkonen sobbed, looking gratefully at Verboden, in his manacled festering cage.

"I returned several times seeking him out, but he was gone. To whither, I could not see. The flesh of man is all that a werewolf craves, and that bite returns it to human form," said Verboden, staring sadly at his Brother of the Faith.

"I have tasted the flesh of children these many moons!" Harkonen wailed. "Let me die, brother, a slow death in this cage. Do not release me, ever! It is the only end to this curse and my sin!"

Verboden grasped his own forehead, desperate for another way. The cage was made of thick steel and chains. There were many scratches and claw marks upon it, but none prevailed against its solid design. Harkonen's body was twisted and tortured, confined to this steel contraption these many moons, whether in human or wolf form.

"It isn't your fault!" Alfred cried.

The Brother attempted a gracious smile but snot and bile spewed from his nostrils and mouth. "Let me die. Save the children. Curse my soul for eternity."

Verboden nodded, grasping Alfred's shoulder, pulling him away.

Murith stood beyond them, peering at the children in the cages. He then noticed two women, Khanafians, suffering as well. They appeared to be the caretakers of this ragged assembly. Murith caught the eyes of one. She was young and frail but kept her gaze upon him. He paused a moment, then shook out of it – something.

"Nubio!" he yelled. He went back to the ascending passage and peered up. "Nubio?" He worried a moment until he saw Nubio come with the frightened boy.

"Yes, Murith?"

"Come."

They stood before a vast array of cages and children. All were ragged and scared. Though gaunt and starving, they had thickset hair, whether stark black or bundled brown.

"They're all so young," Loranna sighed.

"They are your age or younger," said Verboden.

Nubio opened the cages with keys from the goblins. The children were too afraid to come out. The Khanafian women held babies and had many in tattered cribs and cots.

"Babies?" Alfred cringed. "Babies??"

"These evil goblins raided the farms and villages and took their children all these years!" Murith scowled.

"There are a hundred, two hundred children?" Alfred asked, counting in groups. "We must take them, all of them."

Verboden looked up. "How? And to feed them?"

"We have to! We have to," Alfred said, pacing to and fro, looking at them still huddled in the cages. He noticed Nubio slowly enter the cages and nod at the Khanafian women. They seemed heartened to see him, one like them. "Nubio, tell them we are going to free them. We need them to show us where all the food is, all that we can take with us. We'll take them to the hamlet."

Nubio nodded and spoke softly to the women who held the babies and comforted any child that clung to them.

Murith pushed open the lid of a barrel and saw maggots swarming amidst some sort of dirt and grain. He waved off the putrid smell of maggot excrement. "I found their food."

Loranna gagged.

"Hurry brother! Hurry!" Harkonen barked from his cage. "Get them out of this curse..."

They all looked at him. The children cowered and cried with a growing sense of tension.

"The full moon is upon us," Verboden shuddered. "Hurry, take them out of here now."

Nubio was able to get the women to gather the able children to go with Alfred and Loranna. Many of the girls saw Loranna's wondrous stature and stared, but there was no time for that as she waved them along. Nubio led them up the stoneway and out.

There was a small cart the women used. Alfred helped them put the dozen babies who cried and wailed in that. They pushed along with the group of children, exiting up the ramp.

Murith noticed and saw the worn women. "They were sold by the ogres, no doubt, and forced to be the nurses of these babies."

"To have these newborns grow here in this cursed prison for the evil of Gorbogal!" Verboden realized. It drained him.

"Strength, brother! Righteous anger is more powerful than evil or sorrow," said Murith.

That gave Verboden pause, and he nodded, feeling a weight lifted. He snarled at Murith. "We'll save these children, we'll return to Grotham, and we'll fight that witch!"

Murith snarled back.

Verboden stopped to look at Brother Harkonen one last time. Sir Murith was at his side, his sword drawn.

"Be at peace brother, his sword is silver and will end your curse quickly," said Verboden with great strength.

"No!" Harkonen cried out, "No, do not kill me quickly! Let me die a long slow death. Let me starve to death as the beast, stuck in this cage."

"I will not. The curse is not your sin!" spat Verboden.

"It is my sin! It is! I could not resist it!" yelled Harkonen, frantically convulsing in his steel confinement.

Murith shivered and stepped back. "Let him suffer if he wills."

Verboden shook no. "He is my friend, my brother in the Father of Light."

"Then heed my request, Verboden! Unto the Father of Light who has abandoned me! I have cursed too many children. I have suffered untold numbers. I cannot bare to go peacefully in the night," he cried. "Damn you! Leave me to suffer!"

Murith pulled at Verboden. "Let us go."

Verboden, reluctantly, painfully, left his brother there to die a slow torturous death of neglect and starvation.

They hurried along, rushing the weak children out. Though they were free, the children hugged and held each other, many sobbing. The dead goblins outside and the dark shadows of the Black Rock mountain were not comforting at all to the children as they exited.

"Hurry, come! I have a friend to show you," said Nubio, hastening down the path. "Don't worry. It's okay." Nubio waved off the dead goblins and pranced along to encourage them to come.

Still in the dungeon, Murith checked each of the barrels of rotting grain. He knew they needed the food, so he had no choice but to knock one over and roll it up the ramp. As he did, he looked back to see Harkonen stare after him. Murith noticed Harkonen twist and convulse in his trappings as fangs and fur extruded. Murith let go of the barrel as it rolled back down to the dungeon, hitting against the fallen goblins and the wall.

"Red!"

Chapter Twenty-One

Out

"Come, look, your friend Red is here," Nubio said calmly as he guided the children to the wagon hidden amongst the brambles. The children squealed as the Baron in his ghostly form appeared before Nubio, waving frantically for him to leave.

"It's okay. He's a friend," said Nubio, trying to usher them back.

Out of the darkness, Red, partly transformed to a hideous werewolf, leapt through the Baron's incorporeal body and at Nubio. The children screamed, knowing this curse, fleeing in all directions into the treacherous dark terrain of the brambles and bog.

Red bit deeply into Nubio's arm. "AAAAAAAAHHHH!!!"

"No!" Alfred pushed through the retreating children, knocking some over, brandishing his spear. "NO!"

Loranna was in the rear, helping the nurses push the cart through the treacherous terrain. She looked down the crowded path and heard their cries. "Oh no, Red..."

Nubio fell as Red reared up and convulsed. She stared mad-eyed as claws quickly extended from her finger tips. Her fearful gaze was overtaken by a demonic force, and the monstrous expression became fearsome. The werewolf growled and clicked its black claws as it stared down at Nubio.

"Curse you, you fiend!" the Baron said, unable to do anything.

124

The werewolf growled at the ghost but returned to its prey. Nubio shuddered on the ground, rolling side to side, crying loudly. The werewolf howled victory as it raised its claws to rip Nubio apart.

Alfred leapt with his spear through the fleeing children. He could not get his footing on the mushy sod. He thrust his spear and it missed by a mere hair, the silver coating burning just the tip of the werewolf's fur.

In its frenetic frenzy, the wolf took advantage of Alfred's failed footing. It flailed fiercely, forcing Alfred to tumble. It swung at him, scraping his armour and slamming him against the muddy ground. His spear twirled away into the darkness.

"No! Stop!" the Baron cried helplessly, as if all were in slow motion: Alfred falling under the furious flailing of the werewolf. Though Alfred's armour was exquisite, he was not wearing his helm. Alfred lifted up one arm to protect his face, but the wolf's swings were demonically stronger. Only a swing or two more and Alfred's defense would falter.

The claws of the werewolf then broke apart a small clay pot that was tossed up. The subtle sound of clay shattering did not alert the wolf beast to the explosion of silver powder and minute shards twirling into its heavily breathing snout.

It froze. It then began utterances of sniffs and snorts, cackling and coughing. It waved the air, trying to hit away the descending silver sparkles. Its snout quivered as it tried to fend off the burning sensation. Alfred kicked the wolf as he awkwardly rolled away across the suctioning mud. The werewolf, in wretched pain, turned and leapt into the darkness.

Loranna rushed through the mayhem. She tried to get a clear shot but she could not, she screamed into the darkness.

Alfred crawled to Nubio, who was crying and clinging to his wounded arm. "I'm sorry, Alfred. I'm sorry."

"No, no, no Nubio, it's okay. It's okay," Alfred cried thick hot tears.

Verboden hurried to them. Murith yelled as he pushed past the wagon filled with screaming babies and the Khanafian women protecting them with their defenseless bodies. He looked at the young woman. She looked at him and nodded a frightful no. He reached Alfred to see Nubio lying below him with his grievous wound. "Grrraaagghhh! No!"

Out

Verboden looked up, into the dark. He could hear the howl of the wolf.

Loranna heard it to. "It isn't far. I can hear it." She raised her bow.

"Wait... I sense it! I sense HER!" Verboden hurried into the dark.

They hurried past some bramble and saw, lying before them, the werewolf convulsing.

Loranna extended her bow to fire.

"No! I sense Red! I can sense her... the silver powder!" Verboden knelt down next to the sickened beast.

"Not a good idea!" Murith yelled, sword ready to finish her.

"The powder is working, isn't it?" Alfred sighed. He got up from Nubio and went to them. "It will kill her."

"She's not dead yet!" Murith yelled, stepping around Verboden with his sword ready. Alfred picked up his spear, nearby, raising it reluctantly.

"That's right, she's not," Verboden couldn't help but smile. "No, no, I sense it... I can sense the spirits separating. The coil of the curse is being tortured by the silver powder. I need only..." Verboden stood and gripped his staff, swinging it fiercely.

I CAST YOU OUT!
Vile spirit, in the name of Armahn!
In the name of the holy one,
Father of Light, upon us,
I cast you out from his creation!
You abomination! OUT!!

A vile bubbling and gargling sound wretched from the werewolf as red hair suddenly appeared. Something dark and cloudy expelled from Red as she convulsed and coughed.

Verboden slashed at the dark cloud all around. He chortled in insane glee as he swung his staff. The staff began to glow. "Yes, holy light! HOLY LIGHT! Upon you dark shadow, upon your curse! I sense you and cast you out! You have no power here! Hah hah!" He swung wildly, forcing even Murith to duck away. The cloud was like a weak misty demon, and Verboden blew it apart with the Holy Light.

Verboden stood proudly, setting his staff in the mud and breathing heavily.

Alfred stepped closer and looked down at the girl. She was breathing hoarsely but was all and all... a girl.

"The cure," Alfred said. "That's the cure?"

Verboden nodded. Through a beautiful sigh he said, "Ohhhhh.... yes...."

"The powder?" Alfred sighed heavily, trying to catch his breath.

"The powder, not enough silver to kill it outright, but enough to torture the demonic curse! To force it out... And with my blessings... end it!"

"Nubio!?" Loranna yelled with hope.

"Oh yes," Verboden nodded, smiling, dirty and mud-ridden, leaning against his staff.

"Your Brother in Faith, Harkonen?" asked Murith.

"Oh yes, my Brother, I can cure him of this curse if he will have it," said Verboden sadly, but with hope nonetheless. Verboden made ready to return to the dungeon.

"What about the Chief! His brother and his daughter!?" Alfred gasped.

"It will be too late for them," said Verboden, pausing, realizing. "They will kill them tonight, any moment now, when the father and daughter finally turn to werewolf form."

"We have to tell them!" Alfred moaned sadly.

"It is a three or four days journey back if we go straight south. We will be too late," Murith said, still cautiously holding his sword at Red.

Loranna stepped between Murith and Red, kneeling by her as she slowly opened her eyes.

The Baron ghost pondered, tapping his chin. "Well... uhh... Not for me."

They all looked at him, in their steamy muddy mess.

"I'm a ghost," Baron reminded. "This is my haunting. This putrid moorland mess. I can go anywhere. Poof! Poof! Just like that!" He snapped his fingers with a bit of flair and then bowed, his face holding a smug expression.

"Well... what are you waiting for?" said Alfred, stepping toward him with a stern look.

"Oh right!" the Baron realized.

"Tell them we have a cure! Tell them to just hold on till we get back! They must contain the wolfkin!" Verboden yelled as the Baron faded out, cupping his ear to listen.

"Understand?" Verboden yelled at him.

"Use silver powder! To weaken them!" Alfred yelled with cupped hands.

The Baron gave a thumbs up and disappeared in a ghostly swirl.

Chapter Twenty-Two

The Cage of Despair

The cage at the hamlet was made of iron clad bars that had been through many fires. For any that were infected were caged. And when the time came, on a full moon, and they transformed to wolf form, Chief Runnik and his men would light the peat moss and bramble placed within. All who were thusly infected knew their fate. For in battling the wolfkin moon after moon, seeing their own families and friends fall, they hoped and prayed their death would be the end of the curse. But it never was these many moons.

Within the cage this night was a father and his young, beloved daughter. They cowered in the darkness, in the shadows, crying and holding each other. The father prayed incessantly as his young daughter held him and kept her eyes closed tightly.

Armoured men came with torches, standing outside, waiting. A few had pitchforks and spears just in case. Chief Runnik stood with a torch, his face red and swollen as usual, from so many seasons of pain and loss. And this, another loss, a dashed hope from a boy king who had not returned with a cure.

"We could use the silver spears instead, father?" one of his sons said.

"No, we shall immolate them, as all their brethren before," said Chief Runnik, sighing. He raised the torch to see his brother and niece within the cage. They were huddled, holding each other.

"The boy king has failed us," he said, not angrily, not repulsed, just sad, knowing all their fates. "He was victorious over goblins, ratkins, ogres, a bugbear army... but his fate was to fall here in the cursed moorlands. I honor his courage." Chief Runnik looked up to the dark sky and saw the full moon beyond the thin veil of mist. He gasped as if the mist far above were the surface of the water and he was deep within an ocean, slowly drowning.

A growling rumble reverberated from the dark cage. The men shuddered a moment, realizing the inevitable. The other villagers, so very few, retreated into their homes, holding their own dear children and weeping for the fate of their brethren.

Chief Runnik stepped forward with his torch and the light of it filled the cage. The fur of the wolf beasts could be seen now. They were crouched and breathing heavily. Though he had seen it many times before, he still gasped, "Brother, niece, my little niece..."

The father wolfkin turned and leapt at the cage, bashing against it as the whole structure shook violently.

"Burn'em quick. The cage won't hold," the elder son spoke.

Chief Runnik nodded and lowered his torch to toss it.

"STOP!" a voice moaned aloud, from the mist.

They turned, frightened all over again, first from the werewolf growling and banging the cage, and now from an all-encompassing moan that seemed to echo from the fog.

They turned to see a ghost glow and float in from the fog. Several men, unable to bear the sight, hollered and fled. They scrambled away knowing this was the end for them all, that it was the end of the People of the Downs.

Chief Runnik stood, torch in hand, accepting his fate as he snarled at the evil presence descending upon him.

His sons came to stand with him, silver spears out, torches ready, quivering but brave. "Father, we fight with you, to the end."

"I'm sorry, sons. I'm sorry I made you stay to this end," he said, frozen in fear.

They stared as the ghost landed before them – and tripped. "Ooof..."

The Chief and his sons blinked and tilted their heads.

"Ooof, sorry!" The ghost slipped in the sod and picked up his muddied hands. "Dahh... what a mess!" He looked up at the Chief and his sons, waving his muddied hand. "I'm allrigh... allrigh... Haven't flown that fast in a while. I'm a ghost, by the way." He stood, brushing off his muddied hands. "Habit, you know, all this sod and mud. I still can't get over the fact that I can just ignore it!" He looked at his muddy hands and then focused with eyebrows tightening and the mud fading. "See, clean hands! No bother at all!"

The werewolves in the cage suddenly howled with a great long bellow. Baron the Ghost tottered from the roar and grabbed at his heart. "Oh!!! What a fright!"

Again, the Chief and his sons stood stunned, unsure what to do.

The wolfkins, big and small, grabbed at the bars, yanking the cage. It shook and sounded quite fragile.

The elder son grabbed his father's shoulder. "Burn them!"

The father nodded. The incredibly violent growls and metal clanging spelled an impending doom, one more frightful than this clumsy spirit.

"No, stop!" shouted the Baron, rushing forward, standing between them and the cage.

A ping of metal echoed. It sounded as if something was coming undone. A nail flew out as the top piece of the gate seemed suddenly askew.

"Father!"

"Do not kill the werewolf... uh the wolfkin!" the Baron yelled.

"He's a curse! He's part of it!" The brothers swung their swords and torches at the Baron.

"No!" the Baron moaned. He tried to dodge and wave them off. But the silver spears and torches had an effect of blurring him and causing his voice to falter.

"They have a cure!" the ghost yelled as he was being slashed at.

The gate to the cage was coming undone. Nails were popping off as the larger wolfkin shook and yanked violently at it, growling and howling with rage.

The ghost was trying to remember as he was forced to dissipate. He had to yell above the wolfkin growls and howls. "I was sent by King Alfred and Verboden!!!"

Though his sons were hurriedly slashing away, Chief Runnik heard the ghost's comment.

"Ow... that silver and fire does affect me! Ow! Oh wait, I remember! Silver powder! Use silver powder! To weaken the wolfkin

131

until they return! They have a cure!" yelled the ghost as he was breaking apart.

The sons yelled as they attacked. The wolfkin growled incessantly as they pounded against the weakening cage.

Chief Runnik shook his head and fled from his sons.

The sons saw their father leave and became more desperately enraged. They poked at the ghost and used their spears to twirl his form, as if twirling him into a mist. The Baron, realizing his demise, retreated from them, tripping and rolling back through the wolfkin and the cage. This actually helped, for the wolfkin flailed at his incorporeal form.

The sons realized the gate was almost broken. They raised their spears to attack the wolfkin. The elder son yelled, "Burn them now!"

The sons raised torches just as their father Chief Runnik ran through them to the gate. He slammed it closed with one hand, as the village smith with nails and a hammer leapt to the holes, to secure the gate.

"Father! Watch out!" the elder son yelled.

The wolfkin saw him at the gate, easily within clawing distance and leapt at him.

His sons yelled, "No!!!"

Chief Runnik had one hand gripping the gate closed, but his other was a tight fist. As the werewolves grabbed at him, he flung his fist open, releasing silver powder that showered the wolfkins. They all froze, even the wolfkin father who now had its claws upon him. The powder descended as the sons screamed in anguish. The wolfkin stared oddly at the glittery silver in the air. The Chief, ever so close to his brother the wolf beast, sneezed right on his snout.

Then the wolfkins sneezed and snorted. The clawed grip the wolf beast had on Chief Runnik merely slid off without a scratch as the wolfkin fell. The Chief sighed greatly.

The wolfkins convulsed in the cage as Chief Runnik nodded to his smith, who hurriedly hammered in new nails and bent their ends to keep the gate secure. Chief Runnik held it firmly, breathing heavily and looking down to control his shaking.

His sons stood stunned, spears and torches ready. But then they came up to help him hold the gate. He saw their support and relaxed, stepping back. He then went to the cage, taking a torch and peering in. His brother and niece were convulsing and contorting in painful throes.

The Baron Ghost floated in through the other side of the cage. "It weakens them. You must keep them weak and wait for the Cleric. He can cure them. He will return in a few days."

The Chief nodded, staring at the ghost, and then at his brother and niece, seeing parts of them through the wolf curse. He could see the struggle of the curse and saw hope, even in their pangs.

"Verboden will come! It was King Alfred who spurred on this silver powder demise... ending the wolfkin curse once and for all..." the Ghost said, floating ever so close to the Chief and his sons. He smiled as he faded with a bow. "I will let the King know you await their return."

"Is this true? Is it real, father?"

"Oh yes, the boy king is very real."

Chapter Twenty-Three

The Healing Hamlet

Verboden brought Brother Harkonen out of the dungeons and to the wagon. He carried him like a weak child. Though Harkonen had been the "wolf-lord" that had infected the children these many moons, now he was but an emaciated corpse, gaunt and near death. Alfred, Loranna, and Nubio were busy gathering up the children, who were scattered in the moors and amongst the black rocks. Thankfully, it wasn't difficult as the children began to swarm in groups like scared fish.

Considering their disposition, being stuck in cages and in despair, they were all still quite able. All were in rags and ridden with lice and ticks, sores and rashes, but they had a virile inner strength. Many rushed to and fro, hugging and comforting each other.

Sir Murith came up from the dungeon, doggedly tired rolling a grain barrel. He then had to control it, rolling it down the path from the tower towards their wagon. Several larger boys came to help him. He noticed that though they were gaunt, they had strength and determination.

The children rushed away as Verboden came near with Harkonen. The Khanafian women comforted many at their small cart filled with crying infants. Verboden set Harkonen down in his wagon.

"Please, brother, leave me to die," cried Harkonen weakly.

134

"No, my brother, you are free from the curse. The demonic spirit is dispensed," Verboden said, covering Harkonen in a blanket.

"I am not free, not from my sin. I am a murderer of children," Harkonen coughed, trying to move but ever so weak.

"Brother Harkonen," Verboden said, pausing to look deep into his eyes.

Harkonen finally moved enough to look back at Verboden.

"I need you," said Verboden with all sincerity, kissing his forehead. He then left him to help the others.

The journey along the moorland trail took five days. It was difficult for the children, who had to sleep in mounds along the driest of the pathways. Verboden spent much time saving the most ill from their doom. But save them, he did. He grew weak and lay with Harkonen in the wagon, squashed between him and the grain barrel. Nubio, Loranna, and Alfred spent all of their time comforting the children in any way they could during the rests, for there were many.

Murith got many of the children to pick out the maggots in the grain. He found them eating them and sharing them amongst the others. He did not stop them.

Nubio carefully milked the goats and then gave small sips to the weakest, with some left for the two Khanafian women. They were nursing nearly a dozen babies and were quite weak themselves. The children ate the rotting grain greedily, whether raw or boiled. Many became sick off that, as it was difficult to keep them from eating too much. As they devoured their handful, many grains fell into the mud, where the children would then drop and pick them up to nibble.

The Baron was quite helpful. He kept the children from wandering off into the mist. As a sick child hobbled blindly or crazed out into the moors, the Baron would appear as a ghost and usher them back along the path. The children were frightened by him so stuck together. Nubio would notice and wave at the Baron, and then remind the scared children, "You must all stay on the path. There is a ghost out there, but he can't get on the path. So stay on the path with us."

The frightened children hovelled together as Nubio winked at the ghost, who floated off to find any other wayward children.

Murith, Nubio, Loranna, and Alfred did not eat or sleep very much at all for five days.

The Healing Hamlet

When they made it to the hamlet, there was no fanfare or joyous cry. They merely hobbled in, a long train of them in the mist, spanning hundreds of yards. The People of the Down saw them from their sod walls. Chief Runnik stared out at the long line of them slowly treading along.

"Are they ghosts?" he muttered.

"They are children," a woman huffed, hurriedly rushing her maidens along. They went out with wagons and carts, to pick up the children along the way. Many had dropped, lying in the mud, ready for the end. But their end would not be today. The maidens easily picked up the emaciated children and took them back to the hamlet.

Within the hamlet, strewn wherever and however, lay nearly two hundred children. The women and men went amongst them, feeding them a light broth and clean water.

Sir Murith carried Verboden to a room, then Harkonen next. Chief Runnik was anxious and followed them. "Sir Murith, your ghost friend told us there was a cure, a cure for the wolf curse?"

"Yes, Chief, but the clerics are too weak right now. They must gather their strength. We have time till the next full moon."

"Ah, not quite," the Chief said, nodding to the cage.

Sir Murith glanced over. The cage was still there, intact. Within was a sallow wretched looking wolfkin, staring at him with evil malicious eyes. "Whoa!"

"They have been in wolf form all these days, ragged from the silver, but still quite vile and vicious," the Chief said. "They won't turn back until they taste the blood of man."

Sir Murith approached the cage, drawing his silver sword.

"You have a cure?! You're not going to kill them?!" Chief Runnik pleaded as he hurried alongside Murith.

"I merely want to see them up close, in the light," said Sir Murith. He walked up, sword in front for defense and not to attack.

The wolfkin looked weak with aching bodies. Their fur was patchy and had exposed skin, lacerations and burns. Murith noticed the bars and ground had splatters of hardened silver.

"We poured melted silver on the bars! It keeps them from pounding on them to escape," said Runnik.

Murith couldn't help but chortle and slap Runnik on the back. "A cure is coming soon. Your brother and niece will be free. Promise!" Murith sheathed his sword as the larger wolfkin howled weakly.

The father and daughter sat at the table, hugging each other, full of tears and joy. Soup was put before them. Verboden plopped down across from them, still weak, but joyful nonetheless.

The father reached over to Verboden and grabbed his arm, holding it for a moment. Verboden nodded as the father sat back with his daughter, in a great, deeply exhausted joy.

Chief Runnik stood at the end of the table and raised his arms, bowing his head. They all bowed their heads in the large room. It was filled with the People of the Downs, and with Alfred, Loranna, Nubio, and Sir Murith. Many of the children and the Khanafian women were in there too, sitting on wicker mats, sitting wherever they could. Murith could not help but glance at one of the Khanafian nurse, for she had her eyes on him too. Then they both bowed their heads.

"Oh, ohhhh... Father of Light, we give you thanks for saving us from the darkness. For giving us hope in a world without your love. Please awaken and end the suffering of so many. Please come and do not abandon us. We seek your Light. We seek it. We are faithful, ever faithful, even under such darkness. Bring the Light, oh Father. Bring the Light. Amen." Chief Runnik raised his head and looked gently upon his brother and niece. He looked to Verboden and Murith and then set his eyes on the Boy King Alfred.

They all began to sip at their soup, with no spoons, like a drink in a bowl. They sipped gently. After the soup, the maidens came about to pour warm goat's milk – and after that, they brought small crumbly bread. The children gulped with difficulty, but gulp they did. The bread was passed amongst them, and they ate it greedily. Their strength was returning, or forming for the first time. Many children stood outside, not forgotten as the maidens carried baskets of the crumbly bread amongst them.

"Aren't any of these children yours?" Alfred asked Chief Runnik.

Runnik stopped chewing to peer at the children. "They are not known to me. The families in this area have lost many children, but their fate was known. I don't believe these children are of my peoples."

Verboden looked up. "They are not. As a cleric, I can sense the mother and father of a child. It is an invocation we learn as young clerics. I sense no mother... no father... of these children here."

"Goblins raid many lands to the west, farmsteads and the smaller kingdoms..." Chief Runnik said.

Alfred looked at the children. They were eating away. He still couldn't get over their thick scraggy hair. "Then, we'll have to take them back to Grotham Keep."

"Puff uhh... uggg... what?" Verboden spit out his bread.

"We'll have to take them back with us," Alfred declared.

"To Grotham Keep?" asked Murith.

"Yep," Alfred replied. "We have plenty of farmland and an abundance of food."

Murith and Verboden looked at each other, chewing on their bread. They shrugged.

"You'll have to wait till after winter. It is upon us," Chief Runnik said. "At the end of winter, the sun will shine and the sod will be as solid and hard as ice. Then, you can travel quickly. And we will provide for you. We will send goats with milk!"

"But you have so little!?" Verboden worried.

"Oh no, Brother Verboden," Chief Runnik huffed. "With silver spears, silver powder, the cure, we have so much! And we now have Baron Oswahl von Schnikerstahn, our friendly ghost!"

The Baron, now floating amidst the children who had grown quite accustomed to him, bowed. "I am honored to be of service. Finally! Giving... giving... serving! I love it!"

"A ghost could come in handy. Scouting, spying, messenger..." Sir Murith remarked.

"He will help us," said Chief Runnik. "Our clans are scattered, hiding from the curse. But with you and King Alfred, our saviors born of men, we can defend ourselves with silver! We will gather our clans and goat herds. We will rebuild. We will grow!" He spoke joyfully.

"And what of the empty tombs?" Murith asked. "They are unguarded, treasures of unlimited wealth abound."

The Chief thought a moment. "I have no need for cursed treasures. There are so few to trade with. Best keep it a secret till the time when there is peace in the land and merchants upon the roads."

"It is best that none know," Verboden said.

"For now," Alfred added. "But this necromancer did all that for a reason... Chief Runnik, you must keep it secret, until we know what they're doing. And when our kingdom is rebuilt, we'll come for it. Is that okay? Alright?"

"You have saved my land, my people, we are more than indebted to you," the Chief responded with a teary smile.

"The wolf curse has ended. No more will you be attacked by doomed souls," said Verboden.

"Thanks be to Armahn," the Chief said gratefully. "We will provide for you, King Alfred and them. All of them! Till spring."

The Quest of Sir Gorham

Chapter Twenty-four

CRAG MOUNTAINS

It was still the end of summer when the three knights departed Grotham Keep. Sir Murith took Alfred, Loranna, Nubio and Verboden northward to the moorlands. Lord Dunther headed on the road south to Telehistine but would turn westward from there to the faerie realm. And, Sir Gorham headed east to reunite with his long lost cousins of the troll hunter clans.

In a week, Sir Gorham reached the edge of the Westfold and could see in the distance, far far away, the tips of the Crag Mountains. They were gray and pointy, teeth-like. Some would mistake them for the Black Spires of Gorbogal's lair, but these were more rough shod, gray and natural. It was as if mountains exploded upward, and their pinnacles extended a bit farther, reaching upward to the sky as columns of granite. Many looked as if they crashed into each other, tumbling and cracking. They looked as if giants had smashed against one another and then were frozen as they reached upwards with their vast rocky limbs.

Before him and his black steed lay a field of grass, a wide expanse stretched to the horizon. Beyond was a hilly forest, then the land of many rivers and beyond that the Crag Mountains. He leaned forward to his mare's flickering ears and whispered a word, a name, then spoke loudly, "Ride like the wind!"

Gorham had to grasp desperately as his mare took off. His head jerked as his grip tightened. His mount sprinted on the grassy plain faster than he had ever known. It took Gorham several hundred yards to collect himself as his mare flew. He was finally able to lean forward with a controlled momentum, gathering the rhythm of the incredible steed under his mounted stance.

It felt as if he hovered above the land, flying past it, upon an incredible beast whose long, sinewy muscles were as graceful as the wind it rode upon.

His armour was magnificent, gnome made, with the designs of Broggia and Boggin of course. It fit him well and was tight like shiny, metallic skin. It may be the only non-faerie armour that could sustain him upon this enchanted steed as it flew across the plains. Gorham noticed that every once and awhile his mount would suddenly stop galloping and literally fly across the grass. His eyes widened at first with apprehension. But as the horse seemed to land as soft and speedily as ever, then find another subtle slope to fly across, he couldn't help but chortle in joy.

Upon passing through the hilly forests and rivers over many days as the waning of summer came upon him, he reached the rocky terrain of the Crag Mountains. Gorham came to love his steed even more. She was an incredible horse whose grace and strength was beyond anything he had ever experienced.

He gave her many rests and time for grazing. Though it wasn't necessary, he couldn't help himself. He stood with her as she grazed. He brushed her fur and kept a vigilant eye out for any aches or pains. Of which he saw none. What an incredible steed, he thought.

The land rose in large swathes with dry evergreens and rock outcroppings. There was plenty of rough terrain to hide wayward goblins or other foul beasts. Gorham knew the land of the troll hunters was filled with primordial beasts, and it is why they loved it so.

Many trees were felled by weather and beasts. The land had a maze of them like damns or walls, but with no purpose to their settling.

Beasts would tear up trees or knock down giant rocks merely to sharpen their claws. These objects would then crash down from the ledges above.

Gorham and his steed were dwarfed by such destructive mounds. Many times they were blocking their way through the terrain. The dead trees, piled in bulwarks, seemed to be leading them a certain way. He was not sure. There were plenty of the cracked trees across the rocky paths as well. Perhaps these just collected so, with no ambush or trickery.

On one stormy night, rain deluged the area. Rivulets of water turned to floods in a wave of gushing overflows. Gorham and his steed stood stoically on a large granite rock as broken trees rolled violently past, floundering amidst the torrents of flooding water. The darkness showed only massive tangled shadows careening downward. When the lightning flashed in succession, you could see the massive evergreens and dead trees deluged in white water rapids. Then the thunder would explode and cause the mountains to vibrate, sending rock and shale splashing down into the flickering waves.

The trees would catch upon each other, between the jutting granite towers all around them, causing more of it to damn up. The water would crash upon that, swirling violently and sending white foamy explosions up into the battering rain.

Still, Gorham and his steed had found a stable refuge, waiting and resting, drenched in the torrential rain. And the night passed as Gorham sat.

They marched slowly and steadily upward, on a hot moist sunny day. The puddles and rivulets of water from the rainy season were minimal, having rushed downward in rapid successions. The terrain was of giant granite blocks and a cavalcade of fallen evergreens. The ground, now, was mostly of broken granite and shale, collected in mounds against the rocks. There was a hardened pathway in front of them. It wound its way upward in a meandering way, ascending slowly but surely.

Gorham saw the towering granite peaks of the Crag Mountains. Each morning they created giant silhouettes as the sun rose from the east. He was in their shadow each morning, heading eastward, as the beams of sunlight would not come through till just before noon. It was in these long shadowy mornings that he would notice the troll beasts and primal creatures lurking about.

At night, he kept a fire raging. There was much dead wood, evergreens with dried husks and browned needles scattered about for fuel. An occasional wild troll would lumber through. Gorham kept his sword out, ready. They would lick their lips wanting his horse. But as they approached, his horse would neigh out a strange hallowed reverberation. At first, it jolted Gorham, but then seemed soothing in a way. The trolls would listen, become sleepy, snort, and then meander off into the dark.

In the mornings, as they traversed the rocky terrain, he would still have to be mindful and awake. The beasts could show up around a corner, waiting in ambush, or be of the sudden random clash. Many were warthog looking. Some were able to stand upright as some grotesque man-beast. Others were trolls in every sense: giant, rough-scaly skin, and nodule like horns coming out of various joints or extrusions. They had that all around gigantic endangering quality.

Still, Sir Gorham avoided much of the threats. The few that seemed to elevate to a clash of beast versus knight never fully escalated, as he would easily sprint from the lazy beasts or flash his brilliant sword enough to give them pause, causing them to turn away.

Thankfully, there were only a few chance encounters in the mornings. The rest of the hot days with mountain cold breezes were his alone to travel up into the Crag Mountains. The closer he came to the troll hunter abodes, the more he could see lit windows cluttered upon the sheer wall of granite.

He was sure they could see his nightly bonfire of bramble through the towering evergreen trees. With all the violence and turmoil it did seem surprising that many trees were still quite intact on their plot of earth between granite columns. He knew the troll hunters would be upon him soon enough. He shivered, for he could not remember the faces of his cousins.

Chapter Twenty-Five

Troll Hunters

The next cold shadowy morning, as he put out his fire and finished his dried jerky meal, a troll suddenly rounded a rocky outcropping, coming straight at him. It roared in a violent panic, thundering its massive scaly fists, pounding upon hardened earth as it came. It was quite large and bulky, having a similar physique to that of jungle gorilla beasts. It towered nearly twice the height of Gorham and just as wide. Its skin was scaly and wrought with many stuck stones, embedded from this rocky terrain. Its visage was roughhewn, squashed, its features minimized by a large jawbone and thickset brows.

His horse whinnied a fright, knowing no sonorous neigh would quell this enraged beast. Gorham leapt up with sword flashing and quickly put on his helm. He then grabbed his shield from his trotting mare and kept on his feet, allowing the mare to retreat. He readied for the charge, moving from foot to foot to leap from the attack.

Just beyond the rampaging troll, he saw upon the granite wall, silhouetted against the morning sun, the unmistakable shape of a violent hardened troll hunter. The hunter held on to the sheer wall, quite as capable as a monkey to a tree. Gorham gritted teeth in his helm and rolled forward and under as the troll pounded the ground.

Gorham tried to alight upon his feet to swing, but the troll's immense weight shook the ground, throwing Gorham against stone.

The mare took off with such speed that the troll knew it was useless to chase after it. Gorham was still able to slash at the troll's hardened skin, infused with scales, horns and crushed granite rocks. The blade cut some skin while scraping and bouncing off the rest.

The troll spun quite rapidly, its two hammer fists swinging like trees as Gorham tried in vain to avoid them. He was slammed hard and flew up and onto the stone wall. He hit the wall hard and froze a moment. He saw the troll hunter continue to cling to the granite above, watching.

"Grrrrrr..." Gorham breathed roughly as his metal screeched, sliding down the wall and hitting the ground. He was given no time to recover as the troll, roaring, charged in and hammer slammed, repeatedly upon his small body.

His armour, violently impacted, still held, for it was gnome designed in an incredible fitted way to absorb and then bounce off stone and even stone encrusted troll fists. It wasn't, necessarily, comfortable, however. Gorham found a moment to lift up his sword and allow the troll to impale its own hand as it swung down upon the knight.

The troll screamed as it retreated, partially peeling Gorham off the ground. Gorham tweaked the blade to slide it out of the troll's fist, alighting firmly on his own footing. He then lashed upon the pained beast with several well placed thrusts and slashes. The troll stumbled backward as the silvery slasher kept up a continual attack. In pain, the troll swatted the knight away, this time making Gorham roll over and over upon jutting rocks and crumbled shale.

When Gorham was finally able to stop rolling and stood, a giant rock suddenly smashed into him, crashing him against an evergreen's trunk. The tree shook and cracked as it splintered. He was stuck between a hard rock and a splintering tree. He tried to unwedge himself but seemed doomed to wait for the tree to decide its falling path amidst its exploding splinters.

Gorham wriggled to no avail, weakened and stunned. Even his arm and sword were stuck in the snapping splinters. The troll was upon him and gave an intelligent sneer. It grabbed him quite viciously from the wood and rock calamity, yanking him out. If it wasn't for his armour, he would have been yanked in two. His sword flew into the air, fluttering down as a twanging metal shard far away.

The troll raised his captive as he opened his monstrous mouth. Gorham tried weakly, barely alive, to raise his shield. He was able to jam it into the troll's mouth. Its thumb-sized teeth crushed in around it. The shield gave the troll resistance, even cutting into its mouth. Gorham's arm was stuck there, within the buckling shield.

Gorham could just see, as his consciousness fluttered, the shadow of a troll hunter careening through the air with battleaxe ready.

The troll hunter landed atop the troll, torquing his entire body and slamming a bardiche or elongated battleaxe upon the troll's thick skull. The giant troll grunted as the hunter seemed to hang from the immense weapon. The troll turned about, unsure, just as another hunter rushed up from below with a huge spear. The hunter rolled right at the last moment to give himself great momentum. The spear stayed level through the roll so that when he chucked it from the rolling leap, it was thrown fiercely into the troll's side. It sank deep, causing the troll to get sleepy and waiver.

Gorham managed to maintain consciousness, having one arm stuck in the troll's spittle-ridden mouth. Upon being released by the waning troll's grip, he was still stuck to the mouth, as the towering beast came tumbling down.

"Bah hah hah!" one troll hunter bellowed as he pointed at Gorham, stuck under the head of the troll. The other, having easily walked off as the troll crash landed, returned to pull out his bardiche with a unique elongated pick. An axe has a curved blade, but the troll hunter's axe has an additional pick or spike at the top of that curve and on the rear of the head. For though a blade will cause a good wound, the piercing of a pointed pick-spike through thick troll hides was essential for the kill. And it also made for a handy climbing tool.

"Well well well, what do we have here? A fancy delicate knight of some sort? Elvish you think, brudder?" one troll hunter barked from his dark iron helm.

The other, somewhat larger, pulled his huge spear from the troll's ribcage. The spear's head, like the pick, wasn't wide like a spear but straighter, pointed and quite thick. It had just over a foot's length before the quillons, or a crossguard, to keep it from going in too deep.

After all, troll hunters have such immense strength that they need to limit their own potentially deadly force.

"I dunno brudder, looks faerie alright, especially with its fleeting horse," the other responded with a coarse voice.

The mare suddenly appeared from below, peering up at them from behind a rock. It neighed a worrisome cry. Both troll hunters, with their frightful appearance, stared at the wondrous but quite scared mount. They shrugged.

Gorham turned to peer up at the troll hunters. They made quick work of the troll's biting clamp on Gorham's arm and pulled him from it. He tried to get up but was too battered and weak.

One of the troll hunters tried to pull off Gorham's helm, much to Gorham's displeasure and seething grunts.

"It's got straps, dumbkin!" the other said.

"Alright, alright, where are they?" the first said, bending down and peering at the helm. His big hands wrapped in leather and spiked claws weren't nimble enough to unbuckle it.

Gorham waved him off and rolled to one side to try to get up. The troll hunters in black iron armour, black straps and fur, with many dark web-like tattoos and scars, stood and waited.

Gorham stumbled. The larger troll hunter used his spear and smacked Gorham back down. "Stay down."

Gorham tumbled and fell, exhausting any strength left in him.

"Never seen a faerie warrior before," the lighter troll hunter said, leaning on his bardiche.

"Not impressed," the larger said. He stepped toward Gorham.

Gorham was finally able to yell, under abated breath, stuck in his helm, "I am Sir Gorham of the Gorhammick Broor, Brudderin Lineage of Ordoh Brutum, Troll Hunter." He coughed and finally fell still.

The troll hunters paused and looked at each other through their bestial iron helms. "Guess that would be... cousin?"

"Yep," the other shrugged.

Chapter Twenty-Six

Cousins

"Is he little Gorham then, from the Westfold, Brok?" the smaller troll hunter asked, peering at Gorham, as Brok his larger brother carried him over his shoulder. Gorham looked like a small metallic elf draped over a bestial man in black furs and cast-iron, cauldron-like armour.

"Aye, must be, though his family's line ended with the siege of Gorbogal, right?" Brok stopped and pondered. He turned back to see his smaller brethren peering back down the trail. "What is it, Ruuk? I sense no trolls."

"It's that horse of his," Ruuk said, peering down along the trail. "It's following us."

"Humph, like a loyal warg then," said Brok, shrugging to get Gorham to fit better on his massive shoulder.

"There's something enchanted about our little Gorham," Ruuk said, catching up and twirling his large bardiche. "He's got this elvish looking armour and an elvish horse, right?"

"We'll know soon enough, when we take him to vatter," said Brok. "...of the Gorhammick Broor, Brudderin Lineage of Ordoh Brutum, Troll Hunter... and Sir Gorham, from the fallen Gorhammick line, fallen in the Great Northern Kingdom, the Westfold, under King Athelrod, at Grotham Keep... long ago..."

"Taken by Gorbogal..." Ruuk added.

"Uhhnnnn..." Gorham moaned.

Brok stopped. "What's that?" He tried to look at Gorham, who lay over his shoulder. But Brok could only see, through his dark helm, Gorham's derriere.

"Uhhnn..." Gorham continued.

Ruuk stepped up to lift Gorham's helm with the blade of his bardiche to get a look at his face.

"Put me down, you foul brethren!" Gorham finally chided.

"Hoh hoh! Hah! He's got some spirit in him yet," chortled Ruuk. He helped lift Gorham off Brok as they both gladly complied.

Gorham landed hard and wobbly. He hugged his ribs, bending over, and coughed with many pangs.

"My sword? Where is it?"

They both shrugged. Ruuk proffered, "Probably left on the trail back there with the dead troll. It will be gone soon enough. Gobbies will scavenge the place by nightfall."

Just then, Gorham's mare came riding up. She pranced in front of them and neighed a loud whinny. The troll hunters attempted to cover their ears under their great helms, while both considered leveling their weapons at the small yet muscular horse. Its neigh shook them to their core.

Gorham suddenly hobbled over and easily alighted upon his steed. He then pulled his sword from the horse's scabbard.

"Wow, a sword-retrieving horse! Impressive," said Ruuk.

Gorham leaned heavily on his horse, still in pain, barely able to hold the sword.

"Brethren," said Brok, raising his big burly hand. "No need for this. You are seriously injured and put on a mighty fine show against a greater trollkin. Your ribs are surely broken. You need rest and healing."

"Gorham of the Gorhammick line, Brudderin... you told us your lineage in your pain. We are cousins!" Ruuk said, opening his arms. "We are the sons of Ordo Brute, brudder to your vatter, Gorhammick!"

Gorham finally breathed easily, whispering to his anxious mount to ease. The horse stood still as Gorham sighed to ease his pain. "Cousins, I've come for your help."

Gorham fell off his horse.

Cousins

He awoke much too sudden, trying to sit up. He grabbed his ribs under his steel plate, lying back down. A raging fire was before him, but it must have been the sound of tearing and chewing flesh that had awakened him. His cousins most certainly did not close their mouths when they chewed, snarled, gurgled, burped or licked.

He looked up to see his mare standing behind, quite still. Before him were his crude cousins. Both had removed their helms and were chewing on some large pieces of burnt meat. They had thick black hair weaved in thick ponytails, with plenty of loose strands. Their jaws were thickset, and their skin, though flesh colored, almost had the hue of rocks. There were shades of black and gray, giving off a sense of hardened granite. They also shaved, he noted, or more like cut their facial hair, for it was sparse yet stubby.

"Hungry, little cousin?" Brok said, not even looking.

Ruuk tore off a small bone joint and tossed it to Gorham. It hit his shiny breastplate with a burnt greasy splat. He caught it and was not hungry, until he smelled it. Then he was ravenous. He hurriedly unbuckled his helm, throwing it off, and bit mightily into the meat. He noticed his mare looking at him, then looking away. He continued to chew.

"Interesting armour you have there, Gorham? Elvish?" Ruuk asked while chewing.

"Gnomish, with the help of Broggia and Boggin, smiths, who are men," Gorham answered, while chewing.

"Gnomish?" Brok stopped chewing to ask, with meat pieces all around his rough shaven chin. "And men, working together?"

"Yes, we have an alliance with the gnomes. And that's why I've come here, to reform the alliance between Men of the Westfold and the troll hunters aloft in their Crag Mountain lairs," said Gorham.

Brok and Ruuk looked at each other, chewing slowly this time.

Gorham, after many chews and swallows, feeling the meaty nourishment strengthen him, paused to see that Brok and Ruuk chewed silently. He found strength to sit back up.

"You set that rock troll upon me, didn't you?"

Brok and Ruuk stopped and looked at each other with devious eyes. They shared a chortle and then a guffaw at Gorham's expense.

"We like to play with strangers who dare come into our most dangerous lands," Ruuk exhorted. "It's our welcoming gift."

150

Gorham gritted teeth, wiping his mouth.

"We did not know you were brethren," Brok shrugged with a humble grin.

"Would that have changed our welcome?" chimed Ruuk.

Both couldn't help but guffaw again and punch each other's fists with a resounding crack.

"How'd you like the rock troll welcome then, brethren?" Brok asked with a big devious smile.

"We need you," Gorham said.

They looked slant-eyed at one another.

Gorham noticed. "What's the matter? There was an alliance between the Men of the Westfold, the Northern Kingdom, and you troll hunters for many generations. It was an alliance to come to each other's aid in time of war."

"That alliance ended when the Westfold ended. And you never even called for our help," said Brok, pointing a meatless bone at Gorham.

"Gorbogal defeated you," Ruuk recalled. "The Witch of the Black Spires, you know, she doesn't live far from here. At our highest peaks, on a cool blue day, you can see her orc-made spires on the eastern horizon."

"Look like patch of gangly spikes, ugly like. Not at all like our great rock spires here," Brok added.

"You've never been defeated by Gorbogal!" Gorham said with enthusiasm. "She was never able to conquer these lands!"

"That's right, Gorham. Your proud king should have called upon us long ago to help! But he didn't trust us, now did he!? He didn't want no roughshod barbarians amongst his men and his walls at Grotham Keep!?" Ruuk spat.

"Our king was in turmoil then, many things were... weakening him," Gorham said sadly. "But that time has passed. We come now, seeking the old alliance and a commitment to our war against Gorbogal!"

"Whaht? You're at war with Gorbogal? With what?" Brok asked.

"That boy king, isn't it?" Ruuk said quickly.

"Nooh... I never believed those traveling minstrels!" said Brok.

Gorham squirmed a bit in his seat, feeling the heat of the fire upon him. "Yes, we have a boy king."

Cousins

Brok raised his arms in defiance. "Oh no! What a sad, sad story! A boy king as conqueror and leader? Beating goblins and ratkins, they sang! Wee little gobbies and ratkinnicks!"

"He beat ogres as well, from the Orient, slave raiders," Gorham added, gulping.

"Fat ogres? Fat, fat slave raiders? Lazy fat bulbous pig heads from the Orient? Who have little humies and gobbies do all their bidding. Pfft!! My mudder could defea..." Ruuk said, stopping short, looking at Brok who glared at him.

Gorham finally found the courage to argue his point. "Our boy king, King Alfred is from the line of kings. He has saved us."

"Then why do you need our help? Maybe he, this boyyy king, should lead the armies of the West and defeat her?" Ruuk spoke.

"Good point. If he's such a boy conqueror, don't see why he need bother with us. Didn't the minstrels say there were children too? Girls shooting with bows? Boys with spears? Seriously, Gorham, that is who you have fighting for you?" Brok exhorted.

"Oooh girl archers and spear boys! Sounds like a mighty army indeed, cousin Gorham! No wonder she defeated you and your father's line!" said Ruuk.

Gorham stood, making fists in his armour.

"Oooh, upset are we?" Ruuk responded, still sitting.

"Silence, Ruuk!" Brok huffed. He waved for Gorham to sit back down. Brok gnawed on his meatless bone. "No need to insult our brethren."

Ruuk shrugged. Gorham slowly sat back down, submitting to the woe of his feeble attempt at forming an alliance.

"If your vatter's king, King Athelrod, would have called us back then, this war against the witch would have turned out much differently! So now you need our help? Best to go back to your boy king and your army of children and leave us. Leave it as it twas, just like the alliance of olde!" said Brok.

This wasn't going well, but Gorham knew he had to keep trying. "We know Gorbogal has been spreading her tendrils far and wide. She seeks to weaken the lands of men, to divide and conquer. She has sent out Agents of Scourge to keep us from forming alliances! She couldn't conquer our King Alfred directly, so she is planning subterfuge and sowing discord."

Cousins

Brok and Ruuk seemed slow to reply. Ruuk was retying a loose leather-iron piece to his armour, dabbing meat grease to moisten it.

"Well?" Gorham finally asked.

"Well... we go to our vatter, you vatter's brudder, Ordo Brute," Brok said.

Chapter Twenty-Seven

The Mountainside Tavern

It was nearing dusk as Gorham followed behind Brok and Ruuk. Though he was on his great steed, he still looked smaller than his bulky and feral kin. They wore heavy furs and thick cast-iron armour yet stepped lightly. Were they a head or two taller than Gorham and that much wider? One of them could easily take on an ogre, and would probably best it by sheer ability. Also, they were not weighted down by fatty limbs or bulbous stomachs. Their joints seemed thick and knobby, ready for the most grueling of rock climbing, leaping and combat. Their muscle cords were thick and sinewy, insinuating they had feats of strength and speed at their disposal.

They pointed up a winding path. Ruuk turned to Gorham. "You take this path. It winds up through many troll hunter encampments. Ignore all of them and..."

"I know of the tavern. I remember this path from when I was a child," said Gorham.

Ruuk sort of smiled, with a sneer. "Ignore all the hunters who mock and scoff your faerie appearance. And make it to the tavern. We'll be waiting for you."

Ruuk was already pulling himself up and over the granite walls of rock using the spike of his bardiche. Brok pole vaulted, gaining much air as he flew up and over the rock juts. Gorham could just see their intense black shapes as they scrambled along the mountain side and up the cliff walls, where flashes and hues of flames from campfires illuminated the dark granite.

These walls contained the homes and halls of the troll hunters. Many lived within caves and others in encampments scattered throughout the rocky clefts. The tavern was a rare wooden structure, quite large, jutting out from the mountainside, giving an incredible view of the Crag Mountains, evergreen forests, and rolling hills that spread westward to the Westfold. It was almost as if it were built, awaiting the call of the Westfold alliance, a call that never came many years ago.

As Gorham's mare trotted carefully along, he patted and whispered calmness to her. Soon enough he came upon wood and stone frames with stretched skins of warthog beasts and black furry critters. They were making fur and leather-hide materials. Many troll hunters saw him, standing to look at his strange delicate-looking form. A few came up to knock on his steel armour. They nodded, that yes, indeed it was some kind of metal. His steed was still nervous, and a few times he had to control it as troll hunters rambled by. They were a mess of a lot, roughhewn, scraggy in their black leathers and armour. Many had claw and tooth-like tattoos all along their arms, legs, and chest. He was beginning to realize that they were beast marks, tallies of how many and what they hunted and killed.

Their thick hair was always braided or tightly wound in ponytails. Yet there was always a looseness to it, as if once done, they rushed off to something quite violent and disheveling. Their skin, again, had a granite hue, perhaps from constantly climbing and living amongst the grey stones. Many had scars, eye patches, and even a few missing fingers or limbs, casualties of the hunter life.

The encampment was a maze of hunters with their skins and skull trophies. Cages of all kinds, sizes and materials littered the grounds, with many strange ruffian beasts within. Most had the quality of warthog, bestial bat, or mountainous goat. He wasn't sure if they were food, pets, or for sale. Gorham tried his best not to stare at the troll hunters. Most were men, hardened and brazen. He only saw a few women amongst them and even fewer children. Though there were some, it must be a hard life for a child to be raised in. He was sure they were born as weak as any human, and this land either made them strong enough to be a troll hunter or it killed them.

The Mountainside Tavern

Weapon racks abounded, and many smiths hammered away near smoky fire pits. They used what appeared to be large chunks of mixed black coal, shale, and charcoal to make a thick black smoke. It burned hot as they smelted blooms of cast-iron. He could see they had not perfected the secret of steel, but something about their acceptance of heavy cast iron made both their weapons and their brawn quite powerful. A variety of polearms that fit into the category of large bladed glaives or more pointy spears were everywhere, as were the shorter bardiches. Again, bardiches are basically battleaxes with long curved blades attached to thick short polearms. All of them had that added unique troll hunter pick or spike, which could penetrate any troll skin and probably any armour including gnome steel.

Gorham was surprised at the prodigious affair. The smiths were busy at work, glancing up at him only for a moment. He was most definitely a new and quite unique sight. However, it appeared that they had many weapons and armour to make. It looked as if they were preparing for war. But he knew this was just the life they lived in such a difficult land full of trolls and beasts.

He could see the Mountainside Tavern far above as the rock path became steeper. Though his horse was quite nimble, able to take many stone steps, it came to a point where he would have to leave her amongst the troll hunter encampments. Up here they were nestled into the stony cliffs and clefts. He found a decent platform of stone with just a weapon wrack and an empty cage. He whispered for her to stay. She did not like it. A rare child, messy and muscular, climbed up to the landing. Gorham looked and saw the child was curious about his mare. They had no horses here, in this roughshod terrain of rock and shale.

Gorham knew the best trick to get on the feral child's side. He pulled out the last of his jerky and a dry crumbled biscuit. The ragged boy quickly leapt at it, taking both and sitting under Gorham's horse to devour his provisions. "Can you watch my horse for me?"

The boy nodded, chewing on the jerky.

Gorham ascended the steep stones, having to climb in some instances. It was painful with his injuries, but he was determined. Several troll hunters bound past him, up the stone crevices to the tavern. He huffed and puffed and finally made it to the open doorway. Loud boisterous laughter resounded from within. He took a deep breath to get ready for the cajoling and scoffing at his size, at his request, and at his boy king.

He noticed many ruffian giant-like men upon an expanse of decking and rails that stuck out from the mountainside. They leaned upon the thickset wood, looking down at him with huge mugs of ale in their brawny hands. They leered at him and his puny form.

He stepped into a dark abode. He suddenly felt even smaller as everything was thickset and large. The chairs and stools, benches and tables, all had a quality of thickness, from the cut of the lumber to the thickness of the ropes and leather straps used. He stepped forward on solid thick timber. His eyes adjusted easily from the dusk outside to the light of many bestial fat- burning torches within. The place was riddled with thick bones as trophies and placed as part of the structure.

"Gorhammick! Brudderin!" yelled Ruuk as he grabbed Gorham, who was still out of breath. "Come and let me show my hunter brood what softy men we have in the grassy plains of the Westfold!"

"HAHR HAHR HAHHR!" was the loud boisterous hurrah of the hunters as Ruuk easily man-handled Gorham into the midst of a cadre of drinking troll hunters. Before he was able to gain balance, a large cast-iron mug was handed to him. He nearly fell over with the weight of the container, spilling its contents as he lifted it back up with his weakened muscles.

The troll hunters suddenly gaped at his weakness. Silence descended in the room. Ruuk stared until Gorham leveled the empty mug. Ruuk poured in some of his ale. Gorham held it with two hands as if he was holding up a heavy stone.

"BAHR HAHR HARH!" they began anew.

Ruuk slapped Gorham's back. Gorham cringed with pain and had to use all his strength to hold himself and the sloshing mug of ale. He literally lowered himself to his own mug using his knees to tilt it and pour a liberal amount into and around his mouth. He was quite thirsty, and knew their ale, as sour and fermented as it was, had healing and strengthening qualities. Even if it was all hearsay, he didn't care. He was quite thirsty, famished, and in need of a strong drink.

Brok was still the largest of the brood of troll hunters. Gorham looked about as they spoke in a very difficult dialect of the mannish tongue. He noticed many were short and squat and wondered if there was dwarvish blood in them. Perhaps long ago a line of dwarven families joined with the men of these mountains. Their height varied greatly, but not their girth and prowess. All seemed quite powerful and ready to slam any offender to the ground. Gorham was not going to offend a single hunter if he could help it. He kept his mouth shut for the most part, swigging his heavy iron mug that the hunters kept refilling.

"Oooh sent wi'rook trohol uponik dere stranguh whomwik did naught connick as oor own brudderin!" Brok spoke to his brethern.

"Nay, naught, rook trohol beat'em slam ham an finnish wid dem rook toss again! Gorhammnick floo wee like'em birdy splat, splint, treebaum come fallin dooon! Funnik, Brok and me chortle we did!" Ruuk said, getting the whole group of them to laugh uproarously at Gorham's expense.

Gorham couldn't understand what they were saying and wasn't even sure he was listening as he swooned while gulping more ale. He then found a large stool and dropped his heavy mug on the table, plopping in front of it.

"Whad wid duh shiny silver faerie iron den?" someone asked.

"Oooh, dat faerie iron impressuv, tis was, rook trohol slam and ham but heyy... iron stay iron!" Ruuk said. "Course can't say the same fer dem wearer!"

They all laughed again as Ruuk pointed at Gorham, who looked woozy and drunk already.

"Ohh, pooh brudderin, trolls are a tough lot. Can't expect him or any softy man who hasn't been here since childhood to survive such against our beasts!" Brok said in plain tongue – or was it the drink that helped Gorham understand?

Gorham looked up and tried to lift his mug to toast, but he couldn't. Still, as he sat, he felt strength revive him.

"Quite wounded as well," Ruuk added. "How's that healing imbibement?"

"Whaht?" Gorham said, swooning just a bit.

"Heee look like a child dere on dat hunter size stool," a hunter commented, chortling with a few others.

Ruuk sat next to him, ignoring the rest who were still having fun. He spoke softly to him. "It's a healing ale, quite powerful. Wouldn't recommend fighting trolls anytime soon, but it will set you on the healing way."

Gorham suddenly woke and held his hands somewhat over his armour by his ribs as he breathed. "Yes, the pain has lessened. I feel it."

"It dulls the pain but also speeds the healing. Still, we'll get you rested and healed. Your armour held up well against the rock troll. And it looked like you may have had a chance against the beast. Rock trolls are one of our tougher trollkins. We thought you were an elf with magic or something. Wanted to draw that out of you," said Ruuk.

"No magic, cousin," Gorham said, tilting his heavy mug and taking another sip.

"This may not be the place for you, little cousin," Ruuk said.

"Oh, I'll drink to that," Gorham spat. "This is definitely a harsh land."

"No, well softy man yes. But I mean, your seeking of an alliance," Ruuk continued.

Gorham looked at him, with focus. "What do you mean?"

"Alliances, promises, distant cousins, family, the lineage of man," Ruuk said, looking more at his drink than Gorham. "Times have changed, right? The Westfold had fallen many years ago. We have not heard from you. The Gorhammick lineage was considered lost to us. Course we lived high up here in our mountain fortress, away from it all."

Gorham tried to discern what he was saying. "Are you not glad to see me? And know that the Westfold has survived and is rebuilding? Old alliances can be restored and made better. Our king seeks it. I seek it. And will honor it!"

"Honor it? How? Children warriors? How many knights do you have? And are they as weak as you?" asked Ruuk. He had a cordial smile when he asked, so Gorham did not feel offended. It was as if Ruuk were not asking as much as explaining something, but Gorham could not tell.

Brok sat down opposite them, weary of the guffawing and bantering the other hunters were still doing all around them. "What you speak of, bruder?" Brok asked Ruuk.

"Oh, I was just talking, of the situation," said Ruuk.

"No need, right bruder? Vatter will take care of that when he comes. No need to step in our vatter, his uncle's place. Much to say there. That is not for us," said Brok, looking stern at Ruuk.

Ruuk looked dour, glancing at Gorham and then looking away.

"What is this you speak of?" Gorham asked.

"No need to speak of... when he is here to speak it," Brok said, nodding and looking to the entrance of the Mountainside Tavern.

Chapter Twenty-Eight

The Boast of Ordoh Brutum

Gorham thought Brok was the largest of troll hunters and any man, and that none could be any bigger or more foreboding in fearsome potential, until he saw Brok's and Ruuk's vatter, Ordoh Brutum, or Ordo Brute. He was massive, nearly blocking out of view the rest of his hunter brood as he entered. His corded shoulder muscles were as big as an ogre's but his physique was taut and more vigorous. He wore the thickest of black furs with iron plates. The hide of fur wasn't just worn for warmth. Its thickness could absorb the most piercing of arrows, spears and troll claws. It had a webbing quality that was stronger than steel, for it was made from troll and beast hides.

His neck was as thick as a troll's. The jaw on this greater man looked as if it belonged to a beast of burden or dragon. His thick black hair was weaved yet lay upon his head like a great lion mane. It was only seen after he removed his great bestial black helm with spiral horns and a teeth-like visage.

These troll hunters hunted trolls and did a superb job of looking like the darkest and scariest of beastmen themselves. Fortunately for Gorham, Ordo's eyes were not at all like that of a beast but of one looking at a long lost memory – for Ordo was looking at Gorham.

Ordo lumbered forward as the troll hunter cadre of drinkers and partakers stepped aside and gave quick bows. They did not drop to knees or bow like servants but nodded in admiration to a brethren hunter, a great hunter, and no more. Also, he was their leader, and that was not to be questioned, except by battle, and thusly, not to be questioned!

Ordo stopped before Gorham, who stood carefully, still a bit woozy from drink and injury. Ordo looked up and down Gorham for a while. Ruuk glanced at Brok, unsure of their vatter's disposition.

Gorham stared silently, trying to recall if there was any respectful behavior or tradition he was required to do. Nothing came to his sloshed mind.

Ordo finally spoke, and the sound was exactly as you would expect, a deep drumming baritone. "Son of Gorham, Brudderin of the Gorhammick lineage."

Gorham's eyes widened, and he nodded quickly.

"Your father was a sickly child. Our mother took him to the Westfold, where he became a page to a knight. Even sickly, he was the strongest of the men of the Westfold, gaining notoriety and prowess amongst them. She was glad she sent him away, knowing he would not survive here. He came back and sang songs of the glory of King Athelrod to our dear mutter. He was her favorite, even though his visits were rare."

Gorham stared as Ordo bespoke of the past, of their family.

"We all made fun of him, scoffed at his weakling physique and his inability to traverse the crags of these mountains. He fought only one young cow of a troll and would not hunt the greater beasts with us. He stayed with dear mutter. I am grateful he visited our mutter. He made mutter happy. Content." Ordo looked at Brok and Ruuk when he said that. "She died in peace, knowing her weakest son lived, even if far away."

Ordo suddenly turned and bent over to look at Gorham more closely. "I remember you visiting once as a small child." Ordo put his hand out to show a short height. "You haven't changed a bit."

"BAHH HAHH HAHHR HARR!" rang out a loud clamorous laugh from all the troll hunters. Gorham's face grew red, but at least he knew that the insulting banter meant he was welcomed by the great Ordoh Brutum.

Ordo then lifted Gorham like a small child and shook him up and down. The hunter brood laughed harder and pointed. Ordo shook his own head. "What is this? Is this armour? It is sooo light? Is it from far off elves? Have you become an elf, my nephew?"

"A faerie, vatter!" Ruuk added.

More banter and laughter as Gorham tried to nod it off and squirm his way from the grip of Ordo. Fortunately, Ordo set him down and felt the steel plates. "Well, it fits your spindly body. Feels strong. Much too light, no weight behind your swing or punch, hey?"

"Well, no, I don't really..." Gorham tried to explain.

"Did we welcome our little brethren, my brudderin's seed? Nephew and knight from the Men of the Westfold then?" Ordo turned and yelled out.

"HURRAH!" the troll hunters yelled in unison, lifting their drinks. A heavy mug was handed to Ordo, who took it lightly and lifted up the drink.

"To the Men of the Westfold, who it appears have returned from utter defeat! Here is my nephew, Gorham, Lord Gorham!" Ordo announced, taking a long swig as did all the others. Gorham stood not so mightily below all of the towering hunters and even the squat yet full-of-girth ones.

Gorham pondered another drink from his heavy mug but felt he was just coming out of the drunken swoon and so faked a sip, having to use both arms to lift it. They lowered their drinks and all began slapping each other on their backs with mighty swings and bantering and chiding each other of past spoils and future hunts.

Ordo turned to look at Gorham, sitting down at the table where Brok and Ruuk were. All sat with a huge thud as Gorham carefully sat amongst them, diminutive on his large stool.

A squat large dwarvish looking troll hunter with fiery red hair and many troll tooth necklaces and accessories sat next to Ordo. He was boisterously laughing at someone's joke and slamming drinks as he sat down to turn and face the not so impressive faerie knight.

"Sir Gorham, this is my brudderin of the hunt, Furioso!" Ordo waved. "The strongest of us all!"

"Strongest smelling but that's enough to lead a trollkin our way for the fight! Ehy! Ordo!" Furioso laughed, spitting ale in all directions.

"It is good to see my kin, however far away one has gone, and changed," said Ordo.

"Changed quite a bit if he has the blood of troll hunters in him! Much less the blood of Ordoh Brutum!" Furioso exclaimed.

"We are all born weak! In some lands that weakness can be forgiving. But here in the Crag Mountains, we are either strong or dead," Ordo said.

"Aye to that! Strength above all!" Furioso raised his drink and clashed mugs with Brok and Ruuk, the splash of the collision plopping down in front of Gorham.

As the mugs cleared and Gorham looked up, he stared into the deep grey eyes of Ordo, who fixated on him. Gorham tried to hold the look but had to look down.

"Tell me, nephew, why have you come?" Ordo asked amidst the noises and laughter of the tavern.

Gorham looked up at Ruuk and Brok, who waited for him to speak. Furioso had turned to banter with other hunters seated at nearby tables.

"I've come for your aid, to reform the alliance, as kin, between the troll hunters of the Crag Mountains and the Men of the Westfold and the Northern Kingdom," said Gorham.

Ordo tilted his head upward, looking down at Gorham, ignoring all the boisterous banter around him.

Gorham was at first unsure, but an uneasy feeling rose within him, for such a claim was not immediately and surely taken as a blessing.

"No," said Ordo.

"No?"

"No, little Gorham, we cannot form an alliance," Ordo said.

Furioso suddenly turned, snorted and glared directly at Gorham.

"What do you mean?" said Gorham, sobering and sitting up. "We must form an alliance of men, against the evil witch Gorbogal. We need your help!" said Gorham.

"I hear from the traveling minstrels at our base camp that you have a boy king, some savior? With children as his warriors?" asked Ordo.

"Well yes, but..."

"But not you? Not you as their savior? With troll hunter blood, you couldn't save the Westfold and your Grotham Keep?" asked Ordo.

"It's not like that. I am a servant knight to the Royal Knight Dunther," said Gorham, stuttering.

"Dunther? That royal baron? Knight of King Athelrod? Pfft... I've never heard of any exploit or legend about him." Ordo waved him off.

"I served under him, and we serve this boy... this king, King Alfred... and we have defeated the armies of Gorbogal," said Gorham.

"I've heard! They sang about it! Spindly minstrels!" Ordo said. "Tell me, did he, did you bow to girls? Little girls with arrows? Did you get on one knee and bow to them?" Ordo asked. "You knights? Men of renown? Bowing to little girls who fight for you? With the honor of war?"

Furioso chuckled at that. Brok and Ruuk rolled their eyes.

"They helped us defeat the goblin army and the ratkin horde," Gorham said. The assertion didn't sound so epic in this monstrous tavern with monstrous men.

"Ooohh ratkins, they are a pest. Girls with bows can come in handy then," Furioso nodded with dancing eyebrows. He took a big gulp of his drink to avoid laughing.

"Girls, you have girls fighting your wars?" Ruuk sneered.

"We also defeated ants," Gorham said, quickly taking a drink.

"Ants?" repeated Ordo.

"Big ones...hormigs... they were very big, dangerous," Gorham said with a shrug.

Ordo looked at Furioso, who shook his head.

"Ordo! Uncle Ordoh Brutum!" Gorham suddenly yelled out, giving pause to Ordo, Furioso, his sons and few other dangerous looking troll hunters nearby. "We have come. I am the dignitary of King Alfred. I have come to rejoin our kingdoms in mutual defense! The witch Gorbogal is on the move. She plans on laying siege to our castle soon, and we are the only thing in her way from destroying the land of Men in the West."

"I thought she already destroyed it." Ruuk proffered.

Ordo raised his hand to silence Ruuk. Gorham looked to each of them, unsure of where this was going.

"You have merely thrown pebbles into a troll's lair, methinks," said Ordo.

"If she defeats us, she will surely raise an army of trolls to attack you!" Gorham tried to warn.

Furioso guffawed. Ordo and his sons merely stared at Gorham, who looked at them uncertain.

"Gorbogal has never defeated us troll hunters up here in the Crag Mountains! She has tried, but we bring her to ruin! And with no help from any of you soft Men of the Westfold, you who have failed, nor of the spindly corrupt Merchants of Telehistine! We make our own way up here, where no evil force can enslave us! We troll hunters are the ultimate fighting beast, undefeated and unmoved by the call of those who follow boys and girls!" Ordo boasted.

Gorham desperately ignored the insult. "That is why we need you! Your fighting prowess is beyond our skills. I know that. That is why I have come, to ask the blood of my father to aid us in our hour of need. We have fought the good fight and done all we can, but Gorbogal's eyes, and soon her army, will be upon us. We need our alliance reformed!" Gorham was leaning in now, livening with passion.

"No. We can't," Ordo said, waving a hand and keeping a stern grim face.

"I don't understand? Can't?" Gorham asked. He looked at their eyes as they glanced at each other, holding a secret it seemed. "Or won't?"

They all moved in unison, as if to remove a growing tension. They seemed fettered somehow and were releasing a strain.

"What is happening? Why can't you form an alliance with us?" Gorham slammed his tiny mauled fist onto the table. It was unimpressive.

Ordo could have easily risen and squashed this stranger in his land. But Gorham wasn't just a stranger.

"Nephew, your kingdom was lost. We heard nothing of it but doom. The Gorhammick line had ended. We knew nothing of you until minstrels came to our base camp and sang of your foolish exploits."

"Childish exploits!" Furioso added. Brok and Ruuk laughed, but Ordo sat and stared sternly. They settled down.

"Base camp? What is this? Where foreigners come? Minstrels cannot come up here? What do you mean by base camp?" asked Gorham, leaning in too close.

Ordo stood. The troll hunters in the tavern all became silent and looked at their leader. He looked down at Gorham, who sat sulking. "Ruuk, take him to the healing hut. Heal him. In the morning, we shall journey to the base camp. There, all your questions will be answered."

Gorham wanted to speak more, but Ordo suddenly turned, and in a blink of an eye he was out the door and gone.

Chapter Twenty-Nine

The New Order of Ordoh

Gorham awoke from a nightmare in a hot sweat. He was in his linens and on a very large wooden table with bestial fur as bedding. A roughhewn woman in troll hide and bone necklaces was taking care of him. She had troll tooth piercings and many tattoos. She looked like a witch shaman, mixing her pasty concoction in a large pestle and mortar.

He was in a large tent built out of a frame of evergreen timber. There were many bestial furs and skins, trophy skulls and bone furniture. Troll hunters did not waste much from their hunts.

The large woman easily manhandled Gorham as he tried to get up. She pushed him back down and reopened his linen shirt. He already had dried crusted paste on his ribs, wrapped in some strange wet animal skin.

She lathered the new paste roughly on his ribs. He winced, thinking it would hurt, but relaxed as she kneaded in the paste. "Three ribs are cracked. Your armour is tricky, huh?"

Gorham stared wide-eyed at the large yet darkly beautiful woman. Her hair was thick and black, wrapped in braiding bones and leather straps.

"Very good armour for a soft man. Your ribs will heal well with my powerful ointment. No fighting trolls for at least another day!" she said with an oddly cute wink.

Ruuk entered and kissed his bride. Gorham sighed in relief, escaping any fantasy toward the taken woman. Yet Gorham noticed a look in her face as she held her belly. Ruuk nodded to her, that all would be okay. She nodded back. Gorham cleared his throat and sat up.

Ruuk turned to him. "Our journey to the base camp is two days. Keep my wife's secret goo on your ribs, wrapped, ehy?"

Gorham nodded.

"Your armour and steed await!" Ruuk said, exiting the tent.

Gorham tightened his breastplate strap to keep his ribcage firm as it healed. He trotted along at a decent pace on his mare through thick grown evergreens and rocky outcroppings. It was a large forest, easily hiding trolls and giants. But he had no worry as two of the most skilled troll hunters trotted alongside him in their thick armour and heavy weapons.

They came to a cliff overlooking an expansive river system. Far below, the waterways created something of a marshland with plenty of river islands. It was thick with greenery and large buzzing insects. Giant mangrove like trees spread across the many fords. The trees grew thick and tall, their roots were exposed when the waterways were lower. This lead to a jungle like bramble of rooted tunnels and walkways.

"The base camp is down there!" Ruuk pointed.

Gorham rose up a bit in his saddle to look but saw only more of the same. "Not like you troll hunters to reside in such places."

"No, it isn't," Ruuk replied. "But we troll hunters don't mind a challenge once in awhile." He suddenly leapt off the cliff, sliding down the side, using the spike of his bardiche to catch himself with each hard landing. Then he leapt again from the cliffside rocks, latching onto the soft wood of giant mangroves.

Gorham gritted his teeth as he watched Ruuk leap downward with one violent impact after another. Brok turned and motioned for Gorham to go down a different path. There was a very narrow winding way cut into the cliff, going down at a dangerously steep tilt. Brok then leapt off, using his spear as a landing pole, vaulting from rock to tree limb and back.

Gorham got off his mare and whispered to her. She nodded and went her way through the forest. Gorham took a breath and then clambered down the steep ravine.

Before he landed, he could hear the troll hunter banter. Though the rocks and tightly grown mangroves muffled the voices, it still sounded as if many were there. It was more rancorous than what he heard in the Mountainside Tavern. When he came off the path, spread before him under the looming mangroves and amongst their exposed roots were many troll hunters. It was indeed some sort of base camp.

They had made a vast encampment at this raised river bed, where more smiths hammered away, and rows and rows of weapon racks were placed. Many were tarring their weapons to keep them from rusting. This tar gave the weapons a blackened quality and strengthened them. It most certainly weakened the sharp edge of the bladed side of the bardiches and glaives, but Gorham figured with the troll hunters' strength, a dull blade was still likely to hack whatever they swung at.

"You made it!?" Ruuk bellowed, coming forth from a large table where the hunters were feasting on a very gigantic cooked snake that was strewn across it. "I see your mount could not make it down here."

Just then, splashing through some puddles from the side of the cliff came Gorham's mare, neighing as troll hunters stepped aside. She leapt over mangrove roots and clomped easily through the muddy terrain to reach Gorham and nuzzle him.

Ruuk folded his arms and shrugged a positive affirmation. "Good steed."

"She's from a faerie queen – mysterious gift. We freed the faerie queen," Gorham said.

Ruuk gave a smug expression. "Saving faeries, a queen of faeries no less. Impressive."

Gorham wasn't sure if he was earnest or mocking. He petted his mare and whispered calmness to her.

Ruuk turned and went back to the snake smorgasbord. "Come, Sir Gorham! Serpent! Eat!"

The hunters easily chopped up the grilled giant snake with a draconian head. Gorham gave a slight wretch as he came near. Then he smelled the aroma and licked his lips. He suddenly and greedily found plenty of meat scraps left by the messy hunters amidst the line of rib bones and had enough large pieces of roasted serpent to eat.

"I will say, Ruuk, you hunters certainly eat well. This may be the secret to your prowess!" Gorham said.

Ruuk and Brok laughed, meat bits stuck to their rugged chins and armour.

Gorham was curious to understand and could not wait to know. "Why then are you here at this camp? Are you conquering the lowlands and the river areas then?"

Ruuk and Brok looked at each other, still chewing their food.

Ruuk ruminated. "That's not a bad idea, hey Brok. Very few mannish inhabitants here to make any claim to it. We never bothered with conquering. Our strength lies in the Crag Mountains. But to be conquerors! That would be a new era for us troll hunters!"

"Mmmm... I like it. We can conqueror Telehistine and take all their stored up treasure of silver and gold!" Brok said, grunting a laugh.

"What would you do with silver and gold and pretty things?" Gorham asked humorously.

The brothers laughed and agreed. But then they stopped and looked past Gorham. He turned to see Ordo standing amidst the busy troll hunters.

Ruuk sighed. "And now the inevitable. Gorham, to your uncle." Ruuk motioned with his food that Gorham must go to Ordo. Gorham took a last bit of juicy meat, eating it as he left the table.

Ordo turned and entered a massive tent of hides under a giant mangrove. The hides covered the roots. Within was the lair of Ordo at the base camp.

Gorham entered to see Ordo and Furioso sitting on mangrove benches. Gorham sat before them on a root. And though the root was the same height as the ones Ordo and Furioso sat on, he felt he was sitting below them.

Ruuk and Brok entered from behind and stood at the entrance. Gorham felt trapped.

The tent was kingly, in a fashion. Gorgeous and immense furs hung from the mangrove roots and huge troll skulls adorned poles and the frames of the tent's structure. Many skulls of beasts could be found in the furnishings as candle holders, bowls, and cups.

"The new order of Ordoh is what we are here at base camp for, to show you the prowess and intent of the troll hunters in this age of the fallen man," Furioso said with a severity Gorham found disconcerting. "We have gathered the troll hunters from near and far to this base camp. A mustering of the hunter brethren has been summoned. It has never been done before, a mustering for war."

"Uncle? What is this?" Gorham said quickly.

"Your uncle, leader of the troll hunters, has made an alliance already," Furioso answered. "With another."

Gorham was unsure, looking from Furioso to his uncle. Ordo's visage was stone graven, saying nothing, yet revealing everything.

Gorham stood. "No..."

Ordo nodded.

Chapter Thirty

Challenge and Betrayal

Gorham stood with sword and battered shield. He yelled a vicious roar, stepping forward. He stood in a circle of large burning torches amidst the great dancing shadows of mangrove trees. Betwixt and amongst the mangrove roots sat and stood the giant troll hunters, unmoved by his desperate call.

Before him stood Ordo, silent and foreboding, a giant with a huge iron cleaver, thankfully, with no spike.

"Surrender, cousin," Ruuk pleaded with disdain.

"Traitor to our cause, to the cause of mankind!" Gorham yelled with spittle and tears.

"Does he cry?" Furioso chortled.

"Father of Light! Father of Light! Give me the impossible! Give me this victory upon the darkness, the traitors of mankind!" Gorham yelled up into the darkness.

The troll hunters may have moved or rustled amongst the mangrove roots, but the only noise was the wafting flicker of large flames coming from the surrounding torches. They were gigantic, huge spears stuck into the ground with iron cauldrons atop, like metal claws holding flames.

Ordo stepped forward with his immense cleaver.

"You!" Gorham screeched. "Uncle! Brother of my father! Great brother of my weak father! Of the same mother! You betray our kind and surrender to Gorbogal!"

Ordo stopped. Ruuk shook his head, crossing his arms. Brok rubbed his chin.

"You were never defeated by her yet you take her coin as a mercenary!?" Gorham spit emotions as tears flowed behind his helm, easily seen in the shine of the fire's light. "You have become mercenaries for the witch of death, and she will enslave you in the end! She kills and enslaves all!"

"What is it? Kill or enslave?" Ruuk mumbled.

"Silence, weakling!" Ordo yelled, overtaking Gorham's weak cries. "The troll hunters serve no one but our own! Defeater of Gorbogal's armies, we've easily repelled her from our lands these twelve years while your people have cowered in defeat! And now we take her coin, we are the conquerors! We will take whatever we wish! Gorbogal pays us mightily, little nephew! She pays us in coin and treasures, depleting the palaces of the Telehistine provinces and your realm long ago. Better to have a powerful troll hunter rule the Westfold than some boy and girls! RIGHT, TROLL HUNTERS?!"

Ordo waved at his brethren surrounding the arena. They yelled and howled in an uproarious cheer that shook the mangroves and broke the spirit of Gorham. His sword faltered as did his step, flinching from the giant paces of Ordo.

"Weak nephew! Join us! JOIN US! Remove that boy and become conquerors like us! Gorbogal is just a step on our march to conquer and show the real power of man! Not weak men of the Westfold, but real men who are hunters and now CONQUERORS!" Ordo switched from seeking connection to his little nephew Gorham to arousing a roar from the maniacal hunters.

Gorham shook his head. "Never, uncle! Never will I betray man for her! That female dog witch! Never!"

Ordo flinched at such an insult. Though impressed and somewhat giddy, he laughed. "Hah, little nephew... there is still hope for you yet. I say, join us, and we will be the conquerors. We take her coin and her treasures, and we build our own path. And you, dear nephew, you can be King of the Westfold, under my rule! We join the Black Army of Gorbogal, who will lay siege on your unbuilt castle by next summer! Her army is of one hundred thousand trolls and orcs!

They have war trolls, black orcs amongst them! She will conquer your land! We troll hunters, four thousand strong, will be part of that victory. And we will reign over it!"

The troll hunters punched and hammered the mangrove roots, roaring and hollering. The mangroves shook violently as thick leaves and dust rained down.

Gorham listened and couldn't believe it. Next summer? An army of trolls, the foulest breed of war trolls, and the vicious black orcs? The black orcs know no pain and have armour embedded in their thick black hides. They have forked tongues, tusks and horns, and seem more like devils than goblins. Their warthog faces, like the vilest horrors, bring any sane man to a paralyzing fear. Only the most skilled and able of knights could fight them.

Gorham could see them in a sudden overwhelming vision, a vast army marching from the Black Spires of Gorbogal's nightmare breeding grounds. One hundred thousand? That was impossible! It would be a sea of evil swarming over the land. From thousands of wargs chasing down any who flee, to the power and might of black orcs – it was the end of the world of man. It would destroy all villages and farmsteads in its path, leaving a wake of destruction. It would then take over the lands of the Westfold, leaving all to ruin and waste once again. Even the army that felled his King Athelrod and a full complement of knights was a mere twenty thousand. And it was mostly of goblin and ratkin ilk. Gorham stood, envisioning a nightmare before his eyes. And then, "Four thousand Troll Hunters...?" He cried with a soft whimper.

Ordo could have attacked then and finished a paralyzed Gorham, but he spoke. "Her army was built to lay siege to Telehistine and all of its provinces. But now, Gorbogal must divert them toward your boy king, to finish him. And then she will move them south, giving me the throne of the Northern Kingdom. Join me, nephew! Join me and dethrone the weakness from your lands! Remove the boy king!"

"And the girls," Furioso spat.

Many around him guffawed and slapped his shoulders viciously and rowdily.

Gorham looked at the savage camaraderie all around him. He tried to wipe his dripping nose but only wiped his face plate. He quivered and knew this was his end. He pointed his sword at his great uncle. "For Alfred."

He charged.

Ordo immediately spun. Gorham's blade slashed but hit only hide and iron. Ordo used the back end of his cleaver to butt Gorham, sending him flying.

"Fool, the Order of Battle, to compel our leader, only seals our little cousin's fate," Ruuk said with a sigh.

"Poor cousin," Brok moped. "I wanted to, you know, get to know him."

Gorham got up quickly, shaking off the dread of unconsciousness. He turned quickly to see Ordo stand and wait. Gorham eyed Ordo's armour. It flowed with his movements. Gorham ran side to side, circling the great Ordoh Brutum. Gorham tried to rush around, to get Ordo to move. The only thing Ordo really moved were his eyes, as he rolled them. He did not even wear his helm.

The troll hunters began to boo and give thumbs down. Some laughed as others waved it off, turning to leave.

"None leave!" Ordo boomed. The troll hunters stopped and remained.

Gorham leapt suddenly, swinging his sword, and Ordo flinched. Gorham watched the leather and iron plates sway. Ordo suddenly flung his cleaver with an outward arc. The blade smacked Gorham's armour and flung him. Ordo looked, expecting to see blood on his blade, but it was clean. He looked at Gorham, who got up slowly.

Gorham straightened to look at his midsection. The armour held.

The troll hunters began to pay attention with interest. Some pointing and nodding.

"Impressive armour," Ruuk shrugged.

"For now," Brok said.

Gorham raised his sword. There was blood trickling from it. The troll hunters pointed in curiosity with many brows raised.

Ordo noticed it and wondered. He then looked down to see a cut under his arm. It was under the swaying leather and attached iron plates. It dripped.

"Whoa!" Ruuk said. Brok perked up. Furioso shifted on his seat but then shrugged and waved it off.

Ordo gritted his teeth, then took his cleaver in both hands, even as the slice trickled blood to his grip. He rushed forward, low and ready to swing. Gorham trotted back, trying to figure out the weight of Ordo's momentum. Yet Ordo swayed side to side quite evenly. Gorham saw his chance and charged in. He slashed and then twirled his sword to pierce Ordo's exposed underside, but he was too slow. Even moving at the fastest and most furious speed he could, Ordo was faster and stronger and more violent.

Gorham folded around Ordo's horrific cleaver. The heavy blade should have separated Gorham's torso from his legs as he bent over and received a gut-wrenching blow. Ordo realized he had not cleaved his nephew in two, for Gorham hung limp on his blade once again. He pulled the cleaver out, trying to add a devastating slice to the death blow.

Gorham flew less far, falling to the ground, crumpling under the pain and shock. Ordo twirled to show his cleaver again. This time there would be blood, no doubt, but he was stunned. It was as clean as before. The troll hunters gasped at the reveal, many nodding and wondering about the faerie armour.

"Bahh, just some elf magic," grunted Furioso.

"Pretty good elf magic," Brok added.

Ordo turned to see Gorham stagger up, using his sword like a cane. Once again Gorham's blade had more blood. It had blood on both edges as he wobbled.

Ordo opened his arms and looked down. He pulled open his leather skirting to see another slash. This one was larger and bleeding more. It was across his inner thigh.

"Okay, now that is impressive," Ruuk pointed.

Furioso's eyes widened.

Ordo's leg shook. He grimaced then gripped the wound. Blood came between his fingers. The hunters leaned forward to look closer.

"That's going to need sewing," Brok said calmly.

Gorham tried to stand steadily. His armour showed a crack across the stomach. Blood began to trickle. He held his ribs which had still not fully healed from before.

The troll hunters pointed. They were now confused. Who would be the victor? This was a strange revelation to behold.

Ordo lumbered toward Gorham with his cleaver low. Gorham steadied himself as best he could. Ordo's open hand held his own blood. His leg spewed forth more, but Ordo did not care. Gorham raised his sword. It shook violently as he readied his attack.

Ordo swung, clashing heavy cleaver against blade. Gorham tried twirling upward, nearly slicing into Ordo's neck. But Ordo had another idea. Jerking back, he lifted a boot and kicked Gorham with great power. Gorham slammed down against the ground hard. His horse neighed from beyond the torches, having been latched to a pole.

Gorham coughed a painful exhalation. He attempted to get up, but Ordo was now upon him with no mercy. Though Gorham raised his blade, Ordo's powerful swing cleaved through the blade and into Gorham's armour. This time it penetrated, and blood splatted. Gorham coughed up blood.

Ordo pulled the cleaver out of Gorham's limp body. The sound of iron scraping out of cut steel echoed across the branches of the mangrove trees.

Gorham coughed up more blood as blood seeped from the split armour. Ordo lifted his cleaver again to finish it. Ordo looked to see Ruuk standing between him and Gorham, his bardiche out. "Enough vatter. He may yet live."

Ordo lowered his cleaver. "If he lives, cage him." Ordo turned to leave and misstepped upon his wounded leg.

Chapter Thirty-One

Cage

Gorham coughed up more blood. He squirmed in blood and tears, spittle and bile. He wanted to die. His hands were tied with leather straps to a table.

"Oh, fool of a weakling man!" Ruuk's wife yelled, rushing from another concoction she was mixing to push him back down.

"Let me die," he gurgled.

"Oh you will, fool!" she argued. "But Ordo wants you alive for now. And oddly, Ruuk wants you alive as well."

"As his prisoner!" Gorham wailed.

"Yes," she said. Something in her saw the raw emotion on his face, the suffering when one realizes he has been betrayed, by family, by salvation. "Live and you can fight again, one day..." She did not know why she said that. She held his torso in, tight, to keep whatever she had done, intact.

He lay surrendered, breathing as blood and saliva trickled from his mouth. She gently wiped it. He felt the gentleness and looked up at her face. Her eyes were moist. She looked away before he realized he had a chance to affect her.

Gorham fixed his gaze on her.

She spoke. "You must lie still. I've sewn your stomach. If it breaks, the acid will spew forth and dissolve your innards. I used the gut of a hog as the thread. I've sewn the muscles of your torso. Do not use them to sit up or they'll tear again. I've lathered expensive ointments in layers within your flesh to cleanse and heal the cords

177

quickly. They will put you in a cage soon. The hunters are impatient that way. I must heal you at Ruuk's and my expense, using all we know to heal hunters and their grievous wounds."

Gorham closed his eyes and breathed softly.

"You are strong, Gorham, for a little man. It must be that troll hunter blood in you," she said.

"I have no hunter blood in me, no traitorous blood that would owe a single drop to that witch and her Dark Lord," Gorham said softly.

"That witch came from the blood line of King Athelrod," Ruuk said from the entrance of the tent of healing. He entered and stood above Gorham. "If anyone is a traitor and guilty of all this devilry, of all these wars against man, it would be your boy king, right? Is he not from that cursed line? You, serving a boy king of a traitorous blood?"

Gorham stared at his cousin, seething but unable to move, paralyzed by the pain and restraints. "We fight this tyranny. We do not serve it for coin."

Ruuk leered. "And now you are a prisoner of it. Not a great end to your noble struggle."

Gorham again tried to sit up, but Ruuk easily pushed him down and pressured his wound. Gorham grimaced and seethed in pain.

"Stop it, husband!" Ruuk's wife said. "You made me come all this way to heal him, use all of my healing magic, and then you torture him. He is still kin!"

"Foolish kin," said Ruuk, releasing and turning away. "How many more days till he gains his strength?"

Ruuk's wife thought as she tended Gorham. "Many."

When Gorham sat in his cage, he looked gaunt and emaciated. He still held his bandaged torso but was on the way to recovery from a most deadly gut wrenching wound. He was still exhausted as troll hunters crisscrossed his blurred vision. He lay amongst decent furs within an iron cage under a mangrove tree. He was in sight of Ordo's great tent and could see the blurry giant figure come in and out of the dwelling often. There was much activity in the base camp. Troll hunter brood after brood showed up to meet and greet their leader at his abode.

Cage

Gorham awoke early one cold morning, shivering in his stale fur bedding to see a giant bulbous and quite grotesque frog looking at him. It shot its tongue out, sucking his bare foot toward its mouth. Gorham wriggled to free himself but the sticky tongue was stronger. His foot was forced to extend out past the cage as the frog sought to engulf it.

To troll hunters, these bestial frogs are a delicacy, and soon enough a spiked hammer slammed down upon the warty beast. A troll hunter yanked it up, freeing Gorham's bare foot.

Gorham watched as a group of them roasted the sickly creature and ate it. He fell asleep in his various nightmares of vast troll armies and the burning of the Westfold. He had many nights with hot fevers as red and sweaty as a devil and other nights with cold chills, dry and shivering as a fish flopping on ice.

Smiths hammered away at more weapons and war-fitted armour. It went on even as the days became colder and winter began to set upon this marshy riverbed. Groups and more groups, broods and brethren, came through. The base camp was getting fuller and spreading across the island mounds.

It never became too cold here. Ruuk's wife tended to Gorham, even as the marshland changed from hot and sweaty to misty and cool. She fed him and tended his wounds daily. Ruuk walked by many times but kept his distance and was always busy bantering in their hunter tongue to other hunters. And all of them were talking about Gorham and the boy king and laughing.

Chapter Thirty-Two

Escape

In the early spring, as the sun began to dry up the mist and cold dew, Gorham became strong enough and healed enough to stand in his cage. Ruuk allowed him, in shackles, to tend to his horse, who was growing sickly chained to a large mangrove tree.

"Please, you must let her go," Gorham pleaded with Ruuk. "She needs to run. She needs the grass of the plains for nourishment."

"Bah, let her enchanting magic sustain her, huh Gorham? She's enchanted and faerie," said Ruuk snidely.

"Please," Gorham said, gently touching his weakened mare with his shackled hands.

"No."

In the heavy rain as most remained in their tents, Gorham's mare reached up to bite off leaves, the few left it could reach from the mangrove tree it was chained to. Its hooves sank unsteadily into the mud and its own waste. It tried to rear up to the leaves, extending its sickly tongue to grasp the greenery. It finally gave up and stood quivering in the deluge. Gorham watched from his cage, whispering to his mare what he could.

On one sunny day Ruuk's wife came up to his horse, unsteady and unsure. She had a bundle of grass. His mare neighed and leapt in fear, being slammed back down by the chain. Ruuk's wife looked to Gorham a distance away. Gorham sat up and whispered something odd. She wondered as his horse suddenly calmed and came to her.

She looked with apprehension, unsure of the beauty of this steed. Horses were not part of her life. The mare gently tugged at the grass offering and then ate from the bundle. Ruuk's wife, it seemed, had not seen such a beautiful creature – and up close. The horse stood close to her and allowed her to touch its neck and muzzle as it gently chewed away at the grass. The eyes of the horse seemed like deep-set gems to her, alive and with a spirit of a beautiful child.

The horse suddenly nuzzled her, and she couldn't help but giggle. She said gently, "My name is Shyrha." She then gasped, wondering why she spoke and to whom.

She looked to Gorham in dream filled joy and nodded. Gorham sunk against the cage, relieved that, well -- that relief and nourishment were given to his mare. Shyrha then retrieved a bucket of clean water and let the horse drink mightily from it. She smiled as she caressed the mare. Gorham noticed that her tummy was becoming more noticeable, with child.

Fortunately, Gorham avoided staring too long, to avoid letting Ruuk or Brok or even Ordo notice that Ruuk's wife now tended the horse more than Gorham.

Gorham grew strong in the cage even though he was confined. Something, his anger or maybe his sense of pride, kept him strong.

"You're healing well, my little cousin," Ruuk said, standing there with Brok.

Gorham nodded, somewhat waking from a bored daze.

"Our army is nearly four thousand strong. Summer is coming upon us, and Gorbogal's army is marching. When this is all over, Ordo, our vatter and your uncle, may still consider his offer to you. He was impressed by your swordsmanship. When he sits, Gorham, you'll be proud to know, many have asked of his intimate scar!"

Ruuk and Brok laughed, nodding to Gorham.

"Never!" Gorham yelled, slamming up against the cage. "I serve King Alfred! And King Alfred will end your nonsense, your betrayal! He will defeat you as he has defeated every dark force before you!"

Ruuk and Brok rolled their eyes at their little brethren. They tried to hold it in but began chortling.

"You laugh a lot. You have not yet met my king," said Gorham, plopping back down and looking away.

Ruuk suddenly rushed the cage, slamming his fist against it, roaring with rage, "Impudent fool! A boy! You speak of a boy!"

The cage rocked, tussling Gorham, who merely rolled with it and stared back at Ruuk with angry eyes.

Ordo came out of his tent, peering at Ruuk. Furioso tugged at Ordo to return to whatever business was occurring within. Many troll hunters, with much business about the impending march, were waiting.

Ordo walked over.

"Oh, here comes vatter," Brok said under his breath.

"Is he as stubborn as ever?" Ordo asked, peering at his nephew.

Gorham couldn't help but notice through Ordo's battle skirt the scar he had given him. Ordo looked down at Gorham.

"We march in a fortnight. Already the spreading of calamity and desolation is occurring. Your kingdom shows no defense, no resistance, and does not protect its borders or the mannish folk there in. All flee before the power and might of Gorbogal's Black Army."

Gorham suddenly stood, surprising the brothers and their father. "Her black army has not yet confronted King Alfred!"

Brok shifted. Ruuk threw up his arms and shook his head at Ordo.

"I will keep my offer to you, for my brudder's sake, to the end, Gorham. You are still blood kin," Ordo said. He turned to go back to the tent but in so doing stopped and spoke again without looking back at Gorham. "You must decide before I kill your boy king. For when that day comes and you do not join us, you will meet his fate."

Shyrha spoke to Ruuk. "Let me take Gorham's poor horse to the fields. She needs to run about and eat the grass thereof." Shyrha's tummy was larger, extending beyond her furs and leather. Ruuk caressed it, as if in a dream.

"Let me take Gorham's horse to the fields," she said more assertively.

Ruuk looked at the horse. It was dirty and muddy, still chained to the mangrove. It looked weak and stiff. He shrugged. She kissed him. "I'll only be a little while."

"Keep the chain firm!" Ruuk said after her. She nodded, kissing him again.

She hustled past many busy smiths and hunter warriors carrying on about their preparations for their march and war. The horse came up to her and nuzzled her again. She giggled as she petted the diminutive horse and unraveled the chain from the mangrove.

Gorham looked with great interest, rising up just a bit from the fur bed to peer at them a distance away. Shyrha looked over to him, giving him a caring wink. He whispered something. Shyrha found it odd that Gorham was whispering. She wondered to whom?

The horse nodded as she pranced behind Shyrha, following her. The horse came up and nuzzled Shyrha's neck and made Shyrha giggle.

Then the mare chomped on Shyrha's hand, surprising her. Her hand released, and the horse grasped the chain from it and turned, knocking her into the mud. She held her tummy to protect her child from the fall. Gorham gritted his teeth. Was she hurt?

The mare charged through the hammering smiths and their forge fires, knocking over weapon wracks and smithing tables. The troll hunter smiths were slow to respond, not expecting any sort of an attack or raucous activity as they spent hours upon tiresome hours toiling away in preparation. The chain swung to and fro hitting against and knocking over many iron contraptions.

The mare gained incredible speed. Eventually the chain caught on to something as the horse leapt into the air. The chain broke, twirling violently into the air as hunter smiths ducked and leapt from hot irons and flying bits of chain.

The black steed then raced right at Gorham, who stood up waving her on. Ordo charged out of his tent to see what was amiss. He saw the steed charge to Gorham, suddenly turn and kick the cage door. The entire cage shook but the gate held.

Gorham waved again. The horse neighed loudly, kicking again and again. The cage rattled severely as Gorham held on.

Ordo gritted his teeth and quickly rushed back into his tent. He pulled his great spear and rushed out again. He roared as he saw the gate was now open and Gorham leapt upon his mount.

Gorham stared straight at him, hugging his horse, clinging fiercely to her mane as his bridle. Ordo threw his spear most viciously. He could see Gorham speaking to her. The steed suddenly reared as the spear flew under her and tore through a stone forge, obliterating it and sending hot molten iron in all directions.

Gorham, upon his steed, raced off. For a split moment, Ordo saw Shyrha getting up. She stared at him with fearful eyes holding her belly. Ordo roared and raced off, yelling orders to the troll hunters. "Stop him! Stop the horse! Do not let him escape!"

Troll hunters from across the camp suddenly reared with great spears and battleaxes.

Ruuk and Brok rushed out of their tent to see Gorham racing his steed through the mangroves down the river. Ruuk stared at his wife and then at her embrace of her tummy. She nodded okay to him, indicating that she was alright. He sighed in relief and then, turning his eyes to the scene of Gorham escaping, growled silently.

Ruuk pointed to the cliffs at Brok. They nodded and raced towards the cliffs and quickly ascended them.

A troll hunter stood in front of Gorham and his mare and threw his giant spear. The steed stepped quickly to one side as the spear landed thickly into the mud next to them. The hunter was taken aback by such a quick move.

Then the horse raced off, sprinting across vast mud isles, fords and river ways. It seemed to race effortlessly across various surfaces with the same speed. Gorham clung to his mare, feeling the freedom of the wind. To any orc army or force of men, none would be able to make chase. The troll hunters, though much heavier, could leap and bound with great prowess.

They kept up for a while, landing spears and axes against mangroves and mud as the horse leapt through a deathly rain of weapons. But soon enough the troll hunters tired and faltered amidst the deep slow river or soft suctioning mud. Or they would fall from branches not meant for such powerful blades and swinging bestial men.

Gorham saw a narrow bend with steep cliff walls. He kicked her on, growling for more speed. She complied and raced to a narrow ravine where the river tightened, leaving only narrow banks.

Ruuk and Brok were above, racing along the cliff top, but they were too late. Gorham's steed made it to the edge, where the river's many falls cascaded down in white roars, down a series of rock levees, and spilled into the wide expanse of the Southron Lakeways. To the west, down rock clefts and steppes, was a forest where Gorham and his mount could make their escape. But at the crest, Gorham and his mare froze and stared.

For below him were thousands of fires, smoke columns wafting into a black-ridden air. What was once, from his childhood a memory, a vast lake forest and fishing village, was now a burnt desolation. He saw the village and its many water structures gone, burnt and scattered. Its people, villagers, and families were gone or much worse. And spread across the barren shattered land were thousands upon thousands of beastmen – orcs and goblins in fire camps, war trolls and mountain trolls in a myriad of groups scattered about with servant goblins. There were wagons upon wagons, cages and cauldrons. It appeared that this vast army far below was beginning its march westward, to the Westfold.

"Woe to the Westfold," Gorham gasped. "Woe to man. Woe to my king!"

His horse neighed in panic. It was too late.

Ruuk and Brok, with a giant leather net meant for trolls, threw it with great spears from above. It wrapped with heavy stones upon them, battering them as they fell into the netting and on the hard wet stones of the rushing river.

Ruuk and Brok pulled them up from the water that spilled through the ravine into the widening valley below. Gorham's mare neighed in pain and panic as it struggled in the constricting net. Gorham merely lay crumpled within, staring at the Black Army of Gorbogal.

Brok swung the net and dropped it hard on a landing next to the river. Gorham's horse whinnied upon the painful impact. Gorham convulsed, being strangled by the netting and his limbs battered by his own horse.

Brok and Ruuk landed next to them. Ruuk kicked the horse while Brok stomped on it. The horse shook in shock at the violent pain but had no strength left to cry.

"No! No! Please! Suffer me the torment but not the innocent creature!" Gorham wailed.

"Not so innocent!" yelled Ruuk, kicking again. "It hurt my wife and nearly killed my child!"

Above, Ordo walked to the edge of the cliff, looking down. "Ruuk!"

Ruuk looked up after one last kick.

Ordo suddenly slammed down upon the ground. They all shook as if an earthquake crept upon them. Even the edge of the river splashed a spray of water at his impact. Ordo stood tall and could see over the waterfalls to the Lakeways and beyond. He could see the vast spread of the Black Army marching.

"They will be marching day and night now. The beastmen do not tire when sorcerers compel them onward, in darkness or in the hot bright sun," Ordo said, above the roar of the falls. He turned to look down at Gorham trying to reach his quivering and battered mount.

Ordo stepped to Gorham and easily ripped open the leather net, pulling Gorham out like a doll. Gorham hung limp, shivering with broken ribs, a broken arm, a smashed hand, a cracked skull, a blood-wrought eye, battered and bleeding legs, and all his spirit broken. Ordo couldn't help but smile.

"Look, little nephew," Ordo said, carrying him to the edge of the fall, to set his eyes upon the desolation and the march. "The Black Army of Gorbogal. Built to besiege the corrupt and divided houses of Telehistine, now marching westward to the Westfold to annihilate a tiny thorn, a boy, you claim to be king. I suppose I should be impressed that the witch must give your boy king and his girls this much attention. Because a few foolish knights could not defend the land. Pathetic knights! This world of men will fall, and greater men will rule." Ordo looked at his broken nephew and roared, "JOIN US!"

"NEVER!" was the sudden spat by Gorham, who had nothing left as he convulsed in shock and pain.

Ordo looked at Gorham with rage in his eyes. Then he looked down at the cascading waterfalls and the harsh rocks. He twitched in his grip of his nephew. His jaw tightened. He then looked at Gorham, ready to end this. Gorham looked at the rocks, ready to meet them.

Ruuk stepped forward, a hand raised, not wanting this end for his cousin.

Brok bent down, looking at the unmoving horse. He snickered and lifted up the netting to see. "Hey, what's horse taste like?"

Ordo suddenly awoke from his anger and smiled. He turned to look at Brok. Gorham looked up from his misery.

Brok removed the netting to expose the horse and pulled out a long knife.

Ordo then glanced, noticing Gorham seem to whisper, "Escape. Warn them."

Suddenly, the mare leapt, however many gashes it had with torn skin flaps that exposed flesh. It limped on one leg with some strange enchantment. It leapt up and twisted in front of Brok, landing with its rear to Brok. Strange magical lights flitted about it as one of its legs popped straight again. Brok looked oddly at the lights.

He smiled, unaware of what horses, mighty enchanted horses, could do. Ruuk waved his arms for Brok to react to the danger. Brok merely shrugged at his brother, unconvinced of any danger.

Ordo tried to yell but merely watched, knowing the inevitable.

The mare hind-kicked Brok with such ferocity that Brok could not even react with troll hunter instincts. He flew back, rolling over rocks and plopping into the river. The horse then sprung past Ruuk's open-arm dive and leapt over the waterfalls. Ordo merely stood, holding Gorham, and watched in a daze.

The beautiful mount seemed to fly past him as the sun shone upon its tortured hide. It seemed to look at them, passing by, landing below upon the clefts and rocks, like the greatest of troll hunters. Ordo merely watched as it escaped westward down into the forests that braced up against the mountainside and away from the Black Army to the south.

He saw glints of the steed through the trees, racing away. Brok splashed and rolled. Ruuk leapt after him and handed him his bardiche. Brok reached the weapon and was pulled out. "I can't swim!"

Ordo snorted then looked at Gorham. "You think your magical horse's warning will matter? You think anything you do matters? Your boy king will fall, and I will be the conqueror! I am sick of you. Die with your line!" He lifted him higher to toss him.

"Don't kill him, vatter," Ruuk said, tugging Brok back up to the shore. Both were now wet and breathing hard. Brok lay with severe chest pains. "Let him see! Let him see our victory and know the truth!"

Ordo hesitated as he was not convinced and was ready to throw Gorham away.

Ruuk tried again. "Let him see his boy king fall!"

Ordo paused and looked at his beaten nephew dangling from his powerful grip. He couldn't help but leer at him.

Ordo walked back and stood above Ruuk and Brok, holding Gorham. "He will be at the front of us, when we attack Grotham Keep, to see the fall of the Westfold."

Ruuk nodded.

Ordo dropped Gorham down next to Ruuk. "Crucify him!"

Chapter Thirty-Three

The March of the Barbarians

Gorham was shackled to a pole on a cart. Two mountain goats were reined to it. He lay crumpled in the cart with his hands painfully hung from the iron rings. He was slumped in his tattered linens, a beaten gaunt man. He was the larger of the knights, having brawn and stature, but now was reduced to a tortured soul.

Ruuk seemed pleased at his contraption. Brok did not look impressed. He plopped a few provisions next to Gorham, bedding and meager supplies.

Ruuk shrugged. "What? At least I didn't crucify him. He should survive the march."

"Vatter said to crucify him," Brok said sadly.

"He meant hang him up, in bondage, till we get there. That was the deciding factor. This weakling has no strength to be shackled spread eagle across a beam! Everything in him is broken. Besides, vatter wants him to see the fall of his boy king!" Ruuk chortled.

Brok shrugged.

Horns blared. Loud deep baritone horns echoed across the base camp and river valley. Troll hunters used horns made from iron. They looked like they were formed from discarded glaives or battle axes.

"Well, brudder, it be time. We march!" Ruuk said. He tapped the goats with his bardiche. They neighed a bit and then began to pull their load.

The March of the Barbarians

Troll hunters formed in broors, a type of grouping, marching along the fords downriver. It was a mass of the most ferocious looking men. Their helms were charcoal black, with iron spikes as horns, teeth, and ridges. Their helms represented different beasts, whether tusk-like, fang-like or horned. Their furs and irons were bulky and worn over muscular scarred bodies full of ferocity and vigor. Though their armoured bodies seemed larger than life, it was their weapons that truly carried the epitome of their prowess. Many had large thick spears, polearms with blackened blades. All had large extended iron spikes. Many had large bardiches, long battle axes with picks sticking out as scary spikes. Their weapons were as long or tall as they. Some of the blades were as big as shields. And they carried all of that with aplomb.

The broors came out from many encampments spread across the river system. They hailed each other as they joined, and the army grew. Because of their skill in the mountains, the cascading falls where Gorham was caught and his steed escaped was an easy descent. Dozens upon dozens dropped from terrace to terrace amidst the roaring waters.

Ruuk and Brok led their cart, with Gorham shackled, down what seemed a treacherous path next to the falls. The troll hunters had some skill with carts and goats, using them for trading with each other and the transporting of troll slaughter in the difficult terrain of the mountains. A train of many carts followed behind them, holding many provisions and supplies with a few younger hunters as their guides.

As they came to the Southron Lakeway, they marched around the perimeter, passing the desolated fishing village. The village still smoked. No life was present. There were the tell-tale signs of boats, huts, nets, pots and pans, showing what was once, now gone in a nightmare. Brok noticed a burnt doll hanging from a branch nearby. What had happened? He chose not to think about it.

Gorham was able to look up with his meager strength, breathing hoarsely. "This is who you joined with?"

Ruuk and Brok did not respond, silent in their bestial helms, marching along.

Many goblins rushed about, doing the bidding of larger beasts. The terrain was barren of plant and woods, all of that having been scoured to feed the thousands of fires. Left behind were smoldering fires, one after the other, choking the air and burning whatever was left. Gorham choked, coughed and persevered, hanging from the pole. Goblins scampered by, curious at this ragged prisoner. Brok had to swing his weapon to disperse them.

The troll hunters snarled at any goblins or orcs that came too close. The goblin kind quickly moved out of their way, keeping to themselves. Ordo then led the troll hunters past what seemed like giant walls of trolls with huge warhammers and spiked tree limbs. The spikes were merely giant nails hammered through carved lumber, wrapped with animal hides.

There were mountain trolls, war trolls, black trolls, black orcs and goblins spread throughout the vast army. And to manage it all were various sorcerers and their helpers.

The lumbering mountain trolls being larger, about fifteen feet in height, had a crude fat look to them. They were like beasts of burden, like giant oxen. They pushed and pulled the war towers or carried vast roped nettings of boulders, supplies or timber. The mountain trolls stuck out as the pinnacle giants amidst this army, carrying the most.

The marching war trolls, were smaller, but still giant at about ten feet in height, were more muscular, had fitted thick-cut armour plates and fashioned warhammers or crafted giant spears. Some had giant falchions or square-cut swords, others squat thick cleavers. Though crude, they were crafted of thick iron. They carried only their own giant weapons. They were the tanks of this Black Army of bestial men. Their bodies were like those of erect gorillas, lumbering forth ready to attack with great pounding weapons.

And then there were the skulking black trolls. These were quite unique and seemed of similar caliber to the troll hunters. Upon seeing each other, the two groups nearly began a tussle. But a sorcerer in black robes riding in a large war chariot kept them at bay. The black trolls, only slightly bigger than the hunters, had a strange shiny tone of black. Their skin seemed more serpentine, scaly and metallic. Their faces had a more defined look than those of regular trolls. Their features were more man-like yet demonic. They stood erect and walked with a supple gait, as if ready to leap and bound with much ferocity. They bore small thick horns, bloodshot red eyes and sharp white teeth. They wore tight-fitting leathers and straps with minimal armour plates. Their weapons, swords and glaives were made of some sort of evil enchanted steel, shiny and bright.

Beyond those thousand black trolls were tens of thousands of rambling black orcs. These too had a darker tone than normal green or grey orcs. The black orcs were larger, usually with thick white tusks. They bore larger muscles and had a more upright stance. They also had the unique quality of sticking armour plates within their skin, sewing it in place. They were known for not feeling much pain. So this type of seemingly torturous bodily accouterments was the norm, not the rarity. Piercings and scarification abounded amongst this rabble. And they too wanted to harass the troll hunters as they marched aside them.

Sorcerers, in various chariots and wagons, controlled their eager goblin kinds, using strong spells and booming voices, speaking in an ancient and evil tongue. Fortunately, the chariots and wagons were pulled by fat horned dragons and rhinos, which created great barriers to keep the orc and troll kinds in line.

Still, it was the magic of the sorcerers that constantly needed to be evoked. Their dark magics and black words controlled the goblin, orc, and troll kinds, keeping them from fighting others and their own. The sorcerer leaders were in bedizened chariots made with richly wrought gem-encrusted metals and covered with many runes and markings.

There were also zealots and acolytes stationed with specific troll or orc groups, and they were constantly tested by the bestial men. They rushed about on foot or grouped together in crude wagons. Their tasks were many, but the most important was to support the sorcerers or help any goblin and orc war chiefs to enforce order and obedience.

"Their sorcerers drive the trolls and orcs on, even in the hottest, brightest sun! You sure this is a good idea?" Brok asked Ruuk quietly.

Ruuk ignored his brudder as he scanned the vast Black Army before him.

Beyond, in the smoke and dust, past layers upon layers of marching spears and glaives, past jutting troll heads and a sea of bobbing orc heads, he could just see a looming vast tower. It lumbered forward, pulled by a train of great dragons. These behemoths had long necks, long tails and vast bodies with fore and hind legs as big as trees. They pulled it slowly but surely. The Great Tower had giant spikes circumventing its square top. It was built of layer upon layer of thick wood and metal sidings, and it flew many banners and flags, all marked with crude depictions of skulls, fangs, daggers, and eyes. These markings denoted different war clans and orc gangs.

191

The March of the Barbarians

Goblins traversed its varied surface, along the areas with openings and balconies. Horns blared from different ones, each with its own sound. Banners were waved notifying different sects. It was the center of command and the conductor of this horrific symphony.

"Is she there? The witch?" Brok gasped quietly.

"No..." Ruuk whispered back, succumbing to a sense of foreboding. "A great warlock, the powerful servant of Gorbogal and general of this vile army resides in there. A hundred sorcerers and their ilk serve him."

The Great Siege

Chapter Thirty-Four

The Spring Before

"What in blazes did Alfred do this time?" Captain Hedor said atop the walls of Grotham Keep. Winter had finally passed and it was the beginning of spring.

Cory, in his splendid armour, rushed up the white stone stairs to see the view in the distance, while Wilden and the boys trained amidst the busy gnomes and men working on the castle walls. "I want to see! It's Alfred! They're back!"

"Back and with company!" Hedor huffed.

They watched with wide eyes as Alfred waved from the road down the slope. Several small carts pulled by moorland goats slowly rolled up. A herd of the same goats followed behind. There was a large group of children spread amongst them.

"Oh boy... more children..." Hedor said.

Cory rushed down and called the boys. They hurried out the gate and down the road.

"I guess he's got us some more warriors, hey Captain?" Ruig said with a wry smile.

Hedor rolled his eyes. "This children warrior thing may be a bit overdone... Couldn't he have recruited some of those northern moorland ruffians?"

"Aye, a tough lot, slogging through that mud year round. Could use a few thousand of them indeed," Ruig sighed. "But... looks like we've got more children. Just what we needed."

"And to feed," sighed Hedor.

"They brought goats," Ruig noticed.

"Indeed. Mounts no doubt... for the *kid cavalry!*"

Alfred, Verboden, Loranna, and Nubio ushered the children into the grounds. King Gup and the gnomes came out to help and were quite curious about the goats. Families who once lived in the moors came to see the goats and help in their care. They were eager to hear the great news from Verboden, that the curse in the land was lifted. There were many hugs and cries as Verboden the Cleric was tossed to and fro from hugging mothers and wives of the People of the Downs.

Harkonen, still weak, lay within a cart. He sat up, and for the first time in many many long tragic months, a faint smile tweaked the side of his mouth. He felt his face and mouth, trying to discern what was forming on it.

"Are you okay?" Nubio asked.

Harkonen shuddered a nod. "I think I'm smiling? Am I?"

Nubio smiled and nodded yes.

The children rushed along by caring women, pointed at the castle, at the gnomes, and most importantly at the food brought out. They cried and laughed, squealed and screamed. There was an utter joy, overcoming their previous despair... an utter, utter joy.

Alfred noticed that the walls were nearly done. He looked up, twirling about. They were of a white granite stone, solidly cut by the gnomes, perfectly fitted. It was amazing to behold. He blinked and blinked as he circled in place.

Gib and Pep came up to him. Gib spoke. "We worked all winter, Alfred. It's nearly done. The walls, that is. Just a few more weeks! Plus many of your surprises were included. Your defenses, milord!"

Alfred looked down at Gib, smiling. "This is amazing! The walls are so high! I never imagined it was going to be this uh... puh... ponderous!"

"Ooh... hah hah... I like that word! Ponderous it is!" Gib chuckled. Pep stood proud, hands on his hips, swaying back and forth.

The children settled in groups amidst the wide courtyard. It was still filled with a cavalcade of scaffolding and tents. Lady Nihan was beside herself trying to comfort and feed the new set of two hundred mouths. She wanted to complain to Abedeyan and Verboden and her king, but she saw the children and knew she had to do whatever it took.

Sir Murith came in last, as he kept watch of the rear. He made sure the sick and weak children on several carts were handled delicately. The Khanafian women with the infants were also under his protection... or more like care. When Lady Nihan came to see the babies, her tears flowed. She and the maids hugged the Khanafian nurses and took up the infants.

The Khanafian men and women of Grotham Keep also came to welcome the two nurses and their charges. It was a strange meeting, coming from such tragic bitterness to a realization of one's full liberation and joy of freedom.

The Khanafians cried and wailed together in their ancient tongue. They seemed to crowd around the young nurse, wailing for her as she stood. Murith noticed as she looked upon him. There was something about her, which the Khanafians knew, but he did not. Sir Murith thought on it only a moment as he had much to attend to now.

First and foremost, they needed to build a stockade for the goats. They decided to build one right outside the castle in the field so they could milk them often, letting them pasture nearby.

Hedor and Ruig were assigned this task. Hedor muttered something about being a captain and security but wasn't inclined to argue with Lady Nihan, especially with her arms crossed.

Abedeyan worked with the gnomes and men to situate the children. The Great Hall was still just ruined walls and lots of scaffolding. The demolition of the old structure and towers had not yet occurred. Lord Dunther, who was still away, wanted the main walls done first, the defenses ready at all costs. Still, Abedeyan found shelter for them all. It was spring, so the weather was warming, but the nights were bitter cold.

The Spring Before

The old tower, in ruin and shambles, was still used, as were the old kitchens, chapel, and various rooms in the rear of the old Keep and Great Hall. The ladies resided in their cloistered rooms, albeit with cannonball openings, which they covered with woven straw.

Alfred pondered as Abedeyan and Lady Nihan situated sleeping quarters with straw and linen bedding amidst the ruins. "Wow, where I come from," he said, tottering on the old rubble from ogre cannon fire, "these buildings would be condemned, and they'd have police tape across them: 'Do Not Cross'... But here, boy, we just use it all. Uh, King Gup, could this be dangerous? Could it collapse any time?"

King Gup looked at the rubble and skeletal stone ruin. "This, ah well, shouldn't be so bad. It's survived ogre cannon fire!" He pounded the stone wall and nodded an okay.

A large stone dropped, smashing in two on his head. He blinked. "Right, let's move everyone out of here. Children in tents out beyond the walls till we clear it all."

A large procession of children, in the cold evening, had to be marched out.

Captain Hedor, Ruig and his men, in the evening light with many oil lamps, just finished the gate to the goat stockade. "Hoy, ho! Done in record time! Good job, men!" Hedor threw his hammer down and gave a big ruckus laugh, sweaty and filthy as ever. They all high-fived and stretched their achy bones. "All I need now is a good rest in my comfy tent!"

"Look!" Ruig pointed.

Up the slope came Lady Nihan and her maids with rolled up straw and linen bedding, and behind her a procession of many children, ready for sleep. The cart with infants was also slowly brought forth. The Khanafian nurses were dedicated to their task.

"You've got to be kidding!" sighed Hedor.

"Hey... goats, children...kidding..." Ruig shuddered.

"Hedor!" Lady Nihan cried.

"It's Captain Hedor, milady!"

"Right, Captain Hedor, my apologies," the frazzled and sleepy Lady Nihan replied.

"Apologies accepted!" Hedor interjected.

"We need sleeping quarters for these children! And it is getting dark and cold!" Lady Nihan stated sternly.

"What about the ruins?!" Captain Hedor waved up at Grotham Keep.

"The ruins are in ruin and dangerous for the children!" Lady Nihan said.

"Well, they slept in the wild all these days they marched," Ruig mumbled to Hedor and not to Lady Nihan.

"Yes, milady, they can sleep out here in the field then..." Hedor grumbled.

Lady Nihan glowered at him.

Hedor scratched his chin. "They could sleep here next to their goats?"

Lady Nihan continued her glowering as the children congregated around them. Many were yawning in their big scraggy hair and nodding as they leaned together.

Ruig tapped on Hedor's shoulder. "The worker tents?"

Hedor turned. "The worker tents? OUR tents?"

"Those will do just fine!" Lady Nihan said and motioned for the children. In a swell or herd, the children suddenly moved as one large group and headed to the tents and pavilions.

Hedor turned and looked at his men, who had glum, tired faces.

"For the children," Ruig shrugged.

Hedor rolled his eyes as the men plopped down hay and straw amidst the rubble and ruins.

Alfred peered from above with a candle. "Hey, what are you doing here?"

Hedor looked up. Alfred was on a precarious stone ledge. "Sleeping in the dangerous ruins of the Keep! And you, King? What are you doing here?"

"Oh, my room is fine. I'm sleeping there."

"A room?" Hedor posited. "Must be wonderful. A roooom."

"Well, I am the king," Alfred shrugged.

"Right you are King Alfred. Right you are," Hedor said, covering his face with a dirty work hood.

Alfred meekly retracted from the ledge.

Verboden brought a small bowl of soup, bread, farmer's cheese and a pitcher of water into the chapel. Though the rear was blown out and rubble filled half the room, Verboden used it as his quarters.

A small fire in an open pit amidst a circle of small rubble had been built by Verboden long ago. Brother Harkonen sat on a stool and stared over the fire, at the symbol, the circle atop a post. Verboden set the food down on a small bench for Harkonen. The brother sat stoically, looking at the circle.

"It is empty brother, an emptiness. We are waiting, suffering in this fallen world. We are waiting for him, somehow," Harkonen said softly, peacefully.

Verboden pulled up a rickety stool and sat carefully. He looked at the small symbol.

"Some confused it with the sun, the moon, some earthly symbol. No, it is a promise unfulfilled. It is the Father of Light, who came down to us, then in the moment of our revelation, poof, was gone. And we held up our swords, our rakes, our poles... thinking we stood for something. But we don't. Not without him. But... when...?..." Harkonen sighed.

"There is a blessing this day, brother, that you are back, healed from the curse. The curse you and I both sought out a cure for, all those seasons ago -- to absolve. And the missing piece was the knowledge brought to us by Alfred, this boy king."

Harkonen looked at Verboden. "Tell me, is the boy from Telehistine?"

"Telehistine? No, he is from the lineage of King Athelrod, a Northern man of the Westfold," Verboden said.

"Hmm... the prophecy says the fulfillment would come from Telehistine," Harkonen said.

"Prophecy?" Verboden perked up.

"Prophecies from the forefathers of our faith, who walked alongside the Father. They say... in their letters, in their correspondents..." Harkonen turned and picked up the soup and small wooden spoon, his hands still shaking from weakness.

"Letters? Writings?" Verboden wondered aloud.

Harkonen sipped gently at his soup. "Yes, there were many from that time long ago. Most, if not all, are lost now, due to the ages and wars and destruction set upon us by Gorbogal and the Dark One. The brothers scattered. The faith dismally shattered."

"Lost?" Verboden sighed.

"Yes, lost."

They looked at the empty circle.

Chapter Thirty-Five

The Mare Returns

"Look! Beyond the fields, a riderless steed!" yelled Captain Hedor from the highest walls.

"It's her!" Sir Murith gasped, gritting teeth. He rushed down the grand stairs of Grotham's great wall and leapt adroitly upon his own grey steed. His mount raced down the slope as if flying, past moorland goats, past Cory and the spearboys drilling, past shepherds and wood choppers, into the flowering fields where Lord Gorham's black mare stood.

The horses reared up in greeting, then dropped to nuzzle and caress each other's muzzles. Murith reached over to touch and pet Gorham's steed. Then he leapt off to take a look at the condition of the weakened mare. He wept for her wounds and scars. He leaned in to hear her every whisper, whine and neigh, and to feel every twitch from her ears and tail. Murith cried and gritted his teeth.

"How long have they been out there in the field?" Alfred asked from the wall.

"Hours now," Hedor shrugged.

Alfred and Loranna, oddly close, watched from the wall as the sun went down and the field of flowers became an orange glow. Murith walked slowly with both horses as they grazed these many hours.

A Khanafian in armour came up, looking quite solid in form. A few seasons of freedom and good food had given him a new robust physique.

"Well, my watch is over. Hope there's some food left for me," Hedor said.

"The children, they take much of the food – and the gnomes," the Khanafian answered, glaring at Hedor.

"Oy... oy..."

"Gnomes brought ant soup, grey. Still some left," the Khanafian added.

Hedor now glared.

The Khanafian couldn't help but laugh. Hedor chuckled along with him. Alfred and Loranna looked at them, disconcerted.

"But seriously – ant soup," the Khanafian said, gagging.

Hedor shrugged. He looked at Alfred. "Oh! Have I introduced you to Kumbo the Warrior?"

Alfred turned to face Kumbo the Warrior. "Well, we met long ago in the Refuge. You look... fuller?"

"Fuller? What does that word mean?" Kumbo asked.

Hedor laughed and rubbed his belly. "It means you have been fed well! And now look like a free man, not a slave!"

"Oh yes! Fuller I am! And learning your tongue!" Kumbo said as he rubbed his belly. "Yes, fuller. Me eat a lot! But I left ant soup for Captain!" Kumbo pointed at Captain Hedor with a big grin. Both laughed.

"Were you a warrior where you came from?" Alfred asked.

Kumbo and Hedor suddenly stopped laughing and glanced at each other. Hedor had already heard the tale. "Yes, once long ago, I was a warrior. My tribe fought against the great Muhat-tines."

"A race of draconian serpents! Powerful and nasty!" Hedor hissed.

"They raid Khanafian tribes, enslave them, force them to work for the ogres. Many tribes fall to them. And many merchants come to buy. I fight, but maybe not so good." Kumbo said this last looking down.

Hedor grabbed his shoulder. "The greatest of warriors can fall! Do not give up, ever."

"Did you fall, Hedor?" Kumbo asked.

"Oh yes, I fell," Hedor said. Then he looked to Alfred and said, "But I was picked up once again." Hedor nodded and went on his way.

Kumbo looked at Alfred and Loranna. "I have the watch now. My eyes are good in dark. I will protect all the people here, all the free people."

Alfred and Loranna smiled.

That evening, Murith finally brought his mare and Gorham's steed inside. Everyone could see the weakened and tortured physique of Gorham's horse and shuttered to think what happened to him.

Abedeyan and Verboden met him at the gate.

"Did Gorham fall?" Abedeyan asked quickly.

Sir Murith looked up from a sad dream. Verboden clasped his shoulder to comfort him.

"He lives," Sir Murith said. "But his quest has failed."

Sitting in Dunther's dungeon hovel, Murith lay upon the bed once again. Alfred sat in Dunther's chair and peered at the roll-out of the castle plans. King Gup was there with Gib and Pep. Verboden and Abedeyan sat across from him. Hedor rushed in, waking from an uncomfortable sleep.

"The troll hunters are the most powerful of fighting men. Four thousand strong march with Gorbogal's Black Army," Murith said, rubbing his temples in despair.

"An allegiance... to her..." Abedeyan moaned with deep sorrow.

"If they are as able as Gorham claimed," King Gup said, "our defenses could not withstand them. They would take our castle walls in no time."

"And they will be here this summer, weeks away? A month? We are already seeing refugees flee from their terror, those that survived the warg raiders," Verboden said softly.

"Gorbogal's Black Army is one hundred thousand strong," Murith said without emotion.

The rest, however, sunk in their seats and Hedor against the wall. Their frames weakened, and their heads dropped.

Murith continued. "She built an army to ravage the realm of Telehistine. She has been building it these many years, bred to destroy everything in its path. Black trolls and black orcs, legions upon legions. And she has bought the troll hunters, the only men who could stand against the black trolls. All of this is now hers to command."

"We must retreat to the Underworld," King Gup said.

Alfred sat silent, staring at the castle plans.

All looked at Alfred, waiting. A sense of dread and despair came across them as they twitched and fidgeted. Slowly, one by one, their eyes looked toward the floor.

Finally, Alfred looked up, "I don't know why, but I'm not afraid."

They all looked up at him.

"I don't know why," he repeated with a strange comforting smile.

"King Alfred," said Verboden, standing up. "No king can withstand this threat. It is the doom of our day. No kingdom has ever encountered an army as vast as this. Our great wizard is gone. We have not heard from Lord Dunther. The distance to the faerie realm isn't far. Yet neither he nor his mare has returned. And by now, well, his quest has surely failed. The land of men, of the West, will fall to ruin and despair. We have no choice but to flee and hide."

"No," Alfred replied, standing opposite Verboden.

All stared in stunned silence.

Verboden sat down again.

"You want us to fight?" Hedor gasped, waving his arms. "I have maybe two score men at my disposal. Ex-bandits and freed Khanafians! Cory and Wilden command a few dozen. Loranna the same. We have only one knight! One out of three whose quests have succeeded. And that success brought no warriors from the People of the Down but CHILDREN!? Enslaved, beaten, weak, hungry children!"

"You have some gnomes..." Pep said.

"We've got a few score gnomes. All with new families and a new hope..." Hedor continued. "How many, whose wives are with child, will fight and die?"

Pep pondered and looked to Gib, who looked down. King Gup, as well, did not look ready for a fight.

"King Alfred, we must flee... as far away as possible. Now," Hedor said.

The Mare Returns

"No."

Chapter Thirty-Six

Preparations

"You were right, King Alfred," Hedor huffed, limping alongside a farmer's wagon, entering the gate of Grotham Keep.

Alfred hugged Cory as he entered with the spearboys. Derhman, Cory's father, was atop the wagon. He looked injured.

"My father is okay," said Cory, dirty and battle weary. "We saved the wagons of people and repelled the warg raiders." He rambled as he passed by with Wilden, Nubio and the spearboys.

Hedor unbuckled a loose shoulder plate and smiled at Alfred. "The gnome steel held against the bite of a warg, but the straps were torn. Not a bad trade." Ruig and Kumbo came in, both weary from fighting, holding each other up.

Alfred was worried. He looked from wagon to wagon. Sir Murith pranced in on his horse. He was very busy surveying. Once seeing that all were in, without a word, he galloped out again.

Alfred looked after him, hoping to get a word, but the knight was off. Alfred saw what he was looking for, Loranna and her girls. They were seated atop the last wagon, bows and arrows still ready. Alfred rushed up and waved in relief to Loranna.

She looked down with a stern look. "The farmers have been saved. But we are going to lose the farms again!"

"We'll rebuild," Alfred replied.

Loranna easily leapt off and landed next to Alfred in her superb elven cloak and steel armour. "We keep rebuilding. It takes us a whole season to build our homes. Then they burn them in a single night!"

Alfred touched her shoulder. Oddly, she rolled her arm and rejected his comfort. Alfred stared wide-eyed. Verboden noticed this as he tended to the wounded.

"Lead us, King Alfred! Defeat her once and for all!" Loranna said, not looking at him. She walked away with her archers.

Alfred stared after her.

"You were right, milord," Hedor repeated. "If we had fled, the warg riders would have taken us. West, South, North, doesn't matter... the people coming in are from all directions. These goblin raiders aren't a few like the last time. They are a sea of death, surrounding us to all the horizons. At least you have kept us on a fortress island to fight to the end. I'd rather our end be here together than being scattered across the land, fleeing and falling alone."

"King Alfred!" Pep called, running up. "Goblins and ratkins have amassed in the Underworld. They've blocked off many caverns and are continually probing our defenses!"

"Well, it appears there never was any place to run or hide!" Hedor hissed.

"We're holding up alright. We gnomes know we're in the fight," Pep added.

"Keep the Ratkin Road open from the Sanctuary to here. That is the most important part. I want those supplies coming! We need to be fully ready!" King Alfred ordered.

Pep saluted and hurried away.

"Ready against the Black Army?" said Hedor, hissing again. "Who can be ready for such a threat? Against legion after legion? It was a good run while we tried, King Alfred... it was a good run..."

"Shut up, Hedor! And get some rest!" Alfred grunted and walked off.

Hedor shrugged, looking at Ruig and Kumbo, who were lying against the wagons, wrapping bandages to their wounds.

"You talk too much, Hedor," Ruig said.

Kumbo agreed with a shrug.

"Yeah but... " Hedor waved it off and hobbled away.

Preparations

Their first sight of the Black Army was the orcs. Not the big brutish black orcs but the common gangly orcs. These were larger than goblins but not as upright or armoured as the oriental hobgoblins or as muscular and stout as the black orcs. They certainly had armour and mass produced cleavers and clubs with reinforced iron shards, which made them look like oversized goblins. They came in groups of hundreds, scurrying along in some semblance of chaotic marching. When they could see the white square on the horizon, that of the man-keep Grotham... and see a lone knight on a gray steed galloping across the fields before them, they knew to begin their work. Gang leaders with whips cracked them and yelled out orders.

Sir Murith scouted from the open fields as his horse reared and neighed in jostling fear. Murith caressed and whispered bravery and determination to his mare as he watched. Hundreds and hundreds of orcs in scores of gangs began spreading across the fields and forests of the Westfold.

Their task, much to his derision, was the onslaught by a thousandfold axes chopping down every tree and every bush, and eating every flower and plant. Some orcs might die from munching on the poisonous sassaberry plant of the Westfold, but no matter. Other orcs would filter in and eat the weeds and root plants, grubs and worms, fish and fleeing squirrels. The orcs were like a mass of ants or ravenous pigs, harvesting everything from the earth and turning it into a barren grey wasteland.

Trees were cut and their branches piled in pyres. The larger logs were set aside in rows. As more and more orcs arrived, as mounted wargs and warthogs arrived with orc war chiefs and raiders, as legions of black orcs arrived, as wagons and chariots of sorcerers arrived, as war trolls and the black trolls arrived, the day turned into night. The pyres were set on fire, burning, creating huge plumes of flames that rose in the night air. They blotted out the stars and created hell here in the Westfold. Mountain trolls, the big lumbering beast of burden ones, would stroll in with cattle and other stolen beasts, thrusting them into the fires. All would rage and howl, ready for the feast.

Murith spied a herd of farm horses taken from some farms and looked away as he heard their neighing screams. The black trolls, being fast runners, herded them into the fires, howling their venomous evil.

He could not bear it any longer. He turned his shaken mare and rode back to Grotham Keep.

From the walls, Hedor and all his men stared off into the distance, to the horizon. He said to no one, "It's as if the whole of the world were on fire."

It started off as flames bursting up in one area. Then flames would burst up in another, and another, till it seemed all of the eastern sky was on fire. All of the lands were being usurped by a blazing sun or a river of lava going from the furthest north to the furthest south.

"No hope, have we," Hedor said to no one. But Ruig, Kumbo, and all his men heard him.

Ruig came up to Hedor and spoke close to him. "Stop your painful poetry! You weaken the hearts of our men!"

Hedor shuddered and looked at Ruig, then shook his head. Ruig did not know what Hedor's response meant.

They turned to see Alfred and the two gnomes Gib and Pep walking along the wall. They were looking at small scrolls and pointing at the great stones of the wall.

"I hope they know what they are doing," Ruig hissed. "I hope they kill as many of them as possible... before we fall." Ruig patted Hedor's chest, even as Hedor sunk against the stone of Grotham Keep.

Alfred came to Verboden and Harkonen in their ruined chapel. Many farmers were in there, praying and sobbing. The brothers in robes were busy amongst them, comforting them and praying with them. Derhman was in there, in bandages and being taken care of by his wife, as were Loranna's father and mother, who nodded curtly to Alfred and tended to those in need.

Alfred sat before the strange symbol. They called it the "Promise". He bowed before it, wringing his fingers together. He was unsure. He mumbled at first, something dark and maligned, questioning why, over and over, why? "I'm not ready," he prayed as Verboden sat next to him, hearing his words. It made Verboden's shoulders sink, his hope weaken.

Alfred hesitated upon feeling Verboden's presence. The cleric took a deep breath and turned to the Promise, bowing his head. "Oh Father of Light, the Promise is before us, our symbol, to remind us of you. Please come and bless us, save us from this evil, this greater evil.

We have no power to repel it, no strength, but you do. You have all the power and all the strength."

"All we have is hope in good, in the good... in the Father," Alfred added.

Verboden looked up. "Yes, yes Alfred, the good the Father created within us all. Whether we take it or ignore it..."

"We've been taking it, haven't we Verboden? Aren't we good? If there is such powerful evil... isn't there also a powerful good? Isn't there a Father?" Alfred asked. Verboden noticed Alfred wringing his hands. His knuckles were white.

"Yes, Alfred..." Verboden looked down. "There has to be."

Chapter Thirty-Seven

The Siege Begins

Kumbo and Ruig pointed at the smoking horizon. The other men rushed to the walls to stare. Gasps came forth and eyes widened, revealing growing fear. From the black smoky clouds a giant tower came into view. It slowly crawled its way forward.

"Siege towers, many, many siege towers," Sir Murith hissed. "And that is the Tower of the Warlock. He is the leader of this evil Black Army. The Black Hand of Gorbogal!"

Kumbo and Ruig turned, looking down into the vast courtyard. Captain Hedor seemed to have gotten courage somehow. He was training the farmers and all able men and women with sword or spear, and with bow and arrow. Cory, Wilden and Nubio helped, getting spears to whoever wished to fight. It was still a rabble of weak and weary people. Most huddled with their families or tended to the sick and those already wounded from the raids.

The scraggy children, who were saved from the moorland curse, huddled together. Lady Nihan, her maids, and Khanafian nurses gave them the most care. She grabbed her maids and the nurses. "Do not let them up upon the walls. Do not let them see." The nurses and the maids, flowing with tears, nodded. Lady Nihan stopped them again. "Do not cry. Do not let them see you cry. Cry at night, when they are asleep. Stay strong for them in these last... in these hours. And pray for King Alfred, our King, who has saved us many times. Pray for him!"

Sir Murith could not help but notice the young nurse again. He wasn't sure if he nodded or merely bobbed his head as he hurried along. She was nursing a pale skinned baby on her dark breast. She had to feed them. There was no time or convenience of privacy. It was a difficult and sad task but one she did with love and care. She fed them in freedom, even if just for a while. Her eyes followed Murith as he passed, busy on his way.

He stopped and turned to look down at her.

Lady Nihan and her maids rushed to and fro, feeding and caring for so many children. Many cried, for they could sense that their salvation was surrounded by a distant hum of coming death. They were not allowed to see. But up on the walls, Hedor and his men revealed their plight in their eyes and faces.

Murith could not linger. It was rude. He hurried away.

Abedeyan rambled back and forth. He was making sure that all who wanted arms or bows were equipped. He was also busy directing load after load of barrels and placing them at the base of the stairs and under the walls. Gnomes continually went back and forth. Some were armed to fight already. Others were load bearers and carried the heavy barrels and sacks.

Alfred went amongst them, busy as ever, trying to keep his mind off the doom before them all. He would issue orders in a hoarse voice, having been so very busy these past few days. The smoky ash-ridden air did not help either.

"The sky is black... from the filth of these vermin," said Sir Murith.

"Could have used more knights..." Hedor replied.

Sir Murith looked at Hedor. "And more men. More fighting men like you."

"Not much of a fighter, more like a survivor.... until now," Hedor said, looking over the wall at the dark horizon before them.

The towers were nearly complete. Siege towers dotted the horizon of the East. They were dwarfed by the giant Warlock Tower. It was as if a giant castle, several times larger than Grotham Keep, were suddenly built upon a mound. They could just see on the horizon line, the great dragon behemoths at its base with their long necks and swaying tails.

"We call those brontosauruses or... sauropods, I think. Or just plain dinosaurs..." said Alfred, sullen.

"Those dragon beasts?" Hedor pointed.

"Yes, but they tell us they're not dragons. They're just dinosaurs," said Alfred.

"What's dinosaur mean?" asked Hedor.

"Terrible lizard, I think," Alfred shrugged.

"What's the difference?" sighed Hedor.

The nearby forests, a ways down the slope, suddenly began to shake and shudder. The chopping of axes echoed as orcs grunted and hollered. They weren't far now. The orcs were a blight to the land and within an archer's range. Trees, across the rolling hills in the vicinity of Grotham Keep, began to fall. Orcs swarmed in gangs and mobs, taking down tree after tree.

Hedor and Murith noticed an orc drop from an arrow. They looked up to see Loranna alone on one of the unfinished towers. She seemed tired after firing the one shot. She slumped amongst the exposed stone and merely watched as another orc took its place and the trees continued to fall in droves.

"Will the spearboys and archergirls save the day this time?" Hedor asked. "With but one knight left?"

"We still have our king," said Murith.

Both looked to see King Alfred. He had many supplies covered under straw and cloth, hidden under wooden scaffolding and the workers' tents under the walls.

"Why all the secrecy with his plan?" Hedor asked Murith.

Sir Murith shrugged. "I don't know. It's a good plan. But with them, with the immensity before us, not even that plan is enough."

The land before them now, not on the horizon but the fields and farmsteads, once of green rolling hills dotted with groves and farms, was turned into a fiery land of smoke and pillage with thousands and thousands of orcs scrambling to and fro. It was as if a blighted empire were being built right before their smoke-ridden eyes. Everyone was upon the walls now, for there was no ignoring the choking smoke or the epic busy bee noises of orcs pounding and axing away the last of the Westfold and its providing earth.

Lady Nihan held a baby with no mother, no father. She cried with the child. The children from the moorlands huddled together on the walls, their eyes returning to the slavery and desolation they had always known. The Khanafian nurses and their people cried, even after

211

gaining their health and freedom. Kumbo was their chief now, amongst his people, and he cried with them.

"We die free! Understand! We die free!" he said, speaking in the new tongue of this land, perhaps never to be spoken again.

Ruig choked up a cry as he heard Kumbo and saw his people. He twisted his neck and turned away, staring at Hedor.

"What now, Captain?" Ruig spoke through quivering lips.

"We kill as many of them as we can, till the end," Captain Hedor said. "Our swords are sharp. Our armour is good. We'll give them a good fight on these great walls of Grotham Keep."

Ruig quickly wiped a tear away with a quivering hand.

Sir Murith went up to Abedeyan and King Alfred. They were busy looking at scrolls and pointing to positions on the wall. "Why do you wait? Why not now?"

Abedeyan and Alfred looked at Murith. The knight shook in his armour. His sword in its sheath vibrated against the steel of his leg.

"We must wait," Abedeyan said.

"Wait for what?!"

"Until the attack," King Alfred said. "Go and watch the walls for goblin sappers. Make sure Loranna and her archers are taking out any goblins or orcs who get too close."

Murith stood, unsure.

King Alfred and Abedeyan looked back at their scrolls and then realized Murith had not moved and was still staring at them. His face was dark, from soot and ash, like everyone else.

"GO!" King Alfred suddenly yelled, stepping forward, pointing for Murith to leave.

Murith flinched.

King Gup and the gnomes peered up, hearing Alfred's sudden yell. Murith finally nodded and turned.

Fires continued to burst from pyres of bramble across the land. Orcs howled in furious excitement. Soon droves of giant mountain trolls marched into the barren fields nearby, pushing the siege towers. The towers seemed bigger and higher than Grotham Keep. It was as if several castles were rolling up to dwarf the white castle. Alongside, pushed forward by more mountain trolls, were catapults and trebuchets. These were bigger than man-made ones, with crude thick lumber. Not one tree, but several logs banded with iron created the supports, making for a larger more immense contraption. They were resoundingly evil looking, with crude iron and splintered wood. They looked like monstrous machines – which they were.

"Oh boy," said Hedor, watching from the walls. He and his men had settled on the walls with small fires and bedrolls. The walls, crafted by the gnomes, were actually quite wide and sturdy. It gave them comfort in this new world of nightmares.

Gib, Pep and many other gnomes rushed to the walls. They stood atop the battlements and peered out over the blighted land and gasped at the horrors before them. Hedor came up to them. He noticed many in armour with soiled weapons.

"How's it going, down in the tunnels?" Hedor asked.

"We are fighting them off. Each gnome can take on a hundred goblins... but there are always a hundred more," said Gib.

"And a few thousand ratkins! Aye, they breed them fast!" said Pep.

"Those catapults, can they destroy these walls?" Hedor asked, leaning against the solid stone.

The gnomes were slow to reply, looking at the monstrous structures and the haul of giant stones the trolls carried forth. It was still a long and slow process for the Black Army. Dozens of lines of mountain trolls, trailing back to the horizon, lumbered forward carrying stones. Their march was slow and tedious, many stopping and having to be pushed on by acolytes and sorcerers with their dark commanding spells.

"Our stone can hold. For a while," Gib said softly.

Hedor wasn't convinced, grimacing and looking on. "Well, for what it's worth, I like your stone. It is very well done. The best I have ever seen."

Gib stopped his fearful stare and looked at Hedor. They were eye level since the gnomes stood atop the precarious battlements while the men stood on the adjacent walkways. Gib smiled and put his hand on Hedor's shoulder.

A procession of the people came into the chapel. It was on the balcony above the Great Hall's floor. Of course, the Great Hall was still in ruin with only the back walkway left. The kitchens below, though in shambles, were still heavily used. Lady Nihan limited all food usage. Very little was cooked except in preparing things as preserves.

The Siege Begins

In the chapel Verboden led them all in prayer to the Father of Light. It did not seem to matter anymore, any sort of inhibition or indifference about worshiping a Father who was not there, whose promise of coming was not fulfilled. They all cried up to him. They all cried to anyone who was listening. And indeed, the only salvation they could sense was that of a Father. For all sense of pride and ego, all sense of self-worth, meant nothing in this dark hour, in these dark hours.

Sir Murith prayed for the first time, to himself, whispering even amongst all the others whispering their last prayers. "Oh Father, oh one... the Father of us all, please help us... help Gorham, end his misery and torment. Please oh Father, end his torment." Murith cried. "Save Lord Dunther from the foul snares of the faerie queen. Please do not let him succumb to her. Oh Father, return him to us, without her charms and spells. We need him. We need his sword..."

The sounds of howling and axes and burning embers stopped. The people rose from their sleeps and slumbers, from their catatonic states and realized they heard nothing. Even the smoke seemed to clear from the courtyard and not waft in from huge plumes over the walls. Hedor and his men rubbed their eyes and looked at each other, wondering. The farmers and children began to ascend the stairs to look out onto the land of desolation.

They saw smoke clearing. The wind blew it away with no fires or pyre mounds of embers replacing it with more. The sun pierced through the dark ash, and its rays shone upon the land. It lighted the land, revealing the harsh burnt grounds and barren wastes.

The people stared in wonder as the foreboding silence of it all gave them repose. And then the smoke cleared, and the mass of orcs and trolls, and siege towers and engines spanned the earth around them. It was as if all work was done, the fires burned away, and now, a vast army was ready, standing and waiting.

The people shrank in their horror, with their worst nightmare realized. They shook and quivered. There was no strength in crying, for crying meant one still had hope, that one was in pain and suffering, and had not given up. Here, the people had given up. There was no need to cry and no need to spend emotional suffrage to get through this. There was only the need now to end it.

Chapter Thirty-Eight

Bombardment

The bombardment began. When the first round of stones hit the walls and courtyard, exploding the ruins of the Great Hall, no one really reacted. They all stood in deadened states. Much of the Great Hall structures fell, crumbling stone upon stone. Hedor flinched a bit, hugging the gnome built walls. He stared at the people, at Lady Nihan, at the children. They merely stood and looked blankly out.

The stones seemed to come in peacefully, quietly, just before impact. Each collision created a loud crack and vibrating thud that Hedor could feel in his bones. He snarled. Was it because of the attack or the cowardice of his people? Did he snarl at their surrender or that evil would attack the weakest of people with deadly intent? He snarled as more rocks crashed into supplies and tents. Were people amongst them, merely lying on their cots or sitting with their families? He got up and finally, as if reaching up out of a deep drowning swim, yelled, "TAKE COVER!!!"

The people suddenly flinched, ducking and cowering, hugging and huddling. Screams and panicked cries spread amongst them. They hurried and rushed down the stairs and haphazardly throughout the courtyard. Stones rained down as people were indeed killed.

215

Bombardment

"To the walls! Under the walls!" yelled Abedeyan. He led the children just under the walls. The lost children clung to the stones and hidden provisions.

Thankfully, the attack came from the East, where the Black Army marched from. They did not spread the catapults all around but merely sent the stones from one direction. Everyone cowered and crowded themselves under the eastern walls.

Stones flew in from catapults and trebuchets as the gnome walls stood firm. The rocks bounced off the white granite, merely chipping bits off. The gnomes that were there eventually gained courage to peer at the stones' impacts and grinned, giving each other slaps of congratulations.

However, there was not much cover in the courtyard. There were just the ruined Great Hall with worker's tents and scaffolding and the tower remains where Alfred's room was still intact. They all hid under the eastern walls to watch as the stones smashed into and pounded everything to a ruinous rubble.

Much of their supplies and provisions were smashed or exploded as stones tore through them. The farmers, the Khanafians, the bandits, the lone knight Murith, Abedeyan, Lady Nihan and her seamstresses, and the gnomes all watched as stones hammered what was left of their home within the walls.

Yet the gnome walls held. They were ugly and battered, chipped and cracked superficially, but the gnomes knew by the sound of the impacts, that it was all surface damage. They touched their walls on the interior and could feel the flying rocks hitting the wall, dozens after dozens, from sunny day into the cold of night. And they felt the stone and caressed it, knowing it was holding.

"Good stone, have we!" said the gnomes.

Gib scurried along the rubble courtyard. He could easily sense the bombarding stones. Peering up into the night sky, he merely stepped aside as a stone hammered next to him. The exploding rocks from the impact had no effect on gnomes and their stone tough skin. He hurried through.

King Alfred was atop the wall, peering carefully through the battlements. He was waiting for something. Murith crouched with him. Loranna and her girls, keeping low, and mostly on the eastern wall, kept an eye on the gnomes, who were looking about on all the walls and towers. Nothing was attacking or sneaking up while the bombardment continued.

Gib easily climbed the wall. "King Alfred, we've lost the Ratkin Road. King Gup and his guards along with Broggia and Boggin are holding the refuge, the Sanctuary Isle. Cory and the boys and us gnomes are holding the tunnels below to the river, but no further."

"They will attack soon, and there is nowhere to escape," said Murith.

Chapter Thirty-Nine

The Troll Hunters

As the sun rose, the bombardment stopped. Verboden and Brother Harkonen spent all morning praying in the courtyard amongst the people. They went from sitting group to huddled families, even to the moorland children awaiting their fate. Large stones littered the ground, making it tedious to traverse.

"There! Are those trolls coming up the Farmer's Road?!!" Hedor yelled. He clung to the edge of a tower to get a better view of the northern slopes that led to many farms. There was a wide area, not filled with orcs or siege towers, left open. It was an expanse through many rolling hills that were once fields and crops.

Coming over those ridges and filling the slopes below them were horned grotesque black creatures. They were different from the common orcs or the smaller trolls. They seemed more vile and powerful. Their steps were more sure and straight. They were evil men with a fixed gaze for killing.

Sir Murith rushed through the few bandits and Khanafians on the walls. A new exhausting wave of fear spread amongst them. Most began hurrying down the stairs, dropping their weapons and shaking uncontrollably. Kumbo kept a few back but not enough. Verboden tried to bless and comfort them, but the fear was beyond him.

Murith stood next to Hedor and stared through the harsh glare of the sun. The shadow beasts marched not like hobbling orcs, but like focused men, powerful men with great shoulders and strong legs. He grimaced as he sought out one thing and saw it – he saw the cart where upon a pole, shackled, his brother Lord Gorham hung limp.

"Troll hunters! They are here!" he yelled, gritting his teeth.

King Alfred rushed up. "I wasn't prepared for them to attack now! For troll hunters... Is that Gorham? Is that him?"

Murith nodded.

"Is he alive?" Alfred asked, grimacing. "Bring up the archers. We need them on the walls!"

"Their arrows won't penetrate the hides of troll hunter armour," Murith said softly.

"We have the gnome spring loaders but not enough for that!" Gib grunted.

"What of oil, can we burn them?" Alfred said.

"Not before they traverse our walls," said Murith, slumping down against the stone. He looked up at Alfred. "My sword cannot match them."

"If I reveal my plan now, before the Black Army attacks, then it won't work," Alfred said, fretting in a strangely bravado way. "Are the troll hunters going to attack now?"

"Yes. The whole of the Black Army was just a costly diversion – but no real cost since they are slaves to Gorbogal's bidding. The troll hunters, thousands strong, will easily scale these grand walls and defeat us in arm-to-arm combat," said Murith calmly, sitting against the wall, not watching as the troll hunters advanced.

Alfred looked to and fro, unsure. Verboden came to give courage. As he made it to the top stair, breathing hard, he saw the horrific beastmen marching forward. He lost his own courage.

Hedor dropped from the tower stone and turned to Alfred. "No time for your plan. Let us flee to the tunnels and fight our way through the goblins. We have no choice. We must flee! We must..."

Hedor shook Alfred, perhaps too much. But no one, not even Murith stopped him.

Verboden leaned against his staff, looking at the monstrous troll hunters arrayed below them, marching up with all intent and purpose. He saw the biggest of them in the middle, their beastly black helms and their even beastlier battle blades and glaives. He shuddered and felt all strength leave him. "Father of Light...," he gasped as he clenched his tightening chest.

The Troll Hunters

He looked down to see the moorland children huddled against the wall, crying. They were only recently rescued and now this was their fate, slavery or worse, or to die a brutal death. He looked up at the troll hunters beyond the walls. They stood as frightful and powerful men. He knew nothing could stop them. This was the end for Alfred, for the kingdom, for the weak and crying. He looked down at the children... He looked up at the hunters... He looked down... Then up...

"King Alfred..."

Chapter Forty

The Sacrifice

Ordoh Brutum stopped and raised his powerful cleaver. They were not far from the white walls of Grotham Keep. One quick sprint over a field of siege stones and they'd be up and over, eradicating the legendary tales of this ridiculous boy king.

Gorham found what little strength he had left to look up. He had no moisture for tears or for his badly split lips. He was sun burnt with cracked skin and boils and near heat stroke. Brok and Ruuk had lost interest in attending to his needs and were ready for all of this to end and their reign of the Westfold to begin.

Ordo ordered them to stop, for he could not believe his eyes. The clanging of iron armour and heavy hide stopped; the stomp of thick boots and clank of cast iron battle blades ceased. The gate had opened, and there stood the inauspicious little boy... or king... or boy. Ordo glared at the ridiculous situation before him.

"He surrenders. And no fight? Pathetic. I will kill him nonetheless," he said, looking aside to Gorham, who peered and shook in his shackles with his last ounce of strength and spirit.

Ordo turned back, standing in front of his mass of menacing butchers: all in blackened hides and cast iron armour, all with spiraling demonic iron horns and monstrous blades.

The boy king walked out of the gate, and then a robed man, a cleric, followed. Ordo looked to his hunters. "Perhaps he comes to cast a great spell on us?" Ordo boomed. "Those clerics of their false Father of Light haven't fared well against the bestial spirits within us!"

They all howled and raised their weapons, pounding their chests with their huge fists. It was their incredible sound that stopped the boy king and cleric at the gate.

The Sacrifice

Ordo rolled his eyes. He raised his weapon to signal their charge to end this charade of a boy king. "No coward boy will waste my hunt!!"

But he froze, his weapon stuck in the air.

The cleric and another, a much weaker looking robed man, ushered many children out of the gate. They formed a rather large group, and with much prodding and pushing, the clerics ushered them through the field of large stones. The boy king marched toward the troll hunters – with no weapon.

Ruuk came up to his father. "Those are his warrior children!"

Ordo could not help but laugh. His laughter sounded more like the roar of a lion, a beast lion in his helm.

Ruuk turned and waved his arms and great weapon. "Behold! The boy king and his children warriors!"

The troll hunters laughed, producing a loud ruckus.

"Behold the mighty spearboys!"

The troll hunters beat their weapons against their iron.

"Behold the mighty archergirls!"

The troll hunters hollered and howled, waving their weapons. The roar shook the barren land and the siege stones.

Ordo stopped laughing as they neared. He was stunned. He could not believe it. The boy king, two feeble clerics and a cadre of wretched children came up. Ordo thought it odd that the children had no spears or bows as their legend bespoke.

Ordo shrugged and walked forward. "Which one of you is the boy king?"

Alfred was obviously the boy king. He was in armour and looked quite different from the rest, who were in ragged squalor and very emaciated.

Alfred hesitantly raised his hand. "I am."

Ordo looked down, and his shoulders shrank. Ordo turned and looked back at Gorham, who shook in his shackles, in a weak sort of desperate sobbing.

Ruuk came up and shook his head. "Let us just take them, sell them to slavers and be done with this."

Ordo turned back and saw that Alfred was oddly closer, standing below him with no weapon, in simple steel armour.

"Hi, I'm King Alfred," he waved.

"Boy, bring out all your people. Your line has ended. There will be no more tales of children kings. We'll spare the able ones. You, unfortunately, must go to the witch – dead or alive."

Alfred looked back at the children and then past them to Grotham Keep. Upon the walls he saw Loranna and her archers. He could see the tears streaming from her eyes and the anguish in her face. Murith and Hedor were not doing much better. Gib and Pep pounded the stone with angry fists.

Alfred looked back up at Ordo. "Oh, I'm not surrendering."

Ordo was always in movement, whether shifting on his feet or swaying his muscular body under heavy armour. But in this moment, he froze and stared down at the frail boy king.

Ordo began to chuckle.

"I have something for you, for your men," said the boy king.

One of the clerics brought forth a child, the little girl with blazing red hair.

"The other children call her Red," said the boy king.

"Father, kill him and let's go," Ruuk grunted behind Ordo.

King Alfred suddenly stepped past Ordo. Ruuk raised his great bardiche to hack the boy in two as Ordo turned his gaze through his great troll hunter helm, curious and in disbelief at Alfred's audacity.

King Alfred announced as loudly as he could to all the troll hunters who stared in disdain, "My cleric, Brother Verboden, was taught a supplication early on, a simple knowing spell!"

"We are resistant to the false Father and his spells!" Ruuk shouted at Alfred.

Alfred shuddered and stepped fearfully away from Ruuk but continued. "MY CLERICS CAN SENSE THE FATHER OF ANY CHILD!!! Their supplication gives them this knowing... the father of this child!" Alfred pointed to Red and the other children. Red stood scared, quivering as Verboden pushed her forward, perhaps a bit too roughly.

Ordo shrugged. Ruuk looked to his father and raised his weapon. Ordo nodded.

Ruuk stepped to Alfred to hack him and end this. Alfred fell back upon the ground, raising his arm in useless defense.

Loranna yelled, "No!" from the towers, but no one heard her hoarse cry.

The Sacrifice

Troll hunters pointed and laughed at the pathetic boy crawling on the ground.

Verboden brought Red forth, closer to Ordo, and looked up. Red shook violently, ready to run in any direction in utter fear.

Ruuk raised his bardiche, not fully, for fully was not needed. Ruuk paused to look at this pathetic situation. He turned to Gorham. "Why on earth did you sacrifice yourself for this boy?!"

Just then, Furioso burst through, knocking Ruuk back and marching past Ordo. And Ordo KNEW. For Furioso fell to his knees, a huge giant in black foul armour, his shoulders as broad and wide as Ordo's – sunk. Furioso's weapon – never in a thousand troll kills – fell to the ground next to him. Furioso's huge ironclad hands reached out, quivering with no strength. And they touched the small diminutive shoulders of Red as she stood in utter fear.

Verboden nodded and stepped away.

Ruuk stared in confusion, his battle axe just above Alfred, whose only defense was a raised arm.

Furioso yanked off his bestial helm to reveal his flaming red hair, taut in braids. And to reveal his eyes, bursting with tears and quivering with a loss greater than any fatherless man has known – the loss of a child.

Red, like a small stick, bent backwards with her head reared. She could not see through her tears and paralyzing fear. With frail countenance she stood under the massive brute of a man. Yet he was before her on his knees. She suddenly focused on his red hair. In her weak state she suddenly reached up to touch his red beard – and in that saw her own scraggy red hair lying upon her arm. They were the same.

Furioso gasped with tears and hot air. He gasped as her tiny fingers touched his red hair. He could not hold himself up any longer. His armour suddenly weighed upon him. He had to drop and sit. He had to try to stay up to look at her, only a few feet tall, but he could not. He fell to his hands upon the ground, with his head slumped. A power greater than Furioso was defeating him.

Still, she focused on the blazing red hair all about her. She touched it more and more. It was as if a bright field of red flowers blossomed before her and told her of EVERYTHING. Who she was and where she came from and the love she deserved forever and ever.

Verboden then sensed another connection. He brought forth a baby held by a girl. The small girl wasn't much bigger than the baby boy she held. Verboden took the child and walked past Ordo, past Ruuk, to a troll hunter readying to slash at the cleric. The troll hunter was ready and able, leveling his weapon, ready to leap. Troll hunters all around stood with dismay. What was this? What was happening? One yelled out, "He put a spell on Furioso!"

"He won't put a spell on me!" roared the hunter, ready to strike.

Verboden merely pointed at the antsy troll hunter. Then he showed him the baby boy with a birthmark on his forehead.

The troll hunter leapt, not at Verboden, but away, back into his brethren. He leapt back in a panic, trying to look away. The troll hunters looked at their own as he tried to hide amongst them. His weapon seemed suddenly to get heavy. They had never seen their own try to flee. He pounded up against the wall of them who were confused by his cowardice.

Verboden walked forward. The baby boy's lips tightened, and he sputtered choking sobs. He stared at the nightmare monsters before him. He knew he was defenseless and knew, even as a baby, to fear them.

The troll hunter's legs weakened. He misstepped and put up his weapon, not as an attack, but as a wall, a barrier to keep the baby away from him. "No! No!!!" He swung his weapon, not like a weapon, but like a father trying to keep a son he had abandoned away from him.

The baby cried in fear. He could not yet speak or walk yet knew to fear all the bestial men around him. The baby boy clung to Verboden and did not want any of this, wailing in an awful fear, the fear of an innocent and helpless child.

The troll hunter collapsed to the ground. Verboden knelt beside him with the baby, the mark on his forehead clearly visible.

"He is casting an evil charm!" someone growled.

"No, no..." the hunter moaned. "I know that mark... I remember it."

"It is a lie, a curse from a sorcerer!" someone yelled. A blade was raised above Verboden and the crying boy. But another blade came between them and slowly moved the threat away. The troll hunter wielding the blade came forward through the pensive crowd of troll hunters, lowering his weapon. "I gave up a boy," he said. "He would be three now."

Verboden looked up and nodded. He looked at the fallen troll hunter and motioned for him to take his child.

"I don't...no... I can't..."

Verboden waited as the baby cried. Verboden spoke a soothing blessing, and the baby stopped crying, but his tearful eyes and fearful face dissolved the strength of any man. Verboden looked at the troll hunter. "This boy, your son, he has no name."

The troll hunter took off his helmet. Upon his face were tears. He nodded and took the baby... his son, gently.

Verboden looked up at the inquiring troll hunter. "I sense your son. Come."

Though Verboden was very small, in robes only, the massive armoured troll hunters moved out of his way.

Verboden took the inquiring hunter past Ruuk, past Ordo, past Furioso, and through the children. They opened to a frightened little boy with scraggy black hair. The troll hunter, wailing, took off his helmet, revealing the same black scraggy hair. The children were at first afraid, but this troll hunter dropped his weapon and helm and fell to his knees.

The three year old boy gazed up at a tower of a man. An older girl whispered in his ear, and the boy could not help but do something he had never done before – gaze in joyous wonder.

Other troll hunters passed through their four thousand, here and there, coming up to Verboden or Harkonen. They sorted the children and their fathers. Troll hunters fell to their knees, helmets came off, weapons dropped, and weak troll hunter arms reached out to their small children. The sounds of weeping from troll hunters permeated the muscles and tendons of all the hunters. It spread like waves across the four thousand and defeated them all.

Ordo stood in silence, like a statue unmoving. He stood as troll hunters walked in burdensome gaits he had never seen, as they went to the clerics to find their children.

"What devilry is this!" Ruuk said, leaving Alfred where he lay.

Alfred stood up and walked to Ordo with his sons, Ruuk and Brok. "We rescued them from an Agent of Scourge, a sorcerer who served Gorbogal in the moorlands to the north. They were being sacrificed to a werewolf. You'd call them wolfkins... The bite would turn the child into a wolf beast that would go out and kill the People of the Downs. Gorbogal had one bitten each full moon and released, left alone in the moors as a scared child, with the curse. The People of the Downs lost many warriors to the werewolves. The Men of the Downs hunted and burned the wolf beasts – your children. One by one, they were used like that. These are all that are left."

Ordo stood, watching. More troll hunters came to the clerics, asking them to find their own. But as the children were spread amongst the emotional hunters, there were now more troll hunters inquiring than there were children left unattended.

Many of the troll hunters took off their helms to show their hair or appearance, or put a hand out to show a height they thought their child might be. The clerics, looking, could not fulfill their wishes, for the children they had sacrificed were not amongst the children that lived. The troll hunters then began to hold each other. Many faltered while others held them up.

"Father, this is madness. We are at war! This is evil charms and false magiks!" Ruuk hissed.

Ordo saw the troll hunters spread amongst the children. Not one was standing. And he saw the other troll hunters with the clerics, whose children did not survive. There were many gathering.

Ordo turned to Ruuk but said nothing.

"Gorham said you defeated Gorbogal's armies. She could never beat you? All these years?" asked Alfred.

Ordo looked down at the boy king Alfred, then back at Ruuk. "We made a deal."

Ruuk suddenly shifted in his stance. It was at first menacing and ready to attack, but now it sunk and was weak and frail.

"We made a deal. Every three years, we'd give up our newborn children – to her. And she'd leave our lands alone. We were safe from her attacks."

"The ritual!? Where all the wives go... it wasn't a ritual... a trial of strength?" Ruuk asked.

"I made a new deal. It was to end now, with our allegiance to her war!" said Ordo.

"Allegiance?" Ruuk looked at the troll hunters amongst the children. None carried their weapons or wore their helms. He looked to the other troll hunters amassed, awaiting a fight, to go to war.

Furioso finally stood. "ORDOH BRUTUM!!!!"

The Sacrifice

Ordo and Ruuk turned to look at Furioso. Red held his leg. Furioso leaned heavily to one side so as to not to hurt his daughter. His emotions wracked his face with deep pains.

"Ordoh Brutum! You did this to us! You did this to me? These twelve years of peace?! I never forgot her!" Furioso gently turned to Red and gently pulled her small hands off of him. For in his ironclad armour, any sudden movements, he knew, could hurt her. She nodded no. She nodded staring, not at his eyes but at his red, red hair.

Alfred quickly came to hold her hand. "Let him go. He just has to talk." Red looked at Alfred, a familiar face amidst the huge bestial men. Furioso gazed at Alfred, who looked back. "Boy king..." Furioso whispered. But then his eyes flicked and a madness came over him. He rose.

Furioso stomped toward Ordo. Ruuk stepped between them with his bardiche raised. Furioso looked at Ruuk. "Get out of my way before I rip that axe from your hands and cleave you in two before your father!"

Ruuk glared, but Ordo put his giant hand upon his shoulder. Ruuk stepped aside.

Furioso came up with a thick finger. "Ordo, I'm as guilty as you in this, you sick fiend! You got me to sacrifice my own child! My own flesh and blood! My daughter! Her name is RED!"

Furioso cried furiously, pulling at his hair. "The Father of Light will never forgive you or me! And never will I!" Furioso turned as Ordo lifted his weapon.

Red reached up as Alfred slowly turned to see what was about to happen.

Brok and Ruuk stared in dismay as Ordo swung his weapon.

Chapter Forty-One

Slaughter of the Troll Hunters

Ordo merely swung his weapon at nothing, turning away as Furioso walked back to Alfred and Red.

Ruuk and Brok stared as Ordo walked away, marching by himself to the East – to the Black Army.

Furioso dropped to Red's level, and she leapt upon him. She was like a small red flower alighting upon a giant mound of earth. Furioso was unsure how to hold her, but he did nonetheless. Then his tear-ridden eyes gazed upon Alfred. "King Alfred, the boy king." He choked. "Thank you."

King Alfred nodded, wiping a tear of joy. He turned and gazed after Ordo, who continued marching eastward, away from them with his weapon raised.

Furioso looked as well, still holding Red.

Ruuk and Brok hastened after their father.

"Vatter, what are you doing!?" Ruuk demanded to know.

Ordo spoke to his sons. "Your mother did not die hunting alongside me."

Ruuk and his larger brother Brok looked at each other. Ruuk stopped walking. Ordo walked a few paces and then stopped and turned to face them one last time.

The other troll hunters were unsure what to do. They began to grumble and form back into their broors, into their clans.

"Your mother leapt off a cliff. She never got over what I made her do."

Ruuk and Brok looked at each other, then at their father. Ruuk took off his helmet and breathed in the air. He stared at his father. "What did you make her do?"

"You had a sister," Ordo said. "She was the first. She would have been his age." Ordo nodded to Alfred.

Ruuk and Brok did not move.

Then Ordo turned to the troll hunter army. "All those who will, follow me to your death! March with me to the slaughter! For we go to kill the witch and her Black Army! All those with children, those who despise me, go and serve the boy king, King Alfred! Conqueror of the Troll Hunters! And conqueror of Ordoh Brutum!"

Ordo turned and marched toward the fields full of orcs and trolls, waiting by their siege towers and catapults.

Ruuk and Brok stared after him. They turned to see the troll hunters amongst the children and the other troll hunters in the broors standing about, stunned. Then each troll hunter and each broor of hunters began to decide its fate.

While nearly two hundred fathers and the scores more who lost their children remained with Furioso and King Alfred, the rest, slowly in pairs, then groups, marched behind Ordoh Brutum.

Several leaders came up to King Alfred, kneeling before him. This was something troll hunters have never done.

"Conqueror of Ordoh Brutum and the Troll Hunters, we go to fight the Black Army and witch for our crimes against vatter... against the Father of Light. We go for the sins of our clan and brethren."

King Alfred wasn't sure how to respond. He merely nodded, slowly.

The troll hunters, nearly four thousand, sans the two hundred or so, began the march toward the Black Army.

There was no strategy, no tactic to their march. It was merely a straight march toward the nearest orc boss and his gang. The orcs were unsettled at the coming of the troll hunters, but not defensive. They merely assumed they were marching to join them. The front line of orcs attempted to move out of the way of the intimidating force of troll hunters entering their amassed army.

The trolls and the bigger orcs were in the rear of the army. Though the mass of the army saw the movement of the troll hunters, they thought nothing of it. They were impatiently waiting for new orders, to charge and attack. The sorcerers were chanting and invoking dark incantations in their groups amongst the Warlock Tower's many openings and in their surrounding wagons, meditating and controlling the masses of beastmen. All were merely waiting for the call to victory and did not detect the change in the troll hunters' allegiance.

Ordo and his troll hunters marched far into the mass of orcs, who were moving out of their way. It began to be disruptive such that the orcs began barking and howling at each other due to the crowding. The rising disorder spread amongst the legions till finally the orc bosses began to confront the troll hunters along the lines. Almost surreptitiously, as the orc bosses were cut down, the other orcs backed off, thinking they were just being warned. For that, brutal slaughter, a most decisive response, was the main language of an orc.

Ordo finally saw the first of the black orcs, gangs of larger orcs standing near the siege towers. Their four thousand was just a small triangle of men in a field of orcs and trolls and siege machines. The giant mountain trolls were waiting to push the score of siege towers forward. The war trolls, bulky giants in front of the towers, waited with heavy weapons, wearing thick armour. The serpentine black trolls were farther away -- by the great Tower of the Warlock.

The black orcs were not like the common orcs. A brutal slaying of one of their own was a challenge and, in this case, the start of the battle. For when Ordo slew the first black orc boss, a great war chief, the black orcs roared and charged forth. The four thousand troll hunters immediately swung furious flails in the midst of a hundred thousand orcs and trolls.

Sir Murith rushed to Gorham on the cart, pulling Brother Harkonen with him. "Heal him! Save him!" he cried. Murith slammed against the cart and furtively sorted through the chains and shackles to release Gorham from his bondage.

Harkonen spoke healing spells and touched Gorham, who did not move. "We must get him to the chapel! Together, Verboden and I may have the strength to save him."

Murith tried but could not release Gorham's chains. He gritted his teeth in anger at seeing Gorham near death. "The gnomes, they can break this iron!"

Harkonen took the reins of the goats and led them quickly back.

"We must get back to the castle," King Alfred shouted, albeit somewhat meekly.

The children and troll hunters were too focused on their emotional reunions to grasp the situation.

King Alfred stepped toward them. "Hello!? Everyone? We must get back to the castle!"

Still, only a few near him began to slowly get up. The rest cried and cried. And oddly, it was the big warrior men who cried, while the children merely stared wide-eyed and in wonder at the men, their fathers, before them.

Furioso, holding Red's hand, stood and stepped toward King Alfred. "Hey! Everyone! Troll hunters! Get your child and get on to the castle! Per King Alfred's order! NOW!"

The hunters suddenly awoke from their emotional state and looked up at Furioso, who stood with his child.

They rose and picked up their own weak children, then their helms, then their weapons.

"Come on yee brudders and now vatters! We follow the boy king!" Furioso cried out loud.

Suddenly, they heard a boom across the sky, then the sounds of horns and fighting, the sounds of orc cries and troll hunter howls.

"Let us hurry!" Furioso yelled.

Alfred and Verboden led them through the field of siege stones and into Grotham Keep.

Ordoh Brutum was of the Order of Brutality. His cleaver swung in huge swathes where nothing really slowed it. Using all of his body in a swooping motion, from taut muscular thickset legs to thickly corded muscular arms, Ordo swung better than the mightiest of trolls. And his troll hunter broor clans were almost as good. Their swings led to line after line of orcs falling.

The troll hunters swung massive weapons in droves, wiping out gangs of orcs as they advanced. Hundreds upon hundreds fell as the massive battle axes, glaives and polearms swung viciously through their ranks.

It was the black orcs that tried to form up fighting gangs near Ordo and the wedge formation where Ruuk and Brok joined in. They were hacking away at the vile creatures. As vicious and armoured as the black orcs were, they still were no match for Ordoh Brutum. He ripped through gangs of them near the siege towers. They began to howl and bark, spreading a warning amongst their ranks. More started moving their way

One managed to blow a horn before being slain by Ruuk. The warning carried across the massive bloated Black Army, to the orc war chiefs, the black trolls, and the Tower of the Warlock.

Sorcerers raced to the balconies to peer across the fields of their army, past the catapults and siege towers with their mountain trolls, to the small area where the troll hunters were. There, in the midst of their ocean of orcs and trolls, was this blackened arrowhead of furiously hacking and smashing troll hunters. The sorcerers hissed in vile contempt and signaled to hundreds of goblins clinging to the tower. They rushed to the horns and banners, blaring strident calls and waving the signal flags.

The orcs and trolls waiting across the land suddenly woke to the charge of the booming horns. They peered at the Tower of the Warlock and saw the many banners waving. They grunted and growled as they moved forward.

The sorcerers watched as the troll hunters decimated the black orcs and took down war and mountain trolls near them. They were like demons flitting about and toppling giants. The sorcerers hissed and called down, speaking in guttural tongues to one of their own below.

A sorcerer below waved up and turned to focus on his goblin servants, speaking chitter sounding commands. He rode on a chariot with an orc driver. It raced off as goblins riding upon it blared their horns. The nearby black trolls seethed in hatred hearing the call and sallied forth amongst the ranks of orcs. The sorcerer waved at them and pointed toward the fighting along the edge of the Black Army. He too spoke in a chitter-guttural tongue, yelling at the black trolls who peered across the crowds of evil beings. They could easily go forward toward the Keep amidst the organized ranks, along the open lines. But to cut across, toward the chaotic fighting on the western edge, the black trolls had to push their way diagonally through lines of orcs and giant trolls. It was a difficult affair requiring the acolytes and sorcerers to cast many spells of control.

The black trolls had to kill several orcs just to pass through as they hurried to the troll hunter betrayal.

It was their movement, like that of troll hunters, that made them so dangerous, even more dangerous than a black orc or war troll. They had greater intelligence and a more focused desire. And here in the Black Army, thousands of them began to converge on the troll hunters.

When the first black trolls broke through the failing lines of orcs and trolls, it was a furious response. Their shiny steel blades easily broke through the thick brittle cast-iron blades of the troll hunters and through their hide armour. It was a thunderous clang of steel versus iron. Troll hunters had already killed hundreds upon hundreds of orcs and scores of trolls and were somewhat worn from the onslaught. The black trolls charged in with no exhaustion and no pain. They swung great oriental swords, thick blades of shiny steel. Some swung them as giant swords. Others had the blades on steel poles. It was a flurry of massive steel blades cutting into the troll hunter lines.

The mix of troll hunter death screams with the black troll banshee howls alerted Ordo that their end was near. He turned to face a cadre of the black trolls and saw their blades swing through the troll hunter weapons. He was next to a siege tower felling a mountain troll and was given a moment of fortitude, of respite, to see the black troll attacks upon his falling brethren.

Brok and Ruuk were next to him, dealing death blows to black orcs and war trolls. Ordo quickly climbed the tower and saw below as the black trolls were decimating his hunters. He cried an angry howl then threw his useless cleaver into a black troll. It bounced off the steel skin of the demonic beast, and Ordo leapt.

The black troll turned too late as Ordo leapt upon him and grabbed him by his foul horns. Ordo twisted, quickly breaking the troll's neck. He rolled as steel blades swung upon him. Brok raced to his father's aid, only to be cut down by the oncoming trolls.

"No!" Ruuk, the smaller brother yelled, fighting his way through black orcs.

Ordo rose with a steel blade in his hand. He held it and liked the balance. He roared a vengeful roar as black trolls converged on him. He swung the steel in circles, twirling far greater feats of skill than the black trolls' own brilliance. He cut through them, and they fell one after the other. And with each fall, he kept focus on his plan. Ruuk leapt forward and was able to catch a black troll's blade thrown by Ordo.

He grabbed up other black troll weapons quickly and tossed them to his brethren. Ruuk tossed his bardiche at several black orcs, ending their charge. He raised his new weapon and quickly met the swing of a black troll. It was a powerful swing with great strength that would have easily thrown a knight across the field of battle – but not Ruuk, who pushed back and kicked at the black troll's legs, causing it to drop. This gave him just enough time to best the black troll and behead it.

Troll hunters down the line also quickly surmised the superior quality of steel the black trolls used to cut them down. Many retreated or avoided the black troll onslaught by rushing into orcs or around the siege machines and dimwitted mountain trolls. They would rather deal with a war troll than face the black troll's deathly steel.

Ordo climbed further up the siege tower and yelled out to all of them, "Take their steel! Take the towers!" He swung his steel blade around as the troll hunters below saw their only chance. Arrows flew at Ordo, but his armour and skins repelled them as he swayed and circled about. He climbed along the siege tower's frame and then leapt down upon groups of chasing black trolls. They were so intent on killing the troll hunters on the ground that an attack from above devastated their ranks.

The fighting was vicious, close and brutal. But there were only so many troll hunters. Even as they killed thousands, there were thousands more to come.

Hedor rushed down from the stairs to meet King Alfred at the gate. He stopped and nearly fell over.

"Oh, I didn't realize how big and scary they actually are!" Hedor cried, as troll hunters rambled into the courtyard with their children.

Abedeyan called from the wall, quite scared. "You sure they're not just using the children as a ruse?"

Alfred gave an odd smile.

Hedor composed himself. "King Alfred, those troll hunters out there are fighting like mad men. But they won't last much longer. We've got to help them!"

As if time had stopped, Alfred watched as the gnomes easily removed the shackles and chains from Gorham. The broken knight collapsed into Murith's arms. He carried him to the chapel. Brothers Harkonen and Verboden went with him. Alfred surveyed the troll hunters... the moorland children. He then looked up to Kumbo and Ruig on the walls with their men and then at Loranna atop the towers with her archers, her gazed fixed upon him. He saw Cory, Wilden and Nubio with the spearboys, who were still a bit nervous – for who wouldn't be nervous with more troll hunters in the courtyard than all of his men and children on the walls?

Alfred passed Hedor without responding, quickly going up the wall to see the fighting beyond. Hedor, unperturbed came up, as did Gib and Pep.

"Oh, they put up a good fight, those troll hunters. But their task is impossible!" Gib said.

The sound of horns blared again, this time across the whole of the Black Army. It was evident that the troll hunters had merely stirred the hornet's nest – a vast nest of a hundred thousand evil beastmen.

"They're on the move!" Gib said as Pep jumped up and down pointing along the front lines of the orc army. It was a massive shuddering, like a wave of energy across thousands of bees. The orcs began their assault toward the castle. Siege towers suddenly shook into action, pushed forth by mountain trolls. The catapults and trebuchets lay silent as their troll crews abandoned them, picking up huge war mattocks and giant spears.

A shriek across the sky jolted the group on the castle walls. The shriek seemed to blast at their very nerves as many panicked and fled the walls, tumbling down the stairs and off the walls. King Alfred waved his arms, yelling for calm.

Hedor hid under the wall, grasping his chest. He spat angrily, "How many more frights can a man take!?"

Kumbo and Ruig ducked and yet tried to keep their men atop the walls. The scream had a powerful magic to it that sent chills into the bravery of all men.

King Alfred stared up, following the flying vulture beast, the source of that terrorizing shriek. It was as if the Dark Servant, mounted upon it and Alfred were staring right at each other. Amidst the unfinished towers, Loranna and her girls still had courage. The towers did not have their final tops with battlements or roofs, but were still higher than the walls. Loranna, firm atop the stone, aimed her bow, and the girls followed suit.

However the monstrous vulture that slowly waved its fowl feathers was high up and circling at a good pace. It shrieked again, causing more fear to echo throughout the castle.

Alfred watched fearlessly, waiting.

Hunched below the battlements, Hedor watched as King Alfred, in full armour with a great spear and shield, kept his eyes fixed on the Dark Servant. "How is he so fearless?!" he grunted angrily.

The giant vulture made a full circle and then, obeying the Dark Servant, veered and flew off. Its flight seemed slow and lumbering as it soared far out past the vast array of the oncoming Black Army.

"Gnomes!" King Alfred yelled.

Gib and Pep looked at King Alfred, who looked at them with a nod. They smiled and chortled as they leapt from the battlements and stood at the edge of the walkway.

"Gnomes! Gnomes! Carry out the plan!"

Chapter Forty-Two

Alfred's Plan

At the public library, Alfred was rummaging through many books. He had a complimentary library book sack. He took a light happy skip as he found book after book in the "APPLIED SCIENCE 600" section. He whistled a little tune while pulling books and scanning the pages, then putting them in his sack.

Wooly passed by with a single book, *Windows 10 Made Simple.* "You ready, Alfred?"

"Almost! I gotta go ask the librarian for some help."

Wooly nodded and went to the reading area.

"Shhhhh..." a small quaint looking librarian said, coming down the aisle with a cart. He was actually surprised to see a boy so enthusiastic about books.

"Hi," Alfred said softly, tiptoeing up to him with his heavy bag.

"Well, nice to see a young man so interested in books these days. How can I help you?" the librarian asked, noticing the bag. It gave him a sense of hope that the next generation would be into reading.

"Now, I've done a ton of research online. But I really find books to have way more detail in them that you just don't find on websites."

"You are sooo right. The blogs and websites online are so thin compared to the research and thoroughness of a good printed book! They mostly write those for web surfers and not for serious research!"

The librarian stopped himself, realizing he had spoken too loudly.

"Yeah, so I was wondering if you could help me out. I want to read and study everything on this," whispered Alfred sternly.

"It's so great to have a boy your age in the library wanting to read books. It's so rare. My faith in the next generation has been renewed."

"Oh uh, thanks," Alfred smiled.

"No, thank you! Oops, too loud." The librarian gave Alfred a goofy smile. "Anyway, how can I help you?"

"I'm looking for every single book you have on medieval cannons and mortars, plus how to make black powder."

Chapter Forty-Three

The Great Battle

Gnomes suddenly rushed from the tunnels below, up into the courtyard, through fallen rubble and piles of siege stones from the bombardment. They brought forth ropes and pulleys, easily scaling the very walls they built, and ran braided steel cables through deep-set iron rings. Deep holes had already been carved out in the walkways at the base of the battlement walls, and rings had been set in the holes. Other gnomes pulled away the tent coverings and hay and wood pallets to reveal the cannons taken from the ogres. There were a good dozen of them, cleaned up and secured to thick mobile carriages. Alfred had them hidden in the courtyard at the base of the walls.

"I knew you gnomes were up to something!" Hedor said, smiling on the edge of insanity, blinking crazily.

Gnomes placed steel plates against the walkway edges so the cables would easily slide up and over. They pulled up the carriages, which rolled up the walls via their wheels, to the walkway using pulleys and counterweights.

"Hey, don't even need to dismantle our battlement weights. Just use the siege stones! Hah!" Pep said. He and many gnomes quickly carried up all the bombarded siege stones. They gathered them and put them into leather sacks. A dozen gnomes clung to the counterweighted sacks and quickly lowered them while a cannon rode up against the inner wall.

Hedor and his men rolled the cannons to different spots on the walkway as gnomes revealed the deep-set rings. They quickly used bits of steel cable running through the rings to tie the cannons down.

Other gnomes carried leather bundles of cannonballs, some large, some small. The weight of iron and stone to a gnome was less than that to a man. The men, of course, helped, bringing up powder and fuses.

All of this happened rather quickly as the huge force of orcs and siege towers lumbered forward toward the castle. Thankfully, the main attack with the siege towers came from the east up the broad slope. The southern wall, with the main gate, already had a small force of orcs with ladders threatening it. The western wall was the same. These forces weren't as large as those of the main attack, but a few thousand strong could easily overwhelm the castle walls if no one defended it.

King Alfred had something else to welcome them with. Gnomes raised several cannons that had come up from the tunnels and were not for the walls. They were shorter than the other cannons. They were squat iron cauldrons – or massive mortars. These were placed in the courtyard. Gnomes pulled out the carrying poles and stretched their wee'lil backs.

Gnomes filled them with black powder and smoothly fit stones and then waited for the signal from King Alfred. These devices fired high-arcing stones that would come nearly straight down with a massive explosive force.

"Loranna!" King Alfred shouted up to the tower.

Loranna hopped over some stones to get to a side so she could see him. She was still far off along the opposite side, up on the western tower. She waved back.

"Keep the orcs busy. You must hold them off!" Alfred yelled, pointing to the southern and western walls.

She gave a thumbs up and went back to her position. The girls began a rain of arrows from those towers. They were conspicuously not at the towers or wall facing the major attack.

King Alfred waved to Cory, who brought forth his boys from the tunnels. "How goes it below, Sergeant Cory?!" King Alfred yelled.

"Wilden and a squad are holding the tunnels with a crew of gnomes. The goblins have taken a beating, and their attacks have lessened!"

"They are expecting the victory to come from here," yelled Hedor, above the rising din of the oncoming horde.

King Alfred cupped his hands and yelled, "Take the western and southern walls!"

Cory raised his spear and nodded affirmation. He led one squad to a wall, and Nubio led another squad to the other.

Furioso and his troll hunters saw the busy work of King Alfred: the cannons being setup with all their provisions, the archergirls shooting, the spearboys heading to their places, and the many gnomes pulling up odd steel tubes with handles and many, many bundles of steel javelins. The hunters gathered in their groups, deciding what to do.

Hedor stood close to King Alfred. "I hope they decide quickly. We're gonna need them, King Alfred's plan or not!"

"Here they come!" Kumbo yelled out, nervous before the onslaught.

"Could use a knight or two as well!" Captain Hedor said, looking out upon the massive siege towers, whose shadows were looming near. The sun was rising in the east, behind the orc hordes, the giant war and mountain trolls, and the massive towers. It made them all stark silhouettes, appearing darker and more scary looking than they already were.

"Awfully close," gulped Captain Hedor.

King Alfred stood and watched. He felt strange. Fear and horror should have overtaken him. But oddly, he was at peace. In his vision, he saw the troll hunters with their children, the moorland father with his daughter saved from the wolf curse, and he saw Verboden praying with Harkonen in their ruined chapel. It was extraordinary. It wasn't fear but love that permeated his being. He stared in awe at the scene before him. He almost felt an admiration at how incredible this was, to see such a horde of monsters coming forth – to see the Black Army of Gorbogal. But then he heard the cries and wails of the children below. He knew that before him was pure evil, brutality, cruelty and no sense of a soul or compassion. It was a horrible massive machine focused on killing anything that got in its way. He gritted his teeth, and finally felt rising fear as a force of determination. He saw his father, training him in swordsmanship. He saw his mother and father before him. He realized perhaps why he didn't fear. He knew he could leave at any moment, escape to the safety of his own world. He realized that this was why he could drive on, in this world, because he knew he could easily escape. "I will not," he uttered.

He looked to see the troll hunters leave their children, the very ones they had abandoned to die, as sacrifices. They had only just met in an emotional surrender. But now, once again, they were having to part from them.

Lady Nihan, the maids, and Khanafian nurses knew their role. They went amongst the children, taking their hands and separating them from their long lost fathers. The troll hunters knew that they had to fight, and they had to win, in order to ensure that these children knew no pain and suffering again.

Furioso could have easily leapt up the stone walls to the walkway by King Alfred, but he chose the stone steps, ascending them with determination. The other troll hunters gathered below, all two hundred of them looking up, fiercely resolute.

"I've come to you, King Alfred. We have all come to defend your Keep, and fight to the very last for our children, and for the boy king," Furioso said. He looked upon the massive army and siege towers coming to the walls. He gritted his teeth, grimacing at the fate before them all. "I have never..."

King Alfred smiled, though he shook with each huge thunderous creak and clang from the oncoming siege towers and the roars of mountain trolls lumbering forward. Even so, he smiled. "Take the walls. Spread your men out and defend the walls!"

Furioso nodded and waved to his men. The troll hunters immediately knew what to do and within seconds were upon the four walkways behind the battlements.

"Oh, they fill out the walls nicely!" Captain Hedor barked at Ruig and Kumbo, who shook each other, clasping in manly joy. But their elation quickly diminished as they turned to witness the slow vast onslaught before them.

Orcs rushed forward, thousands of them with bows, between the mountainous towers. Horns blasted from the siege towers. Hundreds of goblins upon the towers, like ants scrambling along a mound, raised their bows to add to the massive volley.

"Incoming fire!" yelled Hedor. His diminutive soldiers, only a handful mixed amongst the larger troll hunters, passed the warning down the walls and into the courtyard. "Take cover! Incoming arrows! From the east!"

Loranna and her girls merely lowered into the towers. Cory and his boys, in splendid steel armour with shields, turned and formed turtle-like groupings with their shields covering them.

The women and children sought the eastern wall, under Alfred, or dropped into the crevices and tunnels where parts of the kitchen still stood. The gnomes crawled and buried themselves under stones and rubble.

The orcs unleashed a rain of black arrows. The arrows poured upon the castle and courtyard with a mighty volley. The men atop the walls were suddenly pulled within the cover of the troll hunters, whose iron armour and hides easily took the incoming fire. Arrows upon arrows skittered and scattered amongst them like black hail. The sound of thousands of arrows hitting rocks and stone and armour was utterly deafening, like coarse dirty rain or hail, and it seemed to go on for a long time.

The orc archers howled in joy at their grand attack. They waved their bows, hitting and smacking each other with a huge ruckus. But a few pointed, and then the rest looked up and saw a handful of arrows returning. They laughed at the arrows lit with flickering fire, only a dozen or so dotting the sky. They wouldn't even reach the siege towers. The arrows reached their pinnacle and then descended in amongst the orc archers. A few hit orcs, who shuddered and fell, rolling over. Other arrows hit the muddy slippery ooze of the earth. Orcs were used to all kinds of foul and muddy terrain. They lived in it. And this ground they marched on was the same to them: foul, dark, black, slippery and oh yes – oily.

At first, the oil lit slowly. But then the fwoomph blast, from fire sensing the fuel, exploded all around them.

"So ends the field of archers," Captain Hedor said, standing up from behind a battlement, brushing off arrows from the battlements and walkway as if to keep it clean.

Thousands of orcs screamed and flailed wildly as the fires spread through the field of muddy black oil.

"Could have used that oil for the walls. But okay, works there too," Ruig huffed.

"How goes it on the eastern and southern walls?!!!" Hedor yelled.

Loranna looked back and waved a thumbs up as the orcs with ladders amidst the fields scrambled in terror and pain, for they too were being chased by many smoking flames. And the girls did not let up on their continual firing of arrows. Cory and Nubio shrugged, quite bored on their walls.

"Girls... Archers!" a troll hunter said to another, each nodding with a smug look.

Back at the main front, the flames spread out, stopping the rest of the attack, or so they thought. But the mountain trolls pushed the vast towers through the flames, smothering them. Not all areas lit, and the flames did not last long. The mountain trolls and war trolls began lumbering through, ignoring the feeble fires. Hordes of orcs were still pushed on, stomping out flames as they went.

They slowly rumbled their incredible force through the pillars of smoke. The towers literally towered over the walls. Trolls barked and roared, knowing they were so close to a brutal slaughter. Black orcs raced behind the siege towers, leaping upon and crawling up their many scaffolds and footholds. There were no ladders or stairs. There was merely a massive frame of wood and iron bindings, spikes and points, which goblins and orcs climbed upon and hung to, ready to leap off and over the walls.

King Alfred raised his armoured arm.

The gnomes all went into action. "Spring loaders! Eastern wall!"

Furioso peered down as dozens of gnomes scrambled along the rubble and through a field of black arrows, each carrying several steel tubes and bundles of steel javelins. He did not know what they were and was curious to see what they would do. Down at the base of the wall, the gnomes got the children to make room. Each gnome loaded a javelin into a steel tube and then cranked a handle. Then each lifted a small steel lid from a hole in the wall and shoved his tube through it. A gnome hung from the pulley above them with his hand raised, waiting for the signal.

Hedor peered down. "I thought those were just gnome decorations!"

King Alfred stood, waiting, watching. Hedor looked to Alfred and then to the oncoming war trolls. The oily fields of fire that devastated the orc archers and kept many orcs at bay made the war trolls advancing seem even more frightening. The flames gave them a fiery orange hue, and wisps of smoke surrounded them as if conjuring them from the pits of hell. Hedor grimaced as he looked from the trolls to a silent Alfred. He went back and forth, grimacing a tad more as the trolls got nearer to the walls. Alfred was not moving. He looked again at the trolls, and then at Alfred.

"King Alfred!?" Hedor screamed a tiny bit.

"Not yet!" King Alfred said as the war trolls slammed against the walls, hammering away at the stone. They pounded the walls with their heavy war hammers and mattocks.

"Oooh, let us have a go at'em!" Furioso exclaimed.

"No..." King Alfred said patiently. Hedor rolled his eyes.

They then saw the towers coming through the thinning black smoke and bearing down upon them, teaming with hundreds of goblins and black orcs ready to leap.

"FIRE!" King Alfred waved.

The gnome on the pulley waved. The gnomes below, mixed amongst Lady Nihan and the children, winked at them, then pulled their triggers.

The war trolls suddenly howled a different sound, not a mean cruel bark or roar, but a wail, a painful confused scream. They dropped, grabbing their thighs and shins. Some still stood. But to see dozens of their bestial brethren drop and roll was quite disturbing, especially for simple-minded war beasts.

The gnomes loaded javelins into the shooters again, cranked the shooters, and chortling amongst the children and Lady Nihan, then re-inserted the shooters in the tubes. The children, though not as giddy as the gnomes, at least had a respite from their paralyzing fear.

"Fire!" King Alfred yelled.

Another round of devastating steel javelins exploded from tiny holes at the base of the walls. The steel projectiles shot into the fallen trolls or those still standing, and this time many stopped moving completely.

Some began to stumble and crawl away, but the ground before the siege towers was now blocked. The fallen war trolls made for a good mound of blockage that no mountain troll could push a massive siege tower over. Those trolls would have to be moved out of the way. And it appeared no one was inclined to do so.

"Cannons!" King Alfred yelled. He turned to look up at Loranna as Gib and Pep and the gnomes gave a thumbs up along the dozen cannons.

She gave him a thumbs up and pointed down to the center of the courtyard.

King Alfred nodded. He yelled into the courtyard. "Mortars! Turn to the eastern wall!"

The few gnomes with the mortars amidst the rubble turned their squat short weapons to the east. They had to brush off or pull orc arrows out of the mortars, but this was not a real bother. The ground was littered like a pin cushion with arrows, but the gnomes learned to live with it. After all... there's a war going on!

The gnomes on the wall got the men and troll hunters to clear out. Not a problem for the hunters, but Hedor and his men had to use normal clumsy men movements to get around or scramble over the cannons to get clear. Some aided in the loading of black powder and cannonballs as well as readying the fuse, but most got out of the way heck-a-fast!

Gnomes lined up their cannon sights on the stalled siege towers where orcs and goblins scrambled about wondering what was next. Mountain trolls roared as acolytes tried to order them to the front to pull the dead war trolls out of the way. Their dark magic was not strong enough, especially when the mountain trolls saw only a few surviving war trolls crawling back or wailing amongst their dead.

The troll hunters looked down with disappointment. "Too easy! Too easy!" they complained bitterly.

Furioso couldn't help but smile as he watched the boy king, standing amidst the cannons, making sure they were all ready. He did not know it, but he whispered "Alfred" in admiration.

"FIRE!!!" was the call of the boy king.
And then the cannons fired.

Great plumes of black smoke exploded above the walls of Grotham Keep. It was so loud that even Ordo and his struggling troll hunters heard it from their failing lines deep within the masses of the Black Army. Across the devastated land, the orcs and trolls all stopped to peer at something that could possibly be more threatening and grand than they were. The Warlock Tower seemed to shudder with the booming echo as hundreds of goblins and acolytes poked their heads out from it, trying to comprehend the explosive force emanating from the tiny walls of the small castle.

Cannonballs ripped through the siege towers, exploding wood and brittle iron into devastating shrapnel. The towers were not greatly engineered, and the frames were put together more like patchwork than an engineered structure. Chunks of supports shook and collapsed. Goblins and orcs were flung into the air.

The entire scrambling upon the towers and trolls clambering all about suddenly froze as the tops exploded into a shower of debris.

"FIRE!" yelled a small voice atop the castle wall.

And Boom! Boom! Boom! went the cannons along the wall. The siege towers exploded again and again. Orcs and goblins flew in all directions. Timber twirled like devastating spears into cowering trolls and flailing black orc regiments. Cannonballs blew through and bounced along the ground, exploding ranks of orcs and trolls in their path.

Ordo, from his vantage point on the siege tower that his hunters took over, saw the devastation. The black trolls climbing and fighting upwards turned as well. They showed for the first time in their bestial lives – doubt.

"Well done, boy king," Ordo managed to say, amidst the fight of his life.

King Alfred then waved to the mortars in the courtyard, "FIRE!"

The gnomes lit the fuses and scrambled away, many being a little too devious in their excited expressions.

"This black powder may be a little bit more fun than our coiled steel spring contraptions!" Gib said, peering down from the walkway.

Pep shrugged, "A bit more dangerous!" He patted their cannon.

"Exactly!" Gib huffed back.

Both nodded and laughed a most devious laugh.

The mortars blew huge plumes as giant boulders flew into the air.

"Oooh, like fourth of a jewel's eye!" Pep said.

"Hey, Alfred says that!" Gib responded.

"I know! What does it mean again?" Pep answered and asked.

"No idea."

Everyone watched as the giant stones rocketed high up and over the walls with a thin wisp of smoke, then descended down upon the siege towers, ripping straight down and exploding the structures outward.

"Ohh! Like fourthy jewel's eye!!" they screamed and danced their little gnome feet.

Another mortar bomb hit the earth, rupturing the icky mud into a huge splash of kinetic energy. Orcs flew, and giant trolls whirled about like rag dolls, slamming against each other and the collapsing siege towers.

Furioso rubbed his helmet. Troll hunters were shrugging, standing a bit stiff and bored.

"You have to admit, it's still a good show," Hedor commented. Though taller, he was much smaller than the squat Furioso.

Furioso looked beyond the wall of devastation, the collapsed debris and panicking trolls. In the distance he could see several stalled siege towers. Upon them were Ordo and his remaining troll hunters. They had taken the siege towers and fought from those. The troll hunters were adept climbers and found refuge in them when fighting the superior armed black trolls. Yet the inevitable was obvious, as the troll hunters and Ordo were surrounded, and the raging fight for their lives was dwindling their numbers.

"We have to help Ordo!" Furioso said under his breath, slamming the battlement nearest him.

Hedor shrunk back but knew the red haired hunter's frustration did not lie with him. He looked to King Alfred. "Best you seek the King's orders on that. We still need to defend the castle."

Furioso nodded and quickly leapt over cannons and battlements to King Alfred. "Ordo is still out there. We need to meet up with them and bring as many back as we can!"

King Alfred looked out to the distant towers to see the calamitous battle that was taking place beyond many lines of the foe. Hunters fell as black trolls ascended the towers. It looked brutal, with many losses of the evil beasts, yet the numbers were against the hunters.

King Alfred looked at Furioso. "No, I need you here, to defend these walls."

"But..." Furioso reared up and then, in a sudden exhalation, realized something. "Yes, my king." He bowed quickly and climbed away.

Furioso bounded back to his position aside the cannons. The troll hunters began to move. "No!" Furioso yelled. "Stand your ground!"

"But we have to fight to Ordo!" another troll hunter yelled.

"No! The boy king has ordered us to defend these walls!" Furioso yelled. The troll hunters, clinging to the wall, stared at each other and solemnly realized the fate of Ordo and their brethren on the siege towers. They climbed back up and stood stoically.

Furioso looked on as the gnomes and men reloaded, and King Alfred again yelled "Fire!" As the cannons boomed their plumes of smoke, cannonballs flew across the fields of orcs and trolls, exploding through the siege tower rubble.

Round after round of cannonballs tore through the lines of the Black Army, forcing it into retreat. Hedor and his men yelled and hollered in joyous relief, clasping each other and hopping like children. But they noticed that the possible victory was bittersweet for the troll hunters, as they knew the fate of their brethren deep within the enemy lines.

Sir Murith suddenly appeared on the wall next to Hedor. "Have I missed anything?"

"Oh, no, no, only the devastation before you!" Hedor said, waving at the crumbling siege towers and flailing, crawling, wailing war trolls.

"Oh," said Sir Murith as he peeked over.

"How's Sir Gorham!?" Hedor asked a bit too casually leaning against a battlement, picking at his ungloved fingernail.

"He'll live. He will live. But he will sorely miss this fight, I'm afraid," Sir Murith sighed.

"Ah well, can't fight every battle," Hedor shrugged, biting a loose nail.

However, the siege was not over. The Black Army was still massive, and the major part of the force was not fully affected by the artillery annihilation. Actually, even the front lines, as blown and battered as they were, still had many numbers, even if they were scrambling and routed. As they formed up with the other forces in the rear, they were conscripted back into the lines.

And the Tower of the Warlock had not yet played its hand. Suddenly, goblins upon it began pounding their drums and blowing their horns. A gigantic troll, the biggest mountain troll, it seemed, pulled out a massive horn and blew it long and hard. From the tower a booming chant seemed to echo across the field. It was a sorcerer's chant. Red smoke emanated from the massive structure. The red enchanted smoke seemed to spread against the wind or nature, winding its way amongst the evil army. It spread even as Ordo and his hunters fought the black trolls. The tendrils spread and then dissipated over wide swathes as the sorcerer chants continued in a mysterious yet amplified way.

And as suddenly as it happened, it seemed to fade, and the whole of the Black Army awoke. Fury and rage spread amongst them, from lowly orc to mountain troll. They all suddenly raised their weapons. A sea of waving iron and steel glimmered in the harsh sun. Banners were raised across the ocean of orcs. Like a mass migration of suicidal monsters, they began a sudden and crazed charge straight for the walls.

Ladders were brought forth, as were a few remaining siege towers. They rolled them, seemingly twice as fast as the last, around the sides of the destroyed ones.

Though Alfred ordered his men to hurry and load the cannons and fire at will, the orcs and trolls poured around, amongst, and over the destroyed towers like waves of a massive flood. They ran straight for the walls.

The gnomes with the spring loaders fired a volley, ripping down many. But many of their javelins merely pierced the already dead war trolls at the base of the walls. Goblins easily ascended the stone walls as the troll hunters went into action, fighting off the scurrying beasts. Hedor and Murith had their portion to defend as goblins leapt up. It was a sudden, up close and fierce fight.

Orcs reared ladders in a crazed rabid way even as cannons ripped through their lines. War trolls held the ladders steadfast as orc after orc hurriedly climbed up.

King Alfred yelled, "Furioso, the trolls!"

Furioso saluted then waved at his hunters. They leapt over the fray and down, plunking their spiked weapons into the war trolls that held ladders or hammered away at the walls. Just as quickly as they dispensed with the trolls and climbed back up, more trolls would charge in, slamming into the climbing hunters, causing the fight to be horrendously close and bitter.

Loranna and the archergirls ran to the nearby towers facing eastward. Arrows suddenly came down rapid fire from each tower, decimating climbing orcs.

War trolls rounded the wall from the east to the south, where they congregated at the main gate, pounding on it with their war hammers. Several troll hunters leapt upon them, killing them and raging in victory.

Cory and Nubio scanned the western wall where there were only a few orcs with their ladders.

"You go! We can defend this wall!" Abedeyan said with a few farmers with weapons, bow and arrow.

Cory nodded and waved the spearboys to the other walls.

"Of course, keep an ear out, case I call you back!" Abedeyan yelled after them.

Cory waved back as they hurried across the walkways to the other side.

Orcs and goblins poured over the walls but were no match for Cory and his spearboys, who were a wall of spears and steel shields. They literally cleared the side walls as they trudged along, taking out orcs and their ladders.

The fight was still raging. It was a mass of destruction, and the orcs and trolls did not care. Even as cannonballs exploded amongst them, as mortar bombs crashed down upon them, as arrow after arrow flew into them, and as troll hunters alighted upon and swung piercing blows through their thick hides, the beasts came on, wave after wave.

Furioso and his troll hunters gave up the ground and walls and retreated to the walkways, fighting alongside Hedor and his men. The ground was packed with orcs and trolls, piling atop each other, climbing up a variety of ladders, some shoddy wood, others iron banded.

A siege tower finally impacted against the southern wall where troll hunters and Cory's squad met them. Goblins and orcs leapt from the tower onto the walkway. War trolls climbed up between the tower and the wall. The troll hunters met the onslaught brutally, even leaping back onto the bristling tower to fight them there. But it was sheer numbers that mattered here. Hundreds to thousands began filling the ladders and tower, even as the troll hunters and spearboys fought fiercely and with great skill.

Furioso cleared many orcs off the walls and could see beyond the massive sea of orcs and trolls piling over the collapsed towers and many dead. He did not see a victory in this. He saw beyond as he fought side by side with Captain Hedor.

"There, beyond the Black Army to the south, there are more trolls coming out of that forest!?" he groaned.

Hedor found a moment to look up, fighting off a black orc with much strain. "No, it's a storm amongst those trees!? An evil wind!?" he gasped, leaning for a brief moment against a battlement.

Sir Murith managed a moment of his own to peer where they looked and were pointing in utter fear. He saw, beyond the legions of orcs, a vast forest of trees, either billowing as trolls pushed through it or swaying in a great storm. It was a strange sight to see when the smoke all around them was rising steadily upward. "That is the way to Telehistine!" Murith cried. "There is no forest of trees along the Southern Road!"

"Doesn't it lead to the Faerie Realm as well?" pondered Hedor.

They all looked at the new forest of billowing violent trees.

Chapter Forty-Four

The Quest of Lord Dunther

A tale to tell, of the Lordly Knight, a royal baron.
And a queen, a magical faerie, of the elvish acclaim.
Some say this is a tragic story, but not yee,
oh not yee, for this is a story of love reclaimed.

A knight began his journey, from the boy king,
A task set before him, to unite the realm.
But 'for we speak of his journey,
remember his trap.
For saved he did, this queen,
and his heart, the queen had wrapped!

A curse he felt, many seasons, a burdensome call,
and when the boy king let, the knight did his all.
A horse she sent, enchanted mount,
to bring her love, straightway announced.

He rode from summer to fall,
down the treacherous Southern Road,
Away from Telehistine, and to the faerie hall.
But the elves of the forest land'of ole!

254

The Quest of Lord Dunther

And female were they – no man betold!

Slept he in dark forests, awaiting her call.
But she came naught, for faeries kept her soul,
and in darkness she rested,
from years of slavery she had fester'd.
The faeries watched the knight, espied him they did,
awaiting the moment, to kill him they w'd.
But the horse belayed and neighed, prancing a rout,
making a fuss, what 'tis this, all about?
The knight knew naught his fate, cooing his horse,
as the faeries surrounded, ready for worse.

So they captured his mare, and tied him up too,
in his deep sleep, he could not fight through.
The mare spoke whispers to them,
but oh angry were they, for a woman's scorn,
a millennial had they.

No man t'were allowed, in their Faerie Realm,
guardians had they, giant trees all around.
But even so, thusly they lived,
sorcery and black magics
were their loathing distress.

A battle they had, these many years, against an evil man,
and the knight, they surmised, was another to end.
An Agent of Scourge was there, at the edge of their realm,
testing their magic and cursing their land.

Lord Dunther his name, Alfred he claimed,
who was this knight, and a boy king he named?
The faeries beat him and charmed him,
deluding his mind, spiteful were they, not very kind.

The men of the Westfold, no savior to they,
For men had failed, all had gone astray,
the women elves, faeries of old, lived without them,
glad and safe, was their realm.

255

The Quest of Lord Dunther

Hidden in their forest, but Dunther had heard,
little they knew, his mare whispered, how absurd!
Under attack, was their realm, no safety, no way!
That Agent was destroying and taking away!
Their guardian trees to make them betray!

Dunther listened as the mare, being nice to them,
cooing and neighing, listened within.
Fights had the faeries, but losing were they,
versus the Agent of Scourge,
and the trees were his play.

How could faeries lose trees, Guardians of the Realm?
How could their queen be asleep?
Not knowing her knight
Was so close to her life?

Dunther listened and waited alone,
in his dark cell, betwixt a tree and a'shroom.
Under roots and moss, he crouched in his cell,
angry at them, angry to yell!

There was no time as he yelled, no time at all,
he yelled and yelled, but t'was no avail.
Then one day, many days past moons and nights,
for he could hear their fears as the trees did fight.
He told his mare, to go find the queen, to awaken her,
no matter her dream.

And awaken did she, even as the horse,
galloped then sprinted, past faerie guards and spirits!
Wounded near death, with darts amidst,
Dunther's mount fell before her, breaking the mist!

Leapt from her slumber, she saw before her,
her gift to her love and the faeries destroy'r!
Anger'tis not the word, tenfold nay a hundred,

The Quest of Lord Dunther

then the word be right, for how she felt that ver'night!
Healed her horse she did and watched it trot,
where she did not know, but followed a lot,
to the cell, to the hole, dark within the roots,
tears flowed from her eyes, to see him so brute.

Faeries, faeries all around her, she wept.
She knew their anger, for it, she did let.
And yet lain before her, upon the soil,
lie a man so weak, she knew he was dying.
Let him! Let him! They all did cry, for no man needed
her, a burden she knew why.

Her gift to him, the mare, came and chose him,
above all the faeries, even the queen.
The mare chose him, as it lay aside him,
the faeries knew not, for she chose to chide them.

The queen healed him, brought forth her love,
even as the faeries called for death, not a dove.
For the forest was failing, man was the cause,
the Guardian trees were turning, and no one could pause.

The queen needed her powers, to fight off that man,
and not be weakened by another, this man.
Dunther is my name, he called forth aloud,
even scaring the faeries who hated his fame.

To touch her he tried, but flew away she 'flied,
let him go, she called, the faeries pretended to bide!

Dunther saw the Guardian trees, fighting each other,
some turned, some free.
An Agent was causing calamity,
turning the faeries, upon their own kin!

Gorbogal was the cause, he knew it for sure,
turning his mount, he returned to the Realm.
But faeries would not let him, catching him again,

The Quest of Lord Dunther

even as their queen was striving against her guardians.

They took him to a hidden site, where sacrifice remained,
and to some dark god they gave blood, for shame.
His mare could not escape, for they ended its life,
it screamed a horrible cry, even the faeries knew – 'twas not right.

For the queen heard, came hither, knowing their dark hearts,
and she stepped forward to stop them,
but the faeries claimed forest rights!

And Dunther, bound, saw his end by a dagger,
bleeding out his blood to their darkest wager.
But he had one last request,
since faeries love games, heard his behest.

Who was their dark god, who was their Truth?
Where did this come from, a wager or moot?
The faeries did laugh for long have they held,
this was their truth, this was their noose.

And who was their god, that he was to be
blood let?
Shut up, they said, not wanting to know,
that their ways of sacrifice, were not proud to show.

I am their way, the queen finally said.
Stepping forward, of the faeries she was the head.
Is she then your truth, your god,
the faeries she led?

The faeries realized, a queen was not just she,
but their god, their truth, and in her they heed.

So if your god is her, a person before thee,
then your truth can change, as the wind upon a loose leaf!
The faeries raised their knives,
ready to kill, no man will insult them,
and their worship of nil.

The Quest of Lord Dunther

Oh Father of Light, unchanging are yee,
but this Queen is in love,
and in love,
WITH ME!

Obey me, my queen, the love of my life,
loosen my cords and I do what I please!

The Queen loosened his cords and set him free,
before them he stood, the faeries could see.
One rose her blade, not believing the Truth,
and her Queen stopped her, completely, through and through.

The faeries stared, realizing the Truth,
that their truth stood on a whim,
and now the heart of a man.
And their dark god and dark truth, was all just a sham.

And Lord Dunther held sway, upon the Queen that they
worshiped.
They saw him take her, fully to kiss,
and they knew finally,
what they had completely missed.

Before they could start, a new religion or folly,
Lord Dunther made charge,
to fight the evil sorcery!

His mare they laid rest, for no life remained,
the Queen wanted anger,
but he soothed her mad aim.
And refocused her mind, on the doom before them.

Heed not the Guardians, that the Agent has charmed,
go around them!
Lord Dunther said, leading the charge.
To the Dark Tower, where the Scourge hid,
no need to fight the forest,

The Quest of Lord Dunther

when faeries flew 'stead.

A new mare the Queen tamed, this one the daughter,
of his mount, lost in shame.
And flew fast it did, past trees who swung,
and trees who craned.

The Agent of Scourge was not ready, for such an attack,
by faeries no less, alighting his stack.
The Tower was filled with golems of wood,
made by his hands but useless as, well wood.
For faeries came down, lighting his crown,
with fire and fury,
powers unused for an age.

And Dunther raced to the Tower, too late it seems,
as faeries sat upon it quite dour.
Why are you sad, Lord Dunther asked.
The faeries responded, why did it take a man,
to complete our task?

No matter the man, or the woman it takes,
we fight for Truth, a never ending state.
Lord Dunther called out, as they reclaimed their trees,
the Guardians lined up, and before him on knees.

No, no, no, I am not your god, nor am I your king,
but there is a boy, who needs your fighting.
We go forth to him, I ask you, as a man.

The Queen said she'd go, but no other must be,
for their Faerie Realm needs healing.
The faeries and trees, giant Guardians are thee,
had free will to choose, so they chose mightily.

Then forth shall we march, a boy king needs we!

Chapter Forty-Five

Turn of Events

Hedor screamed back. "Did that tree hurl an orc?"

Sir Murith dispensed with a black orc and stood upon it to get a better view at the horizon line of swirling, swaying trees. Dozens of orcs flew into the sky as the trees seemed to sway mightily, furiously. Long extended branches or limbs swung into the air, and orcs were hurled from them. Dozens more and more, all along the line of trees, flew like leaves in a storm. "Those are not trees, are they?"

Hedor grimaced, "Well, they aren't tree TREES!"

"It's Lord Dunther and the faerie queen!" yelled King Alfred, thrusting his spear, pushing an orc back off a ladder.

Hedor looked at Ruig and Kumbo, midgets betwixt Furioso and the troll hunters. They gritted smiling teeth then suddenly hurrahed, even amidst the flurry of frenetic sword buckling action.

"No time for reunion celebrations!" yelled Sir Murith, fighting back orc after orc ascending a ladder. A troll claw suddenly grabbed a battlement, climbing precariously up. It clamped down so powerfully as to make Sir Murith fall back. Furioso quickly punctured the giant hand with his battleaxe spike, and the creature released, falling back down amongst the horde of orcs.

"Gib, Pep! The long steel cables, tie them to the rings and to the hunters!" ordered King Alfred. The gnomes glanced at the steel cables about the unused cannons and the troll hunters all about. They got it and scurried. They quickly untied them from the cannons and unraveled them a bit, measuring them for a specific distance. Then to Furioso, they rushed under. He was fighting furiously and at first didn't notice the tiny gnomes.

"Furioso!" King Alfred yelled. "Let them tie the cable, secure you to the wall!" Furioso found a moment to pause as Kumbo and Ruig filled his spot. He was unsure of what the boy king was saying but glanced down, nearly swinging at them until realizing they were the gnomes. He stopped just in time.

"Watch it, big fella!" Gib warned.

Furioso couldn't help but smile as the two gnomes quickly leapt upon him and tied the steel cable to his belt.

"Oh yes!" He understood quite well the physics of an apex. Furioso turned to the ladder before them. Though hunters were smashing the ladders at the top and killing orc after orc, common orcs to black orcs, the attackers kept coming and would tire out the defenders soon enough. But Furioso now had a way to return from bringing down a ladder. He grabbed the ladder and with great gusto leapt from the wall, pushing the ladder out with a dozen orcs clinging to it. As he reached the apex, he let go, and the ladder fell back, crashing orcs down upon their own. Furioso merely swung back, easily contacting the wall above the mad swinging trolls and puncturing the skull of one as he pulled himself back to the top.

The other troll hunters saw his move and immediately looked to the gnomes for their attachments. All along the wall, gnomes with their strong nimble fingers tied steel cables to the giant warriors. The gnomes were crafty with their steel-made springs and thin wires. They threaded the wires to make the perfect rope. It wasn't very thick either, maybe a dozen to a score of steel threads twisted to form very strong cables. And the gnomes knew how to unthread the ends and quickly braid them as intricate knots to anything.

Troll hunters began leaping, pushing ladders out. Small rickety wooden ladders and iron bounded thick ones -- all came crashing down upon the mass of orcs and trolls below. The hunters merely swung back to the walls, just above the orcs, bashing against war trolls. The trolls were mighty giants, pounding their warhammers or spiked clubs at tiny weak humans fleeing in terror below them. But a great warrior, on a cable, swirling about them was not something they could comprehend with their limited brain capacity.

Most swung wildly as if blind and most certainly unsure. Even when the war trolls managed to hit them, the hunters scoffed at such weak blows. The hunters' main attack upon trolls in the Crag Mountains was from above, leaping down, in many cases from great distances. This arrangement on a cable, however, gave them second and third leaps, bringing them much glee and joy in their furious flying feats.

Troll after troll fell, crushing orc after orc, giving defenders on the wall breathing space. Sir Murith, Captain Hedor, Sergeant Ruig, Warrior Kumbo, Squire Nubio, and Sergeant Cory most definitely needed it. All leaned against battlements or each other, breathing heavily, weakened from the fight.

Gnomes scurried back and forth, killing any squirming orcs, for hundreds lay fallen behind the walls. The children and women of Lady Nihan cowered as orc after orc fell before them. Thankfully, the gnomes were there to finish them off.

The horns of the great Warlock Tower suddenly bellowed forth again, a resounding order that had every orc and troll that still lived suddenly turn and march back. It wasn't that the army was weakened, for more war trolls and orcs with ladders were coming, climbing over their own dead. They would soon have had enough dead piled by the walls for the trolls to reach up and the orcs to climb over, but that all ended with the blast of the horns.

King Alfred and the defenders looked up and saw that the Tower was maneuvering the army to the south, where the onslaught of the trees was formidable. The orcs and trolls moved away from the walls and toward the line of trees.

"Looks like the trees are moving northeast, toward the Tower," exclaimed Sir Murith. "It must feel threatened by them!"

The few brazen black orcs and angry trolls that tried to stay were quickly dispensed by the troll hunters and by Loranna's archers. But the mass of them retreated, marching to the trees.

King Alfred turned to Furioso. "Furioso! Save Ordo!"

Furioso suddenly bounced atop the battlement wall and looked at his hunters. "Yes, my boy king! Yes, my lord! To Ordo!" He raised his battle axe, and all the hunters cheered in resolution. He leapt from the wall only to be jerked back by the steel cable. "OOOOFF!" he slammed against the wall and meekly climbed back up.

"Oh yep, here yah go," Gib mumbled as he quickly untied the steel cable.

"Much obliged," Furioso chuckled, then dropped from the wall. Dozens upon dozens of troll hunters landed with him, amongst the mounds of trolls and orcs. It was easy enough for them to trample upon them as if they were soft rocks. "To Ordo!!" Furioso yelled. And softly to himself he said, "To his salvation."

They hurried through the carnage and siege tower rubble. Though many of the orcs and trolls were heading south, there were still plenty to fight. For many were passing through from the northwest, and when they saw the troll hunters on the ground, they immediately engaged.

As much as Furioso wanted to get to the siege towers where Ordo was surrounded, he couldn't. For legions of black orcs were between them and beyond that. The black trolls remained at the Siege Towers to finish off the surrounded brethren.

"Oh, doesn't look good for them!" Captain Hedor said.

King Alfred stared after them and then surveyed the fighting to the south. It was an incredible sight to see. In the middle was a sea of bobbing orcs with polearms and banners, dotted with many, many trolls amidst. They were waiting in massive ranks to get to the battle front of giant trees.

The trees were massive and swinging methodically through the line of orcs. Orcs flew side to side as the trees lumbered forward. Just then King Alfred could see the faerie magic shooting from the treetops. Faeries, holding on to the trees as if riding them, seemed to fly or flit from tree to tree, getting the best position to fire. The shots looked like piercing volleys of sparks, as fast as gunfire, yet with magical glimmers or faerie dust. These shots burst out as if from a gun turret down into the ranks of orcs, but more importantly into the larger trolls. As a troll neared to bash and smash the limbs of the trees, faerie fire would suddenly blast away at it. It would take many shots, but the trolls would eventually flinch or falter, and the trees would overtake them with giant limb bashing.

Still, some of the war trolls could best the trees. Though shorter, there was a speed and ferocity factor that enabled the war trolls to swing their iron weapons and smash the trees limbs, cracking and splintering them. And those with huge battle axes or cleavers severed the trunks, causing the trees to fall over with great crackling explosions.

And orcs in some regions managed to gather archers and light their arrows. They rained arrows of flame upon the trees with enough to cause leaf and foliage to ignite. The other trees would cower from the fires, only to be attacked by trolls swinging giant axes.

"King Alfred, there! In the center!" Loranna pointed from her perch atop the tower.

Alfred leapt atop a battlement to get a better view, covering his eyes from the glare of the hot afternoon sun. In the middle of the charging trees, he could see a lone knight on horse. It was Lord Dunther, racing along the line, swinging at the trolls. He could not best a troll, but he could wound it with his great steel sword. He was upon a white steed, racing between swinging trolls and leaping orcs. And there, riding with Dunther, sometimes flitting with her wings, was the Queen of Faeries. Her fire was like blasts of hot light, one shot wounding any troll it hit. Dunther was directing her to shoot the war trolls. King Alfred could see that Dunther realized they needed to decimate the troll numbers.

"Cory! Loranna!" King Alfred yelled.

"You're not thinking of going out there!" Captain Hedor suddenly said, rushing up.

"Cory! Line 'em up!" King Alfred yelled above the courtyard to the other wall. His voice sounded deep and manly. Cory heard and saluted, motioning his spearboys to move.

"Loranna!" the King yelled above to the tower. "In the spear wall!"

Loranna saluted and waved her girls down from the towers. She couldn't help but smile.

"King Alfred," said Captain Hedor. "You are the King! Stay in the castle! We will go!"

"No Captain, you must keep the walls. Only our maneuvers can get to them." With this, King Alfred quickly descended the stairs.

"We'll go!" Captain Hedor said as Sir Murith rushed down, Kumbo and Ruig following.

"We'll man the walls! We farmers and the gnomes!" Abedeyan said, trying to scramble through the rubble strewn courtyard, filled with siege stones and orc arrows. "You'd think I'd be skilled at traversing our courtyard in ruins and rubble by now!"

King Alfred looked at the desperate and resolute faces before him. He shrugged with a smile. "You all could come in handy!"

Sir Murith, Hedor, Ruig, Kumbo and their mix of merry ex-bandits and ex-slaves smiled proudly, all dirty, grimy and in need of a bath.

"You'll watch our rear!" King Alfred said as he hurried to Cory and Nubio, who were forming up the spear wall. Wilden came up from below with his contingent as well.

The band of jovial men gulped a not-so-humble look. Sir Murith waved his sword to follow, in a not-so-gusto way, and they followed behind. "We'll take up the rear..."

The gate opened, and the wall of spears came out, Cory on one side, Nubio on the other, ordering the wings of the spear wall to maintain formation. In the middle, with Wilden in support, King Alfred yelled, "Forward! To the north, the siege towers first!"

Loranna and her girls rushed through Murith, Hedor and their men, lining up behind the spearboys. Loranna came up to King Alfred and kissed his dirty face. "I love you, by the way."

Proudly, to all, King Alfred looked at her, as a King, ready for action. And she loved that.

Sir Murith and his humble men hobbled behind them. They didn't look so excited but were ready to do their duty.

Captain Hedor and Ruig had a mumble-off: "We're here in the rear once again. Whatever. If we're even needed. They've got nice shiny armour. We've got the left-over armour, still – can't complain. Perhaps we could clean up their kills for them. Oh yes, drag them out of the way. Most handy! Pick up their arrows. Plenty of work there. Be useful for sure. Oh, grateful. Shine their armour. Did you bring a rag? I am a rag!"

Kumbo and Sir Murith stared, unsure of what they were hearing.

Between them rushed Gib and Pep, fully armed with spring loaders and a bundle of steel javelins. "We're coming too!"

King Alfred turned to them. "Fine, but tell the gnomes to clear us a path north!"

"Oh yes sir, be right back!" Gib said, tossing Pep his spring loader and bundle, rushing off.

"Ooof!" Pep said, taking the load.

266

Chapter Forty-Six

Sally Forth

The cannons on the wall raised up, their line of fire going above the siege tower rubble. Beyond that was a sea of orcs and trolls, like a vast murky river in the monsoon season slowly drudging along. They were moving to the trees to bury them in their evil sludge. It was a rich and deep target. Beyond the vast Black Army was the great Warlock Tower, sitting there orchestrating the motions of this massive sea of orcs.

The cannons, secured again with the cables, blasted out great plumes of smoke as iron balls flew out and burst through the ranks of oblivious orcs. Line after line of them splatted or were obliterated as a rain of cannonballs bounced fiercely among them. Giant granite balls, blasting from the mortars, dropped from far above, blowing up huge expanses of ground, shattering stone shrapnel and throwing orcs out and twirling the giant trolls.

Then the cannons went silent. The gnomes waved down from the walls. Gib turned to King Alfred and yelled, "That's all the fire we got left! They're all out."

King Alfred peered at the wall of smoke and dust before him. A slight breeze moved it, but it descended slowly as the sky above began to show. All seemed oddly silent, as if the dust and smoke absorbed all the sounds of the horrific battle. The wall of spearboys settled in nicely around him. It seemed he was in a mobile steel castle, steel spears poking out on all sides. Behind him Loranna and her girls waited with abated breath. Alfred could hear the taut cords of their bow strings, readying.

As the dust and smoke settled, seeming to blot out even the vast sounds of the orc march, the sounds returned, as did the Black

Army before them. Yet in front of them vast areas were blasted out, giving them space to advance, quickly albeit with much fighting to come.

The land below them had thousands of dead orcs and mounds of fallen trolls, but there was still a sea of orcs and trolls ready to fill the sudden terrific voids.

"March!" ordered King Alfred. "To the siege towers of the troll hunters!"

They were coming from the gate. They would have to march northward around the siege tower ruins and then veer to their left, westward, to where Furioso and his hunters were embattled with legions of black orcs. Then they would march through that to the stalled siege towers. Black trolls, a thousandfold, had the three towers surrounded, having ascended up into them, fighting Ordo and his hunters amidst the wooden bulwarks.

"That's a long arduous march," Captain Hedor huffed.

"What you complaining about? Just keep up the rear!" Ruig sighed.

Hedor looked back and saw a sea of orcs forming behind them. "Uh oh."

They both gulped.

Fortunately, most of the orcs were heading to the fighting against the trees, but some turned when they saw another target. They formed gangs to pursue the small formation.

"Uh, Loranna?" Hedor quickly rushed up to her, tapping her shoulder and pointing back.

"Girls! One, on me!" she immediately said. "Two! Three!" Within a moment their lines formed in the rear and fired upon the gangs of orcs. And within another few moments all but a few fell from arrows. Those decided to go back to fighting the trees.

"Oh, not bad!" Captain Hedor huffed as Loranna returned to the march forward.

"We could have fought them," Ruig shrugged. "But yah know..."

Furioso and his hunters were doing quite well against the black orcs, taking down line after line, but more filled each spot. The black orcs were unafraid to die and their hatred and blood lust kept them charging forward. The swing required to kill them was exhausting for the hunters, no matter their effectiveness. Many had to pull back, giving themselves a moment, while other hunters filled their lines. It was still an arduous task, and time was a factor.

For Furioso could see that of the nearly four thousand troll hunters that went with Ordo, only a few hundred remained, fighting desperately against black trolls, which had superior steel weapons. They barely hung on, literally, upon those few towers.

"If those black trolls would have made it to the walls of the Keep, we would surely not have survived. Well done Ordo, well done," Furioso said under his breath.

His hunters stalled amidst the line of brazen black orcs, each side yelling and bantering back and forth. More vicious orcs filled their ranks, swelling their lines, as his two hundred hunters grew more and more tired. They held a line, unable to break their adversary. Even if they could, it did not seem they would be in time to save Ordo.

Suddenly, a new energy came crashing down against the line of black orcs. It was a rain of steel arrows. Hunters at the front stared in disbelief as orc after orc, once barking and gnashing their teeth against the hunters, began jerking and collapsing, convulsing and then dropping. Arrow after arrow, like fierce steel rain, pierced their thick hides and iron plates. Orc upon orc fell, in droves, layer after layer. It happened so fast that the rear orcs did not have any time to come up and fill the lines.

"Girls... archers..." the troll hunters nodded with grim smiles.

"Advance!" Furioso yelled. "At pace!" They marched forward solidly, with renewed energy as the orcs, unsure of what was amiss, kept jerking and falling.

Furioso saw, to his right flank, the spindly wall of steel and spears marching. Orcs tried to advance there, but most fell from arrows while those that did make it, died immediately from very, very sharp spears. It seemed more like a steel beast, like some mysterious giant metal turtle -- not tall but very low and wide, with no head, and a steel casing and spikes that organically moved all along it. Any attackers would meet their doom with spears that pierced through anything.

A war troll leapt in pounding its heavy hammer. Oddly, the steel wall merely moved away as the war troll hit the ground. It had no time to react as arrows and spears converged. It retreated weaponless, grabbing at its many wounds, falling back into the orc ranks dead. And the steel wall of spearboys suddenly converged into a solid wall once again.

269

"Spear... boys..." Furioso caught himself saying. He turned quickly, though, to refocus on the task before him. He could see the clearing as orcs fell one after another. He realized then that his weapons were no match against the black trolls. He saw why the troll hunters fell, for many lay before him. He saw the black trolls swing their great steel swords and finely crafted glaives up at Ordo and his brethren. A few of them had acquired the black trolls' steel and were fighting back, but Furioso and his broor had no such weapons. For the first time in his life, he hesitated.

On his right, the steel beast of King Alfred kept moving forward. King Alfred stared through the openings of his spearboy shields and could see the demonic looking black trolls. Past the falling orcs and many fleeing orcs from his archers' rain of terror, the black trolls were a new breed altogether. He saw a hunter on the tower try to swing at their skin, and his weapon glanced off. He fell amidst their great steel swings.

"Hold here!" Their skin seemed like steel in a way, black scaly steel. "Loranna, focus on the black trolls!"

Loranna came forward, peering through the spear wall. "Open up for us."

Wilden waved and shouted "Mid open!" The spearboys opened suddenly. Loranna quickly hurried out amidst the field of dead orcs. She went a bit further up than Alfred liked. "Setheyna! Watch her back!"

Setheyna peered forward. "Two! On me!" Her squad formed up and kept an eye to see if any orcs would attack Loranna. But none did. All who were alive seemed to be scrambling to and fro, amongst their fallen. Her cloak hid her well amidst the bright glaring sun and the squinting eyes of the orcs.

But not the black trolls, for one of them, with serpentine tongue and bloodshot eyes, turned to see her. It smiled fang-like teeth and leapt toward her. Alfred saw it and without notice ran out of the lines with his spear and shield in hand. Wilden yelled after him, "King Alfred!"

Cory and Nubio were still holding their lines, keeping their walls solid, for there were still plenty of orcs and trolls rushing about, whether scrambling around them or trying to find weaknesses in their lines.

Sir Murith saw King Alfred take off and pursued him, leaping through the spear wall. "Hold the line. I'm going!"

The black serpentine troll was closer, easily charging toward Loranna. She stood and watched it. She seemed still, as if paralyzed with fear. King Alfred had to trudge and trip through a field of dead orcs. Sir Murith wasn't making much distance either.

And as the black troll adroitly raised its glimmering steel sword, Loranna raised her bow and fired three arrows. The black troll's great blade fell to her right, and it fell to her left with three arrows in its neck. She bent over to look at it.

"What are you doing!?" Alfred said, dropping behind her in exhaustion. "That was too close!"

"Wanted a closer look," she said, shrugging.

Sir Murith finally reached them, breathing hard.

She walked back past them to the line of spearboys. "Better hurry back!"

Murith lifted Alfred as they stared after her and ran back.

"One, on me!" Loranna yelled.

"Two, on me!" Setheyna yelled.

"Three, on me!" Niranna yelled.

"Come!" Furioso waved his hunters to get closer to the spearboys and King Alfred.

"We've got to move to Ordo!" a hunter yelled out.

Furioso raised his black iron bardiche. "Not with these weapons!"

The hunters stared after him and then followed, never feeling so many shames in one battle.

King Alfred's head oddly poked out from the steel wall and peered at Furioso. "Furioso! Take out any orc legions that form up! And the war trolls! We'll deal with those snake looking trolls!"

Furioso waved from outside the line. "Aye, we can deal with war trolls alright! Hunters on me!" Furioso led his broor more to the rear where orc gangs and war trolls were forming. The hunters attacks there were brutal and effective.

Hedor and Ruig watched their rear as the troll hunters passed by to fight off any flanking enemies. "Well, looks like we're quite useless once again."

"Speak for yourself," Ruig said, holding bundles of javelins for Gib and Pep, who were supporting the archers with their heavy spring loaders.

Black trolls turned to see the spindly turtle of spearboys advance. From the tower, Ordo could not believe it. From his vantage point it looked like a silvery shimmering pool of water. Facets of reflections scintillated off its surface, yet spindly needles poked out of its front and sides. It seemed like an enchanting deadly spirit slithering over war torn terrain.

To Ordo, the black trolls charged like black leaping bugs at the silver turtle. They raised their steel weapons and bounced along like the best of the troll hunters. But they merely met the steel arrows and javelins of children and gnomes. The arrows rained through their steel scaly hides while the javelins pierced through several at a time.

The first and second line of black trolls fell before the spear walls. The third had a few make it in close as they swung their blades. But they were shocked to see that their dark magic swords did not shatter the spears. The spears merely swayed with their swings while others appeared where the trolls leapt. The spears pierced what the black trolls believed to be their very own impenetrable skin.

Black troll after black troll hit the spear wall, only to shudder in death throes. Each black troll fell when the spears retracted. Then as a line of dead black trolls formed, the spear wall advanced over it. And again, another line of black trolls would drop amidst the wall of spears, and another row, as the spearboys advanced.

"Archergirls and spearboys," Ruuk commented, hanging next to Ordo, his brows dancing.

One black troll broke through the spear wall, and the boys, with great skill, knew to leave it, not panicking or faltering, for Sir Murith and the men had their rear. The black troll rolled within the wall and for a moment blinked at the odd spectacle of seeing so many boy backs and girl archers firing outward.

But it had only a moment as Sir Murith charged with swinging sword. The black troll quickly swung down with its sword, knocking Sir Murith flat upon the ground. The knight's sword deflection and armour held, though not his strength. Hedor and Ruig charged with their swords, clanking their blades off the black scaly hide. Kumbo pierced fiercely with his spear, yelling in ancient gibberish.

The black troll smacked him away, but Hedor and Ruig screamed bloody murder as they leaped to Kumbo's spear and pushed it in further. The black troll howled hot spittle into their faces as it dropped.

"That's enough black troll fighting for me," Hedor huffed.

"Complete agreement," Ruig shuddered, rolling off the dead thing. They fist-bumped.

Ordo could see the scintillating steel form of spearboys make its way through black trolls charging at it, and the black troll lines falling one after the other. He sighed in great relief.

"Vatter, it looks like you and I will live for another day," Ruuk said, sadly.

"We deserve death," Ordo said calmly, letting go of the tower and dropping. He landed from black troll to black troll, using his newly acquired steel blade. Ruuk, with a black troll's glaive, followed. They descended past their hunters, barely holding on within the webwork of the towers. They cleared the way of the black trolls to get to the boy king and his proven spearboys and archergirls.

As Ordo lumbered through black trolls all around him, they fell. Arrows flew past him, and finally the spear wall opened for him. He walked in amidst the tiny grove of armoured boys. And there stood King Alfred and his diminutive men of valor, the ones who saved the great and mighty troll hunter warriors.

Ordo took a knee.

Furioso came up from the rear, picking up black troll weapons and passing them to his broor hunters.

"King Alfred, I came here to destroy you, the boy king. But now, I am your servant, forever and ever."

Ruuk took a knee next to him.

"Thank you, Ordo! Get your men armed with steel. We must fight on!" King Alfred yelled.

Ordo couldn't help but smile as Furioso came up and tossed several steel weapons to Ordo.

"Gather the hunters. Get them steel weapons. We must make way to help Lord Dunther and the faerie queen!" King Alfred ordered.

Ordo got up and returned from whence he came. He and Ruuk carried weapons as the spearboys and archergirls advanced behind him.

Black trolls were felled by arrows and rolled away. Ordo felt as if he was in a dream, a slow motion dream. He carried a bundle of weapons as he would a child, a girl he once had or could have had. He looked down to see black waving hair bobbing as he pounced through the glory of battle. A girl stared up at him, a beautiful young girl unknown to him yet like him. Then she faded, and it was his wife, the wife who was the mother of his lost daughter and his lover who never forgave him. He peered at her even as Ruuk yelled slowly after him, trying to warn him, as a black troll began to swing its great blade right across his neck. But the black troll turned its head, faltering before Ordo, having met the arrows of Loranna. His tears flowed as the woman in his arms, the love of his life, faded and was replaced by steel blades. "Forgive me!" he cried.

He reached the base of the tower and yelled a painful angry roar up into the scaffolding. Hunters and black trolls looked down to see his pained stance, his heavy breathing. The black trolls stared in confusion, licking their lips with their forked tongues. The last of the desperate troll hunters saw their chance and leapt down to him, discarding their brittle broken heavy weapons and taking the light strong steel.

Ordo fell to his knees, weeping. The hunters couldn't believe what they held in their hands. They always believed the heavier, the mightier. They never had to meet true steel as they fought wild trolls and mountain beasts with thick iron-cast weapons. But these blades and glaives felt as light as the wind and as sharp as the ice of winter.

The black trolls leapt down to meet their end at the skill of troll hunters wielding these superior weapons. It was still a furious fight. The black trolls knew no fear and never surrendered. Even with a limb cut off, they'd fight with the other or bite with deadly poison. The troll hunters had to fight hard, but now they could defend, counter, and swing with assurance.

Chapter Forty-Seven

Ordo versus Loranna

A blast of power unleashed upon them. It was a like a vast giant flameless fire that pounded from above. It dropped the spearboys and archergirls, throwing them to the ground. Their heads exploded in pain and delirium. And with it was a screech that pierced the northern sky, a howl that surrounded and drained them.

A foul green gas exploded and forced them to grab for their necks as their very life was being choked out. None could withstand the searing vile air or the bitter heat. All fell to their knees upon the ground, grabbed at their chests, troll hunters and men, black trolls and orcs. Many of the lesser orcs died immediately, unable to withstand the very black magics from whence they came.

A great shadow darkened their eyes, and hot foul air choked their breath over and over, back and forth, pushing in poisonous gas while sucking out the very air they needed to survive. Great talons came in. And King Alfred was crushed between claws and lifted from amongst his guardianship.

"*Kurehnde, buht-egree nemesis! Ovuht!*" boomed a voice.

Those that could, could see a shadowy figure illuminated before them with a pointy hat. Its arms splayed out as the foul gas dispersed and the breath of life returned.

The figure faded immediately, and there stood Verboden, who shook then collapsed. Sir Murith rose in a delirium to catch him. Hedor and his men coughed, still in distress, struggling to stay from death's door.

"ALFRED!!!" screamed a voice. It permeated through all their bones and their very souls.

Loranna screeched as she ran out from her fallen comrades. She aimed high as all the fellowship looked up to see Alfred thrust aloft, caught in the talons of a great vulture, flying away. She coughed foul poisons and had sickly throes but still...

"ALFRED!!!" Loranna screamed as she flew past everyone and through black trolls and legions of orcs, firing up arrow after arrow into the body and wings of the great flying behemoth.

But the arrows pierced what seemed – to be nothing. They broke through crusty feathers, exploding them into showers of dust and dried filaments. Beneath the feathers were just bones of a vulture that had been dead a thousand years. It thrust its dried old wings up and up, taking aloft its own dead body away from her.

Loranna continued on, screaming in a rage and fury, at a loss that was unbelievable and not possible, yet right before her very eyes. It was these very moments that could not be, but were set in motion to destroy her love forever.

"Move, we must get to her! Loranna!!" coughed out Sir Murith. He lifted Cory as Hedor lifted Nubio. "Get everyone up! Loranna is too far!"

They rose, coughing and hacking. Sir Murith looked to see Verboden lying there, spent of all his blessings and prayer. "Is he dead?"

Kumbo felt Verboden's neck and shook no and held him nonetheless.

Sir Murith was relieved but still unsure of Verboden's condition. Would he survive? But Murith turned. "Hurry, we must get to her!"

He looked beyond the spearboys, who were getting up and forming their lines. He could not see her beyond the wall of black trolls and orcs standing up and reforming amidst the siege towers in front of him.

Ordo watched as the great vulture beast flew above and past him. He saw it carrying Alfred in its talons. He saw the Dark Servant push the vulture on and up and away.

He leapt atop the tower, climbing fiercely to meet the great vulture as it spread its wings aloft. He clambered quickly, past leaping black trolls and defending hunters. He reached the pinnacle of the tower and leapt as the vulture climbed higher. He jumped with all his might.

He missed the great beast as it flew beyond his grasp.

Alfred did not look up or down, for he lay limp within the great talon grip.

Ordo fell to the earth and thought, "I shall see my wife now, dying as she did, leaping to her death. I shall die as she did, and I deserve it so."

Instinctively, he landed, skidding down a great mountain troll. He cut the beast open with his steel blade, holding on to the blade as he yanked to and fro. He fell down next to the mountain of a troll, rolling into the midst of some Greater Black Trolls. These were the leaders of the black trolls. The black serpentine trolls had great strength and agility – but these Greater Black Trolls were bulkier with greater ram-like horns and mightier tusks. They turned to see Ordo and sneered at his coming demise.

One charged, twirling his oriental blade with great skill. Ordo lifted his blade knowing he was in for the fight of his life. But it was all for naught as three steel arrows pierced its upper chest and eye. The other Greater Black Trolls roared demonically and leapt forward. He fought one as two others fell with arrows. Though he shoulder-bashed the one, it threw him back, and he lay there as it reared up its giant glaive. And once again, much to his surprise, arrows zipped over him and forced the Greater Black Troll to convulse and then die.

Loranna leapt upon the mound of dead beasts and watched the sky as the vulture flew over the Warlock Tower and beyond.

"Alfred!!" she screamed. It was a blood curling wail.

Ordo looked up as she wavered in her stance. Another black troll tried to take her, but she shot it without looking. The beast fell at the girl's feet upon the mound of four very dead Greater Black Trolls.

Ordo stood up next to this little girl with her bow in hand. He stood stunned, peering at her.

Loranna turned and looked at him, tears streaming. She screamed with great vehemence, "We are going to rescue King Alfred! UNDERSTAND!!"

Before Ordoh Brutum realized it, he had nodded.

Book Two

Chapter Forty-Eight

Collapse

When the remaining black trolls began to retreat, the battle was over. Their numbers fell over and over again against the spear wall and archers, a small silver slither of armoured children within the mass of orcs. Behind them, on both sides, like wakes of waves, were the troll hunters expanding their flanks. When the black trolls retreated through the ranks of orcs and trolls, panic spread like a shuttering ripple.

No horns or waving banners from the Warlock Tower could stop it. And as the space between the Black Army and the trees widened, the trees paused and began something new. Those in the back ranks shook violently, crackling and crumbling, resounding like booms of thunder. And the front trees reared back, grabbing giant rocks that were being dug up and passed forward.

Lord Dunther raced along the lines, sword drawn, his Queen sitting behind him, "Take their siege stones! Fire upon them! Destroy them with their very stones!!!"

She hugged him tight, her face resting upon his gleaming armour.

The faeries floated aloft as the trees picked up siege stones, even buried stones, and in waves began a monumental obliteration.

"Oh, I think we should slow down our advance, just a bit," Captain Hedor yelled, looking up at the stony sky. Yes... stony sky.

The stones crashed in waves against orcs and trolls, squashing and crushing them. The waves built up almost like a rolling rock avalanche, with scores of bouncing rocks landing in succession until it reached the Warlock Tower. The first few stones bounced off the crude iron sidings, jolting goblins, bashing in horns, and ripping up the banners. Then the tumultuous wave of siege stones began its work. The Warlock Tower exploded in cavalcades of iron, wood, goblins and finally a dark magic.

It exploded from within as stones punctured it. Strange scarlet tendrils of fire came forth. A horrific evil scream wailed as hundreds of acolytes and sorcerers burned and fell within the collapsing temple of doom.

A wave of dark magic suddenly burst out like an evil explosion. It sent a red lightning streak up into the sky that flitted out and then burst into mere dust as the sun shone brightly upon it.

"So ends the warlock, whom ever that vile creature was, servant of Gorbogal!" Sir Murith exhaled as the Warlock Tower collapsed into ruin. Its dark scarlet flames turned to the natural oranges and reds of an all-consuming fire.

The troll hunters charged in a great flurry, and the crashing rocks continued to decimate the fleeing beasts. It did seem a bit cruel at this point, but no one bothered to stop them. Only King Alfred could order standing one's ground after a great victory, but he had been taken aloft by an undead vulture.

Sir Murith took the reins of their small entourage of deadly children warriors. They all stood and breathed, inhaling and exhaling a moment of peace amidst an all-out panic of retreat by their enemies.

Still, this victory, great and legendary as it was to become, as written in song and sung in all the hidden halls spread to the West and to the East and to the South and North, even unto the walls of Telehistine... did not bring joy to these children. They were not crying out with joy. Instead, they were in pain and sorrow over the loss of and fear for Alfred, their King.

For their King, their leader, their friend was taken, and taken to be tortured and killed. This is what they believed, what they knew. Captain Hedor peered at them, tears running down his emotionless face. He slapped at his cheek, thinking a bug was creeping down it. He peered at the line of spearboys, all downcast, some crying for Alfred, and then looked at the girls, hugging and holding each other, crying and knowing they had failed. Ruig held Kumbo, as Kumbo wailed the most, his arms in the air, asking why, why, WHY?!

Verboden was awake and ashen looking, drained of his energy.

Loranna returned with Ordo behind her, as if protecting her, though it was not needed. For the raging slaughter was spreading beyond them, down the barren slopes and into the burnt hills.

She looked at them all, at their fallen state, of her archergirls and the spearboys. "Get up! Get up!" she screamed.

The children looked up at her, their next in command.

"Get up! We're going to him now! Get up!"

Ordo stepped forward and spoke carefully. "No. That's not possible."

"Get up!" Loranna yelled frantically, charging in and amongst them.

Sir Murith stood next to Ordo, both watching Loranna and her seeking of vengeance.

"Loranna..." Sir Murith spoke weakly.

"We must go! Get up!" yelled Loranna.

The girls wept more. Cory stood but faltered. Nubio shook and could not get up. All of them were ashen, muddied, many with cuts and bruises, drenched in sweat and tears, even in their victory.

Lord Dunther galloped to them, waving his sword in glorious victory as his horse jaunted up to their group. When he saw their condition, he sheathed his sword. Behind him, the onslaught of siege stones flew, the trees advanced, and the faeries made chase.

Before him, Lord Dunther somehow knew without anyone saying a word. He rode in close, galloping about them, peering with intensity. His Queen flew aloft and landed near them, looking closely at their eyes. She was as beautiful and enchanting as ever, but no one noticed.

"Where is Alfred!? Where is my King!" Dunther yelled. Upon meeting Loranna's red and enraged eyes, he looked up and scanned the horizon, the skies.

"The Dark Servant?" he hissed through his teeth. He leapt from his horse and knelt before Loranna. He stared deeply into her eyes, trying to get her to nod no, to say something beyond what was true.

He turned to his Queen, "Florina, your faeries, take flight. Now! To the East!"

She looked up at him. She stared at his desperate eyes.

"Do as I say!" Dunther said, turning and walking up to her, towering over her. "I command it! Take them! Destroy the Dark Servant! Stop him!"

She looked fearfully at him, at his sudden change, his vile contempt, his anger building to something possibly evil and enslaving.

He grabbed her fiercely. Her wings fluttered about him. At first she melted into his painful grip.

"Listen to me, witch! Use your powers! Do it!" he yelled at her.

Her eyes darkened to a slick oily black, and she burst forth a bright light. Dunther tottered back, quickly drawing his sword and pointing it at her. He glared at her darkened face as she stepped back. He gnashed his teeth and roared, "Why won't you do as I command!?"

"Why do you command me as such!?" she hissed.

He stepped forward then saw Hedor and the children looking at him with an empty exhausted look. He saw the tip of his sword near her. He focused on that and wavered. He pulled off his helm, his face grievous with straining emotion.

He fell to his knees, dropping his sword. "I'm sorry. I'm sorry. I, I..." He covered his face with his gauntleted fingers.

Her black eyes faded, and her stance softened. She looked at him with a moment of doubt.

Sir Murith stepped forward. "Forgive him. He is of this world. His prowess cannot withstand... from victory to utter defeat... so suddenly."

"He, he just wanted to save Alfred..." Captain Hedor added hesitantly, for Hedor had never stood so near an enchanted being such as the Queen of Faeries. Her beauty, whether in victorious approach or a sudden darkness of contempt, was a bit much for Hedor and his simple mind.

Dunther stood weakly, blinking crazy tear-filled eyes. "I will never raise my hands upon you again," he said. "Never."

She remained, almost statue-like, for a long moment. She wasn't breathing, and her wings were not scintillating. Her aura seemed so very still, even as the dust and smoke wafted around them, as the children sniffled and sobbed, and as the retreat and slaughter continued beyond.

"What is that word?" she finally spoke.

"What word?" asked Sir Murith, finally choosing to speak amongst them.

"For-give..." she said.

"Forgive?"

"Yes, what is it?"

Sir Murith looked at the Queen of Faeries, then at Dunther bent before her.

Verboden stood up weakly, touching Sir Murith's armoured shoulder and then leaning on him. He spoke. "It is the word that affords all things in love. It is the word that asks you to sacrifice everything, for practically nothing in return. It exposes you, and reveals you... it is everything... for nothing. So it is – everything."

Dunther raised his face to her. She slowly nodded.

"Why do I love you so?" she finally said.

He hesitantly stepped closer. She stepped away, and he faltered. Then she took his hand and held it. "You stay with them. I must go back to my sylphs. Their strength is within the trees and our land. We cannot venture out far from each other or our strength weakens. We become lost the further we leave our realm."

Dunther nodded. She let go of his hand and flew back to the guardians and the faeries.

"Phew... that was close..." Hedor said softly. "She forgave him, right? Don't want to lose that alliance. Or that enchanted mistress, if I may say so."

No one laughed... he stretched out his chin. This was no time for bad jokes or goading.

Dunther turned, picking up his sword, and breathed.

Sir Murith came forward. "The Dark Servant flies east, to the Black Spires."

Ordo stepped forward as everyone began to rise, knowing more was to be done. "It is a three week journey, past our Crag Mountains and through treacherous lands, no matter your fastest horses. We troll hunters can make it in one week, no more than two, but we must leave now."

Dunther looked up at Ordo. "I'm glad Sir Gorham was able to get an alliance with you troll hunters. I am Lord Dunther, knight servant to King Alfred."

Ordo looked down, removing his bestial helm. "Sir Gorham lies in your castle from grievous wounds given to him by me. I am here... surrendered to your boy king."

Dunther looked unsure, glancing to Sir Murith and Verboden.

Verboden spoke again. "The troll hunters had an alliance with the witch, to come here to destroy the Men of the Westfold. It was Sir Murith's Quest that brought back forsaken children, who through my incantations were revealed to be the troll hunter's very own offspring. Alfred and I brought them forth to the troll hunters as they advanced upon us. We broke them not with sword, but with the truth, the alarming truth of their evil sacrifices, that a father would give up his child."

Ordo stared at the ground and then saw the children before him. He saw strong boys with spears and strong girls with bows. They looked back at him with courage and resolve.

Ordo spoke. "I will take the troll hunters now. We will live off the land and make straightway for the Black Spires of Gorbogal. We will attack to the very end to save King Alfred."

"I'll go with them!" Loranna said.

"No," Ordo suddenly responded. He turned and went to a knee, looking straight at Loranna.

She was about to argue with him, with contempt, but saw the look in his eyes. She saw something beyond a brute or hunter.

"You are a great warrior, the greatest... and but a girl... her age..." Ordo began, looking down for a moment. He took a breath and looked back up into her eyes, his bearing tears. "The road we take is beyond the farmsteads and grasslands. And however great an archer you are -- for great you are! -- the travails and treacherous road we take will be fast and furious. You are still a girl. Even a man from this land cannot keep the speed of foot we will be on. But meet us there, you will! Get them ready. March forth! We will siege that evil fortress and call out for Alfred! And we will not stop till we get to him and await you!"

"We must heal and supply ourselves for the march," Sir Murith said behind them.

"But march we will!" Lord Dunther added.

Loranna nodded, tears streaming from her eyes.

Chapter Forty-Nine

Loss

Ordo and several hundred troll hunters immediately left. Furioso and his contingent stayed behind to be with their children. They were in the blasted courtyard, clearing it of what rubble they could and trying to set up the torn tents and pavilions -- much to no avail, for all of it was shredded in ruin. Lady Nihan was beside herself yet still so grateful to be alive and to see fathers reunited with their children. When gnomes dug out the kitchen provisions from amongst the stone ruins and brought them to her, she hugged them. Then she set up the few pots that remained.

"Some of the troll hunters are returning to the Crag Mountains, choosing not to go on the suicide mission," Sir Murith said to Lord Dunther and Loranna. They stood upon the walls to survey the land.

They looked beyond the battlefield of devastation as the troll hunters hurried away. Lord Dunther sighed. "Let them choose. We have much to do, spread so thin."

"We must leave as soon as possible! We must leave as soon as we gather enough food and water together! Immediately!" Loranna cried. Verboden and the knights looked at her. She stared off in a delirium of pain and exhaustion. She finally fainted, and they caught her.

"I shall take her to the ruined chapel, our only house of healing," Verboden said. "My brother, Harkonen, is there. We saved him in the north. He will aid in healing."

Loss

Dunther and Murith watched as Verboden left. They then looked at the faeries and great trees slowly lumbering southward.

"We sure could use them, Lord Dunther. Aren't you their king?" Hedor said, climbing up the stairs and peering over the wall with them as the trees slowly migrated southward.

Dunther stared a long while as they receded. He could see the Queen amongst them, riding along the guardians. She stared back at him from afar. "No, I am not. I will never be."

Murith and Hedor looked at each other.

"Their magic will fade if they remain. They will be susceptible to the dark magics. They must return to their realm."

Hedor sighed. "Not even a hello? A thank you? A good bye?"

"No, not even that," Dunther said.

"Perhaps, in peace, we can visit them, and thank them there," Kumbo chimed in.

Dunther raised his head, and a breath of emotion came out. He looked at Kumbo with sudden gladness. "Yes, yes, that would be appropriate. But first, we must heal, and ...Alfred... our king..." They all bowed their heads.

Broggia and Boggin arrived from the tunnels, and with them came a large group of gnome smiths. They scoured the battlefield of fallen enemies, collecting the massive arms and armour. After vast piles were formed, they had to build carts to move them. It would take weeks and months of this. They had to use goats and many ropes, devising teams of bridled beasts to pull the dead trolls and orcs into vast piles. The stench and rot were apocalyptic. It seemed as if the land was filled with the wretched dead, rotting and bloated. A gazillion fat flies floated amongst them.

Collecting wood for such work was even a more arduous task, for all the nearby lands were burnt by the Black Army. The goats they got from the moorlands were all killed. Thankfully, the People of the Downs came with more, providing much needed milk. Farmers from the west brought food. Within days many small hamlets, villages, and farmsteads in lands untouched by the Black Army came to help the famed and legendary folks of Grotham Keep. Food and labor and beasts of burden were given, the folks knowing their very lives and lands were saved this great day.

Loss

As the sun beat down on it harshly, cooking the dead bodies where they lay or where the tiresome men and gnomes could pile them, not even the breezes of summer could rid the land of the foul decay. The healing process for the children and men was slow. Brother Harkonen and Verboden spent the days nursing wounds and dealing with fevers: from the children and farmers, to gnomes, and many troll hunters.

A contingent of farmers and Hedor tried to gather and march to rescue Alfred. They were angry and frustrated. Loranna, sick and in delirium, was unaware of this. Lord Dunther and Sir Murith rode out to them. They had no choice but to strike them with the flat of their swords, hurting several, to stop them from leaving. Sir Murith destroyed the cart of provisions, killing their goats. The rage and near murder was almost tragic. But before the group could attack the harrowing knights, their horses galloped them away. From a distance Dunther and Murith waited, as the group raged at them. Thankfully, none of the archergirls were there. Hedor, not as upset as Murith, merely sat staring eastward, exhausted and remembering Alfred. After two days the group succumbed to depression. Exhausted, they and the knights returned to the castle.

Strangely one day, Lord Dunther and Sir Murith went out on their mares to meet a large guardian tree. It had come back and seemed to plant itself within the ashen fields.

"I have been sent by your Queen," the guardian rumbled.

"My Queen?" Lord Dunther asked.

"Your Queen," Sir Murith repeated.

"I have chosen to come, to remain, and to sleep," the guardian said. It dug its thick-rooted feet in deeper, and its limbs, hanging like arms, stiffened as they rose. "I will heal the land and awaken life and wood upon this scoured ground. Trees will grow again, soon, and the wood and life will be for you. I am just a tree who wants to be."

It stiffened completely. Its man-like visage of eyes and a mouth closed and sealed over as thick bark. Before their eyes it became a massive wonderful tree. They stared up at it, confused. A bird landed on one of its many limbs, chirping.

"I suppose we can make this a war monument to the guardians," Sir Murith said.

Loss

"To remind us of the alliance," Lord Dunther sighed.

As they turned back, for much was still to be done, Sir Murith said with emphasis, "Your Queen." He reached over and punched Dunther's shoulder.

Loranna, cleaned up and rested, rushed into the chapel. Lord Dunther sat in loose linens next to Gorham, who was lying on a cloth-covered mat of straw. He was healing well but still weak and wretched looking.

"It has been three days! We must go. It will take us too long, and all is lost!"

"Whatever time it takes, Loranna," Lord Dunther said, "we will be too late."

Loranna fell to her knees. She looked at the wounded, still healing, crowded everywhere on the floor and benches. Her own archers, the boys, Nubio, the gnomes, and the many troll hunters lay anywhere there was room. Torn tents covered them from the hot summer sun. The ruined walls of the old Keep afforded them shade and something of a shelter.

"But, we will still go," Lord Dunther said, sitting beside her. "We need just a few more days. Provisions are ready. We will use the carts Broggia and Boggin return after they cart off the spoils of war, the spoils we will use to rebuild our army, our arms."

"We won't need an army nor our land without King Alfred!"cried Loranna. "He is now being tortured to death by Gorbogal! We must leave! We must go!"

"I'm sorry. We can't. We have so few, and Gorbogal's Black Spire is still surrounded by her elite guards. I remember them well from the days of old, from the first wars against her. We... there isn't..."

Loranna stood up and stared at him, then walked out.

Chapter Fifty

Gorbogal

Alfred awoke in a nightmare, flying through hot decaying air. He gasped vile parched breaths. His sides were crushed, constricting his ability to fill his lungs with air. His arms and legs lay limp as they swung slightly with each thrust of the slow methodical working of the wings of the undead vulture.

With what strength he had, he tried to look up at the beast that carried him thousands of feet above the earth, slowly across burnt lands. It was flying over the path on which the Black Army had marched west. His helmet came undone and tilted, finally falling off and fluttering down and away, becoming a minuscule speck. He spit dry phlegm, for his lips were parched and his face bloated and reddened from pressure of the talon's grasp.

The repetitive crackling whoosh of the vulture's dried husk of wings constantly echoed in his delirium. Alfred could not tell if he was in a nightmare or some other reality. He could not remember who he was. He couldn't remember his name or what sort of existence he was part of. Things like boy, human, life, history, his past, present, or future were not coming to him. He only knew pain and a dizzying sickening whirlwind of air and frightening heights, far, far above and beyond anything.

He blacked out again and again, wakening to the same exhausting nightmare. And this was all he knew, for it never ended. It was eternal. He wanted to die but knew not what that was.

When the vulture finally landed, Alfred could not tell or see, but only knew, he could breathe differently. His ribs could move, and he could feel a surface, a cold hard surface. He could sense the giant beast lumber and then loft away. And he heard the pattering of many feet scraping around him. He felt the cold rush of foul water upon his lips. He could hear chattering and grunts.

Many guttural voices echoed in his dark mind. He felt a strange sensation of cold and hot coming into his mouth, dripping on his parched skin. He was not sure. He lay limp and dizzy as mean hands gripped him and rolled and dropped him many times.

His eyes finally fluttered open, and he found he was lying in a dark cell. There was a small hatch of light far above. The cell was square. The stone surrounding him was black. It did not have the texture of brick. Rather, it looked more like solid stone that the room was carved out of. He lay on a tattered mat wearing a tattered hide. He could tell it was goblin like. His memories suddenly began to return. He remembered that he was in a fantasy land, and was a boy king. He remembered Grotham Keep and then saw Loranna and Dunther. He remembered the great siege. Did they win? No, they must have lost. And now the end, he was here, and it was all over.

He then thought of his mother. He remembered her and sat up. In the dark cell he looked up into the light and sobbed, "Mom?"

He said it softly, scared someone might hear. He sensed a vast evilness out there, beyond the small window of orange light.

"Mom? Oh mom, I'm sorry, I failed, as king, as a boy... Loranna – I want to go home. I don't want to stay here anymore. Please mom," he sobbed. He covered his face and curled up in the foul prison he was in.

The door suddenly clanked and then opened. A dark bent-over goblin came forth and grabbed Alfred, easily pulling him.

"Ow, ow, please, stop," Alfred cried.

"Shut up stupid boy king!" the goblin squealed angrily.

The goblin dragged Alfred out of the cell and past giant guards, huge troglodytes in thick armour. They stared down at the weak boy and snorted through their warthog snouts. Alfred was dragged through a procession of them and then past many black orcs in well-dressed armour and helmets. It seemed like they were all lined up to see this boy king, this bane and reward of Gorbogal the Witch.

The goblin finally plopped Alfred into a huge room. It all seemed to be cut out or carved out of one vast black rock, just like his prison cell. The room was circular with a dome ceiling, quite high. He was sitting in the center of a vaulted hemisphere of a black rock. At first, he blinked and stared at the stone. He could not discern things past the line of troglodytes and black orcs on either side. They had lined the corridor he was dragged down and were now spread along the perimeter, standing a ways from him. He could see to his right an opening, a balcony with no rail. And past that into the distance, he saw the stars twinkling far away. They were so very far away.

Before him, blinking to focus, he saw many robed men and women, foul looking in their dark attire. He wasn't actually sure if they were men or women. They had a strange demonic look. They seemed to be wearing dark makeup or tattoos. He couldn't tell. They stood and looked at him. He then focused, past his sweat and fever. He could see the mound behind them, something with roots or webbing that filled the expanse up along the dome. It was huge and pulsating.

As he sat on the ground, trying to stabilize, with his heart pounding and his nerves still twitching, he was able to see more and more. The mound was a mound of flesh. It had venous, bulbous skin and sinewy limbs that seemed to stick out of it. They were muscular arms, claws, and talons. He wasn't sure. It was difficult to see. The mound was vast, sitting behind the many sorcerers and witches.

And then, he saw her. He could see her. At first, it wasn't frightening because she seemed to be part of the massive mound of flesh. As he realized it was her, his fear rose. She was encased in the flesh, engulfed in it, part of it. It was as if she sat hunched in it and in a curious way *was* it. Her face was that of contorted old woman, with bulbous features and a scowling visage. Her eyes were evil dark orbs, and her skin was flesh-like, as if it were turned inside out.

Her hair was stark black and moist, sweat and spittle-ridden, matted to her deformed skin. She had something of an upper body, with two limbs and shoulders, folded like a gluttonous mutated human. She sat, bloated and hunched within her own flesh.

Then he saw her more clearly, as she began to crawl out from her flesh. She came out on her hands, her upper torso only. She had a long snake-like midsection, ribbed or muscular extending from the fleshy blob. Limbs from the mound aided in her crawl toward him. Alfred shrank and stood still, ready to run away.

Gorbogal suddenly stopped, as if worried that she had frightened him. She put a hand up to her mouth, covering it as if gasping in delight and not wanting him to be embarrassed.

Alfred stared wide-eyed and shook.

"Nephew!"

Alfred became woozy.

"Dear, dear nephew," Gorbogal gargled, pacing on her two strenuous limbs, back and forth like a tiger yet attached to her own mound of flesh. "You have been such a delight!" she yelled, cackling in a scratchy laughter.

She twirled a moist muscular limb to her audience and spoke further. "You see, my servants! It is in my own flesh and blood that power resides! My blood is god! Only one with my blood could contest me! And this boy king, my nephew, the... Alfred, son of that handsome Bedenwulf, Knight of the fallen House of Utharian, Knight of the Order of Light and son of my dear little sister... boy king of the Men of the Westfold and the great Northern Kingdom... only one such as this... could be the only challenge to my divine authority!"

Alfred stared, breathing heavily.

"And a trouble you have been, my dear boy! Such a trouble. Such a trouble. TROUBLE!!!" she finally screamed.

Alfred flinched.

"And now before me you are. Before me you are and can do whatever I wish to do with you." Suddenly, a limb burst out of her flesh, out of her own stomach, smaller than the rest but still quite sinewy and strong looking. It had two elongated finger appendages at the end. It extended and grabbed Alfred by the arm. It squeezed hard.

Alfred cried and fell as his arm was raised painfully by the limb. Gorbogal scowled as she gritted her teeth, grabbing his arm painfully. Alfred cried more, like a boy being grabbed by the utmost evil. She did not let go but merely enjoyed the pain she inflicted upon her nephew.

"I have been wondering how you came to be. Where has your mother been hiding you? My victory over the Westfold and immolation of your father made me forget! I thought I burned her to ash... toooo.... and with you in her! Hmph! But oh, pretty boy, your kingship, how surprising! And how vexing you have been! Delays... delays... have you caused me..."

She finally let go. "Hah hah, hah... torture you. That's all I want to do, my dear nephew. Just torture you, for a very long time."

Alfred looked about, at the floor, at the feet of the troglodytes standing down the corridor. He rubbed his arm and then quickly spoke!

A little mouse, small in size,
powers of might, deduce, minimize,
powers of light, reduce!

He ducked and lay on the stone, staring away from Gorbogal.

"What trifles is this?" Gorbogal sighed in bubbly utterance. "What pathetic trifle magic do you wield? Is that what destroyed my armies thrice?"

Alfred looked and saw he had not changed. He was merely a boy. He looked back at the horrific mound that was Gorbogal. She stood with two strong arms gripped to the floor, holding up her torso. And two more arms formed as her regular arms and were crossed, across her chest, in defiance.

"Who taught you magic, little incantations, boy? Who?"

Alfred stared, shaking.

"All the wizards are dead or turned! I have several here, as my slaves! Warlocks and witches! Sorcerers and necromancers! The Dark Lord has power over the dark magics! And so do I, of course! Tell me then, who taught you such a trifle, an incantation such as that! Cowardly! A rodent! A runaway, run along feeble mouse!? How pathetic! But I still must know... who taught you this pathetic spell?"

Gorbogal's two-fingered limb, lying limp on the stone floor, suddenly awoke and reached up to grab Alfred again. Alfred gritted his teeth and wrestled the limb. It was stronger than he but not its two elongated fingers. He quickly grabbed them, twirling his whole body and breaking the fingers.

Gorbogal squealed in pain. Many of the witches near her screamed in anguish, reaching out to care for their master.

The limb revived with more strength, yanking free from Alfred. It then bashed him, and he fell to the floor as it retracted into her mound of flesh. Then out of her mound came a new limb. This one was bigger and had thicker fingers with talons. It grabbed Alfred whole, squeezing his torso and pulling him close to Gorbogal.

She stared at him with evil bloodshot eyes and gnashing sharp teeth. "Hurt me!? How impressive, nephew! See my servants!" She turned to gaze at her cabal of sorcerers. "Only my own flesh and blood can hurt me! I am impressed, little boy king. And torture you more shall I! Hee hee hee!"

She squeezed him hard. He gagged in awful strained pain and blacked out. As he lay limp, she shook him violently. He awoke in a nearly neck breaking convulsion. He cried in horrific exhaustion.

"I'll tell you what, little boy king," she said, licking her black lips. "If you vow to worship me, and only me, I will turn you into a slave sorcerer. And maybe, just maybe, I will allow you to serve me alongside my entourage!? After I torture you for a long time that is! What say you? Worship your dear dear aunt!?"

"No."

"No!??? Hah hah-eee..."

"No."

"How... curt! And disappointing." Gorbogal spoke through dripping sharp teeth. "I will have fun, making you say yes... yes... YES! I will do as I do... and make you say..."

Then a hot white light burst through the vast dome. It came so suddenly and fiercely that Gorbogal did not know what had happened. Her flesh seemed to rip from her limbs and face, though that did not seem to affect her as much as the bright blinding light.

"Tirnalth!?" Gorbogal growled as she cowered. "That's not possible! You're dead!" The limb that held Alfred burned and dropped to the ground. Alfred lay limp as Gorbogal saw the shadowy figure emerge from the hot light.

Troglodytes and black orcs fell back. Her great sorcerers could not surmise the power before them. The witches screamed and wailed.

"No!" Gorbogal hissed.

Ethralia stepped from the light and picked up her son. She held him and looked at her sister. "You are your own god. And death all around you is your master."

"So that is how you escaped! A gateway!!"

Gorbogal peered at the hot white light. Her black eyes narrowed to fine points within a pool of blood red. "Did Tirnalth the fateful wizard do this?! To quell the Dark Lord then, before his fall!?"

Ethralia quickly pulled Alfred into the light. A sorceress attempted to grab at him, but Ethralia vaporized her.

Gorbogal reached, strangely, with a human arm and hand. Though bloodied from being extruded from her flesh, it was a real woman's arm. It reached toward the light, which had become a vast swirl of air and turbulence.

The beast servants panicked and retreated from the great clash of powers. Sorcerers cowered as witches wailed and wailed once again, reaching for their master, petting and hugging her mound of flesh.

An intense storm of air burst in and out as Ethralia held up one hand to her sister Gorbogal while pulling Alfred into the light. Great turbulence tore at Ethralia, but she held Gorbogal's powers at bay.

With her great magic force, Gorbogal tried to pull Alfred and Ethralia from the light. Alfred's limbs seemed to dangle in the air, sucked at by a vortex draining toward Gorbogal. Incredible thunderous claps of air and wind burst the room as panic overtook Gorbogal's once brave servants. Ethralia, windswept, her hair fluttering in the mad storm, was able to resist and pulled Alfred within the hot white light. It collapsed to nothing, and they were gone.

The dome was suddenly dark, pitch black. The candelabras and torches relit as the screams and wails of Gorbogal's servants returned. They were all lying strewn about the stone ground. Gorbogal ignored all of their wailing and fright at the sudden burst of magics – for in her tightly gripped hand lay several strands of Ethralia's hair.

Chapter Fifty-One

ቫ.

At Home... Alfred cried in his mother's arms. They lay on the floor of their apartment. They were back home. Her hair was in a frizzy and slowly settled down upon them both. She held him tightly, rocking slowly as he sobbed in great pain. She saw his injuries and spoke soft words. As she rubbed him, as she spoke the Father's name, close to his ear, his contusions and abrasions healed.

Alfred looked up at his mother and felt great power within her, greater than anything he understood. She kept it all at bay, far away, deep within her green eyes. She never used it. And there it was held, the greatest power of magic stored all these years. It was something she had never wanted and had denied, but she used it to get her son and heal him, giving him strength.

He sat up, looking at the evidence of his physical suffering. It faded yet left scars. They were scars that could not be healed, ever. He lay back in her arms and sobbed. For though she healed his body, she could not remove the fact that he now knew great evil. He experienced it, that soulless evil that suppressed all compassion and heckled at suffering. It took his memories away through pain and torture. It took his very being away through the ultimate fear -- not just of pain but of a pain that promises to be inflicted through sadism, for the twisted joy of inflicting it -- not only to hurt but to kill slowly. It was as if the complete opposite of the Father were there, the absence of the Father, of the Light, of joy, of hope.

Did the Father turn away? Did joy and hope leave him? It felt so empty and frightening, as if one who was surrounded by joy merely took a misstep, and evil suddenly exploded into all of one's senses and imprisoned one forever and ever, swept away from the light and into a vast choking darkness.

Alfred shuddered. Ethralia held him tighter, rocking gently, tears rolling down her checks.

A sound of heavy thuds hurried toward the door. The door burst open, and Wooly rushed in with a broken sword drawn. He was in a hot sweat and stared at them, and then around the room.

Ethralia put up a weak hand, waving that they were at peace. Alfred remained in his mother's arms. Wooly closed the door but kept the broken sword drawn. He continued to look around. Ethralia seemed to cry more, trying to wave at Wooly to settle down, to stop moving so much.

Wooly sat on the couch next to them and kept his sword close. He looked at them, unsure, sweating. Ethralia reached up a weak hand and Wooly took it. She held his hand, not for her sake but for his, to soothe his heavy breathing and darting eyes.

"It's not over," Wooly said. "I sensed it. You opening it. I sensed it."

Ethralia looked up at him. "I had to. He called me. I felt her. I felt her anger. At us."

"I know," Wooly said, covering his scarred face with his hands. "She now knows."

Ethralia cried and shook her head no. It was the most desperate no.

The woman from the immigration office came out of the crusty elevator with a man in a suit holding a briefcase. He did not look impressed with the place.

She looked at him, shrugging. He shrugged back. "I've been to worse. A lot worse."

She motioned for him to follow her. She looked in her manila folder at some notes and then at the door numbers down the corridor, following them to the end of the corridor where Ethralia, Alfred and Wooly lived.

H.

"Okay, his face is pretty scarred up, so don't freak out," the woman said.

The man rolled his eyes. "I've seen plenty of scars on immigrants. This is what I do. And don't think I don't appreciate you giving me this case."

"Well... we may be on the opposite sides of this agenda, but this is a way for me to give you something, and it's a pretty unique case. I can't pigeonhole it."

"Well, I appreciate that, but I'm getting every immigrant the rights they deserve, including this family," said the man. "Let's make this quick. I've got to catch a train outta here before it gets dark."

"You mean illegal alien, not...nevermind," she shrugged and gently tapped on the door.

Wooly looked up. He stared intently at the door and then back at Ethralia and Alfred. She nodded a short no, not knowing who or why.

Wooly stood up with his sword but realized he should not wield it. He hesitantly put it down and then covered it with her sewing work.

Outside the door the woman smiled. "You're gonna get a load of fun out of this family. I guarantee...." She looked down the hall. Dark blue webbings of light suddenly burst from a fine point.

The man saw the hues on his sleeves, coming from the same direction, and looked.

The light burst into an oval shape and seemed like a frame for a dark tunnel into nothingness. A loud cackle burst from the shimmering hole.

The man suddenly shook and stepped behind the woman. "What the flip?"

The woman, reacting more like a law enforcement person than a desk worker, crouched slightly, putting her hand on a hidden gun.

"What is that?" asked the man, pulling up his briefcase.

"I don't know," said the woman, pulling out her gun and raising it.

"A gun? Really?" said the man with a sneer.

They could hear it, something grunting and coming. The corridor was not a corridor anymore, at least not where the shimmering oval of light floated. It was large enough for them to leap through. They could distinctively see a rock-hewn tunnel receding

H.

deeply into it. And a shadow was coming from that tunnel. It scampered like a bent-over man, strangely misshapen.

"What the flip? What the flip!" The man quivered and stepped back.

The woman raised her weapon, for whatever it was, it was fearfully beyond comprehension. From fantastical lights to a depth perception miscue, to a demonic shape coming straight at them, it made both of them spasm with sensory overload.

A grotesque little man came out of the light. He was green with a bulbous face, like some fantastical creature. He wore distinctively medieval armour and carried a crude bent sword.

The man with the briefcase hurried back down the corridor to a stairwell door. He hit it and dropped the briefcase. Papers burst out and fluttered to the floor. He fell at the door.

The woman stepped back, knowing the creature was dangerous, for it snarled at her and raised its sword. It quickly hobbled toward her. She shook and quivered, not knowing what to do, but her training kicked in, and she fired.

It bent over unsure of what hit it. Then it growled again and began anew its charge, raising its blade. She fired again and again, and it finally crumpled to the floor in front of her.

The man covered his ears, shaking violently, pushing the stairwell door open. The woman stared down at the creature stunned from the blast of firing and all that just occurred. She looked back at the stairwell door. The man leapt through and fell down the stairs with a grunt. She was not sure of his well-being. She looked back at the creature and then at the shimmering light. She didn't know what to do.

She heard more skittering growls coming from the dark tunnel. She saw more silhouettes of the same grotesque-looking man coming toward her.

The door to Ethralia's apartment opened, and the woman pointed her gun at Wooly. At that moment he looked like a beast, a monster. Wooly quickly deflected her hand and pulled her inside. He shut the door behind them. She skipped and fell over the couch, putting her hands out to catch herself. Her gun plopped along the cushion and rattled to the floor. Her hair flailed over her eyes as she peered down at Ethralia holding Alfred.

H.

She shook but managed to gain balance, crouching to pick up her gun and wave her hair back. "What the flip? What is it? What is... who are they?"

"Why is she here?" Ethralia hissed in her spittle.

Wooly pulled out his broken sword from under the folded sewing work. "We came through a gateway," he said. "It's magical. There is one in the hallway now."

"A gateway? Magical?" the woman repeated, stunned.

"It's not from us. This one is from her, the enemy," Wooly said. He motioned for Ethralia's hand.

"The enemy? Her? Who?"

The woman breathed, gaining some composure with her gun in her hand.

Wooly looked up and down the woman as Ethralia sat with Alfred. "You have training. You know fighting?"

The woman nodded her head. "Marines, a long time ago. Military police."

"Kill them, understand?" Wooly said, leveling his broken sword.

She stared at the broken blade. It still had a sharp edge with a broken point.

Alfred stood, as if awakening, not from a nightmare but from a coma. He shook out of it, grabbing his head.

Wooly listened at the door. They could hear the grunts and groveling of the creatures. "Goblins," he whispered. "Scouts."

Suddenly, another door was heard opening and a scream.

Wooly reacted quickly, bursting the door open upon a goblin, who was looking down the corridor. Wooly quickly sliced that one. Then he raced out. The woman leveled her weapon but remained inside, thinking to protect Ethralia and Alfred.

Still frazzled from experiencing this terrifying unknown, she could barely move. Her muscles felt numb and her legs weak. She put one hand on the couch to balance herself while trying to steady her gun aimed at the door.

They could hear the growls of goblins. Then they heard a man stepping, grunting and slicing quickly. This was followed by the gurgles of dying goblins. Then they heard the calm voice of Wooly. "Keep your door closed and locked."

Ħ.

He returned opening their door and rushing in. The woman almost fired and then stopped, letting out a breath of air.

"Ethralia, can you close the gate?"

Ethralia nodded, stood up and rushed to the door. She looked at the shimmering blue glow. Shadows were racing to it, a multitude. She mumbled something and waved a hand at it. The blue light suddenly flashed out.

The woman looked at Alfred, blinking slowly.

Alfred looked back and smiled strangely. "I don't have a sword, at least not in this realm. I think I might need to get one."

Wooly and Ethralia turned back into the apartment.

"She will try again," Wooly said, grimacing.

"I can close her gates, but I must concentrate," Ethralia said. "I can sense her seeking." Ethralia sat, furrowing her eyebrows. She then looked up. "She will open a gate further out."

"Further out?" asked the woman, trying to regain composure.

"I can repel her magic, her seeking. But the further I push out, the further she will find a way," said Ethralia.

"Further? I don't flipping understand!" the woman said, stuttering.

Just then, they heard a scream from the window – outside. A car suddenly hit another car, and more people screamed.

Wooly rushed to the window. "Darkness is upon us. She won't stop!" He turned and grabbed at Ethralia. "Come! Now!"

No one understood his need to go. But they went nonetheless, for only he seemed certain of his task. They came out of the corridor, and the woman saw the dead goblins, a half dozen lying about in dark pools of black blood. She stopped to see that they were steaming and melting, turning into a black ooze.

They hurried to the stairs and saw the man lying at the bottom of the first flight. He lay crumpled and lifeless. As they neared him, the woman shuddered, and tears finally poured down her face. She tried to stay, but Wooly pulled her along. "We must go!"

As they reached the apartment's lobby, they could hear sirens blaring past. Wooly waited for the police cars to pass and then opened the door. People ran past him in a panic, screaming in terror.

Distant growls burst against the building walls. Wooly peered out.

"Where are we going?" the woman asked.

H.

Wooly waved them out as he ran next door to his cordoned off workshop. Ethralia and Alfred ran out and looked. Cars were piled up in the narrow block. Behind them a police car with red lights flashed. The red lights mixed with a blue hue and electrical lights from the gate beyond. Many people were rushing away, but many others had their phones out recording. Two police officers were pushing them back and yelling. Suddenly, screams and gunfire erupted. Everyone ran in terror.

Wooly, Ethralia, Alfred and the woman got to Wooly's shop. The front door had a huge bolt lock on it, courtesy of the police, that Wooly could not open. He went down the narrow side-alley to the back. There was a large empty lot there full of weeds and trash. It must have been the parking or holding ground for the old fire station, but now was an abandoned space behind squalid apartments and old brick buildings.

"Those policemen came with me," the woman yelled as Ethralia and Alfred rushed down the alley. "Let's go to them. What are you doing?" the woman yelled as Ethralia and Alfred rushed down the alley.

She saw the policemen pointing their guns at the shimmering blue lights beyond the jammed cars. They were waving civilians back and yelling, "Get down! Get down!"

She wanted to go out to them but realized it was hopeless. The only people who knew what was going on were behind her. She ran down the alley to them. "I need to get back to the office and report this! You guys may be in for some kind of asylum or beyond. This is way above my pay grade."

Wooly wasn't listening, as he was yanking open a small window. He adroitly climbed in and put out his arm for Ethralia to climb up and through.

"Stop! Stop!" the woman said, huffing. "We've got to get back to the Federal Building. We've got to get the FBI, uh... no, National Security needs to be in on this!?" She pulled out her phone.

Alfred stopped to look at her. "I've seen those reports on TV."

"What?" she asked while dialing.

"Terror attacks," Alfred said. "I've seen them on TV. You need to call this in as a terror attack and block off the whole area."

"Absolutely, I'm calling an agent I know at Homeland," she said, finding the contact on her phone.

Ң.

Alfred stepped in closer. "She will never stop. Gorbogal the Witch will never stop. And even after she gets me and my mom, she will never stop coming here."

The woman was about to push dial but stopped, looking into Alfred's eyes. She could hear the growls of monsters and the screams of people fleeing. She could hear the bang bang of gunfire and the swing of steel and horrific growls – and then the terrified pain of human suffering not far away.

"So this is what you could not explain."

Chapter Fifty-Two

B.K.

The Black Knight... Wooly leapt through his crowded workshop to a dusty wooden chest at the bottom of some metal shelves. He yanked it out, opened it, and looked at his black steel helmet. It was crusted and burnt from long ago but still held its shape. A flash burst into his memory, of his former face and the all-consuming fire that entangled flames in his helm and burned his skin, cooking his head within. He plopped it on the worktable and then all the clanking pieces of his suit of black armour.

Ethralia rushed up and aided him, knowing exactly what to do. He pulled on an old crusty gambeson or padded coat. It had many moth holes in it but had retained its shape.

"You don't know about mothballs?" Ethralia suddenly said, a momentary lightness to the impending terror. She swooned. "And you haven't washed this since that day."

Wooly shrugged, pulling off his work boots and pulling up the chausses, or thick woolen leggings. She coughed but got to work putting on his rotted gambeson. A thin coat of rusted mail was pulled from the chest. He threw it on. Everything was a bit rotted, decayed, and thirteen years old, stewing in that wooden chest.

B.K.

She gagged, rolled her eyes, but continued. She put back on his modern work boots as he sat on a bench, buckling his arms. She tied on his sabatons, small boot-fitted plates to the boots. It was relatively easy for her to untie his boot laces and affix the sabatons.

With each new piece, even in the rotted padding or rusted chain, Wooly felt stronger and more virile. When the breast plate went on, Wooly was transformed into a great warrior, the Black Knight.

Before putting on his black finger gauntlets, he rummaged through other hidden shelving and from the bottom of it pulled out a long plastic wrapping. Ethralia helped him cut open the taped package.

Alfred crawled through the window and opened the back door for the woman to walk in. She hurried in while on her phone.

"Yes, a terror attack. You have got to get everything in ten block radius down here and cordon this place off. I am not pooping you, Randy. This is on the line."

Alfred stood and stared at his father. The woman looked up and stopped talking even though she could clearly hear a voice on the other end yelling at her.

Ethralia pulled out a new modern longsword from the wrapping. Wooly had ordered something in this modern world, just in case. He took it, even as the price tag still swung from it.

"Cold steel. It is made well. Has a good balance," Wooly said. He then pulled out a small workmen's axe. "From the hardware store. Made well too."

"What the heck are you?" the woman said gulping.

"He's the Black Knight," Alfred said, gaping himself.

Wooly turned to Ethralia and kissed her deeply, a man encased in medieval black steel kissed his love.

The woman watched and swooned a little, catching herself.

Wooly released Ethralia and put on his helm. "Draw them to me, Ethralia. Draw them to the back." Wooly motioned for the rear.

Ethralia nodded no.

Wooly stopped to look at her again through his helm. The strapping and padding were new, for the former burned off and melted against his skin long ago. He replaced them, ever knowing he would have to wear it again. He put on his gauntlets.

"Others, innocents of this world, will die unless you draw them to me," he said. He then looked at Alfred. "My King, you must form an alliance with this world, with the United States of America. We are the target for Gorbogal. We must be taken away from the people of this city, to their fortress."

Alfred thought a moment as Wooly stomped past them and into the back lot. "He's right. We have to form an alliance. The thing is out of the box! The pandora thing!"

The woman blinked, thinking... "The Pandora's Box has been opened?"

"Yeah, I remember reading that in my Greek, uh, myth studies, except... this isn't a myth. It's for real."

Ethralia sat down. She seemed to waver as she concentrated on something.

The woman and Alfred stared at her, breathing heavily in the sudden silence of the dark room. They could hear the distant growls and panic from the front.

"Magic and those goblins, they're for real?" the woman asked, as both she and Alfred quivered suddenly.

For outside, the growls of beasts raging could be heard getting closer. Their stomping and clomping was just outside, passing down the narrow alley, echoing inside the dark dusty workshop. Ethralia was drawing them as she concentrated.

The woman ducked back behind a work table where Ethralia crouched. She was muttering to herself, transfixed in some spell casting state.

Alfred snuck to a window. The woman tried to wave him back. She realized she had her phone still on with the yelling voice on the other end. She got back on as Alfred was peering out the window. She whispered hoarsely as she cupped the phone. "I'm here. I'm here.... did you hear that? Good, get everything to block off the area. What? It's on the news? Everywhere? Then you know I am in the gosh darn middle of it. The abandoned fire station! And get the president, get the highest level you can on this. And Randy, there's a man in black knight stuff, in armour. He's a knight. Like medieval times. I'm gosh darn serious! Listen to me, gosh darn-it! He's fighting them, fighting the... the... the flipping terrorists. Okay, let them know. Let them know. You'll see him and know what I'm talking about. He looks like a black knight. A knight in black flipping armour! Yes, gosh darn-it!"

Alfred, crouched low, stared out the dusty window. He could see the dark shape of his father, flying through many many flailing bodies in the back lot. Tears came down from his eyes. "Dad..."

B.K.

A Special Weapons and Tactics truck, known as SWAT, rolled up to the police cars and traffic jam as the grey of evening turned to the black crisps of night. Its members rushed out of the truck, guns aimed. They peered beyond the cars with their harsh headlights. Whatever had transpired on the block was not clear. Several policemen lay lifeless, lit in the bright headlights of stalled cars. Some civilians were lying amidst the cars or under streetlights. One was cradling a bloody arm. The SWAT saw that they had gruesome wounds.

"What the flip?"

An old man from a window waved and pointed behind them. "They're monsters! Many of them! They all went that way! Oh dear God... Oh dear God..."

The entire cadre of SWAT members turned their guns and moved to the alleyway to which the old man pointed. They could hear growling and clashes of something. They were unsure. They hit the wall, lining up on each side as the front ones aimed their guns toward the noise. They peered down with weapon-mounted lights. The narrow alleyway was dark as they cut through it with their misty beams of light.

They waved as team members filed in, hurrying down the narrow brick corridor. Several stayed back. They had bolt cutters and were opening the workshop's locked door. Several readied to go in that way.

As two came to the back lot shining their lights, they could hear the strangest noise, like a muffled lion growling. They weren't sure. It definitely shook the resolve they acquired from many years of training and experience. Before them they could see a figure lying on the ground. But it wasn't a person. It had two legs and two arms splayed out, and it was wearing something akin to body armor. They weren't sure.

The harsh shadows and their contrasting flashes of light beams danced, making the visuals all too surreal. It was real yet incomprehensible. Was it a crazed large man? It looked too fantastical, like something out of a monster movie. It must have been homeless crazies or gang members wearing Halloween costumes and grotesque masks, something of this reality, this world, this comprehension.

And again they heard a strange noise like what they had heard only in movies, steel hitting steel, growling and gurgling. They got to

306

the opening and flashed their gun lights about to see a crazed movement and some person or thing flail and fall, as another, a dark shadow, seemed to pierce their beams of light then disappear again.

A member fired a three-shot burst, unsure of what he was aiming at.

"Hold your fire!" the lead officer shouted, raising his hand. He slowly moved his light beam across the dark lot. A row of SWAT members lined up. Members within the workshop adjacent them began yelling at whoever was inside.

"Hands up! Show yourselves!"

"Hold your fire! I'm a government agent. Janice Wood! Immigration Law Enforcement! I made the call!"

"Civilians! Officer on site. Intact."

The leader's beam of light saw bodies, many bodies on the ground littering the weed ridden abandoned space. They were odd, some were small and gangly, and some were large and hulky. It was strange to see, for all of them had grotesque faces and grotesque skin. But before the members could focus their harsh lights on the impossible before them, they saw the black figure. Was it a robot? Some dark big black robot?

Their beams finally focused on the figure, hunched over and holding a sword and an axe. Both were bloodied with some sort of dark black blood.

"Put your gun... put your weapons down!" the lead officer yelled, fixing his beam of light on the figure. They all pointed their weapon at the man, who they now could discern was wearing medieval armour.

"Put your sword down!"

Wooly dropped his weapons and raised his arms.

The SWAT team slowly stepped forward and then stopped, for they saw steam rising, and a putrid odor permeated the area. They were amazed as all the grotesque bodies began to steam and melt into a black ooze.

"What the flip?!" one said, stepping back.

"It's okay. He's the Black Knight. He's with us!" Janice finally yelled from the workshop, waving her badge as several SWAT members came out with her.

Chapter Fifty-Three

C.

"Containment... We have got to have full containment on this!" Janice yelled in her phone as Wooly, still in his bloodied armour, sat on a bench across from her. Next to them, huddled inside a truck, Alfred held his mother. The siren of the vehicle blared outside as they were heading somewhere, anywhere.

Filled in around them were SWAT members, staring at them, unsure of what the heck just happened.

"I am bringing the subjects in.... wherever you want them. They are willing and able. This is another world event or something. Containment is crucial. Some kind of terror attack has got to be the report. Make it some kind of flash mob, gang related, drug war, whatever story your team on the ground can come up with. And this is all hands on deck! Yes sir, this is way above my pay grade. I'm bringing them to higher ups... Yes sir... Containment."

To Alfred it was a series of the strangest truck transfers. Each one was done somewhere odd. Different men came each time: first the police, then soldiers, and then just men in suits. He slept through much of it, unsure, exhausted. Much of it was waiting. Just waiting... cloistered in a steel truck, whether still or rumbling along.

He could see a bridge and a seaport where big cranes were. It was night once again. Helicopters and trucks and police crowded the area as they led Wooly out, then Alfred and his mom.

C.

They went from the police to the military, this time out in the forest somewhere. He could see evergreen trees and street signs but no buildings. He wasn't sure where they were. His mom was in a strange trance. She was muttering to herself. Her eyes were open, but she acted like she was in a nightmare.

Finally, the men in suits crowded around and took them out of the military truck and into black SUVs. After that they were placed in some sort of train or subway. The men they met there looked different as well. Some had dark uniforms on while others were in lab coats. They brought other vehicles too, with many carts or gurneys, and upon them were things wrapped in thick plastic bags. A flurry of people in lab coats rushed to them, some to Alfred and Wooly and his mom. Alfred was so exhausted that he couldn't discern where they were, how much time had passed, and who they were with.

He just remembered Gorbogal and her wicked hackle. He saw her come at him. She grew to overtake his vision, as if taking him away. And then Ethralia awoke from her nightmare and looked at Alfred.

"Don't you dare let her!" she said, looking close at her son as she hugged him. She kissed his forehead. "Don't you dare let her have power over you!"

Alfred gazed up at her calm face, even though there was a flurry of activity around them. Wooly had taken off some of his armour - the shoulders, the arms, the breastplate - but was still in his mottled gambeson and leg armour. He sat beside them, waiting patiently for each new order.

Men in suits with assault guns and men and women in lab coats surrounded them on the seats in this strange mysterious subway. Lights flashed across them, as they went deep down within the earth, far far away from everything Alfred knew in two different worlds.

Chapter Fifty-Four

B.

In a Bunker... they were in some kind of bunker or fortress. Alfred couldn't tell. He was wearing a simple grey t-shirt and the scrub-like pants nurses and doctors wear. He had cloth sock-like shoes on. He felt as if he was in a hospital. Maybe he was a mental patient in a hospital? They were cleaned up and waiting in what looked like a meeting room. There was an expanse of windows across the walls facing them. They had sheets hanging behind them to block off the view. The room looked unfinished, with exposed wires and concrete floors. The door was open. Guards stood outside. The opening showed a wall across from them, but to the left was a very large room Alfred only saw in passing. There was a flurry of activity out there. Many people or agents at computers were speaking. Orders and questions went back and forth. They were ushered in from the right through stark corridors. They could hear a lot of electronic voices. They were talking to higher-ups on phones and video calls.

B.

They saw agents rush back and forth, many with papers or their phones out, peering at stuff. On many occasions, heads would poke in and peer at them. The younger ones, male and female, tended to smile politely. The older ones tended to give stern looks and go away.

Alfred looked at his mom. She was very distracted in her mind. She looked mentally tired. Wooly stared at her, sitting in a business chair, wearing the same grey t-shirt and scrub pants.

"Can you maintain it? Does she still seek?" Wooly asked her softly.

"Yes, ever and ever... and she has sorcerers and witches..." Ethralia said, furrowing her brows and looking not at anything in the room but beyond.

Alfred touched her arm. It seemed that contact was as supportive and strengthening as an army of enchanters.

Janice, the immigration agent, came in. She looked frazzled and was not given the time to shower or put on the new set of patient garb that Alfred and his parents wore. She was holding a coffee cup and drinking from it. Her hands were shaking. She sat across from them and slowly looked at each of them but fixated on Ethralia and her strange distant look.

"What is she doing?"

"Containment," Alfred responded.

"That light? That gateway?"

Alfred nodded slowly.

"She's holding it off, from opening again?" Janice gulped.

"Yep, her sister is trying to get us, wherever we are," Alfred said.

"So she can come right in here? Through that glowing gateway thing?"

Alfred nodded again.

Janice gulped more of her hot coffee and got up. She waved a single finger at them, signaling for them to wait a moment. She left.

The buzz of talking and responding and electronic voices suddenly stopped as Janice spoke to everyone in the bigger room. Alfred couldn't make out what she said but knew it was something to the effect of, "We have a containment problem."

After a long silent moment a military general walked in the door.

311

B.

"What if I shoot you right now? Will that be our containment!?" the general yelled.

Alfred's eyes widened, gazing at this old man in an army uniform with a few notable stars on his chest pocket. He was not wearing anything fancy. It was definitely more of a military work attire with the noted general stars versus combat or formal attire. Wooly sat up, ready to pounce.

The general's eyes flitted back and forth between them. Agents crowded at the door opening, pushing the guards aside. Several heads peered from the windows, pulling away at the temporary sheets. Alfred could just see the expanse of computers, desks, and agents beyond.

Alfred stood up.

That actually surprised the general. He was focused on the man with the scar face.

"I am King Alfred. This is my mother Ethralia and my father Bedenwulf the Knight. We come from the Northern Kingdom in the Westfold."

"Holy moly if that ain't some bull mularky poop dung!" the general yelled.

Alfred covered his ears.

"What the flip is wrong with him?" the general asked Wooly.

"You are swearing. Perhaps you should not swear," Wooly said with his guttural voice. Several younger agents swooned and had to be held up by the others.

"What the tar nation did you say, scar face?" the general grunted. "My gosh darn swearing is too much for this boy who claims he is a gosh darn flipping king from wazoo land!?"

Wooly gritted his teeth. Alfred cringed more.

Janice walked in and patted the general on his shoulder. "Okay, bad cop, I'll be the good cop."

The general crossed his arms. "I want some dag nabbit answers here. What the heck kind of a cluster mess have you three gotten us into!? A whole dang city block, a whole dang city sector has been put on terror alert, with people dying, and you're worried about my gosh darn pooping swearing!?"

Alfred slowly lowered his hands. "Your swearing will only darken what is already so dark."

The general looked at Alfred.

B.

"General," Janice said softly, "I've seen it. What happened is for real. I've seen it, them, the gate. You're being a real big booty head right now."

The general looked at her.

"I am King Alfred. Shooting my mother will not stop the gateway. Right now she is the only thing stopping it from reopening."

The general listened. Agents suddenly burst through the door: one was holding a camera, recording everything, and the others had a cart with a widescreen monitor with many cables dangling from it. They rushed to one side to set it up while the agent with the video camera positioned himself in the corner. Another agent came in, having just retrieved a tripod. They quickly set up the camera to record everything. All of the activity looked new to the group, as if they were figuring this out as they went along.

"What is this gateway?" the general asked.

"To another world," Alfred said.

"Holy moly, the nightmares are true," the general said. "We got real flipping monsters!"

"There is also good! Knights, farmers, girls and boys who can fight. We were winning. Only – only, she got me. She kidnapped me with a Dark Servant and his giant vulture."

"Giant..." The general couldn't finish the repeat.

"They caught me! She was going to kill me, but she wanted to hurt me first, for a long time," Alfred continued, swooning slightly with the realization.

"Who is she?"

The General suddenly looked tired, as if all of this were so very true and beyond just some strange hoax or false report by news outlets, many eyewitness agents, and fallen police officers.

"Gorbogal, the witch... she is my mom's sister. She has been building armies and destroying the Westfold, all the people, their kingdoms and farms and families. She didn't know about me, about the gateway. I can make this gateway too. I can go between both worlds. I can't do what my mom and... her sister can do. Gorbogal didn't know about making the gateway till now."

"Till now? How?" asked Janice gently.

"My mom, she had to rescue me, using the spell. She didn't want to. She came here to this world to live quietly and not use magic. She wanted to raise me in peace, away from the Westfold and that world that had fallen into darkness. She didn't want to be around the darkness that uses dark magic to control everything... everyone..."

The general rubbed his forehead. Agents peered from around the camera. Others lowered their phones, looking in from the door and screened off windows with stunned looks.

"My mother, when she used the gate spell to rescue me, well, that's when Gorbogal knew about it. She now knows about the spell and that this place, that Earth, exists. Even I don't know how it all works exactly. Or where the Westfold is... if it's just a planet far away or in another dimension. I was born here."

"What about all those things? Janice said they looked like goblins?"

As he said this, the general pulled out a chair and sat down. Then many other higher-ups and agents came in. Most were older, a mix of men and women, and most had civilian suits on. Two were military, possibly different branches, since their uniforms were not the same.

The agents in the room awoke from their staring and quickly finished setting up the monitor, inserting different cables to different devices. The screen went on, and there was a familiar face.

"The president!?" Alfred gasped.

"Hullo, is your name Alfred?" the president asked, fumbling quickly with an earpiece.

"Yes, yes, I'm Alfred," Alfred said and waved too giddy.

The president nodded back, giving a warm smile. "Hi, I'm President Mount of the United States of America. And we've gotten some incredible reports coming from there, about you and your mother and that man. Some incredible reports. A real situation where you live, right?"

Alfred nodded.

"My question to you is, what is going on? Speak plainly and clearly."

Alfred nodded.

Everyone waited.

Patiently, quietly, Alfred looked at all those staring at him. There were many faces at the door, the window and beyond. The guards with their assault rifles peered over the agents. The President of the United States of America gazed from the screen.

Alfred gulped.

B.

"Alfred, we need you tell us the truth," President Mount said through the monitor. "Now, I heard what you just said. But now that we can see each other, I'd like you to explain it again. Take your time."

"There is another world."

An agent fainted.

"And there is a gateway. And my mom and I can open that gateway. Magically. Also, Tirnalth can open that gate. He was the one who made the spell. He is a great wizard. But I don't know where he is. He is preparing to help, though. He is very strong. But he had to go away, to finish or complete his powers... So my mom, she had to rescue me from Gorbogal, who was hurting me, badly, and..."

Alfred quivered, remembering. His mother touched his arm as she focused, awaking into this world.

Ethralia stood, peering oddly at or through them all and spoke. "And in so doing, I revealed the secret of the gateway to my sister, the witch Gorbogal. She can now open the gateway between these two worlds. She is using locks of my hair to focus. Right now, she is trying to reopen it, to send in more goblins and far far worse. She is mustering far more dangerous orcs to come in."

"Orcs!?" the general burst out.

The voices of the agents and leaders suddenly burst out, many considering war footing or national defense or security protocols.

"Silence!" President Mount yelled from the TV. It wasn't necessarily loud since the volume wasn't. But his voice still resonated. "Are you saying, Alfred and Mrs..."

"Ethralia, just call me, Ethralia..." she said, sitting back down, exhausted and still trying to talk while focused on something altogether otherworldly.

"Are you saying we now have... or can be invaded by fantastical creatures from another world led by a witch? A powerful witch?" the president asked.

Alfred nodded. "Yes."

"And she's your mother's sister? Your aunt?" the general interjected, pointing at Alfred.

"Yes."

The general threw his hands in the air. "Situation not normal! Still flipped up!"

Alfred cringed, grasping his ears.

"Language, general! Language!" President Mount burst out.

B.

"Sorry, Mr. President. My apologies," the general grunted.

"Alfred, how do we stop this invasion?" President Mount asked. Everyone froze and looked at Alfred once again.

Alfred glanced at all the guards with their assault rifles. "We must kill Gorbogal, the witch."

Chapter Fifty-Five

S. F.

Special forces men sat in scattered chairs. There were over a hundred of them in the low-ceiling cinder-block room. Alfred stared at them with incredible wonder. He sat on a stool at the front of what seemed like some unfinished presentation room. He compared them to the troll hunters, having that killer look, but these men were much more varied, though smaller in size. There were all kinds of races and creeds. Some were big and burly with muscles and beards. Others were skinny, scrawny, with clean-cut looks. Some wore military looking garb while others were in sports clothes. A few were in expensive looking suits.

Wooly entered with the general. They seemed to be hitting it off. Alfred could see that the general admired the warrior spirit. And Wooly, his dad, was definitely that. Wooly was wearing one of those dry-fit tight shirts and new jeans. He had military boots on and was even allowed to carry his sword. That was weird, Alfred thought. Several of the men sitting in the fold-out chairs noticed.

5. Ͳ.

Alfred remembered the fast and furious work over the last few days. It was practically non-stop. Before, when Alfred first told them they needed to kill Gorbogal, the meeting room echoed a huge vacuous hush.

Then President Mount said, "Well then, that means we have to take the fight to her. That means your mother, who I see is in a struggle with her sister right now, has to open a gateway directly to her, right?"

Alfred nodded.

"Can she transport a spec-op team? Right there, near her, to eliminate the target?" President Mount asked blankly.

Alfred sat up. "Heck yeah!" He looked at his mom, struggling with her resistance of Gorbogal. "Or at least I think so."

"Son, we don't operate with think so. We either do or don't. Lives are at stake here," the general warned.

Alfred touched his mother's arm again. She grabbed back, surprising Alfred and everyone else. She huffed, resisting something powerful so far away yet so near. The lights flickered, and the monitor with the President flickered. Everyone stared.

Ethralia gritted her teeth and then suddenly turned and focused on Alfred. "Yes, tell them yes. I have to."

The general plainly heard. "So she can open a gateway back, and we can rush our team in and eliminate the target?"

Alfred nodded. "Yes, I think they can detect or feel each other."

"Like homing beacons," the general said.

"Yes," said Alfred.

"Excuse my stark remark, just need to restate the obvious here, but if we eradicate you all," the general pointed at them, "wouldn't that end any possibility of otherworldly contamination? Of her targeting this world?"

Even Wooly understood his comment for what it was – a serious consideration for the very survival of mankind in this world.

Alfred wasn't exactly sure. His mother did not answer from her trance-like state. Something was happening, and she was concentrating. She looked exhausted. Alfred did not think she could last much longer. She needed sleep. He doubted Gorbogal needed any sleep at all.

"I'm not sure," he said. "But... I know the realm now, the other world. I know places there. And I... I can teleport there, where I have been..."

S. F.

"So once you know the place, it's basically been marked?" the general asked.

"Yeah, I think so," Alfred said. "But just so you know, I don't even know how I teleport and... I can't really control it. Not the way Tirnalth the wizard or my mom did when she saved me. I've never done it like that. Mine doesn't seem as focused as hers did. Not in the place I show up... or even the time."

They looked at him, staring thoughtfully but unsure. Many looked down, unable to comprehend that this was really happening.

Alfred looked at his mom. She was sweating and mumbling to herself. Wooly sat close to her, watching.

Wooly addressed the general. "Sir, I think you should have a force here, an armed force ready."

The general nodded. "You mean ready to go in."

"No, I mean for when she can't keep her sister away."

The general turned to an adjutant, some agent assistant, and spoke to him rapidly. The agent nodded and left the room.

The general turned back. "We'll make it so. We've got a pretty high level of security here, but we'll put them on high alert, internally."

"Are they trained in sword? In melee?" Wooly asked.

"In what?" the general asked.

"In close combat?" Janice added.

"Not modern close combat. More like medieval," said Alfred.

"I think our modern weapons of warfare, our firearms, can do the job," the general said.

"When I fired at that... at that goblin, I fired, and it like didn't seem to register it was shot," Janice said, trying to remember. "It didn't react the way we do. It wasn't shocked or stunned. It carried itself forward. I had to put in several more rounds before it dropped."

Wooly thought for a moment and then spoke. "Their pain awareness is different from ours. It's dulled, slower. Their senses are not the same as ours. They are muted, and they do not feel pain easily. They can struggle through pain. We knights must train knowing this, striking them to impair or kill them outright. We cannot slash their skin and expect a reaction. We must cut deeply, wounding severely, to stop them. Medieval weapons are slower, not so sudden. They are more effective. The firearms of this world – their power is different. It is like lightning. That power is beyond their understanding and feeling."

319

5. F.

The general clenched his jaw. He looked at the other military men in the room. "Knight, or whatever your name is..."

"You can call me Wooly. That is my name here."

"Wooly?" the general replied. "Well Knight Wooly, I think you need to give my security personal an orientation, a training session A-S-A-P."

"He wants you to train his men how to fight goblins and orcs," Alfred added.

Wooly nodded.

"Goblins and orcs!" the general huffed.

Later that evening when Ethralia had finally failed, she screamed and fainted in exhaustion. She was in a small room with several beds. Alfred hit the alarm button on the door and ran out. Several guards were there and sent out the alarm to all sectors. They spoke through their ear pieces and raised their arms.

It wasn't hard to find the bursting blue lights and crackling electrical sparks. A corridor not far away shook and burst as the gate was opened.

The entire complex's monitors and lights flickered and turned off for a brief moment. The backups were well engineered. Immediately, screens turned back on, the operating system maintained itself and issued programmed responses to the klaxon alarms and red flashing lights down the corridors. Everyone jerked into high alert. Something that only happened on occasional and mundane drills was now tearing through the psyches of every agent and operative inside the bunker fortress.

Wooly was in a padded training room with security officers when agents rushed in. He was looking at their equipment, light plastic riot shields. He was not impressed.

Everyone had to yell as the klaxon alarms were blaring.

An agent roared instructions. "Team suit up! The light show is on. Wooly, I'm here to escort you back to your room!"

"I must go and fight," Wooly replied.

"Negative. General's orders. You come with us," the agent said.

The others rushed off to their lockers, putting on vests and loading magazines into handguns and assault rifles.

Wooly looked at them unsure but complied.

S. F.

The general was in a command center. "How much longer till we get the team here?"

An agent responded, "Two hours. They're loading the sub-train."

"God help us!!"

Agents turned on security screens above them that provided live streaming from the many corridors.

The general looked at the screens with gritted teeth. "What the heck am I looking for?"

An agent pointed to one screen. The visual was severely impaired as a glowing light was blasting the lighting correction on the camera.

"What the heck is that?" the general yelled.

"It's the light or energy of the gateway. It's messing with the electronics," the agent said.

Suddenly, from that screen, shadows burst forth. Flickering images came out of the glaring white and showed themselves to be bestial shadows running through. Gunfire could be heard and screams – human screams.

Growls and swinging metal hitting things echoed from the scratchy speakers.

"They're breaking our lines! They're coming!" yelled a frantic voice as gunfire erupted and horrific grunts and screams mixed into the limited static-ridden speakers.

A technician tried to adjust the speakers, to soften them. Then they could hear the same horrific fighting coming from their doorway, leading out into the corridors.

Wooly rushed out of his room as guards stood there listening to their ear pieces. Alfred followed, shaking.

The guards looked up at him with fear.

"Get me to my armour! And my sword!" Wooly commanded.

The guards got up and hurried with him down a corridor. Gunfire echoed from a distance behind them, as did growls and screams.

"Sir!" an agent said, pointing to another screen.

Small goblins and a large hulking bestial man lumbered into view from another camera that was not affected by the gateway's burst of lights. It was still difficult to see. The electronics were still flickering. But they got the point.

"Holy hellfire!" the general said, staring.

More beasts came through, charging down the corridor.

Wooly turned to Alfred, "You must get Ethralia to close it. You must get her to wake up."

"I can't! She's exhausted. I can't," Alfred cried. "SHE will keep coming."

"I will fight to the end!" Wooly said, pulling on his gambeson. Alfred helped with the buckles and straps of each armour piece. He knew exactly what to do, even as tears of fear flowed.

Wooly looked at his son. "Alfred? Alfred... use your fear. Use it. Do not let it overtake you, freeze you. Let it empower you. Understand?"

Alfred looked at his father.

Wooly said, "In all the fear and death I have always known, none of it mattered, for I have known love. Your mother and I... and you... have known love. Of the Father, for each other. That will be forever. The fear... and pain... even the sadistic torture... It is only momentary. They will never own your soul, Alfred... Use it!"

Alfred stared at his father and froze a brief moment. Then he continued with the buckling and fitting. Each piece he finished he slapped and tugged with growing conviction. Wooly flexed his muscles from within. His inner strength rose with each strapped piece. He raised the sword as Alfred buckled the shoulder pads and tested each with a hammering fist.

At the door, the two agents flinched and cowered, guns ready. They listened to their ear pieces but could easily hear the gunfire and growls blast from down the corridor.

The general grabbed his stupid little headset in frustration, yelling, "Get all security back to operations. Seal the gosh darn doors!"

A group of lab coat technicians rushed into the command center from a rear door. They looked young: an Asian boy, a black boy, and a white girl. The three had one thing in common. They looked like nerds. With them was an older fat guy in an obviously non-issued flannel shirt and dirty jeans. The Asian kid muttered aloud, "General, General, we got an idea!"

S. F.

"Not now, kids! We are under gosh darn flipping attack!"

"We have an EMP device!" the kid said as the others urged him on.

The general and all agents stopped to look at the lab coats. "What?"

"The gateway, the stargate... it's electrical. If we can get this device close enough, maybe it can disrupt the energy of the gate," the kid said.

The general looked at the anxious crew and the older fat guy gripping a shoddy looking device. It was a baton with coiled wires in a loop and looked like a toy wand or bubble maker. Affixed, just under the loop, was a small circuit board attached to a row of batteries taped up against the handle. It was clunky looking. The fat engineer held his device, not proudly and a little worried. It was duct taped and wrapped in a hurry with what equipment they had in their workshop.

"An EMP device?" the general queried, staring at the glowing white screen where the gate was. He could just see electrical flashes at the edges of the glaring image.

"Best we could do..." the old engineer muttered.

"We just need to get it close to the gate!" the Asian kid said. He then gulped, looking at his team. They all realized that that was one part of their plan they had not thought through. The engineer swallowed and set the clunky device down for someone else to pick up.

The general stared at the device and then at everyone in the command center. There were many civilians, agents, and lab techs, but none with combat experience. The agents sat at their respective computers, staring at the general. Two guards stood at the door, guns drawn and cowering.

He motioned to a technician next to him as he adjusted his earpiece and mic. "We need a security team here. Is anyone able to make it to the command center?"

They listened to the loud speakers. There was constant gunfire, screams and grunts. There was the slashing of weapons and the cry of men. The agents and technicians flinched in the command center with each gun burst and scream. The monitors were not much help. Every screen seemed to flicker or produce static, badly degrading the video.

"It has a pulse, an electro-magnetic pulse," the Asian kid said. "This will work."

5. F.

"It's got one charge! If it's strong enough..." the old engineer mumbled.

The general nodded, sweating. He pulled off his coat and revealed his holster and gun. He grabbed the EMP device.

"What, what, you?" the Asian kid gulped.

"You just aim the wire coil at the gate and push the button on the bottom," the engineer said quickly. "Simple. But remember, we only had enough time for one charge."

"You can't go," an agent said. "You're the general."

"I'm a soldier first," the general replied. He hurried to the door, waving for the two guards to come with him.

Wooly burst from the room. His fighting prowess against goblins and the hulking troglodytes was difficult to discern on the screens. On the monitor the technicians saw him rush through a corridor as the Black Knight. The movements of Wooly were like the mix of a ballet dancer and a football player, only way more aggressive yet graceful. The shadows of beastmen flailed and fell as he went.

A technician grabbed a large microphone that was on a separate stand. He punched a button. "Wooly, the Knight?! You must get to the gate. You must help the general! I'll lead you there!"

Wooly looked up only a moment as the voice burst through speakers along the corridor. It was somewhat difficult to discern as the klaxon alarms continually burst out their repeated horn sounds. Fortunately for Wooly, the troglodytes before him paused at the voice as well. Wooly recovered first and leapt between the troglodytes, slitting throats and piercing spinal cords.

"Go straight down and turn to your right. To your right!"

He turned to see goblins hurrying along. He quickly hacked his way through, twirling and tumbling amongst them.

"Oh my gosh, that was awesome! Whooh hooh!" the speaker voice yelled.

Wooly looked around a brief moment but realized looking was unnecessary. "Where to?!" he yelled back.

"Oh, oh, sorry, keep going down. Straight ahead!" the electronic voice replied. "Then right again!"

Alfred hurried with the two guards back to his room. He wanted to get to his mom. Several goblins rambled by and noticed them. They hurried after them. The guards turned and fired. Three goblins fell as the guards frantically changed their magazines. One goblin was left. He growled at his fallen comrades and then leapt with his crude blade.

Alfred charged in front of the guards, swirling his father's handaxe. He quickly killed the goblin and posed, ready for any more. The two guards reloaded and aimed over Alfred, but none came. They could hear the fighting beyond, somewhere. There was very little gunfire but many monstrous screams and metal clashes.

"That's my dad," Alfred said to them. Both nodded with a modicum of panicked relief. "Come on! To my mom!"

Alfred rushed between them. The guards looked at each other and shrugged, following the boy who said he was a king from a faraway land.

Wooly turned a corner in the corridor to see the general and a guard running back to him. They were being chased by a big lumbering troglodyte with a heavy war axe. The general looked old and beaten, even with his gun out. The guard fleeing as well seemed delirious.

Wooly ran forward. The general moved aside as Wooly met the charge of the troglodyte. It was a brutal bashing of plated armour and thick muscular beastman. The general stared at the incredible horror before him. He tried to aim and help, but the movement was too frenetic. And then the troglodyte smashed against the wall to its death next to him.

They saw the guard unconscious on the floor with a big gash in his back. The general, however, old and breathing heavily, was still a soldier. He waved for Wooly to lead him back the way he fled.

"This device…" the general held the odd EMP device under his arm so he could quickly change out his gun's empty magazine… "should close that darn gate. I need to get close!" He breathed heavily, barely able to hold up his gun or the device.

Wooly nodded and charged forth.

The general rambled forward, trying to keep up with the Black Knight as he charged through the smoke filled corridor. Out of the choking mist leapt monstrous shadows. Wooly in his medieval armour bashed up against each beast, knocking it off balance, and then quickly swinging his sword in two or three flashing strokes or a sudden piercing jab. The goblins and bigger brutes flailed and fell.

The general wasn't sure how close to the blinding flashes of light he needed to get. The gateway was just beyond the furious flurry of fighting. He looked up at the corridor speaker, waiting to hear any instructions. He could just discern, over the vicious growls of dying orcs, that the speakers were only spitting static.

He ran up behind Wooly's furious attack and pushed the button on the flimsy device. When the general pushed the button on the duct-taped hand held EMP, the electrical gateway burst a sudden flash and then disappeared to a dark smoky cloud. It worked! He fell forward, hitting against the Black Knight and falling to the ground. The red lights of the emergency backups filled the corridor, and before him stood something completely different. It wasn't a monster, a goblin or bestial humanoid. It was a gaunt bald man in robes and long necklaces and bejeweled chains.

The general was utterly shocked, and then the word "wizard" or "warlock" came to mind. Was he really experiencing the fantastical invading the reality of his modern world? The warlock stood before the Black Knight. Both suddenly posed in their accompanying attack stances. The Black Knight raised his sword, ready for the warlock. The creepy, gaunt enchanter twirled his hands about and then stood straight and brought out his fist, gripping the static charged smoky air between them. The red klaxons going off and the red flashes of light made the whole experience that much more nightmarish.

The general stood up as best he could. He dropped the spent EMP baton and raised his handgun figuring he might as well die from a fireball or magical blast firing away at the darn thing. The general and the Black Knight stared at the warlock, unsure what to do.

The warlock or sorcerer, with crazed tattoos and piercings, clenched his fist again and again. The Black Knight raised his sword, ready to receive whatever blast of dark magic the warlock was trying to expel upon him. The general hesitated as well. He wasn't sure what was happening. Was it a mind spell? Was something mentally torturing the Black Knight as he stood there with his sword upright in front of him?

And then he saw Wooly raise his sword above his helm to strike. And he stood there, unmoving. The sorcerer must have paralyzed Wooly, the general figured. He raised his gun to fire upon the warlock. Just then the warlock began cringing. He was convulsing and locked in painful contortions. Black ooze started rupturing from his skin and eyes. He looked up and spit black ooze and moaned an awful guttural cry. Then he fell to a pile of black ooze.

Chapter Fifty-Six

S. F. 2

Alfred shook out of remembering what just happened, he returned his attention back to the present. In the large meeting room with the special forces gathered, the general stood with Wooly, staring at the hundred-plus men seated in foldout chairs on a dusty industrial carpet.

"Men, you are the elite of the elite. You are soldiers, martial artists, assassins, special forces, criminals and warriors. You have been collected, called, taken, and abducted. However, this job is strictly voluntary. Believe it or not..."

Everyone, glancing and judging each other, suddenly stopped and looked up.

"This is the moment of your gosh darn flipping lives, an opportunity to serve your country, the United States of America. And for you foreigners, whom we got through political and not so political means, it is your chance to know the ultimate answer to the question that drives you to do what you do. Are you the best? The elite of the elite?"

The men, who at first looked suspiciously and oddly at each other and at the boy, the general and the man with the scarred face at the front of the room, now looked on with something a bit less than arrogance.

The general pointed to the door. "That door. You can leave. Each of you will be paid one hundred thousand American dollars for your trouble if you do not choose to stay. You cannot tell anyone you were here. Anyone can leave. Again, this is strictly voluntary. You will not know the details of the mission unless you decide to stay. But if you stay... you cannot change your mind. If you do not leave now, you will never be allowed to leave until you are dead or the mission is accomplished. Either way, this can never be mentioned to anyone. If it is, we will hunt you down and kill you."

He stood and looked slowly across the room. There were Europeans, Asians, Africans, Americans, and Hispanics. It was an incredible mix of men, all with faces that knew fighting and surviving, having experienced it.

One stood up, a German looking man in expensive sporty wear. "Excuse me my English. I am not... uh, a soldier. I am a martial artist, the best in Germany. I compete. I have won martial arts competitions in Europe, Asia. I am not like this. I just compete. I do not do this..."

The general motioned to the door.

The German, nervous, carefully walked through the row of other men who sat silent. He quickly made it to the door but was still scared to open it.

"We aren't going to kill you. The boy here and I agree. We must be explicit to all of you that this is voluntary. You have every right and freedom to leave. And yes, one hundred thousand dollars paid right now, no questions asked."

The German still shook, afraid to reach for the knob.

"Who is the boy?" a big burly bearded guy at the front asked.

The general answered, "What boy?"

Alfred blinked. The general stared at the bearded guy.

The bearded guy shrugged.

The general continued. "I can tell you all this. This mission has a high level of failure. And if it fails, your bodies will never be found. And you will probably die a most gruesome horrific death. There may even be torture involved, and no one will be able to rescue you. Your supplies and ammo will be limited. Your communication will probably be nil. This will be the cluster cluck you have nightmares about. I can tell you no more. You all must decide for yourself. Freely."

Alfred covered his ears, cringing.

The general looked at the German. He walked over as the German looked down, about ready to cry. The general opened the door. The click of the knob made the German martial arts master flinch.

"There is absolutely no dishonor in leaving. None. This mission is beyond even my understanding."

The general motioned for the martial arts expert to leave. Beyond, the German could see the vast bunker-like warehouse and the sub-train waiting for any who wished to exit. He stepped out and walked fervently to the train. A small group of agents at the train waited and handed him a small bundle of cash. He took it nervously and then hurried into the train.

Others peered through the door. Suddenly, and somewhat surprisingly to the general, many got up. Men in suits, in fatigues, in expensive sporty outfits got up and walked out. At first, it seemed like all were leaving. The general couldn't tell, for many men passed by blocking his view.

One mumbled, "Can't kill us all."

The general closed his eyes as he felt the men pass – the many men.

When the way cleared in the large meeting room, the general was somewhat relieved that some of the abducted special forces had stayed. The cost of agents researching thousands of candidates across the agencies from the F.B.I., to Homeland Security, to the C.I.A. and many off-shoot branches, was overwhelming. The cost in time and pay for agents to find warriors, elite and able enough to take on this mission was daunting. When the president put his full endorsement, albeit top secretly, behind this, it was as all hands on deck. To scour the planet of all warriors showing a multi-faceted ability to deal with such a fantastical mission as this was incredible. Not even the intelligence agents doing the recruiting were aware of the mission. All they knew was that they needed the most dangerous and physically capable soldiers in the most varied combat and hand-to-hand fighting situations.

Many agents failed to acquire their targets. Some targets came willingly while others got away by threatening low level agents who approached them. Others got yanked into vans, which then drove off.

There was a strange array of conditions and circumstances across the globe and hundreds of millions of dollars used to acquire these special men. On top of that, there was the cost of travel: from first class tickets to military helicopters, from taxicab rides to social app driving services, it was as varied as was the possible recruits. And here they were, most now leaving with a hundred thousand dollars in their pockets.

It looked as if maybe twenty were still sitting. Would that be enough? The general wasn't sure. It was kind of devastating actually. He was proud of the twenty that stayed. And yet he was saddened at the immense work in such a short time to get the toughest of the tough that led to only a handful staying. He couldn't be too judgmental. The conditions he set forth were not fathomable. And most of these possible recruits were of the individual ingenious type. Perhaps, he should have just gotten some loyal U. S. Marines. In hindsight, that probably would have been the better choice. He wasn't sure. This was all new territory.

"Could have just got a bunch of marine grunts, hey General? Or us Navy Seals – would have gotten a lot of guys..." the bearded guy said.

The general smiled at the coincidental notion. He then noticed that a small tight-knit group of men was led by the big burly guy with the beard. He recognized them as former Navy Seals. "We chose men of fighting prowess, who did not have any immediate kin, wives, children..."

The bearded man looked at his men, then back at the general, and nodded.

The general stepped weakly from the door as he closed it. The door was stopped by a small Japanese man who returned. The man bowed and looked once more into the room. A bead of sweat came down his forehead. He stared a moment, then stepped in and nodded for the general to close it.

The General followed behind the Japanese man as he walked back to a nearby chair, bowing to the other warriors within and then sitting. Many nodded back.

Alfred sat glum. He looked at the few left, spread across the hundred plus chairs. It looked quite empty. The general met Alfred's eyes and then tried to give him a reassuring look. Alfred grinned politely.

"Now that we're here, can you tell us who the boy is?" the burly bearded guy asked again.

The general nodded to Alfred.

"I am King Alfred. I am really just a boy who grew up here, in the city. But my mom and my dad, well..." Motioning to Wooly, he said, "They're from another world."

"What?"

"A third world?"

"Another world," Alfred said. "Another dimension. Like outer space, only magical."

A strange Asian man in the back stood up. He was a rough-looking guy with a goatee, balding with long side hair. He was very muscular and had many scars. He wore strange Asian metro fashions. All of it looked dirty as if he had been partying all night. He was older, with wrinkles, but still quite deadly looking. He rambled through the foldout chairs, kicking many over. He came closer and pulled up a chair closer, then plopped down. Everyone stared back at him. "What lies is this? If cowards get paid one hundred thousand for leaving, what do I get paid for killing?"

"One million," the general answered.

Everyone turned and stared at the general.

"It will be paid to whatever account you wish and to whomever you wish, tax free," he added. "I suggest you make sure to fill out the paperwork properly and thoroughly. Again, none of you has immediate family, wives or kids. So find a next of kin... before we give you the rundown of this mission, let's get an intro from all of you: Who you are, what is your training and what skills do you have." He motioned to the scurrilous looking Asian street fighter.

He stood and said, "I am Kwan Thai Suex. I fight anyone, anywhere, for money." Then, realizing he had nothing else to say, he sat down. He stared at Alfred, who bravely stared back.

The Japanese man stood up quietly. He wore a simple suit and bowed. "I am Masamu. My father is a renowned sword maker in Japan. I am his son." He bowed again and then sat.

The burly bearded man looked back at the few men who were there. He had three with him. He stood up. "I'm Riley. These are my men, Jake, Brubaker, and Loud. We're former Navy Seals. We get the job done."

He looked back at the rest who were still there and then at his men. He turned to the general. "Who is going to be in charge of this mess? On the ground?"

"Not sure, maybe you. Maybe him," the general nodded to Wooly or maybe to Alfred. Both sat to his left on high stools.

"Who's scar face?" Riley asked, looking at Wooly.

"I want to know about that old face back there?" said the general, peering at a big bald black man sitting in the back.

"Me?" The man seemed to wake out of a dream. The general smiled, nodding as if knowing him. "Me? Me. I'm just an old warrior. Heavy weapons... My wife died of cancer. And I do have a son! Your agents missed that. But that's okay. That's okay... my son hates me. He got that education thing from those professors at a fancy university and now hates who I am and what I do. He marches for the rich while complaining about the rich. So I don't have much left to live for. And you can keep your money." Though he was big and tough-looking, his voice was soft and quiet.

"What's your name?" Riley asked.

"The Duke. Just call me Duke," he said.

"Well, you're still getting the money. You do have a sister," the general said.

"That I do," the Duke said, smiling at the general.

"I'll take care of the paperwork."

"Much obliged," the Duke replied.

"And you?" The general nodded to another guy, a somewhat clean-cut blonde with an old Western-style mustache.

"I'm Rudy, Marine, mercenary, security. I get around," he said shrugging. "I don't plan on dying. I plan on collecting."

"Oh, that's a good plan. Hope it works out for you," Riley said.

"Oh, I intend on it," Rudy replied.

The general moved on, "And you?"

"Me?" A tough-looking muscular guy stood up. He wore cool fashions, European, that he barely fit into. He also wore gold plated sunglasses, even in the pale fluorescence-lit room. "I am Russian. Heavy weapons like the black man."

The Duke looked up. "Oh-okay, I'm the token black man, alrighty."

Some snickered.

The Russian tried to smile and be oddly polite, though his muscles, haircut and fashion revealed his vanity. "I am Rostislav."

"Rosti-slav?" the Duke whistled. "Heck, might as well just call you Russki then?"

"My name is Rostislav," Russki said.

"Okay Russki," the Duke said, sitting calmly behind him.

"Then I call you black man. Token black man," Russki sneered.

"Whatever floats your boat, man, whatever floats your boat," the Duke said.

Others snickered, the Navy Seals, Rudy...

"Alright, you guys can whip out your pride some other time..." the general said, waving his hands.

Alfred cringed.

A man in a suit stood up. "I am a hit man. I guess international law isn't at play here. I don't think this is my line of work. But I also am quite familiar with sword play." He bowed curtly to Masamu, who stood and quickly returned the bow.

"Got a name?" Riley asked.

"No." The man sat back down.

"No?" Riley shrugged. "Okay, No it is."

Others spoke. There were military men, most of the mercenary sort. Many were patriots and American, with a few from other races and nationalities. But it was a few indeed.

The general waved them to be quiet. "So to recap, we got ex-Navy Seals Riley, Jake, Brubaker and Loud. We got two Asians, one a Muay Thai street fighter and one an honorable swordsman from Japan. We got two heavy weapons guys from the Cold War or something, the Duke and Russki."

"Rostislav."

"Rostislav," the general nodded and continued. "We got No, some mysterious international hit man, and I recognize Rudy and the half dozen Marines and handful of Rangers. So we got a bevy of fighting men. None of you is my first choice..."

They laughed.

"But you'll have to do."

"What about scar face? And the kid?" Riley said. "Now that we're most definitely in."

"...till death do us part..." the Duke chimed.

The general looked at Riley and nodded. Russki sat down, very curious to hear who they were. Alfred was about to speak, but the general put his hand up to stop him. Alfred complied and grimaced with a smile.

"What these two are going tell you... you have never heard before. Remember this, you have no choice after the choice you just made, your choice to stay. Whatever they tell you, you will believe, and whatever they tell you, you must follow their orders. There is no turning back now. That door is sealed. The only door you have now is victory or death."

"Does that apply to the kid?" Riley asked.

"Yep," Alfred spat.

"Lemme guess, he's the heir to next kingdom here on Earth!" the Duke sang.

Alfred's eyes widened.

"Settle down and let them explain," the general said. He looked and nodded to Alfred.

Alfred scooted off his stool and stood like a boy in a recital about to give a speech.

He froze and stared at the men peering at him. They were all seated in folded chairs too small for their bodies. Even the smaller-built warriors looked big and bulky in their seats. Aside from the Duke, all of them seemed bent forward, not using the back rests but hunched over with intent.

"I am, I... I am King Alfred. I have defeated rat...men, goblin men, beasts and monsters," he finally said.

The men remained quiet, glancing at each other.

"I have been at war with my aunt, a powerful witch in another world. Her name is Gorbogal. She now knows how to connect to this world and send in goblins and far worse stuff. She is trying to get me and my mom and my dad. He is the Black Knight." Alfred motioned to Scarface. "You call him Scarface. His face got burned by Gorbogal when she was a dragon. Uhhhh... we are going back through a gate to kill... uhhh eliminate the target, eliminate her."

"Oh come on!" Rudy burst out, standing up and waving his arms. "Come on! This is total poopy doop!"

Alfred covered his ears.

"Rudy, sit down," the general said. "And watch your language."

"What? My flipping language? You asking me to fight and die, probably for this kid, and I gotta watch my mooky flipping language!?"

Alfred cringed, for the words most certainly disturbed him. Wooly stood and raised his hand at Rudy.

"And who is Scarface? Whip it out? Who the heck are you, Scarface?"

"He is the Black Knight, Bedenwulf," Alfred said, yelling at Rudy angrily. "His face was burnt by my aunt, the witch, when she was in the form of a shadow dragon!"

"Is this a friggin fantasy game? A reality show? Huh? Seriously! You telling us all this poop about dying, no choice, the doorway or stay and die? What the dooky man!? Oh my God!" Rudy spat.

The soldiers all glared wide-eyed. Riley slowly blinked.

"I don't like your swearing!" said Alfred, sitting down and crossing his arms. "Just show them the video!"

Chapter Fifty-Seven

P-4.

P-1

Part of their Preparation was to watch videos of the fight in the corridors caught on electrically over-charged cameras. The men bent closer, squinting their eyes as if that would help them discern better what they were seeing. The large widescreen mounted on the wall was playing back the corridor cameras and the battle that had just taken place within the very bunker fortress they were in.

An agent had a laptop connected and was playing various videos. Each one showed something, a furious shadow rush by or a blurry figure that didn't look human, or did it? Was it a hairless gorilla? Wearing armour and carrying a sword? One video looked somewhat clear but too fast. When the agent paused it on a frame the motion blur obscured the passing figures. Only on quick playbacks of several seconds, looping in a disconcerting fashion, could they see the monstrous creatures running by. Finally, the clarity of a bestial man running down a corridor followed by several small goblinesque creatures was apparent in one of the playbacks. These were things that didn't surprise the deadly men in the room. After all, they'd seen better in movies.

"I've seen better stuff come out of Hollywood," Rudy chuckled.

"This is real. It ain't all that Hollywood bull malarkey," the general said, showing frustration at the poor video quality. "Fought these darn things in our own corridors and we ain't got but poop-a-doop midnight video capture at a convenience store."

"Show them the melted bodies," Alfred said with a shrug.

In a laboratory, the men stood around with crossed arms as the young lady from the lab coat team peeled open a thick plastic body bag.

"They degrade rapidly in our atmosphere. We're not sure why. They're comprised of similar inert materials as we are: oxygen, carbon, nitrogen, water based," she said. There were dozens of these bags on carts crowded to one side of the laboratory workshop. The other team of lab technicians was busy studying samples.

Another young lady came by to pick at another sample. Rudy noticed and danced his eyebrows. "Hey?"

She rolled her eyes and carried on with her work.

Steam wafted from the bag. Most covered their noses and gagged. Wearing surgical gloves, she pulled up what looked like some sort of metal armour piece with leather straps and buckles, dripping with black goo.

"Is that poisonous? Could there be some alien virus coming out of that poop?" Rudy asked, plugging his nose and standing back.

"If there is, it's too late for all of us. These things have contaminated the corridors," she said. "We've spent the last few days with them in here and have not found any element foreign to us. However, something is missing," she said.

"The dark magics," Alfred sighed.

"The what?" Riley asked, standing close to Alfred.

"Gorbogal, she is a witch of the dark arts," Alfred answered.

"You're aunt, the witch?" Riley asked.

"Yeah."

"And she is trying to come here, invade here using these as her foot soldiers?"

"Yeah, I guess."

"But why? If she is an alien queen, why does she want our technology? Seems she's got way more advanced technology with teleports and making these beasts." Riley stated. The others listened, intrigued as they moved away from the stench of the dead goo. The general motioned for the lab tech to seal it back up.

"I don't know. I know she wants me... and she wants to rule the Westfold, the world I'm from, or well, where my mom and dad come from. She wants to take it over. But I think I'm stopping her. My small castle and my spearboys and archergirls and knights... we fought against her armies and stopped them."

"Spearboys, archergirls? What?" Rudy interjected.

"Yeah, I had them train as spearmen and archers. And we fought her goblin armies and beat them," Alfred said, staring blankly as the young lady sealed up the bag. "Plus the gnomes, they helped us."

Everyone stared at Alfred, the bag, and each other. There was a long silence. Many were rubbing their chins, the backs of their necks, shifting in their stances, and glancing at each other.

Rudy shook his head in disbelief. "General, why don't you shoot me in the head right now, cuz this is total poop-a-doop!"

Alfred cringed at Rudy's – well, rudeness. He turned to look at Rudy. "Why do you swear so much? Why are you so angry and dirty mouthed?"

Rudy looked at Alfred while everyone looked on in a strange silence. Rudy shrugged. "Why not? All the darn evil in this world... and your fake world, why not be angry and dirty flipping mouthed!?"

"Alright, that's enough," the general said. "You need to get in line, Rudy. We're gonna need your demolition expertise and not your bull malarkey. Excuse my French, Alfred."

"That's right! I like to blow things up!" Rudy replied, flashing his fingers into an explosion before Alfred.

"How are you at melee? At close combat?" Wooly asked, stepping in a bit close.

"Oh, I can handle a blade!" Rudy said, posing with a make-believe knife.

"A knife won't work. I mean a sword," Wooly said.

"A sowww... wow..."

P-2

In a large padded room Wooly pulled out thick-set plastic batons. He threw one at Rudy, who caught it and rolled his eyes. He then stood in front of him. Rudy shook out his shoulders and felt the balance of the baton.

The score of fighting men were there. Masamu and Kwan Thai Suex stood peering intently. The Navy Seals Riley, Loud, Brubaker and Jake grouped together. Duke sat on a large padded box, reclining against a wall. Russki sat on a wooden jumping box trying to look cool and dangerous wearing a very tight designer shirt.

The other men, the mysterious hitman No, soldiers of fortune and special forces found places to sit or stand, curious about this new or rather old form of fighting.

Rudy sneered. "Why don't you just use spearboys and archergirls to get this witch of yours? Don't need us fighting men, hey Scarface? Don't need a bunch of bad hombres with the finest military hardware! Huh?"

"Hey," Kwan Thai Suex leaned in, "you talk too much." He stepped back and met Masamu's eyes. Masamu nodded. Kwan merely sneered.

"Alright, alright, let's see what you got, Scarface," Rudy said, twirling his baton quite adroitly.

Wooly nodded, posing with his baton. For a moment all noticed something grand and noble about the way he stood and how he raised that simple baton. And then he tossed it to Alfred.

Alfred caught it, twirling it into a similar position.

"Oh oh, hah hah," Rudy chuckled, flinching a bit at the sudden toss. "Oh, okay Scarface, this is how its gonna be, huh? Gotta use a kid for your fights..."

The warrior men in the room chuckled and shifted, very curious about the turn of events.

Alfred stepped forward. Before he could ready himself, Rudy charged.

Blackness with a slight ringing, and the blue padding was now a wall. Blurry figures walked up and down that wall but oddly standing not up, but to his right. They were walking sideways and their voices were gooey and woozy. The ringing subsided, his focus bounced back to clarity, and the wall of blue padding rotated back to the floor.

Rudy sat up and floundered slightly as he was used to the ringing and the unconsciousness. "Who the flip hit me!?" He knew someone clocked him without him knowing. It had happened to him a few times. And explosives tend to cause this effect from time to time, even when the practitioner makes it to a safe distance. After all, demolition is more of an art than a science.

When he became steady, he saw the kid, Alfred, before him. Wooly then stepped in, patting Alfred on the shoulder and taking the baton. Alfred gave a cool shrug and stepped off.

Wooly turned to the group, looking at Masamu and Kwan Thai Suex especially. "The smaller beasts, the goblins, should not be a problem. They have fear, when confronted, they hesitate. Their desire is to massacre not to fight. But the larger beasts, the troglodytes, and perhaps black orcs, they will be much harder to take down."

"Screw this poop!" Rudy said, tossing down the baton and rubbing his head. "We got AR-15s and fifty cal. We got forty fives and holy hand grenades. We don't need no darn sticks or swords!"

"Are you done?" Riley said, stepping forward, annoyed.

"Man with no faith has gotta talk the most," the Duke said, still lounging, rolling a large padded ball back and forth. "Braggadocio is all he's got."

"Oh yeah, we're talking about another reality man, another universe, another planet! Guess there are aliens... kind of disproves your Bible, don't it!" Rudy spoke, getting up, rubbing his head and eyeing Alfred.

Riley and the Duke shared a look.

"I ain't budging from my faith," the Duke said softly.

"Amen, brother," Riley said.

"Pffff..." Rudy waved and walked off looking for something to sit or lounge on. "Course this sounds like poop-a-doop anyway. I mean look at all the darn cameras everywhere." Rudy pointed to the security cams above. "Just another flipping reality show!" Rudy made lewd faces and stuck out his tongue at the cameras.

Alfred cringed at Rudy's language and behavior. This was how faithless men acted? He looked to his dad who stood and stared at his strange behavior. Wooly did not have that look ever. What was the word? Jaded.

Riley motioned, and Wooly resumed. "The larger ones have armour and thick hides. Their sense of pain is dulled. You cannot just cut them. You must wound them severely, or they will keep fighting. And even if you wound their limbs, they will leap or crawl after you with one intent, to destroy you."

The men looked at each other, knowing this was new territory for them.

Riley stepped forward, raising his hands politely. "General, uh knight... with all due respect, but this is really hard to swallow. I mean, some strange videos, some black goo with armour sitting in it? You got a kid here. I mean, again, with all due respect, but this ain't some Hollywood reality show. The proof for what you're saying is somewhat lacking. You guys aren't pulling something over our eyes here? There's a lot of cameras up in those corners. I can't help it, and the guys here, we're just having the toughest time buying it, that this is real. I'm sorry. We've seen it all. We've seen the real deal, and this just isn't... it isn't real to us."

Alfred stared at Riley, for he was the one man Alfred felt a possible kinship with. There was an honor in him and his men. Alfred felt a dizzying weight come upon him. Wooly looked to the general, who was looking down, arms crossed.

Alfred stepped forward. "Riley, what if... what if... it was a reality show, and you were getting paid a lot of money. And we had a test at the end, a test where you get to fire real live guns and ammo at, uh... at robots. These robots look like goblins and beasts. And you had to destroy them before they... before they even get to touch you. And those that survive or win, you get a million dollars."

"Sounds like a bunch of poop-a-doop," Rudy spat.

"I will do it. I will win the one million dollars!" Russki said.

The Duke walked into the circle of men. "I believe it. I believe it, son. I believe you came from another world, you and your dad the Black Knight. I dig it. You wear some kind of black knight armour? You, the guy in the video fightin' like crazy?"

Wooly nodded.

"Yeah, I dig it." He turned to the other men. "It don't matter if you believe it or not. It also don't matter if you are on TV or not. All I know is that my country has once again asked me to serve. Little old me. I'm old and fat, and yet they still ask. If my country wants me to run into live fire or go down on a reality TV thing, I don't care. I don't care. I love my country, even with the crazy president we got in there. I love it. Always have, always will."

The Duke walked off.

"Well, there you have it," Riley said, looking at his men. "We never question the mission. Suppose we shouldn't start now."

"If it's hard to believe, then just play along. You're getting paid either way," the general said softly. "Just make sure next of kin is on your paperwork."

P-3

The men walked through a corridor. Sitting at intervals were two-man security teams. Each group had carts with strange looking electrical packages on them. The carts had large batteries on the bottom with wires leading up to the top where large circuit boards were secured. Then there were large coiled wires that extended outward. They were quickly made but had all the right components to look quite effective.

"What's with the EMP devices?" Rudy asked the general as they walked along.

"Impressed you know what those are," the general said.

"Hey, demolition... EMP is part of the package deal," Rudy shrugged.

"It counters the gateway that the witch is trying to open to our world. We also had to get them to the city block where she first started this whole gosh darn mess."

"I saw the videos on Facebook and Youtube. People shot some weird stuff," Riley added, moving up to the general and Rudy.

"Those goblins attacking the police and the clean-up crews, that's part of this? Looked like some sort of reality TV promo."

"That's what we had to do," the general said.

"You had to lie to the people," the Duke sighed.

343

"Yep. We had no choice. We don't know what it is. We don't know what to do. But what we do know is that those goblin beasts attack with no remorse, no compassion, and are definitely not human. Several policemen were killed. She can invade and attack us whenever she wants."

"What about the EMP devices?" Rudy asked.

"They're working for now. But she is expanding her awareness further out. Once she marks a point, she can expand outward from that point. She is doing it slowly, but not too slowly. We are going as soon as possible."

"Going?" Riley repeated as they entered the sub-train terminal. "Going where..."

The train was sitting there with its doors wide open.

"Whoo-hooh!" yelled Rudy as he ran forward. Others followed quickly. They could see through the train's windows, quite clearly, the distinct black shine and lines of modern day weapons. They were all stacked on gun racks and shelves, lined up along the inside of each train car.

"Holy moly! This is what I'm talking about. Oh, I'm in, all in!" Rudy yelled, slapping the guns down the row like they were a bunch of teammates. "Oh this is the Package Deal!!! This is the part I'm talking about!" Rudy couldn't help himself from yelling and squealing.

Kwan Thai Suex stepped in quickly, tensing his muscles and fists. He looked down the row of guns on racks. There were various automatic M-16 assault rifles and lots of heavy machine guns. He clenched his jaws, as if some sort of animal anger were rising in him. Others passed him. The train car got crowded pretty quick as soldiers moved in to examine the weapons.

He peered down, and saw rows of handguns and a shiny big .44 magnum revolver. He picked that up and held it, acting like a cowboy.

Loud, one of Riley's Navy Seals, handling a rifle, looked up to see Kwan Thai Suex posing. "You don't know much about guns, do you?"

Kwan Thai Suex looked down the sight of the revolver and then peered at Loud. He pointed the gun at Loud. The Navy Seals all stopped and looked at Kwan. He grinned with dirty gold-plated teeth, lowering the revolver. "I'm a cowboy!"

"You're gonna need to know how handle this," Loud stood up, showing him an M-16 assault rifle. "I'll show you."

"I don't need!" Kwan Thai Suex replied defensively.

Loud walked up, moving the assault rifle in his arms as if it was second nature. "This is your rifle. It is light, sturdy, easy to aim, and easy to fire. You will learn to use it, standing next to us." He handed Kwan Thai Suex the rifle. Kwan glared at it and then looked at Loud's face. It wasn't egotistical or leering. Rather, it was a face of caring and discernment. Kwan nodded and took it. He was surprised that it felt good in his arms. Loud began to explain everything, simply and effectively. "This is not a semi-automatic AR-15 that civilians use, this is an assault rifle. It can fire full auto..."

Masamu stood outside the train, peering at the soldiers busy inside collecting weapons. The general walked up. "We've got everything in there. Swords are in Car Twelve I think, down there."

"I have my sword," Masamu said calmly.

"Gotta be something in there you don't mind shooting," the general said.

"They can shoot. I will wait," Masamu replied calmly.

"Wait?"

"For when the gunfire fails."

Outside the train cars, the men had boxes and crates stacked in their own little areas. Each group or individuals had their own stock of items: guns, ammo, vests and pouches. They were figuring out what and how much they could carry.

The general and agents with clipboards walked amongst them. Agents were trying to inventory everything each group had collected. Rudy looked up at one. "Seriously?"

The general spoke, "In twenty-four hours, we are making this trip. You will load up on as much gear and ammo as you can. Do not forget the body armour. Do not forget rations. You will have a hot meal at eighteen hundred, and get some shut-eye, because at oh-nine hundred, the mission begins."

"Last meal?" Loud said to Riley, who shrugged, focused on loading magazines and examining his choice of weapons.

Rostislav and the Duke showed off their heavy weapons to each other. Russki posed with his Russian made Pecheneg light machine gun and a backpack that had a scorpion-like tail or metal belt of ammo coming out of it. "This, my token black friend, is the Pecheneg scorpion! I am like a super hero! No!?"

The Duke looked up at him, sitting with an even bigger machine gun. "Oh, that is sweet Russki, very sweet. I like the tail. But this is the classic American M-60. It is old, heavy, and reliable as heck." The Duke stood up holding the M-60, his old man's biceps bulging and sweat already forming.

"General, can you get them to stop swearing!?" Alfred said. The general looked at Alfred.

Alfred continued, staring at the men all joking and swearing. "I don't like it. It doesn't feel right."

"Hey kid, it's part of the darn show. It's what the folks want. Even for kids! It's in all our movies! A bunch of mooky flipping tough hombres with guns showing off and kicking some booty!" Rudy yelled out from his little collected area of gear.

Alfred cringed again.

"Sorry kid, these guys are fighting men. They talk like that all the time. It's normal," the general said.

"I have fighting men. My men are knights who have fought desperately in the most dangerous situations and without guns and ammo. They have fought against all odds, against beasts in overwhelming numbers, against giant ogres who enslaved and giant ants that swarm over you and tear off your limbs. They have died defending the lives of our farmers and children. And they do not swear. Not at all," Alfred said, he turned and walked away.

The special forces men all looked as the boy walked off. The Duke couldn't help but raise a smile, thinking of some deep thought. Rudy tried to shrug it off, packing wires and demolition carefully. Yet he too couldn't help but look at the strange kid. Riley and his men looked at each other, nodding subtly.

Kwan Thai Suex stepped into Car Twelve. He found the crates filled with all kinds of swords and hand-held weapons. The only one in there was Wooly, who was examining the swords, feeling their weight and strength. Row after row of medieval weapons were haphazardly placed in there. It was as if they were hurriedly acquired and quickly loaded onto the train.

"You fight with blade?" Kwan asked in broken English.

Wooly nodded.

"I fight with blade. Cut many men. I slice and dice. I fight for money," Kwan sneered. He most definitely had an evil look. His face twitched. He had tattoos and gold teeth.

Wooly tossed him a blade. Kwan caught it and swirled it around most skillfully.

"You will be fighting beasts now. There are only you and the other man, who looks like you, who have skills with the sword," Wooly said.

"Looks like me? You racist!?" Kwan grunted. He opened several of the metal chests and found what he was looking for. He pulled out oriental style weapons: curved blades, hooks and forked style shorter arms. He put down the sword and pulled these out.

"I am not familiar with them. I am not sure they will be effective," Wooly said. He swung an axe in a sudden twirl, hitting a metal shelf. The whole shelf of weapons jolted in a loud clang, as the axe head flew off the handle. Kwan peered and nodded discontent.

"Test each weapon. These are not crafted with the concern for life and death. They are not crafted by one who fears the weapon will fail."

Masamu peered in, seeing Wooly and Kwan. Kwan swung around a curved blade. It was like some sort of ninja looking assassin's blade, easily hidden and brought out for a quick slice. Masamu then noticed a stand with a longer katana and its accompanying shorter blade, a wakizashi. He stepped in and shuddered.

"Daisho? My father's," he said. "Stolen. Twelve years ago." He took the blades.

The general came in behind him. "I was expecting more medieval guys to stay. We got experts in sword fighting. Many Europeans... it appears those who swing a sword for shows and competitions aren't much for the real deal."

"How did you acquire my father's sword?" Masamu turned to face the general. He pulled out the katana to examine it.

"Oh that, most of these were in lock-up, black market relics. We acquired them from Interpol, from one of their secret vaults," the general replied.

"All these years, they had it and never returned it to my father," Masamu said, looking at the katana closely.

"The politics and intrigue of international crime and black markets, no telling what deals or secrets one has to make or hide. In this case, we had to get everything we could, the best..." the general stopped as Wooly tested a sword.

He whacked its flat side against a steel shelf post. It made a loud clang. Wooly felt it quiver along the blade and up his arm. He looked at the general and nodded, "This one is good." He twirled it around and felt its balance.

"Next car over, we got sharpening stones. Even got one of those medieval replica grinding stones. It can be pedaled. Better get to it," the general said.

P-4

Back in the training room, filled with padding and close combat practice gear, Wooly stood with a heavy baton. Pacing in front of him was Kwan Thai Suex. Masamu stood to one side and waited.

Riley and the Navy Seals and the other men hurried toward the training room. They turned a corner as the general, peering at forms and papers with agents, looked up. They rushed by.

They crashed into each other, flailing as they got to the entrance of the training room. Some stopped to stare, right in the doorway, as others piled into them. Eventually, somewhat quietly, they hustled in to see the fight. Alfred sat on a padded box. He seemed quite calm as the flurry of men entered, scooting and sitting all around him.

Kwan held two batons while Wooly held a long one, like a sword. Kwan paced like a tiger. Wooly stood like a lion.

Kwan stared at all the men watching. He was quite unique in his look compared to the rest. He looked street ruffian and deadly in the criminal way. All the rest were clean-cut in some fashion and showered. He looked and smelled like he wasn't used to showers. He stared at them one by one, like a caged tiger pacing, wanting to slash out. Wooly watched but seemed somewhat distant. It wasn't a calmness or a boredom. It was out of curiosity perhaps. He didn't seem afraid at all.

Kwan curtly nodded to Masamu with a wry smile then suddenly twirled a flurry of baton swings at Wooly. Scarface managed to deflect the first few, but then the swings hit hard onto Wooly's head and body. It got to the point where Wooly did not look very skilled at all.

It was somewhat disappointing. Kwan pushed Wooly off the mat with his flurry of attacks. Wooly stepped back outside the mat and looked at Kwan and his victorious stand.

The other soldiers were miffed and gave leers and jeers at Scarface. He didn't seem much like a fighter.

"Well, it appears the host of this reality show got a taste of some real medicine," Rudy smirked.

Kwan ignored Wooly then turned to the other soldiers standing about. He pointed at them with his batons, beckoning another.

But Wooly stepped forward. Kwan turned and waved him off. "No."

Wooly looked at everyone. "He should have finished me."

Kwan turned and looked at Wooly with annoyance. "What? You lose! Get out."

"They will not stop like I did. I have not known fighting like that. It is unfamiliar to me. And it will not work against the black orc."

"Hey Duke, this guy racist?" Rudy chimed.

The Duke responded, "Flip you."

Alfred cringed.

The Duke was near and noticed. "Ah, excuse my French, son. I'm sorry. But your dad out there... not much of a fighter. I mean, you can clock Rudy here, but Kwan is the real deal."

"My dad is the real deal. And he doesn't speak French," Alfred said.

Rudy, the Duke, and the others chuckled.

Kwan waved Wooly off. "No more fight. You no fight. No good."

Wooly stood with his baton, then walked toward Kwan.

"Ah come on, waste time!" Kwan said. He suddenly whirled again at Wooly with a flurry of his batons.

Wooly took the hits on his shoulders and head. They were hard and solid blows. But Wooly was unmoved. He then bashed Kwan with his full body in a lightning quick move. As Kwan flew back, Wooly swung the baton again, breaking it in half against Kwan's body.

Kwan flipped and landed hard on his knees. He wavered as he tried to stand but tottered and flailed when he tried to find something to hold on to. He merely fell.

Wooly looked at the others, tossing his broken baton. "The black orcs are well armoured. A flurry of slices on their muscles will not stop them. You must strike them deeply and in vital parts. Your swings must be important, not wasteful."

"I want a rematch," Kwan said, shaking out of it and finally standing up. "You trick me!"

"No!" a voice suddenly rang out. Everyone stopped and looked. Masamu stepped forward. "I wish to test what you say."

Wooly stepped to the bin of sticks. He rummaged through and found wooden poles. Kwan was somewhat relieved. He sat down, rubbing his head and neck and chest and elbow.

Wooly raised his wooden pole as a long sword. Masamu raised his wooden pole as a katana.

"Remember, slicing will not work, unless it is forceful enough to severe the limb. Otherwise, they will keep coming at you," Wooly said.

"Why do we need this swordplay poop when we got gosh darn guns?" Rudy lamented. "We are just gonna blow them the flip away..."

"Hey, watch the language," said the Duke.

"Yeah, yeah, kid gonna be around us. Gotta handle it. Besides the reality show can beep it the flip out and makes for a crude humor angle," Rudy figured.

"You faithless guys and your imaginations..." the Duke mumbled.

Masamu suddenly moved his practice sword. It made many flinch. Both men stood a long while not moving. His movement was smooth and quick. It opened him up but also made him more deadly.

Wooly charged forward. He swung as Masamu quickly deflected it and swung a deadly blow straight down Wooly's head. The pole cracked on Wooly's head, and he shuddered and stepped back. A slow trickle of blood dripped down his forehead. He reached up and touched the warm drops. He looked at Masamu. "Now remember, it won't just be one coming at you. I am one beast, who will keep charging and others will charge in. Understand?"

Masamu nodded quickly, with his broken pole.

Wooly nodded back.

At the doorway stood the general. The men all turned to see him. They fanned out so all could see, for standing next to him was a frail woman. They couldn't quite place it, but there was something odd about her. She was beautiful yet wore no makeup. She seemed frail, leaning on one of the general's arms, yet she looked determined. She peered at them, one by one. Then she saw Wooly and the rivulet of blood dripping between the scars of his face. She looked to Masamu with his cracked pole. She nodded. He nodded back.

"Well, since you are all here, and she is awake, I thought you should all meet the most important human being in your life."

Chapter Fifty-Eight

Guarding Ethralia

The men were spread out amongst their gear, which was still scattered and piled outside the sub-train. Many were going back and forth between their stuff and the sub-train cars to retrieve more gear. There was a uniform section where the right clothing, holsters, utility belts, ammo belts, backpacks and armor components were available. Many agents with clipboards were there to keep tabs on what the soldiers were acquiring. However, through intimidation and good'ole cajoling, they became like squires or peasants rushing to and fro, helping the soldiers with their gear and searching and retrieving what the soldiers wanted.

Rudy paced amongst them, through Riley's and the Navy Seal's area of gear, through the Duke's and Rostislav's heavy weapons ordinances, and through Kwan's array of blades and even past Masamu, who stood with light armor pieces and his father's two swords, plus his own two, just in case. No, the 'no' named hit man in hi-tech hiking gear, picked weapons like he was some secret agent. Beyond them were the rest, marines and rangers. All in all, they were about twenty hard mercenary types.

The Duke was not amused by Rudy's pacing. Rostislav rolled his eyes. Riley and the Navy Seals merely turned or moved politely as Rudy paced through.

"I don't get it, man. I gotta go through this again. I mean the general, Scarface, the lady and the kid were telling us some crazy stuff.

It's all just rancid hot sauce if you ask me! It's just a load of hooooo-eeey! This is the most flipped-out mission briefing I have ever experienced, man. So she is the sister of a witch, who we gotta get. This princess Ethralia..."

"I think she's a queen," the Duke proffered.

"Queen Ethralia, fine... this queen, she's gonna open a doorway, a magical doorway, and we're gonna walk through it? Right?" Rudy chimed.

"Yep. Yeah. Sounds right. Yup," responded various men clicking and clacking gear.

"And through it we go, probably to meet up with these black orcs. I thought orcs were green or something. Whatever! We meet up with them. We have a gun session with them. I hope these ain't stunt doubles, not gonna go well... And swords as well..." Rudy motioned to Kwan and Masamu as he paced through them. "They better be robots! So, we blow these things away. Then we get the Gorby? Gorba?"

"Gorbo-gal," the Duke answered.

"Yeah, Gorbo gal... a girl... a gal..."

"She's a witch. A powerful witch," the Duke sang in warning.

"Whatever," Rudy continued, "We get her. What does she even look like?"

"Look like?" Riley stopped fussing with his gear. "The Queen, Scarface, and the kid, they'll point her out."

"Amidst a crowd of nightmarish robot orcs..." the Duke hummed.

"Well, I hope so. Yeah in a crowd of orcs, it'll be easy to spot her. She'll probably be some hot actress!? Huh? I'll grab her, oh yeah! I'll do the honors, right guys, right!? That'll be my job!" Rudy huffed. Many guffawed and gave Rudy high fives. He complied most enthusiastically with a bunch of whooh-hoohs and oh-yeahs.

With a thick Russian accent Rostislav said archly, "I wonder how they will do the gateway effect, huh? Probably put us in a dark room. Countdown... lights, fog machine, then a tunnel with flashing lights, and we have to run through. No?"

The Duke looked at the silliness before him. His expression was much more serious. He caught the eye of Riley, who was at first laughing along with them and his Navy Seals, but the seriousness of the Duke gave Riley a chill down his spine.

"Hey, listen to me all of you, for my sake, for your own sake," the Duke finally said, even getting Rudy's attention. "I just got one thing to say. Nothing else. Just one thing."

"What is it, old man," Rudy finally said, calming down, letting out one last chuckle.

The Duke pulled up one cartridge, one bullet. "This is a three oh eight round. It is a real live round that I will be firing from my M60. Ain't no reality show or Hollywood letting us carry live ammo or demolitions, man. Whatever is going on, it is the real deal."

Alfred walked by the mess hall where the soldiers were eating their last meal. He was carrying some of the modern armor pieces in packaging. He had a few pieces on. He almost looked like a mini-size special forces guy. He noticed Riley and his men in there, sitting around with their heads bowed.

Most of the soldiers had finished or were leaving. They were grumbling. "That was our last meal? Disappointing. You'd think paying us a million would get us a rib-eye or turkey dinner. I'm complaining! Can we get a pizza delivery?"

Rudy was sitting apart from Riley and the other Navy Seals, slowly eating his Salisbury steak and watching something on his phone. He looked up, overly chewing, and danced his eyebrows at Alfred.

Alfred kept looking at Riley and his men, heads bowed, in a circle. They were saying something, almost a whisper. He could not hear but wanted to. He stepped in past soldiers getting up and walking out. Some nodded to Alfred, but he did not notice. Something drew him in closer as he hugged his package of gear.

Rudy noticed that Alfred was fixated on Riley and their group praying. He removed his headphones and leaned in. "Hey buddy? Hey?"

Alfred ignored him and stepped closer to hear them. Loud noticed Alfred and looked up. The others looked up. Riley turned to see Alfred.

Rudy spoke first, "Ah, their just praying to their God... no need..."

"Who are you praying to?" Alfred asked.

Riley looked at his men, and then at Alfred. "We're praying to Jesus, for this mission, for our safety, for our families – for you."

Alfred wondered about that. He had heard about Jesus a little, mostly in jokes and when people would say his name. Especially on TV or movies, they would say that name when they were surprised or angry, but he never heard those same people say that name in prayer or quiet moments. He heard kids say his name when they would act up, especially on the playground when they got upset or surprised. "Jesus Christ!" they would yell out for no reason. He wasn't sure why they copied the actors on TV who did this. There was something weird about it, especially since nobody really even knew who Jesus was.

"Who is Jesus?" Alfred asked.

Rudy rolled his eyes and made a long-winded, "Phewwww..."

Riley turned his chair to open the circle. The men looked at Alfred with saddened eyes. They looked at each other, rubbing their hair or their hands that were gripped in prayer. It reminded Alfred of Verboden in his small chapel, praying desperately to the Father of Light.

"You do not know who Jesus is?" Riley asked.

"Nope. Well I know he is here, in those churches here, and that people pray to him. Is he a god?"

It was an earnest question.

"He is the one true God," Riley said softly.

"Oh, oh, no, he is the son of God. There's like three or something, and then they say they're all one. Makes no sense!" Rudy interjected.

"Do you believe in Jesus like them too?" Alfred asked with a smile.

"Ah, heck no! Bunch of bull poop!" Rudy cajoled.

"Then why are you answering for them?" Alfred asked.

"Cuz I..." Rudy leered at Alfred. Riley and his men couldn't help but share a smile.

"He is the living God, the son of God, and a man," said Riley. "He came down to save us all. He was born as a man to suffer and die for us, to show us the love of God. That is what we believe." The others nodded calmly, some whispering Amen.

Rudy rolled his eyes at Alfred. Alfred looked unsure, looking at the calmness of Riley and the Navy Seals in the circle after their prayer. Alfred then looked back at Rudy, who was fidgeting and seemed upset, urging Alfred through his expression to leave, to ignore them.

"Hey, so what god do you guys worship on this other planet, huh?" Rudy finally asked, scooting closer with his mess hall chair. He winked at Riley.

Alfred thought a moment as the Navy Seals looked on.

"Gotta be a whole other system of gods, right? A whole different world, of orcs and witches! Must be a ton of gods, different ones..."

"They worship the Father of Light..." Alfred said.

Riley perked up, wondering. Alfred looked at the Navy Seals again.

Rudy looked oddly at Alfred. "Father of... that's it?" He looked at Riley. "Well, see, guess it disproves this one and only god of yours! Huh, disproves the Bible?"

"He came down as a man and walked amongst the people," Alfred said.

"What?" Riley asked.

"But he's gone. Missing... or gone... I don't know... Verboden doesn't know... he doesn't like to talk about it," Alfred said, furrowing his eyebrows.

"The Father of Light came down as a man, walking amongst you, and... disappeared?" Riley repeated.

Alfred nodded.

Riley looked at his men. They stared at each other for a long silent moment, nodding.

"Yeah, uhhh..." Rudy coughed up.

Alfred looked up at Rudy. At first he thought Rudy was suddenly praying, for he had his hands up to his face, seemingly clasped in prayer. Rudy was actually covering his mouth, his fingers meeting above his nose. Alfred realized Rudy was covering his gaping mouth, rubbing his face to relax.

"Uhhh, isn't this a government run mission?" Rudy finally mumbled.

"A what?" Riley asked.

"Government run... you know, a uh... separation of church and state. We shouldn't be talking about religion man..." Rudy said quickly, not looking at anyone. "Yeah, goes against the rules..."

Riley looked at Rudy a long while, silently. Rudy kept rubbing his face till it relaxed. He then looked back at Riley with a smug expression.

Alfred wasn't sure what was going on. He just felt an overriding sadness. It must have been the mission, these men, Gorbogal. Would their bullets even work? Would the gate work? Could his mom even send them through? And would they just be ambushed by the big orcs he saw in Gorbogal's citadel? He wasn't sure what overwhelming sadness bore down on him. He hugged the package of gear more tightly.

"Hey, general's calling a meeting!" someone suddenly yelled from the doorway.

Several soldiers hurried by. The lights in the mess hall flickered.

"Oh God! Something is going down!" Rudy said, grabbing his phone and getting up. "Come on, kid!"

Alfred stared at Riley and his men. They looked at him as they stood. They continued their prayer for a moment, something joyous in their eyes. Alfred didn't get it. Or did he? He left with a strange smile.

In the corridor the rush of men was exhilarating in some strange way. It was as if the time had come. It wasn't the right time though, as they were going to have a night's rest. A team was pushing an EMP cart through. Something was amiss. Was another gate opening? Alfred wasn't sure. He looked down, remembering that he was holding a package of gear. He wanted to get back to his mom.

He hurried along with the group of men, jogging to get somewhere. He passed by where he, his mom and dad slept. He quickly looked in. They weren't there. He hurried along and realized they were all congregating at the sub-train terminal. It was where everyone had temporarily placed gear. It seemed as good a place as any to meet up.

Everyone was there, his mom, Wooly, in most of his armour, the general, many agents and assistants. The lab coat folks were there too. Several had EMP carts and tons of equipment. It looked as if they were setting up their own area of science data machines. He guessed it was probably to scan or record what was about to take place. Was it about to take place, now? Alfred wondered.

"Hey Scarface!" Rudy said to Wooly. "That knights of the round table stuff ain't gonna stop my M4 or 5-5-6 round, buddy." He smiled wryly.

Some of the others chuckled and gave him high fives.

Wooly didn't get what was funny. He looked down at his black armour, unsure.

"We are moving up the schedule men!" the general yelled.

"We just ate a big meal," someone replied.

"If it's too much, puke it out. The witch is not stopping. We've placed EMP devices in an ever expanding circle around the base, and she continues to push out at an alarming rate. We haven't got hours of rest time. I want this witch stopped now," the general said.

"I guess the show starts now," Rostislav whispered to anyone near him.

"You've got one hour! Then Queen Ethralia," the General motioned to Ethralia, who was leaning against Wooly, "...is opening the gateway and all of you are going. One hour!" He turned to face his assistants, agents and lab coats. Each one had desperate questions and concerns, all of which, it appeared, he answered with many NO's.

The men all turned to look at each other, rolling their eyes and exhaling large volumes of carbon-ridden air. They migrated to their areas, pulling on, pushing through, strapping on, buckling, velcroing, buttoning, zipping up, tying to, fastening, clicking, smacking, punching, clasping, latching, rolling, tucking, snapping and so on, all of their gear, armor, ammo magazines, demolitions, clothing, and guns.

Kwan Thai Suex and Masamu looked at each other. Kwan was overburdened with two assault rifles, one American, one German, and lots of ammo magazines in belts and pouches. He had a very big shiny revolver in a holster that seemed too large for his small body. He carried a variety of Ninja and Chinese style blades in odd places. He looked at Masamu. "It's heavy."

Masamu nodded.

The Duke and the Russki posed with their machine guns. For Duke, he had the M60 with a box style pouch of belt-fed ammo and several more in a pack. The Russki had the Pecheneg machine gun with a metal belt feeder that led to a backup of thousands of rounds. These were meant for tripods or placed atop things, but these guys had big arms and bulging biceps instead. It was obvious they could hold up their heavy automatic rifles for quite a few rounds of continuous fire.

Rudy felt like spending a few of his precious moments setting up his phone and a Bluetooth speaker. It was a really nice one he somehow got from somewhere in this top secret facility.

He began a song that started with church bells, ominous and loud. Everyone stopped to hear it. All the fighting men loading their gear stopped for a moment and then went back to getting ready. A lone guitar was then added, and the men chortled and grunted. Another guitar and drums quickly joined in. Rudy pranced about with a sneer and a leer, holding the speaker and dancing to the drumbeat. He kicked his legs and bobbed his head.

Wooly and Alfred stared from Car Twelve, where Alfred was picking out a sword and shield. Rudy lip-synced the crazy mean sounding song. It seemed to boast of how tough and weak these men were. It seemed to boast of a dark god... with Rudy acting the part. All the men, whether still packing or sitting and waiting, bobbed their heads or their muscles or their shoulders. It reminded Alfred of the bestial men performing a pre-battle ritual.

Even Riley and his men bobbed along, feeling the dark song, like magic, surge through them. It was a scary song, but Alfred noticed it seemed to give them courage, a dark violent guttural courage.

Rudy couldn't help but prance around them, showing off his air guitar or lip-sync acting. He certainly played and believed in the part. He was readying himself for whatever this whole crazy mission was about. Some third world fly-in, some organized crime attack, or some reality TV fake entertainment bit, he didn't care. He was jigging and pumping and rocking through the crowded space of the most high-end warriors he had ever seen. Something was about to happen.

And an hour later...

Kurehnde, buht-thaguhm, muhrathum
Kurehnde, buht-thaguhm, muhrathum

"Holy moly, what the flip is that?!" Rudy yelled.

"That is not *a special effects!* It is not fake?" Rostislav yelled in broken English. "I don't know."

"Holy mother of God," the Duke said.

"SHE'S OPENED THE GATE! GO! GO! GO! GO!"

Chapter Fifty-Nine

Gorbogal's Lair

The electrical gateway was massive. Alfred stood and watched. The men reluctantly walked through even as the general yelled over and over, pushing them, "GO! GO! GO!"

They stared at it unsure. Ethralia stood, holding her temples with her fingers. At first, she looked in pain, struggling with concentration and focus. But then she seemed to transform into a blue glowing witch. Wooly, as the ominous Black Knight, stepped back from her. She seemed to grow in power and looked utterly frightening.

Rostislav went around the vast circle of blue arcing electricity to look behind it. He saw the wall of the train station and all the laboratory equipment. The lab coats and scientists were going crazy with their instruments, turning dials and holding up various recording and radiation devices.

The gateway was thin, like a mirror, to Rostislav. He shrugged, looking at the Duke. He saw men go in one side and not come through the other side to the lab equipment. They disappeared into it as if it was shimmering water. He gazed at the Duke, who gazed back and shrugged for him to follow.

Riley and his men stared at the vision before them: the shimmering blue gateway, the arcing webs of lightning running along it, and the immense glow and glare. They looked behind them at her, the Queen, and saw how intensely unreal she looked. Her eyes were blue auras, sharp lights that pierced into their vision. Riley turned to his men, gritted his teeth and motioned. They went.

The gateway opened to a black corridor, a cave or tunnel. It had straight walls, a level floor and ceiling. However, the surfaces were definitely carved out somehow. It wasn't by a machine but seemed hand carved. It was very solid stone. The men stood close together, staring up at the high ceilings and wide corridor. They weren't sure what to look at. The corridor ran up a ramp to a T a hundred yards or so away. It was at a distance and very dark, with what seemed the hue of moonlight refracting throughout from the immense pulsating glow of the gateway.

"This is her place," Alfred said, shivering.

"What's he doing here?" Rudy asked no one. "I didn't know the kid was going to be in the show!"

"Show?! What the heck you talkin' 'bout? This ain't no darn show!" the Duke yelled.

"Bigger budget than I expected," Rudy shrugged.

Masumu walked through the gateway next to Kwan Thai Suex. They stared wide-eyed at the walls. Masumu drew his katana, shaking.

"Man, that ain't gonna do a darn thing around here!" Rudy hollered.

"You talk too much!" yelled Kwan.

"Is that the only English you know? Just keep your knives away from us men with guns, alright!?" Rudy grunted, pulling out his M4 assault rifle with all the accoutrements. "Let's get this light show started! Gosh darn mother clucker of eggs!"

Alfred cringed.

"Don't worry, kid! They'll bleep it out!"

"Bleep this out," the Duke barked, slapping his M60s ammo belt, double checking.

The Black Knight walked through the gateway. The stark pulsating blue lights of the magical portal created intense contrasts amongst the warriors and the rock walls. Ethralia followed from behind, blasted with a blue aura. Her hair seemed to float along. Her simple army issue shirt and pants floated as if she were in water.

"Alright...alright... Scarface looks chicken-clucking wicked in that medieval dung, you gotta admit," yelled Rudy above the crackling of the electrical arcs.

"That's very cool effects," Rostislav grunted. "Better than Russian movie set."

"This ain't no set," the Duke moaned.

"We've got company!" Riley barked. "Line up, line of fire. Wall to wall!"

Riley and his men immediately spread in one section of the corridor, leveling and aiming their guns up the corridor. Rudy turned to look. The other men joined the line. The Duke and Rostislav stood side by side. They looked like human tripods, spreading their feet the right distance to hold their machine guns firm.

Masamu stepped forward, but the Black Knight touched his shoulder and motioned him back. Masamu was half the size of Wooly in his medieval armour. The Black Knight looked amazingly incongruous. It was hard to take him seriously since everyone else was in modern Kevlar and plastic armor. He seemed like a medieval caricature, out of place.

Masamu had on the lightweight plastic armor, like a policemen or SWAT member. Even though Kwan had guns, he too stepped back. He wasn't as comfortable with the line of assault rifles aimed up the corridor and decided it was better to watch the first round of entertainment.

Riley and his Navy Seals got to one knee or down on the ground for better aim. There was a mix of men, many standing, some on a knee, and a few on the ground like snipers. It was a long row of twenty highly dangerous and brutal guns of furious fire.

"Hold your fire!" Riley barked.

"Who made him in charge?" Rudy asked.

"Guess you missed the briefing," Loud said, lying below Rudy.

"I sure hope they gave us blank rounds cuz those stunt guys or extras are gonna die!" Rudy said, peering along his red dot sight.

Up the ramp, there were many figures in costumes -- or this was the only way Rudy, Riley and the others could fathom it. Even with the setting, the gateway, the magic all around them, they still could not grasp that this was anything but a show, a spectacle.

"Whatever performance this is, stick to your training, your experience," Riley said, loudly, calmly. "We are all professionals here and will act accordingly. Let them be damned who think otherwise."

The men in costumes, up the corridor a hundred yards, were not really all that clear. They carried torches and yet seemed shrouded in darkness. There were all kinds of shapes and sizes, from shorter crazed goblins to hulking troglodyte boar-like men, and then there were the dark green muscular brutes that were black orcs.

Riley eyed them and felt a strange sensation. They didn't move like men or stuntmen in costumes. They moved naturally and with a feral ferocity as they congregated a distance away. Their movements reminded him of a tiger he once saw in the jungle. It moved naturally, lightly, yet with harrowing muscles.

More and more of them filed into the area; a lot more than what seemed necessary for such a production or action sequence. They were crowded at the top of the incline. Many of the smaller more frantic ones were spreading out but not yet charging. They were hopping up and down, waiting for the cue.

"That is some awesome prosthetic work," Rudy said.

"Demons man, this is for real. There be demons!" the Duke moaned, a tear coming from his eye.

"Dad, do they know what they are doing?" Alfred said, pulling on the Black Knight's armour.

Wooly turned to look down at Alfred, who held his sword firm and wore the modern fitted plastic armor. Wooly replied, "I do not know."

"Is it a holograph, some new cool effect?" Rudy mumbled to no one.

Then the charge began. There was a sudden growl and flailing of crude steel weapons. The goblins howled with cackling joy and began the sudden dash and hop down the corridor. Behind them a wall of brute beast men rambled forward. They had brawny muscles covered in thick iron plates of armour. The black orcs had their many pieces sewn into their skin. The troglodytes had thick leather and tied iron plates. Both looked brutal and bestial, lumbering forth and building up speed.

As the goblins got within fifty yards, Riley began the onslaught of lead bullets. "Fire!!!"

But no one fired. They shifted, unsure. Even Riley couldn't fully grasp if this was – what it was.

"Here goes," Rudy huffed and fired into a closing goblin. It tripped from the shot but limped forward as if not registering the hit. Rudy fired again. It took several rounds before it dropped, seeming to just exhale and sleep. Others rushed around it and were closing in.

"FIRE!!!"

A wall of muzzle flash lit up the corridor. The repetitive blast of gun fire, from thin wispy cracks of the German light automatics to the thunderous crackle of M4 assault rifles to the explosive cutting tears of the machine guns, overwhelmed the area. Hundreds of rounds of lead bullets zipped and ripped.

Goblins suddenly twirled and flailed, yet many still charged forward with holes and limbs torn off. They didn't seem to understand the lightning bursts of damage against them. A goblin hit the line of men and cut one with its blade. The soldier screamed as the blade was stuck in his forearm. Another had to kick the goblin back and put several rounds into it.

"What the cluck!?" the soldier yelled, peering down, shocked that the actor would hurt him. He wrenched a blade out, exposing a real bleeding gash. He could only hold it and stumble back. Another goblin leapt in as the men around him were trying to register if this were real or not. The gangly goblin, crazed to the max, slashed at them and cut several before Riley rushed over and shot it in the head with his hand gun.

Several soldiers fell back with grievous wounds, screaming and grunting in pain. Their screams were not as loud as the slow steady gunfire and the oncoming tumbling wave of bestial brutes.

Riley observed the men shooting too carefully, in controlled bursts, not sure what sort of combat situation they were in or if this was real. And then he saw the wounds from the falling men and the wave of beasts yet to come, and coming they were. His men were not fully registering this fantastical doom.

"FIRE! FULL AUTO! STOP THEM!" Riley yelled. "FIRE! FIRE! FIRE!" He had to run up and down the line, hitting his men, yelling loudly into their ears. "STOP THAT ONSLAUGHT OR WE'RE DEAD!"

The Duke and Rostislav seemed to awaken from a dull nightmare. They shook out of it and gaped silent screams as their machines guns suddenly roared into full auto. "Open it up!" the Duke suddenly yelled. Russki gritted his teeth as his stupid sunglasses slid down the bridge of his sweating nose.

A hail of lead bullets finally roared across the tumbling wall of bestial brutes. Goblins were torn asunder and dropped under the monstrous wave. The troglodytes and black orcs flailed and tripped as blasts of impacts sparked and smoked across them like crackling fireworks. Even with the devastation, the brutes tumbling opened up to more brutes behind them. And some reached the line of modern men with modern guns and light plastic armor. The swing and crash-land of a heavy brute beast was ponderously destructive.

With only a score of fighting men, any that were bashed and smashed off the line, severely weakened the small elite force. Several went flying or crushed under as a troglodyte slammed dead upon them. Another leapt over that to swing viciously from behind. The plastic armor of the special forces did not hold up to the heavy iron blades swung by tiger-like limbs of troglodytes and black orcs.

Screams of pain and panic broke the line. Riley fired close range, taking out a large black orc. He had to empty his magazine into it. He yelled and yanked for them to fall back. But where were they to fall back to? Even as many fell before the Duke and the Russki, more brutes leapt in. The rest couldn't keep up the wall of devastation and fell back, shooting frantically at the leaping brutes that broke the line.

The Black Knight was what they saw. When Riley fell under the brutal swing of a heavy iron battleaxe, he could only see the sudden flash and glare of the black medieval armour. He did not fall and die, he fell under, holding up his M4 assault rifle to deflect the blow. It was one of the heaviest blows he had ever felt. His M4 was destroyed saving his life. The blow that slammed him back felt exactly like the time his Hummer crashed from an explosion and threw him and the others hard as the vehicle flipped.

Masamu and Kwan Thai Suex merely stood stunned. Though they were skilled fighters, they were not "trained" as it were like the Navy Seals or the mercenaries with military experience. They were not trained under strenuous circumstances to instinctively carry forward, especially under the thunderous roar of gunfire. The men all around them continued to fire or retreat while pulling their fallen comrades with them. It was as if Masamu and Kwan were in the eye of the storm. Smoke and sparks flew all around them, muzzle flashes and ricochets burst all around them, screams and yells echoed all around them, and limbs and huge crude weapons swung all around them. They seemed to look at each other, slowly blinking.

The Black Knight burst in front of the failing line. His swings were always a succession of furious follow-throughs. As a goblin fell, then a troglodyte flipped, then an orc dropped. Even in his bulky armour, he stepped skillfully through the fallen bodies, through the confining smoke and met the charge of more bestial men.

It gave Riley a moment to assess and see the mess. "Get them up, and get them back!"

The firing subsided as the Duke quickly rushed back, trying to load another swinging belt of ammo into the canvas container attached to his machine gun. The Russki was still firing, having the scorpion tail still feeding rounds from the backpack. But he was careful and professional with his fire as he saw the Black Knight pass him to the front. The knight seemed to hold the line single-handedly.

Riley leapt amongst the monstrous bodies and found Rudy lying amongst them. He picked him up to see Rudy had a gash in his head, his helmet cracked.

"Oh my dear Lord..." Rudy spat through blood trickling down his face. "Oh God... oh God..." he deliriously moaned.

Riley picked him up and pulled him back. A black orc came out of the smoke and charged at him. His men were there and fired upon the beast. It roared and flailed, nearly hitting them with its jagged machete. They looked at it closely as it smashed into the ground next to them.

"Oh my God, oh my God, what is this... what is this?" Rudy muttered, recovering somewhat.

"Come on!" Riley held him up, retreating. Both stood up and then stopped, staring as Ethralia stepped forward. The gateway suddenly closed. She looked at them as the screams of battle still raged.

Alfred stood with her, as if guarding her. He held his sword and shield.

They formed a line in front of Ethralia. Riley didn't have time to assess who was still alive. Most had made it. Many had wounds. He knew at least two must had fallen, and no one was able to pull them back. Were they alive? He couldn't tell in the mess of dark bodies strewn before them and the smoke from their massive wall of gunfire. It was smoky and hazy as the flashing lights of the gateway were subsiding. Darkness was filling the black corridor. The men turned on their gun lights. Beams flicked on and waved about, erratic in the dark curling smoke.

They could hear the heave and crackle of steel crunching and cracking beyond. Grunts of the bestial men they encountered repeated, and many very heavy bodies dropped. They couldn't discern what to shoot at or what was coming. Most were wiping their faces quickly, on the verge of and barely holding back a pure panic. They were professionals, the elite of the elite, and were barely holding it together.

Several had gashes and wounds. A couple were holding guns with one arm. Another was bandaging one up quickly, wrapping the wound. "At least there ain't a bullet in there!"

"Darn nearly cut off my arm! Got any painkillers!?"

"Oh yeah."

"Quiet!" Riley huffed. He held up his hand. The men quickly found firing positions again. They listened intently as the fighting continued beyond the smoke.

Masamu stepped forward nervously, precariously amongst the monstrous bodies. He tried not to look down but did and blinked, slowly looking up. "I must go and help."

Kwan stood behind him, grimacing and trying to build up his well-known crazed foolhardy courage, but he couldn't.

"Stay!" Riley said. "Stay here. Be ready if any break through."

Masamu raised his blade and nodded too quickly, too nervously, his face drenched in sweat.

Alfred waved his hand and spoke a subtle spell. He used the vacuum spell to collect the smoke into a ball.

A sphere of air,
radial out,
seal from me
and come about.

Riley and the others looked surprised, seeing Alfred step forward and mumble the words. To see the air and the smoke suddenly wisp to his command was stunning. Yet more stunning was to see the corridor and the clarity of the situation. The Black Knight swung in ferocious and brutal waves at several black orcs and troglodytes. He ignored the goblins as they easily were trampled by falling brutes or killed merely by his secondary swings. The Black Knight moved in a way that Kwan and Masamu had never seen.

Fighting men in their world had limits. There were minimal requirements of exertion and exhaustion that succeeded in impairing or inflicting pain upon one's adversary. Here, against these beasts, there was no concept of inflicting shocking pain to debilitate them for a final blow. The swings had to be brutal and quick, sudden and ferocious. Masamu stared at the level of intensity he had never witnessed in a fighter. It was almost like the movies yet all there in full view, with no editing or neat camera shots. It was all before him, the full figure of this knight in black armour bashing and slamming against large beast men. And then he would twirl vicious arcs of sword hacks to break, not their tough hide, but the flesh and bone under it.

Beast men after beast men roared in sudden shock and fell to the Black Knight as he stomped and charged forward.

"He can't keep that up forever. Form up. We're stepping forward. Be ready when he steps back. Be ready!" Riley said.

Rudy had to shake out of his pain, wiping blood off his face as he refastened his broken helm. It was no longer a helm but a strapping to hold the blood soaked bandage atop his head. All the men checked their weapons, loaded fresh magazines, wiped their faces and shrugged off their nerves.

"Where the heck are we going? Where's this witch we suppose to be catchin?" the Duke yelled out, his M60 ready.

Ethralia, back to her diminutive form, pointed up the corridor. "She is not far."

"Oh," the Duke shrugged, settling his M60 better.

"We better move fast. She has many more orcs in camps around this place. They will be coming in the thousands," said Alfred.

Riley stared wide-eyed. "Let's move!"

They hurried up as best they could, stepping over many bestial limbs and bodies. The flashing beams of gun lights flickered across a harrowing scene. There were many fallen torches, mixing the cold beams with warm auras of flickering flames.

"Man, this is for real. For chicken-clucking real, man. It's all real," Rudy sobbed, looking quite wretched from his head wound.

"Stop swearing!" Alfred said, looking mean, zeroing in on Rudy. Alfred stepped forward quickly amongst the dead bodies. He looked back at Riley. "Riley, get your men to each side. When we fall back, fire along the edges! We will stay in the middle."

Riley and the others stared odd at Alfred. He was small, barely fitting in the modern gear. His shield, a Viking looking replica, and sword were oddly mismatched to the gear. But he suddenly moved in a way similar to the Black Knight, deftly navigating the uneven terrain. A goblin behind Wooly noticed Alfred and charged at him.

Riley and the Duke raised their weapons. "Can't get a clear shot!" the Duke said. Riley aimed carefully. Alfred stepped between, quickly and summarily dispensed with the creature.

Masamu raised his katana and grunted as he hurried over. Kwan threw off his assault rifles and ammo. Other soldiers greedily grabbed them up. He pulled out curved blades and hurried to Masamu.

"Dang it! It's getting crowded up there. We can't use our firepower!" Riley exhorted. He motioned for them to rush up. "Single file! Marksmen take the front! Help with reduction!"

Riley took the left, and Loud took the right. The rest lined up like a split in bowling, some on the left and some on the right, favoring the walls. The badly wounded limped behind, ready to fill a spot.

The Black Knight could not keep up his devastating attacks for much longer. A score or more of the brutes and dozens of smaller ones fell under his relentless attacks. He heaved heavily, limping back with exhaustion.

Alfred came forward to meet the many goblins hurrying to harass them.

Masamu came up and swung his katana, severing limbs or heads. His movement was at first sublime and controlled, but the reality of the brutal nature of what he was doing was immediately overwhelming and exhausting his senses. His swings became erratic, uncontrolled and awkward. He had never swung at living things before, not even innocent animals. Even though he was swinging at evil creatures whose faces had permanent snarls and evil eyes, it was still the taking of life. And each one seemed to weigh on his sanity, even the philosophical sanity he had honed in swordsmanship, training since he was a child. It was, what he thought, a full encapsulation of his understanding – his understanding of the world, of life, of honor and duty, a professionalism he thought that could match and overcome any threat, obstacle or challenge. But it could not. He nearly decapitated Kwan as his swings became more like an insane rage and panic than controlled guardianship.

Kwan had not yet advanced, for Alfred fought up front while Masamu swung crazily at any goblins that made it through. There wasn't a lot of room as swords swung to and fro. They were not forming a line of medieval warriors but were taking on the mass attack as lone blademasters. Kwan could see that Alfred, the odd American boy, not a weak kid stuck on his phone, was a skilled swordsman with controlled swings and shield skills. It was in those thoughts that he was yanked back by a violent pull.

He turned and quickly slashed in circles at the would be aggressor. But he only slashed at clanking steel as the Black Knight suddenly swung the flat of his blade, throwing off Kwan's flurry of swings. Kwan stopped and realized it was Scarface in his terrifying armour.

The Black Knight let go of Kwan, who nodded and stepped back. Wooly stepped forward.

"Masamu! Control yourself!" Wooly yelled through his helm.

Masamu shook uncontrollably. He stared wide-eyed as he quivered. The Black Knight, however exhausted, advanced. Masamu swung wildly at another goblin, killing it but also endangering Alfred, who was just a few paces away. Wooly swung viciously and disarmed Masamu quickly. He motioned for Kwan to get him.

Kwan nodded and quickly ran up to grab Masamu and bring him back. Masamu weakly grabbed for his katana but tumbled instead. Kwan quickly yanked the thin man up and pushed him back.

Alfred took up the strange floating cloudy marble ball. He hurled it up the corridor into a few orcs and goblins. It fwomped a blast of vacuous air. The smaller goblins smashed into the walls. The bigger brutes tottered.

Riley and Loud fired single shots into the stunned brutes, dropping many of them. This opened the corridor. They hurried up as best they could amongst the fallen grotesque bodies.

Riley fired at more black orcs coming. It wasn't a mass of them, just a few. He focused his shots on the upper body and head. Several dropped. Loud, at the other wall with his precision rifle, did the same.

"Quickly!" Ethralia yelled, marching forward. "She is mustering forces from below. We must get to her before they come!"

Chapter Sixty

Siege of Gorbogal

They hurried up the rampway to the cross section. To their left was a corridor that turned and descended. Against the curved carved walls echoed the growling sounds of distant beastmen – dark horrific armies of monsters. The men with their guns and gear stooped over, breathing hard and staring through sweat, blood, and grime.

Up the other way the wide stark corridor took a bend. Alfred pointed with his sword. "She's up there."

"Let's go," Riley ordered. The men hugged the walls as Wooly marched forward. He was like a brutal black robot. Were they hugging the walls or steadying their weak knees? They got comfort somehow in this nightmarish realm seeing the man in black armour steadily stomp forward. If that scar-faced man could do it with just a sword, surely they could, fully armed with the best modern firearms.

And the boy walked bravely behind his father with sword and round shield in modern plastic armor. He too gave them a sense of purpose and realization they couldn't quite grasp in this hellish nightmare.

Masamu gained some composure with his katana in hand. He pushed off Kwan Thai Suex and accepted his fate. Whether he could handle the fighting or die from the intensity, he was now willing and able. Whatever shaking nerves he had succumbed to were exhausted. His calm demeanor returned.

Kwan Thai Suex continually, slowly, swirled his curved ninja blades. He had nothing to do or prove now. Everyone was in a state of shock and fear. He had only his instinct to fight. However, there was still a shuddering fear in his movements because merely slashing at these combatants wasn't enough. He had to swing and give deadly gruesome blows. He was not at all used to this. Never in his back alley black market arena fights did he have to fight with such brutal viciousness.

When a man strikes a man, there is a known quantity, a pain and shock infliction that gives the better man time to compose or reset. The opponent would falter, back away, or collapse merely from a shocking slice. But here, he saw how the demonic creatures just kept coming and coming, even after slashes and wounds. They leapt forward in their death throes, trying to inflict grievous wounds upon the soldiers. This sent a horrible chill down his spine as he slowly waved his flamboyant blades around.

When they came upon her, they stepped forward in stunned silence. Bedenwulf stood before her in the vast domed room as a lone knight with his long sword. Spread across the vast hemisphere of space were many black orcs and troglodytes standing to the sides, growling and waiting for the order to charge. Behind them rows of the sorcerers and witches stood silent. To their right was an extended platform, an opening to the night sky.

The mound of flesh swirled and pulsated, bubbling gastric whirls within its bloated bowels. The men slowly entered up the ramp, spreading just a bit to Bedenwulf's left and right. They raised their weapons but couldn't exactly tell what or who to aim at. They definitely saw the black orcs and troglodytes staring at them, but they were unable to fire.

Riley stared wide-eyed, training his aim across the line of brutal beasts. He was able to focus and see the strange diminutive humans behind the towering bestial men. They looked like creepy tattoo-ridden night clubbers or post-modern pagans. He wasn't sure. Then, at first a blur, he finally saw the veins and pustules, the quivering mound of skin and flesh. It became more and more visible, the overriding sense of the vast power behind it all. And there, suddenly before him, focused through his sites, was the most wretched, extended gruesome looking witch, woman or bestial demonic thing he had ever seen. He couldn't tell what she was. For seeing the black orbs of her eyes and wet matted hair framing a grim face with extended features froze him with paralyzing fear.

He knew that the horrific beast woman coming out of that giant wall of flesh, attached to it, was Gorbogal.

"Oh my dear God!" Rudy moaned, blinking past the trickle from his gauze-soaked bloody helmet.

"This ain't Kansas anymore," the Duke sang in some strange nightmare swoon. He looked on the verge of crazy.

Rostislav stood next to him, having lost his sunglasses. His face was swollen with fear and sweat. Tears dripped down from his eyes.

The men should have spread out, found cover immediately, but they couldn't. They stood close together with guns raised and shaking, and tried in all meekness to gather strength from the brethren next to them.

"Bedenwulf," the voice rasped, echoing like a thunderous whisper across the dome of the carved-out rock. "I burned you..."

The men convulsed, quivered, and shook in uncontrollable fear. The voice seemed to permeate them as if they were inside a vast concert hall. And yet it was a whisper, a guttural growling whisper.

"Bedenwulf, fallen, disgraced lord of a diminished house. Adulterer with my sister... taking her from her home, from her father – from me..."

The Black Knight, in the helm burnt by Gorbogal's fires twelve years ago, raised his sword.

Gorbogal suddenly crawled forward, her muscular talons pounding on the black stone floor. All the men focused on her, flinching from the realization that she was even there. Only a few had discerned that she was there amongst the bestial men and seductive sorcerers before she spoke. The rest could not focus on the threat. The mound, the wall of flesh before them, was like a living blur that confused their concentration and training.

Now – with her pounding her snakelike torso and her flesh clomping forward, they could see the sinews of her shoulders and arms pulsating in ungodly strength. She was most definitely the Gorbogal they were to take out. And they realized that this was impossible, and that they were all going to die with their bodies imprisoned in this hell beyond their reality. They now knew why they were chosen.

They all shook violently. Their weapons and gear rattled. Sweat and tears flowed. Blood from grievous wounds trickled.

"Hold it together!" Riley yelled.

Gorbogal gazed at him, her curiosity halting whatever death she was intending to deliver in that moment. She gazed with her black orbs. She looked at their dress, their weapons, their belts of ammo and factory stitched boots. She looked at their haircuts and shaved skin, their beads of sweat and the perfectly stamp-formed buttons and zippers. She was intrigued by the zippers and the Velcro and the finely woven polyester threads that made up their belts and straps. Her black orbs darted to and fro, absorbing every detail. She licked her grotesque lips. She saw the modernization of everything they had. She had visions of factories and technologies, of pressure molds and conveyor belts. She saw power.

She stood like some giant lion, extended outward from her cavalcade of conjurers and bestial brutes. She was larger than the beasts. Her sinewy muscles were more sharply defined, even as they seemed skinless. Veins and moisture all across her flesh pulsated in scintillating, blood-ridden sanguinary colors.

Alfred stepped forward from behind his father.

"Alfred!" she hummed. "Alfred, Alfred, did you miss your aunt?"

Rudy, Riley, Loud, Masamu, Kwan, Rostislav, the Duke, the mysterious No, and the others, all glanced at each other, at Alfred, and at this horrible beast in front of them, this nightmare reality. They shook, hearing her talk. They had never heard a bestial guttural cackle. To hear a beast or fantastical voice echoing in the expanse, tore to the core of their nerves.

"You must stop attacking Earth! You must stop opening gateways to their planet. They have come here to stop you!" Alfred yelled above her growls.

She suddenly stopped her gibbering and peered at them, at the men again. "Earth? That is what you call your realm? Its full of soft men with interesting contraptions like cannons – small, little cannons of death. Interesting. I want it. All of it!"

"How do we take her?" Riley asked.

Gorbogal stared at him. "You don't." She raised one of her normal sized limbs – a real arm, it seemed – not a larger sinewy extension with talons. No, the mysterious hit man, rushed in front of Riley, seeking redemption for his sins. She merely flicked her hand. He burst into a vast splatter. Riley choked and floundered from it.

She flicked again, and another soldier burst. The others screamed in horror.

Bedenwulf stepped forward. She raised her other hand as her other monstrous arms held her torso upright. He stood paralyzed.

She flicked her hand again. Another soldier was obliterated. His gear and arms dropped to the ground intact.

"You don't," she repeated.

The Duke roared a tragic howl, but he could not move.

She flicked again. Another soldier disappeared in a burst, his weapons and shreds of clothes and gear fluttering to the blood stained ground.

"Nooo!!!" Riley yelled.

She flicked again at Riley.

Riley looked up in tears. His gun weighed so much that he could not hold it up. She flicked at him again. He gaped, spittle and tears spurting. She flicked again. Nothing.

Ethralia stepped forward with her hand extended, her palm out.

"Ethralia... sister...."

"Kill her," Ethralia said calmly as she waved her other hand to the men. Gorbogal blinked.

"Let's rock!" the Duke yelled. His forearm muscles suddenly lurched and his M60 burst a rain of splattering bursts upon Gorbogal. The intense damage forced her to crawl back as her minions and monstrous limbs came forth.

Rostislav woke from a nightmare and opened up his Pecheneg. He sprayed across charging black orcs and troglodytes. They took many shots but kept coming, contorting, limping, even falling and yet still charging at him and the others.

Bedenwulf the Black Knight charged at Gorbogal. He swung a vicious strike, severing one of the monstrous arms. Gorbogal fell to the ground hard. Her flesh pounded like a heavy beast of burden. He swung again, cutting into the monstrous body. His blade stuck in the sinewy flesh. Gorbogal gurgled and moaned angrily. Her mound of flesh suddenly yanked her, and she slid back into the bulbous womb. Then many bestial limbs and talons suddenly burst out, like an explosion of horrific tentacles.

Bedenwulf was then met by an onslaught of black orcs and troglodytes. He deftly leapt side to side, swinging incredible slashes at limbs and torsos, and then he had no choice but to roll and leap back.

Kwan leapt forward to fend off a massive limb. He slashed at it mortally, but it grabbed his arm, immediately breaking it. He screamed in utter shock. Masamu swung with the perfect katana slice, using all his skill and training. The blade merely stuck into the limb as it tightened around Kwan's arm, causing him to go into shock. Another appendage grabbed Kwan's leg and pulled. Masamu realized he was going to see Kwan torn limb from limb right before him.

He saw the pulsating muscles and veins on the powerful limb before him, squeezing Kwan to death, pulling his leg. Masamu then twirled his katana, slicing around the limb. He could not sever it, so he slashed the muscles around it.

The talons gripping Kwan failed from their muscles and nerves being cut. Masamu had weakened their grip. Masamu quickly swirled his blade along the surface and then quickly pulled Kwan free. Another three-fingered limb extended toward Masamu. He quickly swirled his blade, cutting off the monstrous fingers. The vast muscular limb, squirting black blood, merely pushed at him and then retracted.

Kwan limped back with one crushed arm and a damaged leg. He cried in anger.

The men fired in a steady line, recovering from their fear and magical paralysis. They knew their training and now knew where to hit these wretched beasts for optimal effect. Some sprayed the legs of the bestial men, getting them to slow, and then focused on the head or mid-torso to pump them full of deathly holes. Others skillfully fired rounds into their necks, choking them, or their heads, instantly dropping them. It got harder to shoot as the humanoids charged. The men shook, in that fated way, against the insane brutality before them.

The bestial orcs dropped as the limbs of Gorbogal still protruded forward. Her limbs were more difficult to hit and their flesh much stronger and more sinewy than those of the orc grunts. Limbs would grab a soldier's leg or arm and crush it, cracking bones and bursting flesh, causing the soldier to grimace and scream.

Masamu leapt from limb to limb, trying desperately to slice the tendons and muscles, debilitating the grips. But more limbs came. Kwan, worse for wear, limped and rolled to do the same, slicing at the oncoming limbs and freeing the soldiers. It was his last act of heroism, he surmised.

Wooly took on the charging orcs.

Alfred stood before his mother, protecting her. Only a few black orcs managed to come close. Alfred knew not to take them on with a full frontal slam like his father. He rolled below either side of each orc, slicing at ankles or knees. He then directed a soldier to shoot them as he took on another.

Ethralia merely stood, her eyes glowing in the same blue as her aura. Her hair was still floating in an electrical discharge. She stared not at Gorbogal, retracted into the flesh, but at the line of sorcerers and witches casting spells at her and the men. She held them off. Their spells of dark clouds and mist burst then dissipated. They fell by gunfire until many were suddenly engulfed in the mound of flesh, sucked or pulled in by tentacles. The mound was consuming its own worshipers.

"Her sacrifices!" Ethralia hissed.

Rudy was barely alive as a monstrous limb banged against him. Kwan severed its tendons, enabling Rudy to crawl out from under its onslaught. He limped on his own leg, standing up to reload. He looked down the corridor. They could hear the raging of an oncoming horde.

Riley motioned to Rudy. "Blow that corridor! Collapse it!"

Rudy acknowledged and limped back. He waved a couple of soldiers to come with him as he pulled out charges and wires. But then he realized as he went up to the stone. "I can't blow this. It's too solid. I need a drill! And lots of time!" he yelled frantically.

"You gotta slow them!" Riley yelled back.

The mess of soldiers, many lying with crushed limbs, continued to fire upon the faltering line of orcs and sorcerers. Bedenwulf hacked at monstrous limbs as Masamu deftly sliced them and Kwan rolled amongst the limbs, hacking and slashing them with crazed screams. But the mound of flesh seemed to have an unlimited amount of limbs bursting out from it.

The Duke lumbered over the field of dead and got close to the flesh mound. He unloaded round after round into it, tearing through limbs and bloated skin. In a crazed rain of hellfire he yelled. "Where are you!? Oh, where are you little witchy?!!!"

Though the Duke was courageously in the midst of the ghoulish mound, he was still supported by Rostislav, who burst fire upon limbs, attempting to reach the Duke from his flank. The Russki calmly fired a burst on his left, then a burst on his right, then a burst on his left and twice again on his right.

Rudy set up several claymores, sticking them into fallen orcs. He had no choice. There wasn't much time.

"They're coming!" yelled Loud, firing round after round. Beastmen turned the bend of the corridor, charging up to reinforce the fallen slaves of Gorbogal. It was a horde of orcs and goblins, black orcs and troglodytes. Something larger lumbered forth with them. They had no time to discern the war troll as they fired round after round.

"Almighty! Almighty...this is for real..." Rudy grunted as he hurriedly set the claymores and rushed back, waving the others away.

The explosion was devastating but finite compared to the horde rushing in. Goblins and orcs flew, but the corridor was intact, and the following waves of the horde pressed up.

"Duke, get back here! We need you!" Riley yelled. His men turned to face the horde coming up the ramp. Many of the men were on knees or using one arm, their other hanging limp. Several were lying still, whether in shock or worse.

Rostislav let out an incredible roar above the Duke's firing rampage against the flesh. "Duke, fall back! Now!"

The Duke gritted his teeth and looked back, seeing the horde converge up the corridor and into the arena of the witch. He hurriedly leapt back, pulling out his last ammo belt. He and Rostislav, even as big men with big guns, adroitly stepped over the fallen beasts and floundering monster limbs to get back to the line. He turned one last time, tossing a grenade into the mound of flesh. "Forget you!"

The explosion burst in the flesh, shaking the entire surface. A thousand squeals seemed to reverberate across it, along with a distant howl of an angry raging witch.

The Duke and Rostislav retreated to the line of desperate men.

"Got one belt left! Ammo is low!" the Duke roared.

"Use it!" Riley ordered. He looked to the magical woman next to them. "Queen, you gotta get that witch. We are running out of time!"

Alfred stared up at his mother. She seemed to be concentrating. She was fighting off Gorbogal's spells of devastation. "She can't!" Alfred yelled. "She's stopping Gorbogal from using spells."

Riley looked at Alfred. "We can't hold this attack much longer!"

They looked to see a war troll rear up a massive warhammer.

"Oh my God!" Rudy couldn't help but yell.

The Duke and Rostislav poured their rounds of machine gun fire into it, throwing a fury of muzzle fire, flaring the whole battle into a raging hell. The war troll roared in its devastation, falling back onto its own horde of minions, but the charge barely faltered as orcs and goblins swirled around it. Wave after wave fell to their gunfire. Men were yanking out magazines for new ones and more and more were scrambling amongst their own to find ammo. They were running out.

"Fall back!" Riley yelled.

Rudy tossed grenade after grenade, blowing up the wall of goblins charging forward.

The men pulled and yanked their fallen, many fired with one arm while yanking back another. Many were unconscious or delirious from grave wounds. They held onto whatever Riley was doing, wherever he was leading them. They moved across the domed room, past the quivering flesh, dead orcs, and dead sorcerers.

Alfred tugged at his mom. He pulled her along. She kept up a stare, the concentration, facing the blown out mound, even as he pulled her away.

Riley got them to the balcony, the opening with the night sky above them. Alfred leapt to the edge to see if there was a way out or a defensive bottleneck. Riley rushed to the edge as well.

"We've got to find a defensible position! Is there..." Riley looked out across the expanse before him. A hot breeze rushed up to him as he saw the vast encampments of orcs, trolls, troglodytes, and goblins below him. They were atop a vast black spire, looking down the mountainside to a land full of death camps and monstrous beasts. An army of innumerable orcs surrounded their position, a long line of them was marching into an opening far below.

Riley stared, frozen for the first time in his combat experience, even as the men fired their guns and Rudy tossed grenade after grenade to slow the onslaught. The domed vault was filled with mounds of dead orcs and putrid smoke.

"We destroyed an army of hers, and here she has another. I'm sorry, Riley. I'm sorry for all of this," Alfred said.

Riley awoke, looking at Alfred. He put his hand on Alfred's shoulder. "I'm not. I'll fight evil anywhere, anytime, win or lose, even in this God forsaken world of yours."

Alfred nodded, a tear forming. He looked at the stars out in the night sky. He saw one bright star gently glimmering.

"Get your mom to get us out of here!" Rudy yelled desperately, leaping back from his grenade tossing.

Alfred looked at his mom. She was straining. Something horrible and dark was gripping her fiercely. Alfred realized she was unable to do it.

The Black Knight came back. "We can't penetrate that abomination!" He pointed at the mound of flesh.

Ethralia spoke, "She is healed."

Suddenly, from the flesh, dozens of monstrous limbs burst forth as Gorbogal crawled out once again, in her powerful sinewy form. And the horde of goblins, black orcs, troglodytes and trolls filled the vast space.

Chapter Sixty-One

The Return of Tirnalth

"We must go! We must go! We must go!!!" Loranna cried. Her head fell to her hands. She screamed into them as she clawed tightly at her face.

Her younger sister Niranna tried to pull her hands away. "Please stop! Please, Loranna, stop...!" Then she cried with her.

Loranna's skin was reddening from the grip. She was nearly ripping her own face off from her anger and wailing.

Setheyna patted her back and whispered. "It's okay. It's okay. Alfred is brave. He is brave. He wants you to be brave. It's okay..." Both cried some more.

Lord Dunther stared at her and at the rest. They were all in the King's Hall, in the Great Hall, as it were, the leftover ruins of the Keep. Tents and pavilions were set up. They had just eaten dinner on makeshift tables in the cleared area. Gnomes sat and ate their scrumptious biscuits silently.

Pep put his down. "Doesn't taste the same. Though it is."

Gib put his down too.

Hedor and his men were not hungry either.

Verboden and Harkonen walked amongst them, speaking softly, "You must eat. You must heal. You must gather your strength."

Lady Nihan, the ladies, with the Khanafians and gnome wives, served all as best they could. There were many there, the farmers, the fathers and mothers of the archergirls and spearboys. Cory sat glum, with Nubio and Wilden at his side.

They were covered with filth and dirt, still exhausted after their great victory days before. Many had bandages or splints. Many were still lying on mats or the ground, wherever they could rest and heal.

Furioso and the troll hunters sat with their children, who were gaining strength and freedom, knowing their fathers.

Furioso stood. "I want to thank Alfred, King Alfred, for saving us, for saving our children. I want to thank him for saving my child, Red. Her name is Red."

Red looked up at her father. She couldn't help but gleam with joy, even in the face of sadness.

Furioso continued. "Even now, gaining their freedom, my child and the others know that the world before them is a lost world filled with great evil. They see it in the faces of those who have rescued them, and missing the one face who led them. He is now in the clutches of fear and slavery and death that they have known. I can only pray for him, to that Father. The Father, the one I hid from all these years. What hope is there left?"

He sat there, unsure of what he had just said, holding his daughter and sobbing.

Everyone had a look of exhausted depression.

Abedeyan peered around at no one. He had an untouched bowl of soup and a biscuit. "What pray can we do? What hope is there?"

King Gup stood. "My gnomes and I, we are willing to go. We do not know the way, nor have we traveled across the land. We... we are unsure how to save or rescue our king. We are so very sorry." He sat and cried over his food.

Dunther, bent over but standing as best he could, spoke. "Day after day, we are trying to prepare, to heal and strengthen ourselves." He looked at Gorham, who sat reclined and weak. His skin was still burnt and brittle, and his arm was still in a sling. Dunther blinked slowly. "The journey we have to make, weeks upon weeks, is before us. And we know the evil witch Gorbogal will never let Alfred survive that long. She will torture and kill him as soon as he arrives. It probably, maybe, has already happened."

Loranna suddenly lurched back. Her uncontrollable sobbing caused her to struggle for breath. Niranna and Setheyna held her steady as she cried. And they continued crying with her.

Dunther, choking, continued, "The journey would be only to weaken ourselves, expose us, and get us all killed in a foreign land without any real army or defensible position. There is no way we... All is lost. Alfred is lost."

"NOOOOOO!!!" Loranna screamed. She yanked herself free. She stared at Dunther with evil eyes. She grabbed at her bow, held tight by Niranna and Setheyna. She stared at Dunther, gritting her teeth. Niranna wouldn't let go of Loranna's elven bow. She mumbled a desperate prayer as Loranna yanked. Already she had three arrows in her other hand.

Dunther stood weak. Verboden, walking through the crowded area filled with sulking figures, moved toward her.

She stared down at her sister and Setheyna, who looked up at her with fear in their eyes. She let go, throwing the arrows at them and screamed. She was about to pounce on them like a crazed animal. But she saw them sobbing, her sister, her friend... she ran off.

Verboden tried to reach her, but she scrambled through them all. Some -- Hedor, Kumbo, or Furioso – could have easily stopped her, grabbing her. But they had not the strength.

She ran past them all, toppling a bowl of soup Lady Nihan was carrying. No one stopped her or yelled at her. They were all too weak and forlorn.

She hurried through the rubble and disappeared. Her elven cloak veiled her from their sight.

The Great Hall was almost entirely obliterated from the ogre cannon fire and more recently by the epic stone bombardment. Its few ruined walls and structures were only kept till the gnomes finished the outer walls and then could begin rebuilding a greater Keep within. The old structure still left was above the kitchens. Part of it was the half-exposed chapel and Alfred's room. It was still dangerous to climb the cracked and crumbled stairs but easy enough for a limber, soft-stepping girl.

Loranna entered Alfred's stark, dark room. She closed the door behind her, locking it, and found solace within. The darkness of night was filling the room. Stars twinkled through the refractive glass of the small window. It was quite cracked. She lay upon his bed and cupped the pillow tightly to her face as she screamed and sobbed into it, muffling and hiding her anger and trepidation from the rest of the occupants outside.

She lay crying, exhausted. She sat up and looked at the stars out in the night sky. She saw one bright star gently glimmering. "Alfred, oh Alfred! My love. My King. The one who was to be my husband. I love you. I love you. I will always love you and only you. You are the one who has my heart... Why did Tirnalth send you!? Why did..." She looked down. She scooted quickly off the bed and stepped to the table. There upon it lay a book. It had "Tirnalth" in small letters on the cover. "Tirnalth?"

She flicked it open. The pages were blank. She stared at it as if it glowed with sparking embers and a depth beyond her eyes' ability to comprehend. Tears dropped, and her mouth shuddered. She stopped her stupid trance and sneered, slamming the book shut.

The room was dark, save a modest oil lamp kept lit. Its small flame lit the table. She removed the top half to expose the flame. She held the book up, huffing in angry breaths.

"Tirnalth!" she screamed, not caring who heard her. "TIRNALTH!!??" She waved the book about in defiance, to show it to whoever might be looking from whatever ethereal realm. "Tirnalth! You feckless wizard!"

She could hear someone, perhaps Dunther or Verboden, scrambling through the rubble and stairs up to her in Alfred's room. Dunther tried to open it. He banged on it.

"Loranna, open the door."

"Tirnalth!!!" she screamed. "This is the book Alfred told me about. It is your way back to him!" She looked about.

"Loranna!" Dunther yelled, banging on the door again. "Open the door! Leave the book!"

"Someone get a gnome, quickly!" Verboden yelled, his muffled voice echoing outside.

"If you won't come now, then damn you, wizard!" Loranna yelled loudly enough for everyone to hear. She put the book to the flame. The flame suddenly intensified, licking the corner of the book.

And then the flame flickered out.

"I wouldn't do that if I were you."

Dunther and Verboden burst through the door as Gib, who had opened the lock, was thrown to the ground.

"Tirnalth!"

Chapter Sixty-Two

Obliteration

"Hold the line!" Riley yelled as the men fired the last of their rounds. They were at the edge of the balcony. The twilight sky was behind them, and a horde was charging through the domed room toward them. Some of the men were dropping their emptied assault rifles and pulling out their handguns. One had his knife out, sitting on the ground with broken legs, ready to fight to the last. Duke dropped his M60 machine gun, posing with bare fists. He quickly grabbed up a foreign weapon, one of the black orc's spiked maces. Loud continued to fire calmly aimed shots, one after the other, at heads and necks. Rostislav found a heavy falchion. He swung it awkwardly.

Rudy merely sat, sobbing, crying, "Oh God nooo... Oh God..."

Alfred looked at him, with sword and shield ready. "I thought you didn't believe in God."

Rudy stopped crying, staring wide-eyed at nothing.

Masamu dragged Kwan Thai Suex back, stopping on occasion to deal with a goblin or orc. Masamu screamed in chilling rage with each tussle, seeking a decapitation or limb removal. It almost drove him mad, but the need to save Kwan, who was on the ground trying to defend himself with one arm, carried them both forth.

Obliteration

The Black Knight took the brunt of the oncoming horde. He swung viciously into groups of goblins, limbs flying. He charged orcs, banging hard and flailing. Yet somehow he seemed to take that chaotic movement and turn it into a counter swing, a recovering movement. The special forces men watched, wiping sweat, oil, tears, and blood from their doomed faces as they saw his fighting prowess. He must have been some kind of legend in the land based on how he fought and broke wave after wave of bestial orcs that charged.

When he dropped a war troll, a giant of a beast, they knew he was a superhero. But after that, Bedenwulf limped back. For even in their dire hope that he could save them, he was waning in strength, endurance, and hope. And the horde swelled.

Alfred looked up into the night sky. He saw the one bright star gently glimmering again. He could not help but think of Loranna. He smiled through his fear and trepidation. Even to the end, he was good and kind and felt the hope of love. It was okay. He would miss her but felt somehow... "I'll see you again one day," he said softly.

Then Gorbogal gathered her forces. She waved forth more orcs and trolls, as her strenuous, sinewy limbs with claws and talons clasping mightily stomped forward. And even more burst out of the mound of flesh, oozing and dripping, as they reached toward the surrounded men from another world.

She crawled to them with her lion-like limbs lumbering out and her snake torso following from behind. Her face was monstrous and hag-like, her skin wet with bile and blood. She lumbered forth, grinning a deathly sneer. She was ready to finish them, as she was intrigued by this new world she could invade and study their crafting of weapons of war.

"Mom!" Alfred cried, looking at Ethralia. She shook and convulsed. The blue aura emanating from her was weakening, faltering. She was about to collapse. She was convulsing and sweating. She was in complete exhaustion.

Bedenwulf reached her as she fell. He dropped his sword, ripped off his helm and held her. He then reached for Alfred and held him. It was all he had left. They were all the Black Knight had left as Ethralia collapsed in his steel arms. Alfred looked closely at his father. Bedenwulf kissed his son's forehead. He then kissed his wife.

Then a burst of white light broke upon them all.

Goblins flew, orcs fell hard and slid, and Gorbogal's limbs shuddered. She raised her arms to block the burst of light, squinting and confused.

For before her, stood Tirnalth in the great glow. All could see his silhouette as he stood before them in the middle of the great dome vaulted room. The Navy Seals, the marines, the rangers, the demolitionist, the Russian mercenary, the Japanese swordsman, the Bangkok street fighter, Duke the old Army veteran – all stared in their various states of panic and exhausted pain. And now before them was a great wizard. They knew it.

Alfred stood up. "Tirnalth!"

Gorbogal looked, lowering her arms. She glared at the form through the hot white light.

The light faded, the glowing aura shrank, and many more shadows were revealed. Three knights stood with gnome armour and great swords, and a brute of a man with blazing red hair stood beside them. A line of spearboys formed a wall of steel spears behind them. Archergirls formed lines behind them, bows notched and ready.

As the light faded, all seemed to breathe a moment, to gather where they were and to see what was before them. The beasts surrounding them and coming up the rampway needed a moment too, blinking from the blinding light and slowly standing back up from being tossed to the black stone floor.

Even Gorbogal, staring at Tirnalth, needed a moment. She stared long at him as everyone recovered. She stared as he took a slow calming breath and lowered his staff.

"Tirnalth.... Tirnalth?" she hummed.

Tirnalth slowly looked at her.

"He destroyed you! He took you! The Dark Lord took you! He owns you!" Gorbogal growled as she crawled, lumbering toward him. "You lied? You lied to us?!"

The three knights were unsure what to do. Furioso looked back and forth at them as the gruesome ghoulish witch came closer.

"You made a deal. The Dark Lord had you! He owned you!" she raised her guttural voice, completely ignoring the epic brutal situation around her. "You don't exist!"

"I gave him my mind, but my soul is not for me to give," Tirnalth said.

"He cast you in the pit!" she screamed.

Everyone froze, unable to react. Her voice, or something, was causing them all merely to stand and look on with fear and trepidation.

"You do not exist! You will not exist!" she roared.

Tirnalth raised his staff.

"The Dark Lord wanted to keep you as a trophy. That was his mistake. He let you live... I see now... I will not make that mistake, Tirnalth." Gorbogal said with a leer.

Tirnalth gaped, a horribly frightened look flashed upon his face.

"I remember how long ago you destroyed eternally the Dark Mage, the one who turned on your precious Father... I remember the spell, Tirnalth, remember... when I was a little girl... I was there... hee hee hee!"

"No Gael-Asura, no...." Tirnalth pleaded.

"Oh, you remember my name. How sweet... And I remember the spell and its permanence!"

Bursting forth from her sinewy muscles came the dark hands of her human form. They flicked together in a spidery dance. Her monstrous limbs held up her torso, but her supple arms cast the spell. Tendrils of lightning suddenly burst forth, ripping at Tirnalth, at his staff.

The thunderous sound cracked the air and the stones. It ripped through the dead bodies strewn about and caused the living to convulse and cover their ears in great pain. She ripped lightning strike after lightning strike. Each one was a powerful burst of hot flash, crackling and smoking.

"If the Dark Lord cannot imprison you, then I WILL OBLITERATE YOU!!" she screamed, her voice as loud and piercing as her thunderous lightning strikes. Tirnalth was not powerful enough, not yet, to withstand her. Each strike tore through his staff and finally onto him. His arms burst. He wailed in torturous pain. His skin burned as strike after strike tore through him. He cried, unable to defend himself. His wailing paralyzed all in astonishment, at his suffering, as part after part exploded from his old body. As the lightning strikes ripped across him, every thread of muscle and bone flailed as blasted filaments.

"Mind and soul, body and flesh, I obliterate you with all my powers and the powers of the Dark Lord!" she hissed. This sent forth lightning bolt after lightning bolt, blinding her minions and causing the rest to cower.

"To OBLIVION!" she screamed as Tirnalth was blasted apart in utter destruction.

Alfred leapt up from his mother and father, charging forth. Everyone was still stunned, staring in shock as Tirnalth's body burst apart and dissipated into the smoke and debris. And when his ghostly soul appeared, Gorbogal smiled. "There you are!"

A last stroke of lightning shredded Tirnalth's soul. It keened or wailed in grief as it shuddered and seemed to blink out to a thousand sparks of waning light.

Alfred leapt too late, striking his sword against Gorbogal's monstrous body. It merely cut a little and then bounced off the thick sinewy bones and muscles.

Gorbogal blinked in exhaustion, from such expelled power, from her joyous victory, and turned to see Alfred falter beside her. He cried as he floundered on the ground. She saw him and chuckled, mocking and scoffing at his sobbing desperation.

The knights charged in. Gorbogal turned just in time as her limbs deflected their furious swings and charges. Limb after limb was severed as the knights, Lord Dunther, Lord Gorham, and Sir Murith hacked their way to her. She roared, "Attack them!"

Her orcs and goblins shook out of their daze and renewed their attack. But they weren't dealing with a ragtag group of desperate soldiers beaten down and running out of ammo. The new group was a sudden wall of deadly steel.

"Wall right!" Cory yelled.

"Left step!" Wilden yelled as spears and shields slammed into the horde. Steel spears pierced and punctured orcs and goblins.

Nubio was there, gritting teeth and holding the line. Hedor, Ruig and Kumbo fought viciously against any goblins that leapt in. They yelled vicious growls to invigorate each other.

"One fire! Two fire! Three fire! Four fire!" yelled Loranna as row after row of arrows flew into the orcs and towering trolls. Wave after wave fell before them, and Gorbogal realized she was alone.

Gib and Pep fired their spring loaders. Steel javelins pierced the skulls of war trolls towering before them. The girls knew not to waste their arrows on the trolls. Though a few dozen could drop one, they had plenty of black orcs to drop.

Obliteration

Now she saw the children who defeated her armies. She saw the glorious knights ripping through her monstrous arms. She saw her hordes of black orcs and troglodytes impaled on spears, falling in waves from arrows. Children, of her nephew Alfred, a king, were annihilating the army she bred all these years. She blinked. And she snarled.

"Ghhhatth braggg daahhh natthhh..."

When Gorbogal is exhausted, her powerful spells require a rhythm in ancient guttural tongues. She looked down at Alfred, whose spell merely needed to be blurted out. And blurt it out quickly he did.

A sphere of air,
radial out,
seal from me
and come about.

She was suddenly engulfed in a vacuum of nothingness. Before her, a cloudy marble ball floated. She choked on emptiness. She could not utter and cast her spell of devastation.

Alfred flung his hand and leaped away as Gorbogal choked and looked oddly after him. The marble sphere of air suddenly burst out, blasting her flesh and limbs.

The knights ducked amongst the dead bodies to avoid the concussive wave. Furioso, unsure, took a big brunt of it and was tossed back. Alfred crawled over many bodies in a daze.

Riley rushed up to aid him. Loud came with him.

Gorbogal lay with her flesh torn and her monstrous hag face ripped open. It was odd, like a flesh casing. For from it, lying inside, was Gael-Asura. Monstrous limbs were entangled all around her serpentine body and flesh. The casing still pulsated and bubbled around Gael-Asura. But it was obvious that she, in a woman's form, was cocooned, encased, or armoured by the monstrous form of Gorbogal.

Bedenwulf came forward carrying Ethralia. She leapt from his arms to reach Alfred. She looked at him through burning blue eyes. He awoke and looked up at his mother. She smiled strangely, peacefully.

Dunther, Gorham, and Murith charged in, hacking and cutting away at the flailing and confused limbs. Dunther stopped, seeing Ethralia come forward. Gorham and Murith also stopped, unsure.

Dunther saw her and remembered. He saw her and wanted only to forgive, to ask for forgiveness, to beg her to forgive him. But the moment now was not for that. It was a brutal bestial moment, not for pausing before the greatest evil of the Westfold. Gorbogal had caused the downfall and tragedy of countless men, women and, yes, children. For when one thinks of evil, it is softened by villains who attack soldiers or city blocks in comic books and movies. They are sugarcoated villains. But what lay before them was true evil that they must fight and stop. This Evil caused the death of children, many helpless and innocent, terrified and defenseless children. This Evil laid waste to families and farms, taking out the weakest and those who dared fight back.

Dunther then saw the Black Knight, yet it was Bedenwulf for his helmet was off. Dunther only paused a moment to see the scars and see his years of hiding yet faith to the one they both loved. Dunther finally understood who was the right man for Ethralia the princess. Both shared a quick nod as they charged forth.

Gorbogal may have been blasted, with her true form exposed as Gael-Asura lying within the flesh, but both the monstrous form of Gorbogal and the sister within, hated her would-be captors. And her form, however shredded, was still a brutal fighting beast.

Swords slashed, armour twirled, the knights severed, and the monstrous limbs flailed as Ethralia walked into the gory flesh and pulled out her sister, who was in a fetal position within, cowering like a cornered rat.

As Ethralia pulled on her greasy bloody limbs, Gael-Asura suddenly leapt out, hissing and clawing. Alfred tried to run up and swing his sword at her, but something knocked him back. It was strange, as if Gael-Asura were in another dimension, only somehow connected to this one. Her arms and legs seemed to swing and flail in a blurred magical ferocity. Whenever Bedenwulf or Dunther tried to grab her and subdue her, the limbs' magical contortions merely knocked them back.

Her skin was darkened by many black magic tattoos, scarred patterns and piercings. She had made ugly her entire body to fit her heart. She flailed like an inter-dimensional spider beast or crazed tentacle alien. Riley tried to grab her limbs, but the strange force yanked him, and he flew. Nothing could penetrate the flashing limbs and blurred body, nothing could except Ethralia.

Obliteration

She grabbed her sister from behind, wrapping her own white arms around the crazed body. Though Gael-Asura continued the unrelenting flailing, Ethralia had her in a choke hold, and they both fell back on the ground. Ethralia closed her glowing blue eyes and held tight, even as the crazed black blur swirled. Gael-Asura choked and howled a vicious cry, and scratched violently at her sister. She clawed at her arms and face. But Ethralia held.

Suddenly a blue gate opened behind them. Rudy turned to see it as the aura shined on his sweating skin. Riley, next to Alfred, leapt up in a daze, waving to the men. "The gate's open!"

Alfred pointed. "We have to get her! Before she regains her power!"

Men rambled painfully toward the shimmering hole. They pulled their fallen and limping comrades over many dead bodies of foul beastmen. The Duke came to help but was unsure what to do. To see Gael-Asura in such a state of strange movement beyond human imagining was frightening. And Gorbogal, as blown apart and grotesque an emanation as she was, was still a horrid threat, and she was regenerating, her flesh reattaching, sewing itself back together.

Lord Gorham and Sir Murith fought viciously with each limb and claw, swinging powerful lordly strikes. Gorbogal, gurgling with a half blown face, crawled toward Gael-Asura, even with the gruesome wounds inflicted upon her and her limbs by the knights.

And the mound of flesh gurgled, opening up a gigantic teeth-filled mouth that split vertically from the floor up. Alfred wasn't sure if it was to encase Gorbogal and Gael-Asura to heal them or to begin eating them. Out of it spewed spindly tentacles ready to take in whomever it wished.

"Oh no you don't, she dog!!" yelled Rudy as he pulled the rings of an entanglement of grenades. He had limped to the mound, ready to sacrifice himself. But as he stood there waiting for the limbs to take him in the maw of vile teeth to swallow and chew him, the Duke and Rostislav yanked him back. The mindless tentacles that spewed forth grabbed his wired up grenades and yanked them in.

"Duck!" Rudy swore with a maniacal grin.

They leapt back as the mound blew up into fleshy gory chunks.

As the Duke, Russki and Rudy recovered, as others limped painfully to the gate, Riley looked at Alfred, unsure.

Alfred yelled. "We have to get her!"

Bedenwulf leapt to Alfred. "We cannot touch her!"

Alfred looked at his mom, being ripped and scratched by her big sister. "She can!"

Wooly looked and saw. He scrambled over, tossing his sword and grabbing his wife. He carried Ethralia as she pulled Gael-Asura.

"No!" cried a woman's voice.

Wooly froze a moment as he saw a face in the blur of the spidery black creature. It was the face of Gael-Asura pleading with him.

"No, please," she cried. "I'll give you anything..."

Bedenwulf snarled and carried Ethralia forth. Alfred came alongside the Black Knight, carrying Ethralia, who in her trance-like state held Gael-Asura, and they marched toward the shimmering blue gateway.

The last of the able special forces men guarded the path as the target was being delivered. They stood, leaned or crawled in line, holding up the last of their handguns, knives or acquired orc blades.

Alfred looked back to see the fury of fighting still raging. The spearboys and archergirls were holding the charging horde at the ramp. He saw and met Loranna's eyes. She turned to see him. She had to, even in the midst of the crazed fight. Alfred looked up at his father carrying his mother, even with the dark evil that flailed nearby. Bedenwulf looked down to his son and nodded.

Alfred stood as Bedenwulf lumbered through the gateway, piercing the veil of the shimmering wall and took Ethralia and the Witch of the Westfold in. The Duke grabbed Alfred, who deftly twirled out of the Duke's grip.

"Come on, son!"

Alfred nodded no, slowly.

The Duke was yanked by others. He glared at Alfred as he fell into the gateway.

Riley put his hand on Alfred's shoulder as the last of them limped, crawled or leapt through the gate.

"Great job, King Alfred. You got it done!" Riley yelled above the clamor.

Alfred looked up to the worn, dirty haggard face of an elite soldier. He blinked and smiled.

Riley smiled back as he walked through the gate. It closed forever.

Chapter Sixty-Three

The Slaughter at Black Spires

Alfred turned to see the fight still continued in the vaulted dome. He noticed that neither the cleric Verboden nor his brother cleric Harkonen was amongst his fighting warriors. Furioso was in the thick of it up front, between the line of spearboys.

Dunther and his knights had to hold the flanks of the formations as the archergirls continued their volleys of arrows. The spearboys met each wave of charging beasts that made it through the girls' shooting.

Alfred stepped forward, over the bodies of dead trogs and orcs and over the many limbs that once were Gorbogal's. He was exhausted but had a moment to breathe and think. He looked at the quivering mound of flesh that once housed the grotesque Gorbogal body.

He noticed the carcass, lying limp and blasted on the floor. He stepped over, peering at it. Gorbogal's body was lifeless but still looked altogether vile and powerful nonetheless. Its black orbs still showed, though slightly clouded from permanent death. He lifted a thick-set arm. It was incredibly heavy. He now knew what they needed to do.

"Lord Dunther!" he called.

Dunther, after dispensing with an arrow-ridden troglodyte, turned and rushed over. "Yes my lord!? Glad to see you alive and well!"

"We have to show them that their witch is dead," said Alfred.

Dunther looked down and then at the ongoing fighting, the continual march of goblins up the ramp, even as their death toll rose

394

and the corridor filled with their bodies. "Right you are! Lord Gorham, Sir Murith, to my side!"

The other knights backed away, waving to the other men to hold the flanks. Hedor, Kumbo and Ruig nodded, leaping forward to each side, fighting as best they could. Thankfully, the front line of bristling steel spears and the volley of arrows did their task.

Loranna appeared from her line of archers. "Hedor, gather our arrows!"

Hedor looked at Kumbo and Ruig and raised his eyebrows. But he knew what was best for the fight. "Yes milady, Loranna!" He rushed about plucking, pulling, and yanking steel arrows from the fallen.

With some humility and aplomb, Gib and Pep, being small and agile, rushed amongst the fallen, pulling arrows as well. No large trolls had come recently, and they thought they might as well make themselves useful again.

"Much obliged!" Hedor said, cradling a dozen arrows. Gib and Pep tossed up their score of arrows and continued the work. Hedor rolled his elbows to catch and keep the arrows. "Oh yes, I can be the pack mule, of course." He turned to see Kumbo and Ruig valiantly fight off orcs and high-five each other in manly gusto.

Dunther peered down at the fallen body of Gorbogal.

"She is no more?" Murith asked hesitantly.

"She is no more!" Lord Dunther said, pulling up but unable to hold the slimy dead limb.

"We have to carry her to them!" Alfred pointed to the continually charging orcs. "We have to show them that she's dead!"

"Right! To end their fight!" Gorham bent down with Dunther, but neither could really grasp or lift the large corpse.

Alfred looked to the spearboys. A large warthog-faced trog tried to charge into them, only to get skewered, lifted, and thrown back dead. They were quite expert and coordinated in their response.

"Cory! Your spearboys, bring them here!"

Cory turned and nodded. They had practiced retreating many times. "Wilden, Nubio, close the lines! Shore up! Hold the flanks! Cory's boys, back step with me! One-two, one-two!"

Cory's line back-stepped, keeping their spears forward as orcs and trogs saw the line open. Several tried to rush in, but Wilden and Nubio immediately filled the ranks and met their charge.

Hedor dropped a good amount of arrows behind the girls. Loranna called out, and one girl from each line immediately rushed back to pick up their lot of arrows and disperse them amongst their lines. It was a well oiled machine of orders and compliance.

Hedor knew he had to help hold the flanks, hoping Alfred's call of Cory's spearboys would only be momentary. Gib and Pep rushed to their javelin shooter and watched for any larger beasts that might take advantage of the tightened formation.

"Turn, rush to me!" Cory ordered as his dozen spear boys dropped their forward pose and turned to hurry with Cory to Alfred.

They stopped to see the large dead corpse of the legendary witch. They were comforted that the knights stood about with a calm disposition.

"Cory, can you use your spears to lift her up? We have to get her down that corridor!? Arms out like this!?" Alfred posed with his arms spread out.

"Of course!"

When Gorbogal, the very dead Gorbogal corpse, arms splayed, bobbed and floated forward, the spears of a dozen boys puncturing and lifting her, the orcs, troglodytes, goblins and trolls could not fathom such a thing. They had seen her numerous times, powerful, enigmatic and mysterious. And now, to see her splayed so, defeated by diminutive soft humans stunned them. Their angry growls were not for charging but a crescendo of fear and panic.

They hissed and howled, staring not at the soft enemies in bloodlust killing, but at each other, in fear and trepidation. They began to retreat, to rush back down the winding corridor that led below. It was a vast descending passage, spiraling down and down to the ground level. Their confusion and panic caused trampling, choking, and crushing of fleeing orcs and troglodytes as they met the others coming up. The convergence led to a horrendous trampling. Even the trolls got turned about. They themselves were falling and crushing others as their own lungs were suffocated merely from tumbling and getting stuck amidst the pandemonium.

"Halt!" yelled Alfred, trying to understand what was happening below. They could hear the crushing disaster. He motioned to Cory. They set the heavy body down, resting a bit. Everyone stood or sat, or leaned upon one another or the walls. The panic below gave them respite.

Alfred turned to look at the spot where Tirnalth was obliterated. A burnt spot on the floor was all that was left. He went to stand and then fell to his knees there. He finally had time to mourn. "Tirnalth!" he cried.

Dunther came up, kneeling beside him. "He gave his life to finally end her evil reign," said Dunther softly, lifting his visor.

"He, he can't be dead, right? He can't give up his own life?" Alfred said, remembering.

"Obliteration is an ancient spell... it is permanent... it can only be used at great cost. When Gorbogal cast it, it weakened her. Tirnalth knew it was the only way, he knew, to save you, Alfred..."

Alfred looked up at Dunther. His mournful eyes changed to that of rage. He leapt up. "No, no, no! I don't want him to save me and die!" He pounded on Dunther's breastplate as Dunther tried to hold him. "No! No! No!" screamed Alfred.

Loranna rushed up and then stood with tears forming in her eyes, knowing she forced this choice upon Tirnalth. She tried to step forward but shook with each of Alfred's screams of "No!" and pounding upon Dunther.

Finally, Alfred exhausted himself and fell at Dunther's feet. Alfred choked and then spoke as best he could. "Where's Verboden? Where is he?"

"He and Harkonen spent the last ounces of their strength to heal Lord Gorham, so he could be in this fight," answered Dunther. "They could not come."

Alfred looked up, with some disdain upon the fully healed Gorham. Lord Gorham moved a bit, unsure of Alfred's embittered stare.

Alfred stood, wiping his hot moist face and his flaring nostrils. He was full of anger, and no one doubted why. All stood silent before their torn king.

"Let's go," Alfred stomped through the dead and past all the exhausted fellowship down the ramp.

It took till the hot crisp of noon to reach the opening at the bottom of the Great Black Spire. They had to crawl and stumble over legions of dead and dying beastmen. When they reached the opening, most of the enemy had fled into the scattered encampments. The land was littered with caves and pits. There were many cauldrons and fire pits, bivouacs of tents and makeshift shelters, piled stone furnishings and bones of many dead. Though the beastmen now cowered in fear, the land still seemed like a nightmare one that would weaken and wane the hardiest of warriors.

Alfred came forth, and the spearboys hoisted high the decaying decrepit body of Gorbogal. Their ragtag group of shining steel armour, dirtied and grimy, marched forth from the grand opening.

The hot sun helped keep the orcs away. Even at their bravest, this time of day would be like midnight to humans. The glaring of the light blinded them enough that none cared to look or see what was amiss. Only the magic of evil sorcerers could spurn orcs on in the glaring sun to march and battle, and there were none around. The cursed land was deathly silent, save a few crackling fires and the waft of smoke in a dry hot breeze.

Alfred motioned for them to drop the body. It was heavy and slowed them. Cory waved weakly, and the boys finally sighed relief as they stepped away, letting the bubbling decaying mass drop heavily onto the gravel. Alfred waved again, and all began as quick a march as their exhausted bodies could muster.

The evil of this world was not done yet. Though Alfred defeated the greatest servant of the Dark Lord, he knew the Dark Lord would not be so keen on just letting Alfred walk away.

A shadow alerted Alfred to the vulture's approach. Or perhaps it was the three days riding in its grasp that gave Alfred the awareness of its presence. He immediately called out, "The Dark Servant! Run!"

Lord Dunther quickly looked up to see the shape against the blinding sun. "Scatter! Poison!"

Everyone knew to rush off, whether into the caves or pits or beyond Alfred, whom they knew the foul vulture. They remembered its poisonous choking cloud and wanted to be fit enough to respond. Dunther hesitated, trying to hold his breath.

But Alfred would not have it. "Run Dunther. I got this!"

Furioso charged at Dunther, lifting him and leaping away as the vulture crashed upon the dry earth, blasting gravel and poisonous dust. The Dark Servant reared quickly to lift the vulture up as its talons ripped into the dirt around Alfred.

It wafted its foul wings, lifting upward, as it squawked a telltale scream. The Dark Servant looked down to see gravel and rock crumble from the vulture's grip, but no boy, no boy king, no Alfred.

"Come back here, you fowl excrement!" Dunther yelled from the ground. He and Furioso rolled quickly away from each billowing of the poisonous dust. Thankfully, the foul air dissipated quickly from whence it was dispensed.

The Dark Servant turned, flying back around, and looked, seeing nothing but Alfred's servants and soldiers coming out of hiding, gathering up again. He could not see his famed target anywhere.

Unbeknownst to the Dark Servant, a mouse scurried and climbed, quickly, easily and not minding at all the foul stench of the bones and decayed flesh of a thousand year-old undead vulture. It, he, ...Alfred the mouse... adroitly climbed up through the bones and innards of the hollow beast, up through the foul carrion and, surprisingly, up into the armour and bone dry corpse of the Dark Servant.

As the Dark Servant searched amongst them, he noticed that even the archergirls were not firing upon him. He wondered why. Was Alfred upon his mount? He looked behind himself and saw nothing. He looked to and fro on his mount, wondering what was amiss. Then, bursting from his side, ripping out ribs and armour and the physical manifestation of the Dark Servant, Alfred appeared. He burst out in such a way that his growth was accentuated by his thrusting of elbows, sword and shield.

The Dark Servant wasn't prepared for that and languished to one side in shock. After all, he did not have much of a midsection left to hold himself upright. Alfred slid along a wing and held its furthest feather, causing the vulture to tilt and drop.

A sphere of air,
radial out,
seal from me
and come about.

Alfred pointed at the Dark Servant, who tried as hard as he might to lift or move, but he could not. For as dark and powerful as the evil spirit was, he was, unfortunately for him, made manifest in a corporeal form. And that form happened to have its entire midsection blown out.

The vacuum spell silenced any attempt by the Dark Servant to exact retribution with an evil incantation. Alfred also left within the Dark Servant's blown cavity that familiar ball of swirling clouds.

Alfred found the right moment to let go of the faltering vulture. It dropped and rolled upon the dusty ground, careening toward and then crashing against rugged rocks. The vacuum spell collapsed, bursting the vulture and Dark Servant into a crumpled heap upon those rocks. And oh yes, the marble swirling ball then exploded outward, thusly ending, in a conclusive and most edifying way, the Dark Servant and his vulture mount.

The troll hunters bounded in upon them. Ordo landed with a booming earthquake and faced what was left of the Dark Servant – debris.

Ordo looked at the exhausted fellowship. Furioso rushed to him, giving him a great burly hug. Then, choking on emotion, he stood back and was unable to talk.

Ordo saw Alfred stand up and dust off his plastic armor. Ordo adjusted his fur armour and helm just a bit. "Would have been nice if you left us something to fight."

Chapter Sixty-Four

The Peace at the Keep

On the long journey back, many had time to resolve their differences or expound on what had transpired. Furioso explained to the troll hunters the magical gateway, Alfred's "special forces" men from another world, the comparable prowess of the Black Knight, Alfred's father, killing trolls like a troll hunter, and the tragic fall of Tirnalth the wizard.

Lord Gorham walked with Ordo and Ruuk. They had difficulty looking at him, not withstanding their guilt, but they were also very much taller than him.

"I'm sorry, nephew," Ordo finally said. "I'm sorry I betrayed my wife and the child she bore. I'm sorry I betrayed your father and his son. I... I have sworn fealty and service to King Alfred. It is all I can do."

Gorham spoke softly. "I knew you had not yet met King Alfred..." He smiled warmly. "He changes everything. He defeated you with children, you're very own children. The boy king has this way with us men, with our evil... finding within us... our good, however muddled."

Ordo and Ruuk stared sadly at the ground before them.

Gorham continued, "He defeated us knights with children as well. Children are the future, they are always the future. Lest we forget – they are our future."

Lord Gorham, Ordo and Ruuk looked up, noticing Alfred, Loranna and the armed children marching before them.

Loranna clung to Alfred. It took several days of teary eyes and long quiet walks before she showed any semblance of awareness. As the spearboys and archergirls marched behind them, their spirits of freedom and hope returned. Alfred and Loranna shared in their fears, speaking softly to each other – he telling of his torturous despair enchained to Gorbogal, she disclosing her bitter frustration at not being able to save him.

Days later, they were sitting at a campfire with plenty of meat brought by the troll hunters. Everyone was eating well, gathering their strength, everyone except Loranna. She nibbled at her food while Alfred ate slowly.

"You must eat, Loranna," Lord Dunther said. "You must keep up your strength. Many leagues more we have to travel, and these lands are not safe." He handed her a bone of meat. She took it, and as he passed by she put it down.

Alfred looked at her. "Please, Loranna, for me? We're free now! Free as can be! And with great knights, troll hunters, the greatest spearmen and archers to protect us!"

"Couple of ruffians as well," Hedor motioned with a greasy face and a big fat bone. He, Ruig, and Kumbo snorted as they grubbed.

She hugged his arm as she stared into the fire. "I called Tirnalth with that book. I'm sorry, Alfred. His passing... it was my doing." She sighed a deep sorrowful sigh.

"Loranna, you... Tirnalth... saved us. We were losing. The soldiers I was with, my mom and dad, we couldn't do it. Tirnalth knew. He knew what she'd do to him, but he knew he had to. Please... don't blame yourself." Alfred bit a large piece of meat off and began chewing. "You and Tirnalth saved us!" he said between chews. She still looked forlorn bu thoughtful.

He kissed her forehead. She blinked and suddenly was alive with life. She smiled up at him. She didn't care that there was a big greasy stain on her forehead and a small chunk of meat.

Alfred quickly licked her dirty greasy forehead to clean it......
"OOPS!" Alfred stared wide-eyed. "I didn't mean to..."

"Yuck!" she guffawed. The kids laughed.

"Sorry, it was greasy!" Alfred grimaced.

She pulled up her bone and hit him in the face with it, leaving a big greasy spot on his cheek. He rolled his eyes and then realized she was going to lick his face.

"Oh no!" he leapt up and ran around knights and troll hunters as she ran after him.

"Oh... looks like she's got her strength back," Hedor shrugged. "Feisty strength..."

"Oh good, I was beginning to worry," Ruig said. "Cuz I ain't fighting any random monstrous encounters in these lands! She can take care of them."

Kumbo chortled as he continued to chomp and gnaw, "I see what scares our King."

"Agreed," Ruig and Hedor replied.

"Save your strength!" Lord Dunther tried to order. Hunters and children alike yelled a raucous cheer as Alfred and Loranna made chase holding meaty bones.

"Look!" Alfred quickly wiped his chin. "It's clean! No need to lick it!"

"I'm gonna get you, Alfred!" she growled.

"Already got 'em," Pep chimed between chews.

"Are we there yet?" the children asked. The troll hunters rolled their eyes as they marched along. The spread of a hundred troll hunters, three gleaming knights, a cadre of shiny spearboys and elvish-like archergirls, and a rear echelon of ruffians and gnomes made for an interesting entourage.

"Are we there yet?" still rang out. The days turned into weeks across ragged dry lands. They followed the wretched path the Black Army once marched and devastated. But even that horrible march was short lived, for the land sprang forth grasses and flowers, and the birds and butterflies returned.

"Are we there yet?"

"No, this is the river valley! I told you that leagues ago!"

"Are we there yet?"

"This is the vast rolling grasslands. I told you that at the river system!"

Then they saw the great faerie steeds, standing atop a hill. The knights stepped forward, as if seeing wives, albeit... not wives, but steeds, their great steeds, of course. The horses came to them.

"I wanna ride! I wanna ride too! What about me!"

"Okay, these are a knights' mounts. They are not meant for children!"

"What about children who fought alongside and saved you?"

The knights walked along as the children took turns riding the great faerie steeds.

"Are we there yet?"

Grotham Keep was still in shambles after their few weeks away. The mess of towers and piles of burned carcasses still littered the vast fields. As Alfred, Loranna, the troll hunters, the knights, the archergirls, the spearboys, Gib and Pep, and oh yes, Hedor, Ruig, and Kumbo taking up the rear, finally returned, there were many active and joyful folks still collecting and sorting the immense treasure of victory.

Broggia, Boggin and the gnomes were in charge of the post battle clean-up and organization, picking and sorting the incredible raw materials. Most of it was crude iron weapons. Many of the crumbled towers had large iron ingots that could be used for spikes and nails. There were mounds of rusting iron and steel, and dried and even mildewed leathers and hides. It was a prodigious and incredible affair. But the hardy gnomes and victorious farmers of the Westfold smiled even as they worked in their laborious exhaustion sorting out the vast rubble.

The returning entourage was cheered on by the groups of laborers congregating along the road. They pointed in emotional joy and sang out, "King Alfred! He's alive!"

Lady Nihan and her ladies came with warm broths and clean water, knowing that Alfred and his fellowship would be tired and hungry. Abedeyan hobbled behind, hurrying along with his tongue just poking out the side of his mouth, giggling in joy. "It's Alfred! It's Alfred! Thanks be to the Father!"

The troll hunters who returned with them were met by the remaining troll hunters and their children. It seemed like a battle line of soldiers clashing as they met and hugged, and as they cried tears of joy. It was odd to see such big scary men not only hug each other in great relief, but now have the time to meet the children of their brethren hunters. Some were actually uncles meeting their nieces or nephews. Their similarities made them seem as if all were related through some line of fathers long ago. The troll hunter fathers held up their children, showing them to the troll hunters who returned. It was a swirl of bestial men and laughing children.

Furioso did not expect the great bound and leap by Red, his daughter. In his arms, she curled her small lanky arms and legs fully around his mess of a beard and ponytails. He nearly fell over as she constricted his breathing and choked him immensely with her loving hug.

Many thanked the troll hunters, believing they rescued Alfred. Ordo had to bark that it was Alfred who saved them, once again. The details of that story slowly unfolded at campfires, firepits, and dinner tables, wherever they all met each night before a peaceful sleep after an exhausting day.

Gorbogal was dead. Her symbiotic frail form, Gael-Asura, was taken away to another world. She was a prisoner, gone forever from this world. No more could she rule in terror and tyranny. Alfred spoke to the groups, explaining in the simplest terms how men, soldiers from his other world, took her and have imprisoned her. Somehow in that world, he was sure, her powers were diminished. Dark magic did not work in that world. He would go there soon enough to make sure of it. When he spoke it, he nodded to Dunther, who nodded back.

Verboden and Harkonen came forth from their long slumber, having saved Gorham's life, having saved him from the torturous chaining and travel forced upon him by Ruuk and his late brother Brok. They were weary peering at the troll hunters and Gorham, who seemed as close as ever.

Ruuk and Ordo had many troll hunters to remember. From Brok the son of Ordo to the many who fell at the Great Siege. The gnomes took them to the burial site of the troll hunters. The gnomes and troll hunters who had stayed took care of the fallen hunters weeks ago, giving them a respectful burial mound where all were together as a great broor of the fallen.

The remembrance of Tirnalth the Great Wizard was performed in the exposed chapel. There wasn't much room, so many were atop the walls and scaffolding, looking down into the chapel space.

Alfred held the small book with Tirnalth written on it. He called over and over as his tears flowed. "Tirnalth, Tirnalth? Can you hear us? Come back?" Verboden had to hold him up. Brother Harkonen talked to the children, to Lady Nihan and Abedeyan, trying to comfort them. The knights and hunters stood outside, bowing their heads.

They set the book upon a small table. Verboden performed a funeral prayer and then placed the book in a small stone sarcophagus. "It shall be kept, in remembrance of his sacrifice."

In the busy aftermath, as the cleaning and rebuilding was occurring, Murith could not help but glance furtively and too often upon the young Khanafian nurse. The other Khanafians treated her strangely, curtly bowing to her even as she did the same chores and tasks as they. She would help them wherever possible. She was still in charge of and helping the dozen young babies that the crude brutish troll hunter fathers tried to care for and handle. She would have to smack their arms or punch their shoulders just to get them to treat their very own infants with something of a semblance of delicacy.

Her consternation at these brutes, tossing and swinging their gleeful giggling babies, nearly drove her mad.

Murith smiled from a distance, pausing in his own appointed tasks. She could not help herself, in her consternation with boorish barbarians to pause and see him from afar.

It was Hedor who scowled, noticing Murith's lazy composure. "What's he doing? What's he doing? Dreaming?"

Ruig noticed and looked. Both followed his gaze to her.

"Ohhhh...." Hedor rolled his eyes and pouted to Ruig.

"Hey, Kumbo?" Ruig elbowed Kumbo, who was gruesomely sawing a rotting war troll's limbs from its giant rotting body. It wasn't that hard to do, what with all the maggots and goo bubbling out and tendons nearly rotting off.

"What? Why you two standing! We've got hundreds of these bloated beasts to move!?" Kumbo grunted.

Hedor and Ruig, stained in troll rot, nodded to Murith, who was still staring at the Khanafian nurse.

Kumbo followed their nod. He stopped, holding a dripping piece of troll limb.

She was escorting several troll hunters as they played with their infants out in the barren fields. She was having difficulty focusing on her task while being stared at by Sir Murith. For the most part, of course, the new fathers knew their role and understood their strength as they played with their children. It wasn't that hard for her to keep watch. But still, having Murith stare at her was distracting and invigorating at the same time.

"Oh boy, she's one of your kind," Hedor said.

"What do you mean, one of my kind?" Kumbo sneered.

Hedor rolled his eyes. "She's Khanafian!"

"So!?" Kumbo shrugged, tossing the gooey troll limb. It splatted a bit on Ruig and Hedor. Ruig flinched and tried to wipe the goo off with his gooey hands.

"Don't you want her marrying her own kind and not mixing with us?" asked Hedor.

"Don't be so small... uh... what's the word?" commented Kumbo.

"Small-minded," said Ruig, still trying to wipe goo off with his goo hands.

"Small-minded! Yeah, and besides, an alliance between two kingdoms would be a good thing," said Kumbo.

"An alliance? What you going off about an alliance? A lowly knight with a milk maid?" huffed Hedor.

"Milk maid?" Kumbo jerked. "Dat's Princess Utah-Nalia! She's daughter to the great king of Khanafia!"

Hedor slipped on some of the troll goo bubbling out from the corpse. Ruig caught him, slipping a bit too.

"That's an... ah... that's... ah... an alliance..." mumbled Hedor.

"If he marries her, King Alfred and my king will form an alliance. Then we will fight the evil slavers and Muhat-tines!" Kumbo exhorted.

Hedor swallowed. "How'd she get way up here? And become a nurse maid?"

"Our king and the scattered tribes are at war with the Muhat-tines. They are an evil serpent empire! They slave raid our people. She was captured and kept for ransom. Even though the king paid, they betrayed him and sent her far away."

"Evil serpents, hey? Draconus... Very powerful, cruel, legendary..." Hedor repeated.

"Legendary lords of slavery, sharp blades, sharper teeth, armoured skin, dragon folk," hissed Ruig.

Hedor stared with wide gazing eyes. "Oh boy!"

"Yes... boy... your boy – Alfred the King..." Kumbo stared at Murith and Princess Utah-Nalia. He couldn't help but form a cunning smile. "Fate cometh."

Alfred and Loranna spent many days together, not alone, but amidst the cleaning, clearing, carrying, piling, pulling, lugging, eating, resting, and sleeping folks of the farms and castle. There wasn't much in farmsteads nearby since the evil army raided and pillaged everything. Thankfully, many hidden farmsteads in forest patches further out still held, and farmers busily began plowing and planting.

Farmers from the West, once again, came in with their provisions and stock of goats, cows, sheep, pigs and chickens to gift and sell to Alfred and his great kingdom. Their leaders immediately signed, not an alliance, but a declaration of servitude to this great king. His utter complete victory against Gorbogal gave no doubt to his leadership acumen.

The Great Northern Kingdom was suddenly formed on parchment with quill and pen. Many remote dukes, barons and their knights, hidden in vales and valleys scattered across the Westfold, began to show up and re-pledge their allegiance and service to the great King Alfred, great grandson of King Athelrod.

It was an explosion of strength and men, a cavalcade of knights, dukes, ladies, and servants who trotted into Grotham Keep and sought King Alfred.

Lord Dunther brought the large procession to Alfred, who was sitting at a table in the open courtyard, nibbling on biscuits with Loranna and the other children. Apparently, they had a honey-butter on biscuit fight – something Lady Nihan, it appeared, was most distraught over.

"We have to ration our food till next harvest and our king and his heroic children are tossing the biscuits about!" she moaned, ignoring the long procession of royal figures and their knights.

Lord Dunther clenched his teeth, trying to nod for her to move along and eyed Alfred to act more kingly.

Alfred leapt up and approached Lord Dunther. He stared at the gathering dukes and knights, ladies and barons.

Lord Dunther bowed and waved his arm to reveal the great return. "My lord, my king, the royal lines..."

"Will you apologize for not helping me during our darkest hour!?" declared Alfred most ostentatiously.

Lord Dunther's eyes bulged, his mouth dropped, and his face saddened.

Alfred tightened his lips and squinted his eyes, looking up at the noble yet apparently weak leaders.

Verboden stood up from the table, a distance away, having clearly heard Alfred's ultimate insult. Brother Harkonen gripped Verboden's robe to keep him at bay.

A knight, appearing brazen and haughty, stepped back, ready to turn and leave.

"We fought army after army, and none of you came. You hid in your keeps far away. Why should we welcome you now!?" Alfred's voice grated. His face was still covered with biscuit crumbs.

Loranna came up and touched Alfred's quivering shoulder. Cory, Wilden and Nubio's silly smiles of child play subsided as they looked on. All were caught by surprise.

A lady, in most proper attire, fell to her knees, "Forgive us, my lord! Forgive us!!"

Several dukes and barons fell to theirs and repeated her words with melancholy. "Forgive us!"

The stubborn knight looked with a grimace. He was the leader of the knights who did not come to their aid, hidden in their keeps. It was obvious Lord Dunther knew him. The knight was still jilted by such a truthful revelation of their cowardice. A prideful arrogant man doesn't like to be revealed as a coward, no matter how true. The knight looked at Alfred, whose eyes formed tears and whose face was not of anger now but of tired grief.

The knight could not help but stare as Alfred wiped his tears and shuddered.

The knight fell to his knees and bowed his head. The rest knelt and bowed their heads.

Lord Dunther grabbed and scraped his own face, as if trying meekly to wipe off the horrified expression.

Alfred then went to a knee and cried. Loranna went with him. The procession looked up confused, unsure of what was amiss. Alfred fell into Loranna's arms and cried.

"He's still a boy, you know!" Loranna said to them as she comforted him. "A boy who saved your lands."

Alfred stood up suddenly, lifting Loranna with him. He looked at the nobles still on their knees and quickly motioned for them to rise.

They rose.

"Will you swear allegiance to me? And always come to my aid when I call?" he suddenly blurted.

They stared wide-eyed at him, then at each other, and suddenly rang out, "Yes my lord! We do!"

Awkwardly, he stepped up to the Duke's wife and hugged her. "Thank you."

She couldn't help but hug the boy back. A warm smile crossed her face. Her husband couldn't help but lose his composure, but smile too he did. Smiles suddenly spread amongst all in the company of visitors. Alfred hugged them, one by one.

"Most inappropriate, my king!" Abedeyan huffed nearby. He rolled his eyes. "Hugging the nobility!?"

"Still... apropos..." chimed Lady Nihan.

Even the rough knight lord, looking at Lord Dunther who shrugged, was hugged by Alfred. That hug must have been magical, for the knight felt a warmth rise in him, and that forced a smile. It was a genuine smile with moistened eyes and was one that brought forth a life of loyalty to the boy king Alfred.

Once again, Alfred and Loranna found time to stare up at the stars as they lay on a blanket atop one of the still unfinished towers. They could hear quaint musical strings and laughter below at the many campfires and cooking pits as the night began.

After another long hard day of clearing the great multitude of rotting corpses and battle gear, resting their weary bodies under the stars was a wonderful thing.

"When are you going back, Alfred? To your world?" asked Loranna.

"Soon, I must, I have to – to know what happened to Gorbogal," Alfred said, suddenly saddened by the question.

"Her form is dead, right? All that is left is Gael-Asura, your... aunt..."

"Yes, her... I need to return. I must know."

"And all is in order with Lord Dunther? Abedeyan? King Gup? They know you are going soon?" Loranna sat up to look at him with leveled eyes.

"Yes, all is in order, as they say..." Alfred mumbled assurance.

"Will you promise to return quickly?"

"Quickly? I dunno... aren't you tired of me?"

Loranna looked down at him. He was still lying and staring up at the multitude of stars, galaxies and space clouds. "Never."

Chapter Sixty-Five

Back to the Hidden B.

Alfred sat up in the cold stark room of the hidden Bunker, which he, his mother and his father slept in only weeks ago. He was on the very cot he slept in. It seemed a lifetime ago. The fluorescent lights were on timers, so it must have been daytime when he arrived. The lights flickered just a bit. It was enough to make Alfred anxious and look about.

The room was empty. As Alfred exited, the metal door clicked open, much to his relief. The sterile corridor was lazily lit by more fluorescent lights. Alfred felt compelled to sneak. He wasn't sure what was amiss. Aside from the hum of the air system, there were no sounds.

He hurried down the corridor. He was in a modern grey shirt and pants, the ones issued to him before he left. He had burned his plastic armor back at Grotham Keep. He made sure nothing modern remained in the Westfold, not even the few guns or military gear left at the Black Spire. During their slow descent down the ramp, he had Lord Dunther make sure they were bashed and burned in one of the fire pits. It had to be so. Nothing could be left there, to give any trace to the Dark Lord or his minions that another world existed.

He felt a little nervous. A dark fear crept over him. Did Gorbogal unleash herself here? He felt a sudden rise of panic as he collided with a dark figure. He fell back, ready to strike as he faced an adversary even greater and more poised then himself.

"Dad!"

He rushed into Wooly's arms.

Back to the Hidden B.

Wooly held Alfred's hand as they walked into the medical facility. Many plastic drapes covered a room where his mother was lying. Doctors and nurses roamed the room looking at medical devices and computers. Alfred gazed with timid eyes.

A doctor came forward and looked at Alfred. "Hello, son. I hear you are the king?"

Alfred nodded shyly, stepping closer to Wooly. He turned to gaze at his mother, lying in the hospital bed, asleep. She had needles in her arm, connected to tubes, and a breathing mask on. Alfred could barely see her pale face beneath the translucent plastics.

"Alfred, your mother is in a coma. She has been through a lot. And based on the, uh, fantastical, the magical – that is something beyond our machines and scanners. We don't have a prognosis, at least not on what has put her into the coma. Her signs are stable but low. We are using our machines to keep her steady, resting."

Alfred nodded gently. He could not stop staring at her, even through the breather. Her hair was matted, and she looked gaunt. She did not look like his mother, full of life and beauty. She looked haggard, old, and deathly.

Wooly nudged Alfred gently. "Go speak to her. The doctors said she might hear you."

Alfred slowly went up. The doctor rolled a medical chair in for Alfred to sit on. He smiled gently and backed away.

Alfred looked closely at her. At first, he was reluctant to touch her. Then he quickly lifted his hand to her arm. He did not know where he could touch her. Tubes went into her forearm and hand, with needles at the end taped firm.

"You can touch her gently, just not on the tape," the doctor said, noticing Alfred's hesitation.

Alfred heard the subtle beep of the heartbeat and looked up at the screen. It was slow, so very slow. Below it another beat followed, fainter but slightly faster. He looked at it, then at Wooly.

His dad looked at him. "She's with child. That is the heartbeat of your sister."

Alfred blinked slowly. He then looked at the little line beating behind the other. Though it was slightly faster, they both seemed so slow.

"We're trying to increase their heart rate," said the doctor. "The child's should be much faster. This condition is beyond us. I'm sorry.

We don't know what is keeping her rate so slow and the unborn child's as well. And yet it is keeping them... alive."

Alfred suddenly scooted in closer, bending forward and putting his arms on his mother as much, yet as gently, as he could. "Mom, mom, I love you. I miss you mom. Thank you for saving us, for saving the Westfold and all the people. Thank you for raising me and protecting me... and making me food and working all the time, for... and loving me. I love you, mom, always. I will pray to the Father and thank him for the time he gave us together cuz I love you soooo much mom. I love you."

Wooly stared at his son. His eyes showed he had very few tears left. His eyes were red with the lids swollen, even amidst his scars.

Alfred bowed his head and shuddered.

The doctors and nurses stood silent. The general, quietly parting the plastic coverings, walked in and stood.

Alfred finally looked up. The general was about to speak kind words, but Alfred spoke first. "Where is Gorbogal?"

The general glanced at the doctor, at Wooly, then down at Alfred. He shrugged, straightened from a kind demeanor to that of a general. "She is in lockdown, extreme lockdown."

Alfred stared at him.

The general strangely tried to avoid Alfred's eyes but eventually looked at him as if Alfred were in charge. "You want to see her?"

Alfred nodded.

It was a cold dark elevator that went down further and further. Alfred and Wooly knew this merely from the time they stood quietly in the dark cell as it hummed and vibrated. There were very few buttons on the control panel. The general, several officers and security personnel stood with them. It was a long quiet ride.

Vault door after vault door, they descended along concrete ramps. There were other vaults they passed. Alfred stared up at their numbers and red lights, the yellow and black striped warning frames, and their small thick windows where things hidden within made his brows tighten in consternation. Heavily armed guards paced the long wide corridors. He noticed they didn't just have guns. Some had other strange devices and contraptions.

Gorbogal or Gael-Asura's vault was open. Several medical technicians were there. Alfred recognized many of them from when they opened the gate and from the lab where they had all the decaying orc bodies. When they entered the room, a woman came to them with an electronic pad in her hand. She looked at Alfred with studious eyes.

They did not seem to fear Gael-Asura as she lay upon an elaborate medical bed with many, many machines all around. There were layers of plastic sheets above and below the bed. Those layers could not completely control the black drips that stained the floor underneath.

"What's going on? With her?" Alfred asked, looking at the woman.

She looked at the general, who nodded. "She's decaying. Deteriorating. Much like those goblinesque creatures. She has the same foreign elements... alien chemical compounds that break up in our atmosphere."

"Dark magic," Alfred said, walking past them to see.

The woman noted his comment, quickly typing on her pad.

Alfred stepped closer, past the beeping machines, the breathing apparatuses, the twitching tubes and the pulsating bags of liquids. He stepped closer to see over the plastic coverings and sheets, to look into the eyes of his relative, his aunt, Gael-Asura.

Her green eyes were fixed on him as he approached. She could see him through the plastic before he got a clear angle of her over the sheets. She looked up at him with a fixed gaze.

Alfred looked to and fro at her black sickly face, down at the plastic covering her body. Small parts were exposed where tubes came in. Her skin was decayed black with pustules and boils seeping, as she was literally melting away. She stared for a moment and then closed her eyes.

The machines suddenly beeped rapidly, and the team suddenly hurried their actions. It was over.

"She was fully empowered by the dark magic," said Ethralia, lying in bed, holding Alfred's hand. "And in this world her dark magic is utterly destroyed. It is not allowed here, ever... again."

Alfred smiled, sitting close to his mother, who had awakened and was smiling but still was very weak. "Did you want to see her? One last time?"

Ethralia looked at Alfred for a long time, as if she was examining him for the first time. "No."

"Why?" Alfred asked softly.

"She has caused the destruction of so much. What she did to those children of the hunters is truly evil. I have no need for her. She has gone to the Father in her horrible decay... and now her reign is over. Gorbogal is no more. The sister that I loved died long ago when she chose the dark magics. I am now here with you... and..."

Wooly snored in the chair on the other side. Ethralia smiled and winked at Alfred as he snickered.

Alfred was thrilled to see his mother, not her weak and beaten body, but to see that her eyes twinkled with joy and her spirit was full of life.

"You will have a sister," Ethralia said, squealing just a little, grinning the biggest grin even with her pale gaunt face.

Alfred smiled a huge smile.

Alfred rushed through the corridors. He hurried to the trains where Riley and Loud, the Duke, and Rostislav were standing. They still had various bandages, crutches or high-tech stitches from their grievous wounds. Wooly, the general and his adjutants finally caught up with Alfred as he ran up to the soldiers. Masamu pushed a wheelchair with Kwan Thai Suex in it.

Alfred gazed wide-eyed. "Are you going to be okay?"

"I don't know king boy. Leg, back, arm... who know! He have take care of me!" Kwan motioned to Masamu.

Masamu bowed curtly. "I am honored to take care of him. And to teach him true swordsmanship."

"Ah, that's child play! But me with broken legs, we see. I play child sword!"

Masamu bowed again and smiled.

Alfred put his hand on Kwan's shoulder. Kwan grabbed it and nodded. His eyes moistened. He looked up at Masamu, who bowed quickly.

Riley and Loud came up. Alfred looked about and only saw those two. "Brubaker got back but his wounds... Jake was killed by that witch. I have their tags."

Alfred looked down. "I'm sorry."

Riley put his hand on Alfred's shoulder. "It's the call. We know. Save the world. Another day, another paycheck, and two less friends. Two good friends. We know."

Alfred looked up. They were getting ready to board the train and leave.

The Duke saw his moment as Riley stepped back. He dropped his over-stuffed duffel bag and pranced over. "Hey, my little man, my king, the fighter! Real royalty. You got those knights and archers and spear kids. That's some real fantasy shebang... uh stuff, little king man!" The Duke reached out and hugged the diminutive Alfred. When they released, the Duke couldn't help but shiver a slight sob. But he quickly changed his demeanor when he pulled out and smelled an envelope. "Lookie here. My retirement! You've given me the big ticket. And the worst fantastical nightmare from anuddah world! But hey... I'm gonna open up a donut shop!"

"A donut shop?"

"The best donuts, the biggest donuts, this side of the Appalachians!"

Alfred giggled.

Rostislav walked up. He looked down at Alfred through a new pair of sunglasses. "You are the real deal kid."

Alfred giggled again and watched as they entered the train. A loud beep alerted the soldiers that the train was leaving soon.

"I'm going to pray for you, buddy," Riley said, pointing at Alfred.

Alfred nodded.

Rudy suddenly appeared in a cast and arm wrap. His head was bandaged. He appeared weak but on the mend. Alfred looked up, wide-eyed.

"Hey Alfred, it was amazing. I gotta hand it to you, man, definitely the real deal. You... are the man." Rudy put up his free hand awkwardly to get a high five.

Alfred finally realized and tried to high-five as Rudy hesitantly put his hand down. Then they began an untimely switching of hands till Rudy finally grasped and held Alfred's hand.

Alfred tried a polite smile. Rudy released and weakly picked up his bag. He turned to the train, stopped and turned back to Alfred. "I hope you find him."

Alfred tilted his head. "Find him?"

"Yeah, your Father, uh... not the black knight, but the Father... of Light..." Rudy shrugged.

Alfred scrunched his face unsure.

"You lost him right? He walked the earth, amongst mankind, and then was gone..."

Alfred listened, pausing in thought, puzzled about what Rudy was saying.

"Hope you find him."

"...find him?"

The beep grew into a blaring siren, calling the last of the soldiers to load up. The train was leaving this ultra-secretive base.

Rudy shrugged and gave a polite glum smile, then turned and hurried onto the train with all the other soldiers. They all looked at Alfred through the doorway and windows. Alfred saw that the Duke had tears. Rostislav rubbed his eyes under his sunglasses. Riley and Loud stared with deep gazes. Kwan was outright crying as Masamu stood frozen. Rudy had a forlorn smile.

Wooly stood next to Alfred. The men saluted as the train began to move. It jerked into high speed and was gone.

Chapter Sixty-Six

The Promise

"They assured me the gateway will never be open again. Their great wizard, who invented it, is dead. And they are the only ones who know about it. If that's the case, then we end them, and all of this can go away."

As he spoke, the general sat in a dark cold room with one small monitor. On the screen was a live feed of President Mount. He was seated at a long table with a board of generals, admirals and civilian leaders.

"Mr. President, we can end this now."

The president rubbed his face as many generals and leaders shifted in their seats or fiddled with papers or their laptops. "Let me sleep on this," he finally said. Everyone shown on the monitor and the general shifted in their seats, releasing collectively held breaths.

"No, no," the president continued. "I don't need any sleep. Do not harm that family in anyway. They sacrificed everything to help us, to save our planet, even if whatever happened came through them. It was never their intent. They fought hard for us. And besides, I don't believe this gateway made by one wizard, who is dead, is it? Right? No telling what other gateways there are. So I say they are an asset, an important asset."

"We keep them in the vault?"

"Oh gosh no, no, no... they're not... we..." the president shifted suddenly in his seat, rising and wagging his finger, growing in stature. "We let them be. They've been at that same place ever since they arrived, living good clean lives, and working hard. We keep them there. We let them stay there. That knight, Wooly, in the abandoned warehouse..."

"It's a lot, just a fire station lot..."

"Yes, that lot, give him full ownership of it. Keep them grounded. Keep them put. Get their paperwork all in order. We'll keep eyes on them, just in case we ever need them... IF we ever need them..."

The whole board of generals and leaders seemed relieved, nodding in positive manners. Some typed furiously on their laptops, joyfully, while others shook hands or patted each other on their shoulders. A groundswell of positive discussions suddenly warmed across the secretive room.

"Yes sir," the general answered. He smiled.

Chapter Sixty-Seven

Back Home

Alfred ran through the streets. His backpack bashed his back repeatedly from the heavy books inside, but he didn't care. He ran along, zipping in and out of shoppers and workers along the sidewalks and storefronts.

He suddenly stopped when he saw a large black man directing some workers. They were carefully installing an electric sign above a store door. It read "Duke's Donuts." Alfred blinked and then saw the Duke. Alfred gasped.

The Duke turned and motioned for a hug. Alfred immediately ran up and hugged him. "Whah... whah??"

"I told you I was starting a donut shop!"

Alfred released and gazed up at the magnificent sign. "Biggest donuts this side of the Apple...apple..."

"Appalachians man! You ever been?"

"Apple-lations?"

"Ah, they are the most beautiful blue mountains around. Oh Alfred, you gotta get out more!" The Duke gave a big grin.

"Yeah, get out more... see amazing, fantastical stuff," Alfred grinned back.

"Come back in a week, and I'll be getting you some free samples!"

"Why'd you open a shop here?" asked Alfred, suddenly squinting his eyes.

The Duke looked around, glancing to and fro, making a silly suspicious expression. "Well son, after that crazy fiasco that occurred here, lots of stores closed up, and owners freaked out and left. I got a great deal on the spot. Couldn't pass it up!"

Alfred squinted some more.

"Plus," the Duke continued, poking Alfred with his big finger, "I'm supposed to be spying on you."

Alfred nodded with a glum look. "What I thought. I ain't just a kid, you know."

"Oh, I know, Alfred. Indeed, I know Mr. Royalty..." The Duke stood up, seeming like a giant.

"Mr. Wilson, does this look good to you?" one of the workers asked, ready to drill the sign in.

"Mr. Wilson?" Alfred repeated, sneering.

"I'm the Duke to you!" The Duke pointed, giving Alfred the warning look. "You run along. I got a shop to open!"

"Bye Mr. Wil.... the Dooky! Oops... Duke!" Alfred ran along.

"The Dooky?..... I'm gonna... " the Duke leered and then chuckled. Alfred was long gone. The Duke nodded to his workers and then tapped something small near his ear. "Everything is under control."

Alfred ran into his father's shop. Computers and parts stacked the shelves of the crusty shop. Old ladies and tattooed guys waited with computers, pads, and cracked phones. Wooly was very very busy.

And at dinner Wooly was much too cautious around Ethralia. Each time she lifted a pot or moved her incredible mound of sewing jobs to one side, he'd hustle up to grab whatever... She pushed him and his doltish care aside. She had to wave him off many times. A small bulge showed on her stomach, with many months to go. Wooly was as worried and delicate as any modern man who's seen no war or battle.

She paused between his supportive arms, giggling at the absurdity, and hugging him in the end. Was that hurting her, Wooly could not help but wonder. And she hugged him harder.

Alfred gagged, joyously, with his meal of grainy breads, thick meaty stews, and nut and honey desserts. He couldn't help but eat as he did in the Land of the Westfold.

Back Home

One late night in bed Alfred lay open-eyed, watching as the headlights of cars slowly sneaked like joyful faeries shining across the wall of his room. "Oh Father of Light... thank you..."

He thought of the Westfold, of Loranna waiting by the pond for him and looking deep into his eyes. He could see Cory, Wilden, Nubio rushing by with the boys, ever doing spear drills. Setheyna with her scar and Niranna, Loranna's younger sister, guided the archergirls as they fired their volleys. Red was with them becoming quite able. She led a band of troll hunter girls. He saw Lord Dunther, Lord Gorham and soon-to-be Lord, Alfred noted, Sir Murith at the table, ever planning their courageous defense of the land. Oh those great, great knights! The clerics Verboden and Harkonen were praying for him, he could see. He saw Lady Nihan and Abedeyan busy as ever, huffing as they walked past with much to do and much to argue over. He saw Hedor, Ruig and Kumbo leap in waving. Then they flinched as Ordo, Furioso, Ruuk and the troll hunters, great shadows in his imagination guarded them all – greatly. He saw the gnomes rush through, below his vision, and Gib and Pep leap up to wave. He couldn't help but giggle.

And he remembered the great wizard, his smile, his cautious and tender hugs, and his love of bread and butter. Tirnalth the Great Wizard brought them through this all, sacrificing himself for them, for his mother, his father, and him and his unborn sister. He smiled with teary eyes as he turned in bed, "Thank you Tirnalth." Finally closing his eyes, he sought solace in a peaceful sleep.

"Bedenwulf," he whispered, then felt a presence in his room. He opened his eyes. "Tirnalth!!!!"

"Who?"

Next Up:

Alfred
Versus the
Necromancer
Volume Four

45480458R00260

Made in the USA
Middletown, DE
18 May 2019